G000016207

MINISTRY PROTOCOL

MINISTRY PROTOCOL
THRILLING TALES OF

The MINISTRY of PECULIAR OCCURRENCES

edited by
Pip Ballantine & Tee Morris

Imagine That! STUDIOS
AUDIO · VIDEO · DIGITAL PUBLISHING

Imagine That! Studios, Copyright 2013
All rights reserved.

Cover Art and Design by Alex White
Cover Titles by Renee C. White
Interior Layout by Imagine That! Studios

ISBN 978-0615885193

No part of this publication may be reproduced, stored in or introduced
into a retrieval system, or transmitted, in any form, or by any means
whatsoever without the prior written permission except in the case of
brief quotations embodied in critical articles and reviews.

This book is a work of fiction. Any resemblance to any person, living
or dead is purely coincidental. Any actual places, products or events
mentioned are used in a purely fictitious manner.

www.ministryofpeculiaroccurrences.com

For all our Kickstarter supporters,
you made this happen!

Enjoy the ride!

From the Desk of the Ministry of Peculiar Occurrences Archives

Finally, I have managed to sneak these files away from Wellington Thornhill Books, and gathered them together in this edition. I think our agents stationed all over the world, and all the various mysteries and mayhem they find themselves in, have stories that deserve to be told, even if Welly is a bit *strict* when Ministry protocol and procedure is concerned.

[*Miss Braun, what are all these classified files doing free of their respective shelves? This isn't anything akin to the æthercast I reluctantly host with you, is it?* — W.T.B.]

The growth of the Ministry of Peculiar Occurrences is one of the most surprising and wonderful aspects of the series. It has been a delight to include so many friends and colleagues in this anthology. All of our guest journalists produced stories that delighted and amazed. It is quite a revealing experience to see your world through other people's eyes.

[*Yes, how wonderful to encourage such growth and interest in this, a* clandestine *organisation with Her Majesty's government, dedicated to* discretion *when handling matters most* sensetive *to the Crown. You do know the meaning of the word 'clandestine,' do you not, Miss Braun?* — W.T.B.]

When we set out to use Kickstarter to fund this venture, it was with great trepidation since crowd-funding is the ultimate test of support. So when we funded this project 152% we knew that we'd done something right along the way.

[*Well, I will grant you that the outpouring of support for the Ministry was most humbling. All things considered, I still find it odd having to crowd-fund an organisation of secret agents. Stranger things, I suppose…* — W.T.B.]

A special thanks goes to our editor, Tee Tate, who kept us on the straight and narrow, and added a layer of professionalism—something we truly desired and achieved in this volume.

[*Really? A layer of professionalism, she brought? Perhaps Miss Tate could, in fact, pass along a skill or two upon your own person, yes?* — W.T.B.]

More thanks go to our cover artist, Alex White, and his team of models, make-up artists, and costumers that created for this collection the magnificent cover image, which is so much more than we could have imagined.

[*Some say to be wary of the quiet ones. For myself, it is the far-too-gifted. Note to self: Increase surveyllence on one 'White, Alex' with particular warning that he is considered to be armed and exceedlingly talented.* — W.T.B.]

Additional appreciation is extended to Thomas Willeford and Brute Force Studios for their incredible and ingenious machinations that graced both this cover and the cover of our role-playing game, *The Ministry Initiative*.

[*Thomas Willeford. A name that will live in infamy.* — W.T.B.]

Finally, the dedication of this book is to our wonderful supporters. If you gave one dollar or a thousand, you made this happen, and for that, we give our strongest and greatest thanks.

[*I do so hate it when Miss Braun is right.* — W.T.B.]

We hope you take delight in these stories from around the world, featuring our fellow agents at the Ministry. Tally-ho!

Eliza D. Braun
~~Field Agent~~
[*ed. Junior Archivist* — W.T.B.]

[*This ætherbook will self-destruct in five seconds.* — W.T.B.]

[*Oh bloody hell, Axelrod! How difficult is it to build a gadget that works?! You sodding clankerton…* — W.T.B.]

Table of Contents

The New Recruit

Leanna Renee Hieber

New York City, NY
United States of America
1889

New York City was as compelling as it was deadly. A dizzying, ever-industrialising monster of innumerable, inexhaustible moving parts; human beings were cogs in intricate wheels responsible for turning the axis of the world's hungriest city. Living here was a mythic journey one embarked upon with great caution. The fangs of New York's creeping, climbing skyline sharpened on the souls of the unprepared. If one were not born privileged, mere survival depended upon an exceedingly resourceful, clever mind. Bettina Spinnett hoped hers was up for the task.

New York was all Bettina had, and she prayed it wouldn't be responsible for her untimely end. At sixteen, she had outgrown the orphanage. Gracious Sister Anne had allowed her to stay. But it was time to move on. Even Sister Anne, in tears, thought so.

Wearing her only possessions—a plain blue linen dress, worn socks and tattered boots—Bettina walked out of the modest orphanage building and towards the bustling avenue beyond, praying that the city might deign to help her find her way, here in this land of striving struggle so many had fled to from so far away to call home.

For any woman without means there was always the trade of flesh, and while she was sure few chose that path, many were driven to it. The idea terrified her and she'd frankly rather die first, which was also an option. She put aside her morbid reverie when she set off down the busy and bustling Lexington Avenue, hoping for a sign. Further downtown, she found it.

Gramercy Park stopped her, the avenue running right into the gated garden only meant for residents. Thankful the beautiful Central Park further uptown had no such restrictions, Bettina reflected on fond childhood trips to that glorious expanse open to poor folk like her. Gates barring access to a neatly groomed park, preventing her a glimpse of New York's finer homes, grand townhouses, and luxurious carriages, unfortunately, were more familiar to her.

What really caught her eye of the world belonging to the better-off were all the ghosts.

There was one particular building that was less fine than the others. Its bricks were in need of washing. All the city's steam, soot and grime had turned its once pleasantly cream coloured bricks a sickly ashen shade. Its shutters were all latched, a kerosene lantern burned upon its front stoop, but at a slight angle, its great hook bent and the flame made a black mark upon the glass. She didn't notice an address upon the front door.

But all the ghosts were pointing. They floated and bobbed in the air as one might expect. What was surprising to her was that they were in colour. She would have expected grey out of spirits, not that she'd had a great deal of experience with them. They had occasionally haunted the orphanage, mostly children who had died there, but the nuns were quick to shoo them away, and from what she had remembered, they were generally white or silver, or an occasional silhouette in the corner of the eye.

Illnesses and melancholies in the previous year meant Bettina kept to herself at the orphanage. Perhaps that isolation made her more able to see the spirits now, or perhaps New York had simply grown more haunted with a different variety of spirits since she'd last strolled its vibrant streets.

A throng of them floated before her, undulating like flags in the breeze, facing the unremarkable brick facade. Once Bettina placed her foot upon the slate stoop that sported a faint hairline crack on each step, the spirits vanished. With far finer buildings around it, this one almost looked like it was trying to be uninteresting. Spirits, she noticed, tended to like things that were a bit off. Now that she was paying attention, they evidently had better things to do.

Something buzzed at her when she stepped fully upon the first step. Her slight weight couldn't have made much of an impression, but she couldn't see the source of the sound. It was like a bird's chirp, but mechanical. She mounted the next steps, up to the doorknocker.

A small circular crest above the plain knocker was marked O.S.M: Office of the Supernatural and Metaphysical.

Bettina had never really thought much about either the supernatural or metaphysical, but both sounded quite interesting and exciting. She hoped she could beg for work in an office rather than on the street. Her aptitude for reading and passion for mathematics and science offered faint hope that she wouldn't be laughed at, seeing that she was a girl. Maybe the spirits had done her a huge favour, her prayers to the city not for naught.

Just as her trembling fingers moved to lift the knocker, the door swung open to reveal a spacious entrance foyer, a coat tree bearing hats, a great coat, cloaks and several umbrellas stood to her right, and a mirror to her left with odd fixtures about its frame. If she wasn't mistaken, a glass eye upon a metal stalk was looking at her from the mirror's crest and followed her as her foot stepped across the threshold.

The corridor was panelled in finely polished maple wood. Open wooden doors on either side of the entrance foyer led to sitting rooms and fine landscape portraits adorning the surrounding walls. A staircase swept up behind a hefty woman at a hefty desk a few yards from the doorstep.

"Welcome to O.S.M, young lady," said the stocky, matronly woman. Bettina didn't know what she meant, but the word was pronounced like "awesome". After a moment Bettina realised it was the acronym for the office.

The woman was dressed in plain, thick navy wool, like a police officer might wear, a pin upon the lapel of her smugly buttoned jacket, hair in a pile atop her head, grey strands flecking the brown locks. Behind her sat file cabinets and a fascinating array of metal things that Bettina couldn't begin to describe or place.

"Hello, ma'am," Bettina said, bobbing her head before she turned to see who had opened the door. She saw no one there.

"You could *see* this address," the matron stated, as if that were something surprising.

"Well... yes. Why wouldn't I be able to?" Bettina asked.

"Seeing this place would mean you'd have been *sent* here. We've a system. A subterfuge." She waved her hand at the facade of the building, as if it shouldn't even have been there. "We don't get 'visitors'. Especially not from young ladies like yourself." Her eyes widened. "You're not the Crimson Lark are you?"

"Ah... N-no...?"

"Good. You don't appear to be a swashbuckling pirate, bank robber and international man of intrigue. But one never really knows, do they? We're expecting the Lark within the month, trouble is, we've absolutely no idea who we're looking for."

"I... wouldn't know the first thing about robbing banks... or piracy..." Bettina murmured.

"Well, that's good." The woman furrowed her brow. "But we're not expecting visitors this week. Tell me your name and what you're doing here? I am Mrs Marsh."

Bettina opened her mouth to explain herself, but wasn't sure what to say, even though the woman was a bit odd, and it was, after all, an office dealing with the *supernatural*... should she mention the ghosts? She paused inelegantly with her mouth ajar.

"Let's try again," Mrs Marsh began with a patient tone that contrasted her sturdy frame and expression of sterner stuff. "Why are you here?"

"My name is Bettina Spinnett and I don't exactly know where here is. But I'm looking for work."

"At present the only one working here is me."

"Then I'd like your job. I mean—" Bettina clapped a hand over her mouth, biting at her fingers. "I don't mean that as if I want to replace you, I mean, I'm sorry, what I mean is—"

Mrs Marsh barked a laugh. "You're looking for work? This is New York. Everyone is looking for work. But I don't understand how *that* made you able to see the place. Usually we're cloaked." The woman turned to the wall at her left where two small swords were crossed upon a placard and pressed a protruding seal above their crossed blades. There was a strange sound, like a gate being closed and the light in the room seemed to ripple a bit, followed by a rumbling hiss of some exhaust valve deep in the basement below. "There. Perhaps our curtains needed to be freshly shut. What do you think, Miss Spinnett?"

Bettina just stared at Mrs Marsh, afraid to seem confused when the woman seemed perfectly clear about this mysterious building with its strange contraptions and desire to hide. If this was an office of the improbable she couldn't act like she didn't believe. She had to seem amenable, as if all this was perfectly ordinary. "Of course," she said with a strained smile.

The matron examined her. "So, you can see our building, even when under our SpectraVeil? Most intriguing. I'm not sure what sort of wages you'd be looking—"

"I was turned out of my orphanage, Mrs Marsh," Bettina blurted, feeling her poise escape her for desperation. "I don't need much. Just a dry place to lay my head and something to eat."

"An individual newly granted independence, ready for the world, but already lost within it." Marsh looked Bettina up and down, something complicated at work in eyes that likely had once been bright but were dimmed with age. "You'd have to work for peanuts, girl. If the President isn't all that fond of us, you should see what the Mayor has to say. We survive only because the Ministry of Peculiar Occurrences has better luck with their government in London and keeps us afloat. But seeing as we're a *former* colony, it isn't much to float with."

A nervous Bettina broke the tension by blurting out the rest of her pitch in hopes of assuring the woman. "Sister Anne, who was in charge of my ward, bless her, tearfully told me today that I had to move on. She liked me a lot— she was the only one who ever took interest in me—because I was smart, so she said. She taught me to read and write, and I'm very good with organising. May I help with paperwork? I promise I'm a quick study for whatever you'd need. I've nowhere to go. This place seems very nice." Bettina bit her lip after her breathless rush.

"And you were not... sent here?" Mrs Marsh again looked puzzled.

Bettina shrugged. "No. At least, not by anyone..." She thought of the ghosts. They had pointed up these steps. "Led here maybe, by Fate, perhaps?"

Mrs Marsh harumphed. "Not sure I believe in fate."

Bettina looked towards the button Mrs Marsh had pushed over the odd crossed swords. "But you believe in magic?"

"*Science*," Mrs Marsh clarified.

The place seemed *very* magical to Bettina, but she didn't argue.

"How are you with numbers?" Mrs Marsh asked. "If I were to send you out on a mission to collect data, could you do it? We just lost one of our best analytics men to another office."

"Yes, ma'am, I most certainly could, thank you—"

"Don't get too excited, child."

"No ma'am, sorry, ma'am—"

"Come." The woman stood and her thick wool skirts brushed around sturdy boots. Bettina envied the woman her prim, sturdy jacket and skirt when she herself had quite a chill. "I'll have to assign you a very special piece of equipment." Mrs Marsh turned to face the stairs. "Oh Mister Books, sir!" She called, her deep voice filling three floors above and resonant through the side rooms. "I'm dispensing equipment. Would you like to come supervise and give instructions or shall I?"

A British accent barked back. "How many times will I have to say 'do not bother me, I am on *holiday*,' Mrs Marsh?"

"Well then, next time, sir, book your room at the Fifth Avenue Hotel if you don't want to be involved with the goings on of an O.S.M. field office." Mrs Marsh's scornful tone carried up the stairs like the snap of a whip. She shook her head, returning her weighty gaze to Bettina. "A Mister Wellington Thornhill Books, Esquire, is in town, supposedly 'on holiday' though at the sight of file cabinets he is evidently transported and can't seem to keep his hands out of our own Archives. He is an important Ministry asset, or so he tells us; working with those who serve as our British 'parents'", she explained. "And Lord do they like to act like high born parents; wanting us to be very good little boys and girls, but not caring one whit to raise us themselves."

Bettina smiled at Mrs Marsh as if they were co-conspirators as the woman gestured her into the other room. Shuttered windows made the light of the room dim lit instead by a few small flickering gas lamps. They were as well kept as one might expect of a first floor parlour, it was unique in the massive length of wooden file cabinets going across one wall.

Writing desks lined the wall opposite, all wired to telegraph machines, many of which were whirring away in pleasant faint taps. Long thin paper tickers bubbled up from whatever implement was taking in the code. There were wires all about the room, leading to small sockets that Bettina at first thought were gas-lamp fixtures, but she saw that odd metal spokes went up from their sconces. She thought, perhaps they helped keep the building hidden, but she wondered why she could see it then. Maybe the wiring was faulty?

Bettina drank in the atmosphere of this lush building, a sharp contrast she had seen in the run-down condition outside; a fine reception room, velvet-flocked wallpaper, and fine curios boasted crystal, china or rare old books. All of the office's grandeur was effortlessly coupled with the forefront of technology. Where the magic stopped and the science began eluded her, but she was captivated. She turned to Mrs Marsh eagerly but was stilled by the woman's next grave words.

"Think very hard about what will and what will not scare you, Miss Spinnett."

Bettina blinked at the rather unexpected question.

Marsh continued, pausing before the parade of file cabinets. "Anyone who is in any way involved with the O.S.M must face their fears and overcome them. This work will try the limits of your sanity."

Bettina took in her words. Could anything be more thrilling? One day she'd been a bored and boring orphan sewing clothes for orphanage coffers and escaping in the occasional hard-to-find book. Now she was faced with adventure none would believe.

"I appreciate that you're wonderstruck, child, but choose. Pick a creature. A monster. A puzzle. A mystery. Go after something that interests you and bring us back something useful you discovered. Bring us numbers. Bring us details."

"A creature?"

"Think of all the mythical beasts of legend and fable. Among our many duties and our wide-ranging purview, we try to ascertain what all truly exists, for most of them do. Research and Development has been refining equipment to track their details. Should you choose the thrill of danger, of course, there are always the more deadly monsters we would like reports about—"

"What about ghosts?"

"Ghosts?" She considered this a moment. "Indeed. Very useful. Can never have enough data regarding ghosts. In fact, that's an area where we happen to be lacking on account of so many false sightings and fraudsters."

Mrs Marsh went to the middle cabinet, middle drawer, and rather than pulling out the handle, she pressed upon it. A strange clunking noise and a hiss of steam sounded from within, like a deep metal lever were pulled, such a hollow and reverberate tone when the cabinets themselves appeared mere wood and only the dimensions visible.

As if on its own accord, the drawer lengthened before Mrs Marsh and she reached in, a tendril of what Bettina assumed was steam wafted up from the interior. The woman's sturdy hand plucked up a white linen bundle and her elbow pressed upon the outside handle again, the drawer sliding back once more.

Mrs Marsh approached and instinctively Bettina held out her hands. Marsh placed something lightweight and cool into Bettina's hand and she whipped off the white linen covering that Bettina could see now was a monogramed embroidered ladies' handkerchief. Thoughts of whom the handkerchief may have belonged to were lost in the wonder of what was now in her hands.

A dragonfly. A large brass dragonfly the size of her whole palm, with tiny buttons and screws and wires, iridescent and incredible. She peered at the curious device with great joy, looking at all its special knobs and fine wire mesh. It must be priceless. This stranger must place a great deal of trust in her with something so precious. Bettina's heart swelled with excitement and purpose.

"You will use this to record and bring significant data as soon as you are able. Two days at the most, we don't loan equipment for long. And don't even *think* about selling it. We've ways to track you down."

Bettina nodded. "I wouldn't dream of it!"

"Good."

Bettina bit her lip. This was as good a time to ask as any, though she didn't want to press Mrs Marsh's amazing welcome. "Tonight, though, Mrs Marsh, could you be so kind as to advise me where should I... stay?"

"Ah yes, that. Well it's probably best for the safety of the device for you to return it here. I'll leave the back door open for you and you alone. And here's how."

Mrs Marsh moved to one of the writing desks and picked up a handheld implement that appeared to be a cross between a stamping press and a pair of pliers and returned to Bettina. In the instant, the woman had Bettina's index finger in her hand. The vice clamped down upon the finger and Bettina loosed a resounding: "Ow!"

"There now, all done," Mrs Marsh said. "Touch that finger to the small metal oval on the back door, the one in the alley beyond, and it will unlock for you and only you."

Bettina stared at her reddened finger, then back at Mrs Marsh. "This place does try one's belief."

Mrs Marsh laughed. "This is just the beginning, child. When you come in for the night, keep to that back room. I'll set up a palette by the coal furnace. It isn't much for accommodations, but it'll be warm and dry. I dare not move you upstairs, not while Mr Books is here."

"Is he really so terrible?" Bettina asked.

"A monster," Mrs Marsh grinned, evincing Bettina's smile in turn. "A tedious, meticulous, *librarian*. Utterly unbearable." The women chuckled a moment before Mrs Marsh recovered herself as if she ought not be seen smiling. "I just don't want *His Eminence's* lip, as I'm straying *far* from protocol. We don't... take folks in." Mrs Marsh smoothed her jacket with a slightly nervous gesture, her fingers fussing about the hem.

"And I promise I'll find a way to repay your generosity," Bettina promised. Mrs Marsh gave her a fond smile before shooing her towards the door.

"Now off with you."

Bettina looked at the device in her hand, then at the door, then back to the woman. "But...how do I use this...?"

"Why, you press the button and hold it towards the phenomena you wish to record, of course," Marsh said, moving forward to press the thorax of the dragonfly on a little iridescent panel. In response, the delicate filigree metal wings flapped and a whisper-soft whine came from the device that was as much mechanical creature as property. The little antennae of the device shifted from side to side and one small, bluish light the size of a pinhead lit up upon its middle and then went out again.

Mrs Marsh's eyes went wide a moment before her expression again regained stoic neutrality.

"How do I know how to interpret what its doing?" Bettina asked, entranced by the movement of the device.

"However many lights will determine, give or take one, the amount of presences near you. We've made all our various recording devices look more like fine toys than equipment so as not to disturb or make the subjects suspect. Once the whole of its panels have lit with as many lights as it has in its system, then it will go back to one and begin counting again. When you return we'll attach the dragonfly to one of our readers and the little beauty will tell us the other factors; temperature, humidity, atmospheric conditions, et cetera."

"Do I *have* to rely on the lights?" Bettina asked. "Couldn't I just count the numbers of spirits I see? That seems more elementary."

Marsh's subtle reaction gave Bettina a slight chill. Had she been impertinent?

Instead, the woman asked with great interest, "Have you always been able to see spirits, child?" Mrs Marsh smiled softly. "That's new to our department if you can."

"Is that useful?" she asked with hope.

Mrs Marsh nodded, prompting Bettina's eager nod in turn.

"Well, yes, but sometimes we can't rely solely on our eyes alone, can we?" Mrs Marsh asked with her eyebrow raised. Bettina shook her head. "Good girl."

Suddenly Bettina wanted nothing more than to make Mrs Marsh and this office proud.

"Do note the phase of the moon and the addresses and intersections of the phenomena. In that case, you'd best take these." Mrs Marsh lifted a pencil and notebook from the writing desk. "And this, for the safety of the device." She then plucked a wooden box with a handle from atop one of the file cabinets and handed them over. Bettina fumbled with them a moment before grasping them tight. Mrs Marsh continued with a motherly tone. "And I'm sure I needn't tell you, an innocent young lady like yourself shouldn't be out past dusk. Gramercy may be safer than the territories of the Hudson Dusters and the Bowery Boys, but there is still darkness in wealthy circles. Best not get caught up with the likes of them, however haunted those poor creatures may be."

"Yes ma'am. I'll return by nightfall. I can't thank you enou—"

"Go be useful, child," Mrs Marsh gestured her out.

Bettina nodded and nearly ran through the door.

With a thrill, she was off into the city. The bustling, ever-so-haunted New York City. She followed her instincts about where the most haunted places might be. Further downtown. The eldest parts of the city, the places of fires and shipwrecks and disasters of all kinds, where native populations were driven from their island home and where thousands of immigrants toiled in squalor and harrowing conditions while the successful were moving ever upward upon the vast Manhattan grid.

The first thing that captured her fancy was the harbour, heading directly due west across the Avenues as they increased in number towards the Hudson. And oh, did it yield. Perhaps the device brought out the spirits more by its presence, for they positively thronged around the waterfront. But with so many of them in tattered Union blue, haunting the harbour they departed from, it occurred to Bettina that the Civil War scars would take a very long time to heal, if they ever could. But somehow counting their numbers felt good, as if she were acknowledging their sacrifices.

Just her and a mechanical dragonfly, looking up and meeting swaying gazes as the spirits floated about, tied to the earth by some unfinished business or worldly woe. The fact that they could see her too somehow made her feel even more driven to her purpose of making them count. Her leaving the orphanage opened up whole new worlds, these spirits showing her the way.

Down blocks marred by fires and accidents, the industrial district had their own fair share of ghosts for all the limbs and many lives taken by terrifying machines. The spirits led on, showcasing where their numbers swelled and where they thinned. As Bettina made an eastward sweep along the tip of Manhattan Island, the centuries of spirits sometimes choked the air with transparent, shimmering colour, she had to keep count ten times over at least, marking in her notebook when the dragonfly whirled its completed tally and the numbers of light would begin again. The proximity beacon was flickering nearly the whole time. She was surrounded.

As the behemoth gothic arches of New York's recent addition, the Brooklyn Bridge, began to loom before her, Bettina gasped at the flock of spirits hanging about its grand bricks and spectacular wire ropes. It was an unparalleled suspension bridge, a monument to human ingenuity, architecture, and design, its two towering arches having gained the crowning title of the tallest manmade structure in this part of the world.

At the amount of spectres hovering around the incredible achievement, she was reminded at what cost such wonder was gained.

So many spirits of men floated there, the bridge unable to ferry its dead across to Heaven, keeping them there where they died, countless from caisson disease alone, their forms bent over in pain, as man should perhaps not be so deep underwater, others from any number of perilous conditions. The awe-inspiring spectacle of engineering was haunted down to its watery foundations.

The day flew by in mere moments, and Bettina did not even notice that dusk had fallen. Spirits cast a fine light and she was more taken up in counting them than in the tracking of the sun or the darkening of the sky. Once she noticed she was taking down her notes by downtown gas-lamp, with the harrowing Lower East Side ahead of her, she doubled back and returned up to the square of fine buildings facing the gated Gramercy Park.

Tucking the whirring dragonfly that had seen such lively use into its wooden box, along with her notebook for safekeeping, she raced back to the nondescript façade of O.S.M., then around the corner and down the alley behind it.

She tried the back door and found it locked, but then remembered to lift her finger. Instinct guided her (still) sore fingertip to a small metal oval where a peephole should have been. After a quiet tense moment of pressing the cool metal plate, she finally heard a clunking sound in response, a sequence of latches undoing themselves, and then the creak of an open door, as nondescript as the rest of the building.

Slipping in as silently as she could, Bettina found the rear kitchen to be a small, brick space with a coal burning stove with a long cooking plate, a fireplace with a spit and hooks for kettles and cauldrons, the sorts of things you'd expect in the most basic of kitchens though none of it looked very used. This was a place of business, not a residence. Through the soft gaslight haze, she could see that Mrs Marsh had laid out a palette with a blanket for her as promised, along with a little glass of milk and a hunk of bread upon the pillow. Bettina welled up with tears, feeling suddenly woozy, overwhelmed by her good fortune at having truly stumbled upon her safe haven in a big city that liked to swallow helpless young women whole.

She curled up, her palette close to the big black belly of the coal furnace, and took eagerly to the bread and the milk. On the third bite of the threadbare dinner, Bettina took a moment to consider all the walking she'd done in shoes that weren't without their wear—she'd not noticed all her blisters until now. No wonder she was so hungry.

Bettina also did not realise how exhausted she was until she rested her head against the pillow and soon collapsed into a dreamless, dark sleep.

It was a clank of metal upon metal in the morning that woke Bettina and she shot up upon the straw-filled palette, nearly hitting her head upon a pipe above her.

"Didn't mean to startle you, child," Mrs Marsh chuckled. "I forgot you were there, you were as quiet as the dead. Usually I'm the one that gets startled. Tea?"

"Yes, please."

"Did you have luck yesterday?"

"Oh, yes ma'am. New York City is *very* haunted."

"Ah, so you've something to show. The last person we sent out didn't come up with much of anything. Mr Books was apparently sceptical at the notion of confirmed hauntings, so he may be intrigued by your findings."

Bettina took the small china teacup and saucer Mrs Marsh handed her. It jostled a little in her hands. Funny, she didn't think she shook as much as she'd been lately. Out and about in Manhattan she hadn't noticed, so maybe it was just nerves as her life had been so unexpectedly swept up into this odd new adventure.

Mrs Marsh took her own teacup and moved to the door. "Come show me your findings once you've drunk your tea, and then, perhaps, we'll even get you an egg to eat."

"Yes ma'am."

The idea of an egg made her stomach growl. She heard the sound, though she didn't feel the ache. (She did however feel the tingle of an embarrassed blush rise in her cheeks.) Bettina didn't think herself terribly hungry, anyway. Last night's bread and milk must have done her a world of good, far better tasting than orphanage gruel.

She sipped her tea quickly, scalding her tongue a bit, nearly dropping the saucer, but she got to her feet when finished, wincing as she slipped back on her boots again—so as not to appear rude being seen in torn stockings with toes hanging out in her workplace—and carefully set the teacup in a basin with others that needed washing.

She imagined Books, being British, went through more tea than the average New Yorker. Perhaps she'd meet him and he'd warm to her if she brought him tea.

Bringing in the wooden box to Mrs Marsh's hefty desk and handing over the ghostly tally, Mrs Marsh took up the dragonfly device in her hands, narrowed her eyes on its thorax, and then turned its antennae towards Bettina for a moment. Something passed over her expression, but she quickly masked it, turning away to rise up to the ledge of fantastical equipment, strange devices Bettina had never seen, all stretched out on a long shelf above a series of encyclopaedias.

Placing the dragonfly atop what looked like a metal scale, an instant symphony of whirs and whistles and clicks resulted. The dragonfly sprang to life, stirring all the items around it. There was a device to the side of the scale that bore long wire needles, little graphite tips on their ends, which made marks upon a thin paper that spooled out on a brass spindle. The ticker continued to run down to Mrs Marsh's hands as would thread winding off its spool to a seamstress' latest work.

Mrs Marsh stared at what was before her, looked back at Bettina with her mouth agape. Something was…wrong?

Bettina felt a cry lock in her throat as Marsh scrambled up to her feet and then darted up the stairs. Something *had* to be wrong, surely…

Her instincts, however, kept her rooted. Bettina knew she had done nothing more than what she was told. The young girl sunk into the seat by Mrs Marsh's reception desk and tried to stay calm.

She heard Mrs Marsh's voice, then a gruff British one, a bit of arguing, a cry of *"Well why didn't you tell me she was special?"* and then a pair of strong tromping tread down the stairs.

A fastidiously dapper, brown-haired man in a fine dark suit paused at the foot of the landing, Mrs Marsh trailing behind him with an expression of nervous excitement that suddenly made Bettina feel self-conscious. She rose to her feet once more.

"Good morning," he said with an awkward nod.

The man, Bettina assumed, was Wellington Books. His accented tone was surprisingly warmer with her than Mrs Marsh's. For someone so abysmal, his bark was louder than his bite, clearly. A handsome fellow, a sparkle of tireless curiosity lit his eyes and gave him a charming air. Everything about him made Bettina wish to seem the consummate lady. She dipped into a pronounced curtsey.

"You must be Miss Bettina Spinnett," Books said with a small smile.

"Yes, sir. Mister Books from the Ministry?" Bettina blurted, straightening back to standing with the sort of perfect posture Sister Anne had always encouraged out of her.

13

"Wellington Thornhill Books, Esquire, and Chief Archivist of Her Majesty's Ministry of Peculiar Occurrences," he stated. He glanced over his shoulder at Mrs Marsh. "And I am currently on holiday, but that little detail isn't your fault."

"I am very glad to meet you, sir," Bettina breathed, needing so dearly to impress him, "and *very* glad for your Ministry that has taken to keeping this office alive, for I owe it my life, sir. Orphan girls don't always last long on city streets, sir."

Books opened his mouth as if to say something, but Mrs Marsh pulled him by the arm, facing him towards the dragonfly on the scale and the results it had produced, results Bettina couldn't begin to understand or tabulate.

"Sir," Mrs Marsh murmured. "*Look* at her data. She's taken down more numbers and details on ghostly occurrences in one day than we have in three years."

Books examined the printouts that had been made when the clicking, whirring device had attached to the spider-like needles and spool of paper. He made several noises that Bettina deemed to be sounds of being impressed.

"But that's not all, Mister Books," Marsh murmured. She picked up the dragonfly and turned it towards Bettina. The reader clicked and whirred and something lit. "*That.*" Books' expression was suddenly similarly amazed. There was something terribly unsettling about it. Mrs Marsh placed the dragonfly upon the desk between them.

"What is it?" Bettina asked, picking up the dragonfly in her hands once more, wondering what upon it could cause such a reaction. She didn't know, she wasn't an expert at what all the lit markings along the head and wings meant, but something was flashing, and her heart was in her throat for fear of what it might mean and she fumbled for words. "Whatever I may have done, I am so very sorry. I never meant to offend, I'll learn, and quick, whatever I—Please don't cast me out—"

"No-no-no, my dear Miss Spinnett, you have done nothing wrong at all," Books murmured, as if he were afraid of scaring off something he was observing in the wild. "What a special case you are indeed. I've never encountered anyone or anything like you. So solid. So *powerful.*"

Bettina smiled broadly. No one at the orphanage had ever found her unique, certainly not particularly useful. "Powerful?" She blushed. "I don't know about that, sir..."

"That's why you've had such luck with the spirits, unlike anything we've encountered. You *understand.* Though I'm having a hard time understanding the *physical* properties of this case. These results are unprecedented." Books whirled to Marsh, his eyes wide and excited.

"*She* is unprecedented," Mrs Marsh said, her face flushed.

"What do you mean?" Bettina asked. "I understand what? Unprecedented why?"

Books whirled back to stare at her, approached, placed a firm hand upon her shoulder and stared at his own hand. Then he looked at Mrs Marsh. They shared some sort of look, a dawning of surprise. And then sadness. They turned that look upon Bettina and she suddenly felt very small.

"Oh, no," Marsh murmured, her sturdy hand went to her mouth, tears springing into her wide eyes. "You don't even know, child..."

"What..." Bettina murmured, dread filling her distantly growling stomach. "What don't I..."

Bettina felt her heart sink in a sickening realisation.

She thought of being turned out of the orphanage. She hadn't been well the day prior. A fever. She'd risen and gone about her morning, but no one had spoken to her, and that was all right. No one usually did. When she'd waved at Sister Anne, the nun started on seeing her. Bettina now understood why the Sister had said:

"Go on now, Bettina. You can't stay here anymore. You must move on."

Bettina had looked at the floor, unable to face Anne, knowing she'd aged out of the orphanage long ago and that this day would eventually come. But in that moment, she'd thought Anne meant her age. No. She'd meant her spirit.

She was dead.

The fever had claimed her.

She'd been out counting her own kind.

A searing pain coursed through her body. Or whatever constituted a body.

Suddenly Mr Books' hand that had been placed upon her shoulder dropped to the side, with no mass to support it. The beautiful dragonfly device slipped from her hand. *Through* her hand. She watched as her solid hand became less so, her own colours and those of the carpeting blending together.

Books bent to catch the dragonfly before it hit the floor, but it jostled in his hands and shattered, the pieces seeming to linger languidly in the air. One of the fine antennae snapped off and tapped quietly onto the floor next to two large teardrops that fell from Bettina's paling face.

"You didn't know you'd gone, dear girl, that's what," Books murmured gently, seeming not to care about the device, wholly more concerned with Bettina, his eyes wide as he looked back up at her. "That's why. Not until now."

"I'm so sorry, my child," Mrs Marsh choked.

Bettina walked backwards. No, it was more like floating. A few more tears splashed upon the floor. All that could manifest anymore, evidently, was her sorrow.

"No. Stay, please stay Miss Bettina," Mrs Marsh gasped. "Don't go."

"I...I can't...I don't...know what to do...what do I do?" Bettina felt all her faculties drain from her. Her floating form took to the chair again but didn't feel the seat beneath her.

"Do you *want* to stay?" Mrs Marsh asked. "Do you want to help us?"

"Mrs Marsh," Mr Books began with a soft tone, "This... girl... is not a replacement for Katie. Please. You can't think of her like that..."

"I...I know, sir, I shouldn't..." Mrs Marsh nodded, that stoic face suddenly red and ashamed, tears falling as she turned to stare agonisingly at Bettina. "See, you're a lot like my girl, gone from this world about your age," Mrs Marsh explained. "Trouble is my little Katie doesn't haunt me. Wish she would."

Bettina felt her sense of self spin. Maybe she could stay on. For an adventure. For as long as it might last. Why not?

"Well, I... I do like it here," Bettina whispered. "And I like the... ghosts. My fellow kind... I suppose my perspective could be useful?"

Books lowered himself to one knee, looking up at her with a delighted smile on his face. "It would be most unprecedented in the intelligence community to have a ghost agent," Books said, trying to keep a casual tone but it was clear he was utterly captivated by the concept. "But you'd have to *want* it, young lady. Truly want it. You were mistaken for human because you had no idea of your state. You have to *will* yourself into being."

"But...you want me to stay?" Bettina asked. She'd never had a home. She'd never had a family. She'd never been taken in. Never wanted.

A yearning so pure welled up inside of her. She wanted this indeed. This hope. This belonging. A distinct new happiness filling an old empty void. Suddenly, she was conscientious of the floor. She understood what was solid and what was shade and the coexistence therein.

"Yes!" Mrs Marsh exclaimed, all stoicism cast aside, a mother longing for a child, no matter what kind of state that child was in...

Bettina smiled, rose and glided to the door. As she did she heard Mrs Marsh hiss a breath, as if she was about to beg her not to go again. Bettina turned, feeling movement in a new way. It was interesting, fascinating. And yes, it was quite fun.

Bettina would, most assuredly, tell them all about it.

"I don't need the device," Bettina replied. "I just need to be with them. My kind. And then I'll come home and tell you everything."

It was the first time Bettina had ever said "home".

And she had never felt so alive as she floated through the door and out onto bustling, ever-so-haunted New York City.

A Feast of Famine

Karina Cooper

Galway, Ireland
Winter, 1879

Miss Lobelia Snow was a *natural*. As providence would have it, she had been born with the best of all the world about her: the exquisite appearance inherently guaranteed by excellent breeding, the effortless carriage of one confident with her place in the world, the fortunes of a well-heeled family, an intellect considered to be both clever *and* engaging, and an uncanny grasp of social interaction.

She was, in a word, gifted, and well did London's society know it.

So it was the great scandal of 1865 when at the accomplished age of fifteen, Miss Snow announced at her coming out that she would not be marrying at all, and would all the fuss about it please turn to her four sisters?

What furore this caused became the toast of the gossiping town, yet there was no hoped-for announcement of marriage that year, nor at the next. After three elegant but remarkably unsuccessful seasons, Miss Snow was declared with some heartache to be firmly *on the shelf*.

Some years later, only a fortnight from her thirtieth birthday—and the highly anticipated label of *hopeless spinster*—Miss Snow could claim herself in possession of three rather notable accomplishments. The first being her role as indulgent aunt to seventeen nieces and nephews, the lot of which appeared to be rather more agile, precocious, and sticky than society would have led her to believe children to be. All the better to visit with gifts and spun sugar, then leave them with their rightful parents.

The second accomplishment being the ring worn upon her right hand. With no insignia in place, nor any particular marker upon it, none but those who knew what to look for would recognise it as a tracking ring from the Ministry of Peculiar Occurrences—her truest and most lasting love.

The third accomplishment, Miss Snow reflected as she alighted from the one-man mail-coach kind enough to carry her from Dublin to Galway, was her history. Comprised of a long string of successes, Miss Snow's resume was a laudable one, her reputation that of an agent who could be trusted to get a job done. This would explain why she found herself in possession of the name of a man who was to be her partner in this current endeavour, written inside a mandate from Director Fount:

Have received word of plague in Galway. Mirrors historical activities, research enclosed. Travel immediately. Rendezvous with resident agent T. Kensington Kennedy.

Director Fount, if indeed he had written the letter, was taciturn to the point of rudeness. More likely, this had been transcribed by another, and delivered post-haste.

Nevertheless, Miss Snow was not an agent who questioned her orders. So prepared, she waved cheerfully at the skeletally thin old man who'd manned the levers guiding the mail coach and twitched her coat more firmly into place about her neck. The cold in Galway was bitingly refreshing, and she expected her cheeks to bloom as rosy as that of the hearty Irish folk who lived here.

If a majority of said hearty Irish folk staring at her seemed to be doing so rather too hard, Miss Snow acclimated it to the slim line of her trousers and the impact of her smile—a force to be reckoned with on any day, or so her many suitors had claimed.

That she was British, and therefore the enemy in these trying times, was all part of the game.

Caitriona Kensington Kennedy was a girl who took after her da more than most would like. She was taller than most lads, burdened with his wide shoulders and thick arms—which was useful for the work she'd helped him complete, to be sure, but not at all what a lass should be known for.

That the two of them, father and daughter, had crafted such delicate items as to be courted the world 'round did not seem to matter to the residents of Galway. She should have been married long ago, they said, and did a disservice to her father's upbringing in saying it.

At least, she'd been given a reprieve from such concern while she'd tended to her da, even if it was a reprieve she would have given near anything to not have.

While the tensions between the farmers and their British landlords had ensured that most tongues remained fixated on the returning famine and the rent those bloody landlords demanded despite it, Caity spent the past fortnight at her da's bedside, bathing his fevered brow and coaxing what little food or water he'd accept into his parched mouth.

In the end, only whiskey would do. He spat out everything else—food and water—as if it caused his tongue to swell.

Now that he'd gone, the wake held and the funeral rites finished, she stood at the side of his cold, freshly turned grave and wasn't sure if she was to cry or sigh in relief. The final days and nights had been bad; so much so that she'd felt guilt for thinking it a welcome end for them both.

It wasn't raining today, though it should have been. Ireland lost a good man.

Maybe, she thought as she hunched her shoulders against December's frigid wind, Ireland wasn't weeping because she got to claim him in the end. Buried in the earth as he was, he'd rot with all of the too many good men Ireland had claimed when the famine turned bad enough to starve her sons and daughters.

One day, Caity'd be right there, next to her proud da and sweet ma, who'd been taken by a different fever long before the potatoes went to rot again and the first blood spilled in this sodding land war. Until that time, she wondered if she'd ever find warmth again.

"Are you Mr Kennedy's daughter?"

The voice came from behind her, carried on the wind in such a way that it seemed to float like an angel's hosanna. The educated tones of an English woman did not belong in Galway, no matter what landlords might claim Connacht.

Caity turned, her back up already, though she couldn't figure just why. Perhaps more of the tension besetting the province had affected her than she'd thought.

The woman who stood a respectful distance away was not a sight Caity expected to see. She wore trousers, which was all fine and well for some of the working lasses, but odd on a lady, and her hair was wound into a fetching coil,

21

sleek but for a bit of a wave. It was the healthy colour of good soil to plant in, rich like the darkest wood, and framing a truly lovely face.

From the top of her low hat to the tips of her glossy riding boots, the lady was—well, she was a *lady*. In trousers.

Caity's brow furrowed.

"Oh, dear, are you simple?" The question seemed as if it should cause offense, but it was asked with such a winsome smile that Caity flushed, deeply embarrassed to be so charmed. "I'm looking for the daughter of T. Kensington Kennedy."

Her da's name earned a narrowed glare. "Who's askin'?" she demanded. "We've got no call for entertainin' the likes of—" She caught herself, her callused hands curling into fists inside her father's old coat pockets. *We.* As if her da were still alive.

Sympathy filled the stranger's smile. "I know you're grieving, and I'm sorry," she said gently. "But there's foul things afoot and I'm in need of a partner." She gave no opportunity to interrupt, striding forward with a gloved hand outstretched. "My name is Miss Lobelia Snow, you may address me as Miss Snow. Are you T. Kensington Kennedy's oldest?"

"Only," she replied, accepting the hand and feeling rather more as if the wind had swept her up off her feet to deposit her in this woman's oddly compelling presence. "Me ma named me Caitriona, me da gave me Kensington. I was the only child."

"C. Kensington Kennedy?" Her smile quirked, bringing a lovely warmth to eyes the colour of moss in a clear spring. "Delightfully apropos. You've the shoulders of a blacksmith, but the hands—" her gaze fell to the scarred fingers clasped between soft kid gloves "—of a tinkerer. Tell me, Miss Kennedy, did your father teach you anything?"

Caity snatched her hand back, bothered when it tingled. The sudden loss of warmth from Miss Snow's handshake should not have been so obvious. Her eyebrows drew down so hard, she could see her own black eyelashes as she glowered. "He taught me everything he knew," she said firmly. "I can do anything he'd be needed for." And she would, too, in his name. *That* was the way she'd respect his memory.

That she hadn't quite decided that until this moment was tucked away for later thinking.

Miss Snow's smile ratcheted up to near blinding delight. "Wonderful! Exactly what I'd hoped to hear. I confess, my dear, you are not at all what I'd expected, but I believe providence is smiling." She beckoned. "Come, there's work to be done."

"But I—"

"Come, now," she insisted, much more imperiously than a British woman should on such dangerous ground. She strode back towards the gate, where the wrought iron separated the living from the dead.

Caity shot an apologetic glance to the pair of graves, one covered by winter dark grass and the other a hillock of turned earth, and hurried to catch up with the strange woman before she strode out of sight.

Miss Snow possessed a remarkable sense of people. Although C. Kensington Kennedy did not particularly look like agency material, there was something to the way she held herself—as if she was greatly aware of her height, yet could not be shamed to bow for the comfort of others. She was a full head taller than Miss Snow, who was not herself a petite woman, and the width of her shoulders beneath her patched coat suggested she was no stranger to hard work.

If she was half the master crafter her father was, Miss Snow would return to London with a report *and* a new agent, rather than just the one.

"I understand that there's some protest from the Irish Republican Brotherhood," she began.

"Hsst!" The girl's whisper, emphasised by a sudden waving of both hands, halted Miss Snow's conversational gambit. "The English haven't any right to go talkin' about it like that."

While poorly phrased, Miss Snow understood the gist. "I'm not here to make trouble for either side. Although," she added as she strode down the road, towards the city centre, "if the Irish need aid from the monarchy, I see no reason why Parliament shouldn't grant it. Claiming a country comes with its own responsibilities, yes?"

The girl had the most remarkable sea-blue eyes, as pretty as the waters of the far-flung Caribbean at sunrise. Miss Snow would wager good money that none of the lads here ever paid her *that* compliment. Those eyes studied her now, wary but still mostly bemused.

"I'm not here for that," Miss Snow added. "Rather, I'm here to put an end to this plague taking your folk."

Although her eyes widened at *plague*, Miss Kennedy was already shaking her head. "The famine—"

"'Tisn't the famine that worries me, my dear Miss Kennedy."

"You mean the sickness? A bit of ague here and there, but I wouldn't call it a plague." A beat. "Ma'am."

"Oh, heavens, Miss Snow, if you please." Dismissing the appellation, she turned her valise to the other hand and shook out her arm absently. "This ague. What happens?"

The girl was quiet for a long moment. Just when Miss Snow thought maybe she was rather *too* brisk for a lass who'd just lost her father, Miss Kennedy spoke again. "It starts with a fever in the eyes, ma—Miss Snow. As if they're made of glass and something else is looking out."

Not unexpected, but a rather more intuitive turn of phrase that Miss Snow would have anticipated. "Then what?"

"They stop working."

"Don't most who fall ill do so?"

She shook her head, her long-legged pace not at all ladylike—which Miss Snow appreciated, for her own stride was brisk and she had no patience for lollygaggers. "They stop all work, all services, everything. They pine, I think."

"For?"

This time, a shrug from those broad shoulders. "Then the taste for food and drink goes. In the end, me da only wanted whiskey."

Miss Snow halted just outside a pub, the faded picture on its placard that of a four swinging bells.

Inexplicably, the pub's name was the Bell and Badger. There was no sign of said badger.

"Exactly what I feared," Miss Snow replied, and adjusted the handle of her valise into the crook of her arm. "Come, Miss Kennedy. I'd like to introduce you to a reliable source."

Caity was beginning to wonder if Miss Snow's vocabulary was slightly off from what it should be. Had she known that *reliable source* meant *person of interest who would start a brawl rather than speak*, she could have been rather more prepared.

Instead, as she rubbed at one shoulder—a bruise, no doubt, would appear in the same shape and size as the bar stool that had broken against her back— she glared at the knot of half a dozen men in various stages of cognisance.

Miss Snow perched delicately upon one of four such stools that had not been broken in the scuffle, her hands folded serenely atop the counter and her smile beatific. "I had no inkling that you would be so capable, Miss Kennedy. Truly, you are a delight!"

Caity could not decide whether she should be flattered, surprised, or frightened.

She'd been inside the Bell many times, and never once had the lads inside turned to violence so quickly—or so viciously. Certainly, they must have been inside ranting and raving about the dire decline in the Connacht potato lands, and Caity was convinced someone must have raised a glass to the eviction of the landowners from the land they evicted good honest Irish folk from, but such matters were common these days.

While she was no slouch in a pugilist's match—courtesy of her da, naturally—she'd only had to swing a few times before they were down.

She leaned over, keeping her voice down lest it garner attention from the groaning chorus behind them. "What did you *do*?"

Miss Snow's smile did not fade, not even when the man she watched twitched against the pub counter's surface. He lay slumped over it, as if only resting his head. "A little something from research and development," she said softly, lifting an eyebrow all but hidden beneath her hat. "Unstoppered, the agents mingle and *poof*. Smoke and discombobulation, making them easy prey."

Easy, Caity's foot. She'd seen how Miss Snow moved in the haze, like a serpent. That was not shillelagh form.

"I'm tired of waiting for him to waken," Miss Snow continued, and dug about in her valise. "Be prepared with that pitcher, would you, Miss Kennedy?"

Caity caught herself reaching for the half-full pitcher of ale, horror mounting. "I'm not to *throw* it, am I?"

"Only if he requires it," Miss Snow said, and withdrew a small brass egg clutched in one gloved hand.

Caity gasped.

"Oh?" Miss Snow balanced the oval upon her palm, nearly so large that the oblong ends stretched from one side of her hand to the tip of her thumb. "Recognise this, do you?"

"That's a cobalt series," she blurted, before remembering that her da had cautioned her to secrecy.

Miss Snow depressed a small mechanism with her thumb, but her sharp scrutiny did not leave Caity's face. "So it is. It seems my instincts are correct." Whatever she meant by that, she did not explain. Instead, with a whirring click and clack of moving bits, the egg turned itself into a frog as big as her hand.

Caity held the pitcher at the ready, though her gaze remained fixed on the mechanical information gathering device. She'd helped her da plan it, even made some of the smaller bits when his old eyes got too tired and needed a rest. It was one part working gears and one part alchemy, which she'd learned at her da's knee, as he had his da before him.

The frog's eyes, the brilliant blue of treated cobalt and thus the series indicator, winked and glistened as it twitched into life.

"I trust you know what it does, then?" Miss Snow inquired.

Caity nodded.

"Excellent, saves time." She tapped the frog on the head. "Let's see what he knows about the peculiar wind."

It wasn't the most perfect means of intelligence gathering, but like most of the cobalt series they had created, it operated on a simple theory. Tell it that what you wanted to know, and it would extract the most minimal and direct knowledge from the person it interacted with.

To this end, the frog cleared the distance between Miss Snow and Bertie Bannigan, the pub's barman, and opened its mouth.

Thoop! A tuberous sort of tongue shot out, connecting solidly with the barman's forehead, just over his nose.

The frog's eyes winked madly.

"Such alchemical pursuits are not common, you know," Miss Snow said conversationally. Behind them, a few of the lads were just shaking it off, groaning as various bumps and bruises were catalogued.

Caity glanced back at the waking men, then at Miss Snow. "I told you, me da taught me all he knew."

"It isn't polite to gloat, Miss Kennedy."

A flush stained her cheeks. "Sorry, Miss Snow."

"All is forgiven. Ah! Here we are, all done, now." Right enough, the tongue snapped back into mechanical mouth, and the frog turned back to the women. There was a whirr of sound all but lost in the rising litany of grunts and curses behind them.

Caity shifted, but Miss Snow waved them off. "Their limbs are a bit numb at the moment. It'll wear off after we're gone." She tapped the counter. "Come on, then, give it here."

Dutifully, the frog's mechanical mouth opened, and a bit of parchment ejected.

"Do be a love and read that, won't you?" Miss Snow asked, so sweetly that Caity obediently picked up the ejected report. The frog climbed into Miss Snow's cupped hand, and once more reverted back into an egg.

Caity frowned at the word.

"Well? What does it say?" A beat. "You can read, can't you?"

Of course she could. Problem was, she didn't want to say this one aloud. It felt wrong. She looked up, a knot forming in her belly. "It's best I don't say it."

"Oh?"

Wordlessly, Caity handed the paper over.

Miss Snow looked at the precise printing and grimaced. "Bollocks. I'd hoped for better."

She rose, crumpling the paper and dropping it with a muttered word into the pitcher of ale Caity still held.

It floated to the bottom as she watched, its ink already fading.

Cruach.

"'Tis a word for slaughter," Miss Snow said as they hurried through the streets. The tension she'd noted upon her arrival had not lessened at all. In fact, upon leaving the Bell, it seemed all the thicker.

"Not entirely true, ma'—" A sigh. "Miss Snow."

"Enlighten me." She was glad that Miss Kennedy could speak and move quickly all at once. It seemed that Miss Snow had arrived in Galway just in the nick of time. Any later, and she wasn't positive there'd be a Galway to arrive to.

Somebody was mucking around with dangerous things.

"It's true that the word can mean slaughter, but as a thing, it means a stack of corn, or a heap of it. It also describes something bloody."

She had exceptional lungs, did Mr Kennedy's daughter. Not a pant out of place.

Taking mental note, Miss Snow had no intentions of slowing until they were far enough from the Bell that the gents with cripplingly tingling limbs would not pick up on their trail. "What do you know of Cromm Crúaich?" she prompted.

Miss Kennedy did not disappoint. "Me da said that when St. Patrick drove the snakes away, it wasn't snakes he tossed out but the gods." She tucked her long black braid behind her shoulder as she kept easy pace, her cheeks and nose red with cold and whatever breeding gave the Irish that blushing hue. "He said that Cromm Crúaich lived on Magh Slécht, and even the Ard Rí worshipped him."

Miss Snow noted that the girl's Gaelic was near impeccable, or as much as such a strange amalgam of consonants and syllables could be. Good, suggested excellent lingual talent. She looked up at the sky.

It had darkened between entering the Bell and stepping out. Clouds scudded across it in various hues of black and grey, eager for whatever stormy collision could be managed in the winter wind.

An ill omen.

"How many have fallen to the illness?" Miss Snow asked.

The girl did not look up, though the wind tugged at the tendrils of her hair released from the braid she wore it in. Curls, Miss Snow noted. How quaint and bucolic.

"Sixteen," she replied. "It doesn't look like famine does, anyway. We're poor and hungry, but we aren't starving."

Yet. The Great Famine of some decades back had struck when Miss Snow was just a child. The stories, reports of fleeing Irishmen and deaths tolling in the thousands, was enough to turn one's stomach. That none yet had died from this smaller crop of blight was a blessing.

That left sixteen corpses unaccounted for. More than enough to satisfy the legend's mathematical demands. Indeed, four more than strictly necessary–and such things mattered.

As the wind blew across the oddly silent city, the faint echo of church bells rang through the coming dusk. They shimmered in sonorous harmony, casting a caution for peace upon a city teetering on the brink of conflict.

Of course. She put an arm out, halting them both. "Of the sixteen," she asked the girl, "how many died within earshot of church bells?"

That question confused her, but to her credit, Miss Kennedy appeared intent on working that out. "Peter and Tom, I think, and Nattie Doyle. Me da, too."

"Are you sure that's all?"

"No, Miss Snow. I don't know all who passed, just them."

Miss Snow's mouth pursed. "Would it be fair to assume that twelve of the number lived outside the reach of the bells?"

"A fair guess, aye."

"And how many are firstborn?"

She blinked. "Me da, Nattie, Peter, and Tom. I think the papers said the others, too."

There was precious little that could be called truly coincidence. Miss Snow fished a map of Galway from her valise, gesturing with the folded parchment to a corner of the street where a wagon had been left, its bales of hay tied for whatever purpose it would serve later.

Heedless of the hem of her fine coat, she crouched behind the wagon and spread the map. "Can you read this?"

"Aye," Miss Kennedy affirmed, with more than a little rankle of pride.

Miss Snow bit back her smile. "Would you mark for me all the homes of those who passed?"

It took her a moment, but Miss Kennedy fetched a few of the pretty white stones decorating the patch of dirt beside the nearest building's front stoop and placed six upon the paper. Another five dotted the borders outside. "An estimate," she explained. "They were crofters whose potatoes weren't all blighted. Just some."

"That's only eleven."

"Aye, Miss Snow. That's all I know, and some of them being guesses."

Not nearly enough, true, but perhaps something to go on. "And the churches in the area?"

Miss Kennedy was much quicker this time, fetching different coloured rocks to mark the churches in the city.

There were enough that as expected, three of the white stones placed within Galway were out of clear range, while the five outside the city like as not had to travel to whatever church they favoured.

That was only eight confirmed, but it would do.

She studied the map, then touched the city centre. "Are there no churches here?" A trick question, for Miss Snow remembered passing by a lovely cathedral.

"There is," Miss Kennedy confirmed, "but the bells're down for repair. Me da said it was strange that it was taking so long. He wanted to find out why."

"Oh, you *are* a clever girl, Miss Kennedy." The praise earned another of those delightful blushes the girl gave so well, and Miss Snow did not withhold an approving smile. "Tell me, have you put it together for me?"

The wind tugged at the map upon the ground, rifling through the girl's warm woollen skirts. Miss Kennedy frowned at the map so hard, Miss Snow half expected it to catch fire.

"It seems," she said haltingly, "that there's a strange bit of ague affecting them what live outside the range of bells." Miss Snow waited. "I think it's not been commented upon because of the worry. From the famine, I mean. We're all too busy looking for an excuse to call on shillelagh's law."

"Likely, Miss Kennedy, all the more pity for it." She reached for the map, twitching it out from under the markers weighing it down. "Which leads one to ask an important question, does it not?"

Miss Kennedy's brow was so furrowed as to nearly hide those lovely eyes. "What question?"

She looked up at the blackening sky. "Is the conflict stemming from the hearts of mortals, or the hands of those what play at gods?"

A pall fell over Galway as dusk settled.

In the carriage Caity had flagged down, Miss Snow rummaged through her valise. "According to writings, Cromm Crúaich was either the most important god or one highly sought after by the High Kings of old."

Caity listened quietly, her chilled hands clasped between her knees. She was forced to hunch in the carriage, lest her head bump the top of it when the wheels found a rut in the street they navigated.

"The story goes that he would claim the firstborn in exchange for wealthy harvest, or something of the sort." Miss Snow pulled a number of small vials from a leather pouch, slotting them into place upon a belt with loops meant to carry them. "On that hill you mentioned—"

"Magh Slécht."

"The world abhors a know-it-all, Miss Kennedy."

Caity flushed.

Miss Snow wrapped the belt about her waist and returned her attentions to the valise. "On that hill were twelve stone figures, and legend has it that a particular High King and three-quarters of his men died when worshipping at that place."

Caity's mind raced, slotting in pieces of information the same way her da had taught her to the cogs and gears of the tinker toys together. "You mean to say that something is causing the firstborn to sicken and die?"

"That's what doesn't make sense," Miss Snow replied, withdrawing a wicked little pistol from the pretty valise. She placed it into the holster on her belt, then withdrew another. This, she handed over, carved handle first. "Cromm Crúaich takes the firstborn and delivers bountiful harvests, and all we've got here is famine. The twelve statues are obviously represented by the twelve who live outside the bells—"

"I beg your pardon," Caity cut in, taking the pistol as Miss Snow waved it impatiently. "The bells only matter for the Folk. Cromm Crúaich was a god, or a demon."

"One might say the same for any creation of myth and legend." Miss Snow eyed Caity's hand, and the pistol held within it. "Have you never used one before?"

"A legend?"

"A pistol, Miss Kennedy, do try to keep up." She leaned over, seizing Caity's hand and arranging the haft of the weapon just so, curling her fingers into place. "You hold it like that, and then you fire. Aim, first, though. At a certain range, it's impossible to miss."

Caity looked down at the be-hatted lady, her eyes wide. "Will I be firing this at someone?"

"You might." She tilted her head. "The Folk?" Then, Miss Snow's eyes widened, but not in surprise. The crystalline depth of her gaze somehow managed to make her look both sage and triumphant—an appearance Caity felt sorely that she would never manage. "That's it! Miss Kennedy, you *are* brilliant!"

She seized the door, swinging it open so that she could lean outside into the wind. Whatever she called up at the driver, the carriage lurched suddenly, swinging Miss Snow back against Caity and pinning them both to the seat.

Colour suffused Caity's cheeks as the other woman laughed a husky, merry sound. With excitement clear in her eyes, she leaned over and gave Caity a warm buss on the cheek.

"We'll make an agent of you, yet," she promised.

Caity found herself cupping that cheek as Miss Snow once more found her own seat.

"We're turning back for the Bell."

"What bell?" Caity asked, feeling rather more thick-headed than she felt she should.

"No, no, Miss Kennedy, the *Bell*. The pub."

"Oh!" Caity dropped her hand to clutch at the pistol in both hands, mindful to keep the snub nose pointing down. "The Bell and Badger."

Miss Snow waved that away. "Be prepared for another fight."

"You think so?"

"I do more than think so, my dear girl." Miss Snow's smile, this time, revealed a great deal of even white teeth. "I intend to ensure it."

The barman had not put the pub to rights after they had gone. The stools still lay broken where they'd been left, and the men Miss Snow's smoke concoction had blinded remained where they lay.

They weren't groaning anymore.

"Jay-sus, Joseph an'—!"

Miss Snow clapped a hand over Miss Kennedy's mouth before she completed the gasped refrain. "That's enough of that, I think," she said, not unkindly for all the girl had gone white as a sheet and possibly twice as fragile. "The last some poor fool had called on saints in such circumstances, they appeared." Too much peculiarity about the place. Such things were dangerous.

When the girl swayed, Miss Snow cupped a hand under her elbow and navigated her to the nearest stool.

Only once she was sure the girl had no intention to repeat the names did she remove her hand from Miss Kennedy's mouth. Poor pitiable thing. It was quite obvious that Miss Kennedy had not been prepared for such an outcome.

Unfortunately, Miss Snow had.

The hearty Irish lads trounced so soundly by Miss Snow's alchemical workings and Miss Kennedy's pugilistic fists had not been allowed to regain their senses. They lay where Miss Snow had last marked them, each in a pool of blood, with crimson gashes carved in their necks. Ear to ear, no less.

Someone, or something, had spooked.

The facts just weren't adding up. Miss Snow found herself wishing she had easier access to the archival arm of the secretive ministry she worked for. Surely the sagacious Thaddeus Monk would know at a glance which piece of the puzzle was missing.

The barman was gone, no surprise there. She should have been more cautious. Bertie Bannigan had been listed as an informant in the research delivered with Director Fount's orders, but in hindsight, it seemed odd that *cruach* would be forefront of a common informant's thoughts.

"The universal issue with informants," she said thoughtfully, surveying the pub with great care, "is that eventually, even the extremely thick ones start to put things together."

"You lost me," the girl replied, croaking it a little.

"Did Bertie Bannigan ever work with your father?"

"Some. In fact, the day before he took ill, he—*Oh.*"

"Oh, indeed," Miss Snow agreed. The pub was like most—polished wood and relative bric-a-brac showing off its patrons' love for all things Irish, ale, whiskey and song. There was a certain discrepancy amongst the Irish that Miss Snow had never quite grasped. All their songs about life and love, war and peace, lust and drink, tended towards a merriment that belied the sorrow of a thousand years of death, heartache, and loss.

An extremely resourceful people.

Her gaze narrowed upon a crack in the farthest wall, little more than a seam.

"Do you suppose Bertie made me da ill?" Miss Kennedy asked, a note of steel entering her voice.

Miss Snow looked at her with measured confidence. "And if he did?"

Her fists clenched, roughened hammers of righteous wrath. "I'd like to hear him say it while he's still got teeth to say it with."

Teeth were less than essential for speech, but Miss Snow refrained from pointing this out. "Good girl. Take your coat off and turn it inside out, would you?"

"Why?" The girl did as asked without waiting for answer.

Miss Snow did the same. "Caution. Now, we need somewhere quiet, cool, and like as not to be overlooked. Any thoughts on the matter, Miss Kennedy?"

As she expected, the girl's gaze went straight for the back. "Aye," she said, and strode for that wall. She rolled her sleeves up as she did, baring sinewy forearms pale as milk save where the natural ruddiness of her colouring tinted the skin. The revolver in her hand remained gripped tightly.

As it turned out, Bertie Bannigan was every bit the fool Miss Snow considered him.

The first bullet splintered the stairwell she hurried down. Caity's heart surged into her throat, but she did as instinct demanded and leapt to the floor to hide behind a stacked mass of barrels.

Miss Snow did much the same, choosing another barrel to crouch behind, so that they viewed each other across a narrow causeway.

"Bannigan, cease fire this instant!"

Caity didn't expect Miss Snow's demand to be obeyed. On cue, another bullet cracked against the stone floor, shooting sparks between them.

Her jaw set. The pistol in her grip shook, but she firmed her hold and tried not to imagine that she might have to shoot a body, after all.

The air was wrong down here. It should have been fresh and cool, but it smelled of old rot and forgotten meat.

"'Tis not too late," Miss Snow called, her back pressed to the wooden keg. She spared an encouraging smile for Caity. It faded just as quickly. "You can still make this right."

"You're the one meddling," the barman shouted, his voice sounding not at all as Caity remembered. Hoarse. Shrill despite the rasp. A little bit mad. "All you have to do is go back to where you came from and this will all fix itself!"

"Bertie, come out here this moment!" Caity called, injecting her voice with all the stern authority she'd heard her da employ. "Enough is enough."

Her demand earned another shot, echoing in the dank cellar. "I've unlocked the old ways. The famine will ease, don't you understand? Without your nosey friend, this might have gone on without blood."

"Without blood?" Caity repeated, aghast. "Bertie, me da's dead! Fifteen more, all gone, because of you!"

"I had nothing to do with it."

"Lies," Miss Snow called, her tone sweet but firm. "You might not have intended it, Mr Bannigan, but you know as well as I the nature of artefacts. Especially that of the old ways. What did you do?"

For a moment, he was silent. Wood creaked. Then, "In my family's field. We found a gold idol in the earth."

Caity frowned. "Why didn't you sell it?"

"I was going to," he called back, impatient enough that Miss Snow lifted a finger to her lips. "Then I remembered about... about—"

"You can't say his name, can you?" Miss Snow asked. She sidled along the barrels. "They won't let you."

"They?" Caity whispered.

"Him," Bannigan shot back. "I'm being respectful!"

"You are being puppeted," Miss Snow replied. "Set down your weapon, Mr Bannigan. You know the consequences for toying with artefacts."

"No! I won't let you interfere," he shouted, and another gunshot tore through the edge of the barrel Miss Snow had sidled away from.

Caity flinched. "Miss Snow?"

"I'll duck about," she said, pitching her voice low, but reassuring. Her eyes sparkled, a becoming flush upon her cheeks. "I want for you to pop out and fire wildly at whatever you choose. Keep him occupied so that I might sneak up on him."

Caity nodded, though her heart was beating all too hard and she wasn't certain she could hit anything. Perhaps if she fired, he might duck for cover.

"I am ready," she whispered.

As one, Miss Snow slipped around the far side of the barrels just as Caity leaned out, her shoulder hitting the floor, and fired the pistol gripped in both her sweaty hands.

In that moment, she glimpsed Bertie Bannigan, his hair wild about his head and his eyes so wide, the whites were clearly visible. He saw her just as she fired, and while the panic that filled his face gave her pause, it was nothing to the sudden, pointed silence that followed when the small board set up on the table beside him flew into the air.

The pieces upon it—one gold figure and twelve of bone—scattered over the ground. Blood spilled in a red gleam, to spatter to the floor.

For a long moment, nothing in the cellar moved. Not breath, not body, not time.

Bannigan's eyes bulged.

"Caity, get down!" Miss Snow rushed through the narrow divide, seized Caity by the shoulders and wrenched her from view. A wind blasted through the cellar, so cold and foul-smelling that Caity gagged before Miss Snow covered her face with her gloved hand. "Don't look," she shouted, needing to despite their proximity; the screaming now erupting from beyond the barrel flooded through the ears and turned the blood to ice.

It seemed as it might go on forever. She squeezed her eyes closed, her face buried in Miss Snow's jacket. On and on, the wind howled and raged—but it did not turn over the barrels. She heard no crashing, no splintering.

Just as soon as it began, it was over.

Miss Snow eased to her feet, dusting off her trousers, and then helped Caity stand. Her expression was rather more sad than accomplished. "I had hoped to avoid this," she said, though low enough that Caity wondered if she spoke to herself.

"Where's—"

"Mr Bannigan?" Miss Snow stepped out from behind the stack of barrels. She gestured.

Much to her chagrin, Caity was not wholly surprised at what she found.

Bertie Bannigan lay dead, his neck twisted at an odd angle and slashed ear to ear as if in sacrifice. A bullet hole marred the surface of the board he lay sprawled upon, courtesy of her wild shot, but it was the scattering of white crystals all over that caught her eye.

She knelt beside his twisted body, the first wash of tears pricking at her eyelids. There was no pulse in his limp arm, nor any signs of life behind his wide, staring eyes.

Miss Snow crouched beside her, one hand coming to rest upon Caity's shoulder. "They'd claimed him, in the end." She reached over, brushing the white grains from the dead man's cheek. "The Folk always do. It's the price, you understand?"

Caity dragged a forearm across her burning eyes. "I don't. I thought this was the doing of..." She halted, the name placed already on her tongue but panic gripping her throat when she tried to say it.

Miss Snow's smile was small and compressed. "Being unable to say his name was a subtle clue, but one I should have paid attention to earlier. They wouldn't stand for it, here."

"I still don't understand."

"I mean," Miss Snow explained patiently, "that Mr Bannigan here dabbled in a bit of old magic that should have been left well alone. By utilising the artefact he'd found, he attempted to call forth the god who could end the famine. Unfortunately, his methods..." She reached over the corpse to pick up one of the scattered twigs, stained and wrapped with twine. "The god's symbol is that of a golden figure surrounded by twelve smaller figures in stone. By taking twelve sacrifices, the first born, he would guarantee a harvest."

"That's bone, isn't it?" Caity did not attempt to touch the board, or the droplets of red scattered amidst the crystals. "And chicken blood, I think. It smells like it."

"Correct." Miss Snow sighed. "By failing to uphold the old ways as written, he only caught the eye of them eager to subvert such things. His intent was pure, but the dead are drawn to the dead. No god came here."

Caity clasped her hands together around the pistol she had wielded to such strange success. "The bells were the clue, weren't they? The Folk are said to be repelled by them."

"Some are," Miss Snow confirmed, and looked up as a dull report echoed faintly through the still air. "Without testimony from an archivist, I'm afraid all I can do is guess, but I believe that Mr Bannigan gained the attentions of the sluagh."

"The restless dead," Caity murmured. "Said to be rejected from heaven or hell, and even the Otherworld."

"What Mr Bannigan did not realise," Miss Snow said, her expression going quite grim, "was that gaining the attention of such forces always goes awry."

"You mean the sluagh are here? Now?"

"Indeed, dear girl, and they have not wasted time. In distorting the legend of—" Even her mouth hitched on the name, "—the Irish god, they have created a landscape where slaughter has taken root, not bounty. They will feed on the dead and harvest the innocent for their hungers. That is what toying with artefacts will gain one."

Caity heard it again, the scattered report she recognised as gunfire.

She shot to her feet, a cry on her lips, and dashed up the steps.

"Caitriona, wait!"

She did not. Sprinting through the pub, she pushed her way outside and choked on the wind.

It tasted of hatred, smelled of an anger deeper than any human heart could carry.

Shouting filled the city as calls of violence turned to flame.

Caity froze.

Which side had lit the wick of war?

Miss Snow fetched first the golden figure laying on its side in the salt. She wrapped it carefully. Even touching it bothered her, and she wore gloves.

Whether this were truly the symbol of Cromm Crúaich or not, Miss Snow was not qualified to know. That it contained a power eager to be harnessed was without a doubt truth.

She carefully pocketed the item in her coat, still inside out, and hurried up the stairs behind the scattered Miss Kennedy. She found the girl on her knees just outside the pub, watching in horror as smoke rose from the square.

"Up, you go!" Miss Snow ordered, seizing the Irish lass by the arm and hauling her bodily to her feet. "Can't stay here, the fire's spreading!"

Sure enough, the first tongues of flame licked the dark sky. Given the direction of the wind, it would blow the flames their direction quick as tinder.

Good girl that she was, Miss Kennedy followed. The streets were filling with British and Irish alike, a veritable mob screaming at each other. Fists and shillelaghs flew, fires were set deliberately, and glass shattered in shop fronts as looters seized the opportunity to make a point.

They ran fast as they could, dodging groups of men prowling for Irish and British blood to spill, until the gates of the cemetery loomed out of the smoke-encrusted black.

Remembering the arch, Miss Snow tucked her hand into the crook of Miss Kennedy's elbow and dragged to the locked fence. "Up and over, my dear," she shouted.

The girl did not balk, clambering up the grating with only a minor disagreement between her feet and hanging skirt.

As soon as she was on top, Miss Snow scaled the fence with the easy agility of a trained agent.

Almost immediately, the air lightened, smelling now of tilled earth, burning wood and smoke rather than the wrongness that permeated the rest.

Miss Snow took a deep breath as she landed beside Miss Kennedy, who had wrapped her arms around herself and watched her city burn.

For the first time, Miss Snow wasn't quite sure how to address the situation.

She touched the girl lightly on the arm. "They've taken their payment in fortune and flesh," she said, as kindly as she could. "Twelve souls for the story, and a burning for the end as proper. It's unlikely they'll linger past the night."

"What of Galway?" Miss Kennedy asked, her voice a whisper strained to the point of breaking.

Drawing the girl away from the wrought iron gate—a protection this city did not know it afforded its dead—she tucked an arm about Miss Kennedy's waist. A companionable gesture.

A comfortable one, no less.

"Chin up, Miss Kennedy," she said. "Although it's true Galway is caught in the eye of the storm, the land war was bound to spill over eventually. That they were surely given a helping hand does not change the realities of it."

"But if Bertie hadn't—" She lowered her head. Her breath shuddered out on a white mist—distress fragmented by the bitter wind. "The Folk are known for mischief, but this is cruel."

"Such peculiar beings often are, my dear," Miss Snow said quietly. "That is why we must be ever vigilant."

"What of the fighting?"

"Ah, my sweet girl," Miss Snow said, now a little sad for this harsh lesson. "There are peculiar occurrences, and these require a solution which we are uniquely suited to. Then there are matters of mortals and men, which by and large will only be slaked by blood."

Miss Kennedy said nothing to that, though she did walk away to stand alone on a small hill, facing the orange flame reaching hungrily for the sky.

Thunder rumbled overhead, and the skies opened up over Galway's silhouette. The rain poured from the clouds, a torrential flurry that soaked them both within moments.

Not only did it freeze them to the bone, it tamped the fire down, until the city that burned and the passions that raged cooled abruptly as they started.

If she were a woman to believe in such things, Miss Snow might think that somewhere, a forgotten god—aggrieved to find his legend so abused—might have reached out a cooling hand to shelter his people.

Miss Snow wrapped her arms around her self, huddling to conserve warmth, and watched the tall Irish lass with the shoulders of a blacksmith and the hands of a tinkerer.

Some time later, Miss Kennedy picked her way to where she perched upon a worn stone marker, twisting the Ministry ring upon her finger.

"I think I'd like to see the world, Miss Snow."

Miss Snow smiled. "As the nearest branch is in Dublin, we shall be sure to introduce you immediately. Here, have a rest." She inched to the farthest part of the marker, making room for the Irish girl to sit.

Miss Kennedy perched with care, her arm against Miss Snow's. When her head came to rest upon that shoulder, Miss Snow said nothing of it. "What of the gold figure?"

Miss Snow was very much aware of it, heavy in her pocket. "It shall be archived, as all dangerous items must."

"Good." And that was all the girl had to say of that.

Later, when Miss Snow would compose her report for Director Fount, the news of the near-fire had been watered down to minor reports of violence between forces angry over the famine, the land, the evictions that would not cease.

None knew the story of bloodshed by young Bertie Bannigan—angry at the world for the conflict tearing his home apart, and meddling where those of flesh and blood should not. Although peculiar occurrences were this organisation's specialty, Miss Snow did prefer it when such occurrences came from the minds and madness of men, not gods.

Some months later, as Miss Snow stood in to witness the recruitment of the newest Ministry agent—a certain fresh-faced Irish girl with eyes like a tropical sea—reports from the province of Connacht declared the famine over. In fact, the potato crops were coming in strong and healthy.

The Archivist had confirmed in writing her assertion of sluagh influences, and Director Fount had determined that as the artefact was securely tucked away, Galway would see no more obvious meddling. It was all the Ministry was qualified to do, after all.

"Come, Miss Kennedy," she called, mandate in hand. "There's a rash of vanishing bloomers from County Clare to investigate."

Gods and Folk, magic or madmen, it didn't matter what was out there. All agents should start small. A pattern of missing bloomers seemed a lovely change of pace.

The girl hurried to catch up, eyes sparkling.

"Yes, Miss Snow!"

Chinoiserie

Tiffany Trent

"You can scarcely imagine the beauty and magnificence of the places we burnt. It made one's heart sore to burn them; in fact, these places were so large, and we were so pressed for time, that we could not plunder them carefully. Quantities of gold ornaments were burnt, considered as brass. It was wretchedly demoralising work for an army."

—Charles George Gordon, 1860

Yuanmingyuan (Old Summer Palace), Peking
October, 1860

The Chinese Imperial torturers are excellent at their craft. That is well-known. For twenty days and nights, they kept our English delegation alive, for little more than their own pleasure. When they released a journalist and junior envoy, the men were incapable of speech and could not walk.

In retaliation, Lord Elgin decided to destroy their most precious landmark, that place they call Yuanmingyuan, the Gardens of Perfect Brightness, also known as the Qianlong Emperor's Old Summer Palace.

A vast complex of water gardens and mazes of intricate beauty, the Old Summer Palace has been slowly expanding according to the Imperial desire for one hundred and fifty years. The French, charmed by its beauty, called

41

it the Versailles of the East and sent architects to help design the residence of the Emperor's favourite Mongolian concubine. Or so the Archives said, when I researched under the auspices of Agent Robertson a few months ago.

The Ministry has feared that many Chinese antiquities will be lost in the wars that have rent her apart in recent years. We are ill-prepared to deal with the occult arts of the East. I was sent to recover what I could before more might be lost.

All of them—the archivist, Ministry Director Phund, his fellow agents there and in the Hong Kong office—couldn't have imagined how right they were.

"Burn it all, Georgie," Lord Elgin said to me but a few days ago. "Burn it, and they will at last understand with whom they are dealing."

And so, here I am, hidden in plain sight, leading our infantry to the doom of the very antiquities I was hoping to save.

I can imagine that October in Peking might be pleasant in other circumstances. There's a nip in the air and, ordinarily, the streets are filled with the smells of roasting meat and the little onion pancakes the coolies favour after a long day hauling their heavy loads. I miss the catastrophically loud and colourful performances of Chinese acrobats here, the death-defying feats of their martial dancers.

The streets are largely deserted, except for the troops flooding through the streets to burn the palace to the ground. Three thousand or so men—British and French—shouting and pushing all around me, a wave of fire headed for the green island of the Emperor's private domain.

We breach the gates without much resistance. Some French troops looted through here a week ago, and the Imperial guard did not engage them. Small wonder that they leave us to our own devices.

The grounds are increasingly empty as we move deeper into their silence. I had heard from some of my old comrades in Taiping that the Emperor fled at the end of September and is somewhere high in the mountains of Sichuan, perhaps even fleeing toward Lhasa. It matters little, though. We all knew that Empress Cixi has been holding the reins all this time. If we don't kill him, she likely will.

As soon as we enter the grounds, my skin prickles. It isn't because of the wool uniform, unpleasant as it's been these few years on campaign. Something in the pine and golden rain trees watches us.

I'm on alert, searching for movement, the flash of a bayonet or sudden snap of a gun.

But I know there is nothing. The only sounds are from our own boys, drunk with uncontested power.

The itching becomes a deep discomfort. This is, in fact, why I ended up an agent of the Ministry long ago. I can detect supernatural phenomena. You'd think the Spiritualists would love me, but since I was very good even at an early age for exposing most of them for the charlatans they are, I was reviled throughout the séance parlours of London. Lucky for me, the Ministry found me before the agents of the Illuminati did.

Though it was only afternoon when we entered the grounds, it is now twilight among the trees. The shadows are long.

It is said that the Emperors of old knew how to protect their palaces with more than mortal strength. There are whispers of ghosts, of demons drawn out of the darkest dimensions of Hell, who are forced by dark mages to hold firm where humans cannot. There is something very wrong here. Perhaps no one is here to protect the palace because they don't need to be.

I almost turn our boys back. Almost. I have my orders, and they are paramount to any desire I might have to flee.

"Major," someone says next to me. It's Fred Ward, the American. His moustache is like a smear of tar above his lips. "You ready?"

I nod.

"Then dip your torch so's I can light it," he says, grinning. I don't miss the euphemism.

"I hardly think you are the one to light my torch, sir," I say with as much good British stuffiness (as the American would say) as I can muster. I, of course, ruin it with a grin.

"Been a while, eh?"

It had, in fact, been a while, but I'm not about to discuss that with Fred, much as I like him and joke with him.

So, I dip my torch and let him light it instead. I am the last one. Everyone else lit theirs before we even left the camp.

My stomach clenches as the flame takes.

We march onward until we come between two great water towers. The only sound now beyond that of the boys carousing is that of the water splashing endlessly over the tines and spires. The curved gables of the Emperor's palace rise up just beyond, the white marble like bone in the gloaming.

We are all standing around, gawking and nervous. And then a shout goes up, I've no idea from whom.

Everyone is running forward, the torches fanning sparks out over our heads. It's a wonder we don't catch ourselves on fire.

Everything in me resists. My arms and legs feel like lead.

"Well, come on then! Let's get a move on!" Fred yells. And he's off, hooting like some odd American owl. He'd set fire to the water if it would light.

I follow much more slowly. At the last moment, I turn with a contingent of Frenchmen. They are running deeper into the palace grounds, seeking the most ancient of the buildings. These buildings are made of wood and clay rather than marble. They will burn much more easily than the marble palaces built by the French architects.

We come to a place one Frenchman says is called the Hall of Glowing Both Above and Below. It's at the edge of one of the broad, shallow lakes the Emperor built for his pleasure boat. The Frenchmen go down to the dock and soon are swarming over the pleasure boat, rifling through whatever little treasures they can find, laughing when one of their number falls overboard.

Whatever watches us is still here, and as the first flames lick the boat's lavishly-painted sides, I feel the sensation now almost like a bullet to the gut. I gasp. I'd hoped to avoid it completely by coming here. I was hoping I could wander off. But now one of the Frenchmen calls to me. He gestures toward the Hall and tells me to set it ablaze.

Once, the Ministry decided to test me by sending me into a castle that was occupied by an extremely nasty banshee. They had a notion of capturing the æther of supernatural entities, using it to power some kind of "spirit engine." That test resulted in an earthquake in Orkney, perhaps the first recorded of its kind. Spirits, though they may be attracted to me, do not like me. At all. The rubble of a castle and the ruined spirit engine prototype within it, is evidence enough.

It isn't as though I didn't anticipate spirits in China. She is, after all, one of the most ancient nations of the world. It's just that I'd hoped they'd be a bit friendlier. Still, I suppose, when one's haunts are threatened, perhaps malevolence is to be expected.

I enter under the eaves of the Hall. The Frenchmen are still laughing and shouting outside. I think they must have gotten into some *bai jiu*, that devil drink that will make even the staunchest man a vomiting fool in no time.

The Hall smells of camphor and sandalwood. Great rock formations, like slumbering dragons, curl around themselves on pedestals in the gloom. The Emperors kept them around as interesting testaments to the art of Nature, but I can feel the power in them. Unfortunately, such a hulking object isn't going to fit into my pocket.

Something flutters at the edge of my vision. A bit of white cloth. The edge of a sleeve. The hem of a robe, perhaps.

I follow it down the corridor, every muscle like a coiled spring. The sounds outside seem to have stopped rather abruptly. All I can hear are my own boot heels and the occasional hissing of the torch.

The moment I see her, the torch falls from my hand. It hits the floor and goes out in smoking silence. And yet, despite the darkness, I can still see.

She casts her own light. She wears the long-sleeved, layered robes of an Imperial concubine and her hair is done up in the loops and pins of the Ming Dynasty. She once had the favour of some Emperor.

The horrid twisting in my stomach tells me that she may not have kept it for long.

I am not without my defences, so I step closer. Her gaze freezes me.

Ni shi shei?

I know better than to answer a ghost. I finger the æther-blade in my pocket. It's a small thing, meant to disperse unpleasant, localised energies in a pinch. To anyone else, it would seem to be a simple pocketknife.

But when I brandish it at her, she shrinks before its thin blue glow. I'm thankful she can't see my shaking fingers.

It's as if the world contracts. There's a ripple through the silence and I hear the Frenchmen coming down the corridor. I smell the burning before I see the flames racing along the old, dry roof beams.

She growls something I can't quite make out. I can feel that growl radiate through my bones before she disappears around a corner.

I'm so pleased with myself that I follow. There's only one direction to run, anyway. The Frenchmen have effectively cut off the entrance.

The flames chase me as I follow a wisp of her. The concubine's ghost is nowhere to be seen, however. I suppose we've frightened her off and I'm glad of it.

I search as best I can for items that might interest the Ministry—small things, charms and tokens of old Chinese magic. There's a ginger jar on the table by a door that leads out onto the veranda. It's small compared to most of the pottery other soldiers have tried to carry off with them. A bit of chinoiserie for the missus back home.

I don't really look at it carefully. The threat of imminent immolation is wont to do that to a chap. I stuff the jar in my pocket with the other things and flee out into the smoke-filled garden.

The rest of the night I run through the maze of burning buildings. The malevolence has been replaced with a feeling of triumph. Our triumph. Whatever designs the dead may have had on us when we arrived, they were simply no match for the living.

It's not until I'm en route to home once again that I remember the little ginger jar. A serving man packed it away before I left Peking. With nothing to do while on board, I decide to catalogue all the artefacts of my travels. Unfortunately, the little jar is stowed somewhere in the hold below.

It's a star-filled night and the moon is just rising above the waves. The boat plunges between troughs and I let the fresh sea air fill my lungs.

It's then that I notice a dark shape slinking across the deck above.

I rub my eyes, trying not to stumble across the deck when the ship pitches. I look up, searching for the tell-tale shape.

I would almost swear that a great cat just crossed in front of the railing.

Then, I hear the scream.

It's faint. A fairly good distance off, but it's coming from the direction of the hold. I sprint past the flickering gaslights that line the corridor.

The hold door is open. The screaming has been replaced by ominous silence. I draw my pistol, though firing it could potentially light this place up like a torch. Perhaps the threat of that will be enough to stop whatever is happening.

I creep down the stairs. There's a light shimmering like the moon on water, and for a moment I'm filled with the terrible certainty that the hull has been breached and the ship is sinking. My stomach knots in that familiar ache. I've not felt this since Peking. I had hoped not to feel it again until we were at least docked.

I try to keep silent, but among ghosts, the merest breath is a betrayal of the living.

The woman I saw back in the Old Summer Palace glares at me. She is kneeling over someone. A quick glance tells me he's already dead.

"What are you doing?" I say, striding boldly toward her. "Did you kill this man?"

She is shaking her head softly as if she doesn't understand, but I know she must. I can tell by her eyes that she recognizes my expression.

"I don't know why you've followed me, but I will banish you at the first opportunity, I swear it."

She understands that, too, because her lips curve in a wicked smile.

"Try it," she says in halting English.

She dissolves into fog.

The ship's crew rushes downstairs as I'm approaching the body. It's a man—one of the crewmembers I'd seen helping load heavy crates when I'd first come on board. His throat is torn out. The large muscles of his arms have been gnawed on.

A ghost couldn't possibly have done this. But a tiger or a leopard…

I've seen the damage those creatures can do.

Three sailors gape in horror. I hear the cabin boy weep into another man's shoulder.

"Who would do such a thing?" one of them asks me.

"Not who," I say, standing. "What."

One of the men has the good sense to come and cover the corpse with a sheet. "What do you mean?" he asks.

"Gentlemen," I say, "do you happen to know if anyone has smuggled a leopard on board?"

I am as incredulous at the words coming out of my mouth as they are.

"There were lots of large crates packed up in Tianjin. I reckon one could have been smuggled in then," one sailor says.

"I suggest you have someone inspect those crates then. Its secret lair is likely to be in one of them."

"How do you know so much?" the man who covered the corpse asks.

"I've seen stranger things than you can possibly dream in the wildlands of Asia. I'm telling you—nothing but a cat could do this."

They don't dispute me again.

"I'll tell the captain," one of them growls.

I nod. "I urge everyone to keep their doors locked," I say. "Especially at night." I won't say anything about the ghost following me. She is mine and I must deal with her in my own way. Any credibility I've built just now would be destroyed in an instant if I so much as hinted at anything that smacks of Spiritualism.

It's only when I get back to my room that I realise I'd forgotten to search the hold for my crates so I could begin cataloguing them, starting with the ginger jar.

The murdered man is buried at sea very quietly, so as not to arouse passenger fears on board. I am dubious that this will be the last killing. Once a tiger or leopard develops a taste for human flesh, it can never be sated by anything else.

I conduct my own investigation, sweeping the ship from stem to stern, but there are places I can't go.

When I try to go into the hold, a burly-looking boatswain is standing at the door, his arms crossed over his chest. He shakes his head at me, defying me to protest.

"But I just need…"

One eyebrow rises.

I suppose it's time to talk with the captain.

I've been avoiding it because the captain is an old warhorse, the sort who will wag his jaw until your ears hurt. He'll go on about his own bravery and expect you to corroborate until the sun rises or he sinks under the table from too much drink. Unfortunately, the former is more likely than the latter.

But if I want access to the hold, there's only one place I can go.

When I knock on the door to the captain's quarters, I'm still trying to think of a better plan. I'm in full military dress. That should count for something.

A serving man ushers me in at about the same moment another arrives with tea things.

The captain is already seated. He feeds bits of cake as it arrives on the table to the little white and brown dog in his lap. He doesn't rise when I enter and barely spares me a glance. He is in no mood for games.

"Seat yourself, Major."

"Gordon, sir," I say, trying not to bristle. I'm quite certain he knows who I am. But this is his domain and apparently he will lord it over us as he sees fit.

The serving man pours me tea, and the clean bergamot scent uplifts me almost immediately.

"Look, Gordon," he says, "I hear a man died and you are saying that there is some sort of tiger or such nonsense on board." He lets the little dog lick his fingers before he picks up a teacake and pops it in his bearded mouth.

"Yes, sir," I say.

"Well," he picks up his teacup and eyes me over its gold-ringed rim before he takes a swallow. "I sincerely doubt that a large cat did this. But I honestly don't care whether there's a leopard on board or not. I want you to find it and dispose of it."

"Sir?"

"That is to say…find whatever did this—man or beast—and kill it. Before it harms anyone else. We'll make a big show of getting rid of the leopard so that everyone will know they're safe."

I swallow. The lapdog looks at me with disdain, and I notice the little red bows tied around its floppy ears.

"Sir, let me see if I understand correctly. You want me to find something and kill it and make a big show of disposing of it, regardless of whether it's the cause of the problem?"

The captain leans forward. The little dog grunts in disgust and slides off his lap. "Do you know what happens on board a ship when mass hysteria takes hold, Major?"

I do. And it doesn't just happen on board ships. It can happen in barracks, in the jungle, anywhere people are enclosed.

"People die, Major. Lots of people. We need to send a message to the killer that we will deal swiftly with such actions. I think you're just the man to do it."

"Why?" I say.

"This leopard thing was your idea. You find it and take care of it."

I suppress a sigh. "I will need access to the hold. Most of my things are packed away there." Not to mention the storage crates where something—or someone—might hide. But I still believe, despite the captain's doubts, that I'm right. I saw a large cat on the deck. The sailor's wounds are the sort such a creature would make. "You should advise people to keep their berths locked and not go abroad at night," I add.

"Fine," he says. "But I want this dealt with swiftly. The longer people feel unsafe, the more hazardous they become."

There seems to be no room for further discussion. "Yes, sir."

I dislike the way he commands me. I am not, after all, in the Navy or any other such marine division. He truly has no call to enlist me in giving aid. But he is right in that something must be done, and I will not shirk my duty to protect the citizens of the Empire.

I have a gut-wrenching feeling that my solution may not be as neat as the captain would like it to be.

After I leave his quarters, I return to the hold where the boatswain still stands, arms folded.

"Let me pass," I say.

He shakes his head.

"Captain's orders, boatswain! Send the cabin boy to confirm, if you don't believe me."

That seems to do it for him. He knows I wouldn't say that unless it was true. He also knows he can find me if I'm lying.

He grumbles something rather rude and deprecatory and steps aside.

I venture down into the hold. I find a lantern secured in an alcove by the bottom of the stairs and light it carefully.

Things have been re-arranged, crates opened. I poke around for a bit. There is nothing to suggest that my theory is true. But then, I've already begun to suspect there is more to this than anyone would guess.

I can't search everything right now, but I divide the hold into quadrants and search the first one. Nothing. No hair, no scat, no blood other than the dark stain where the sailor fell.

I kneel down and place my hand against the cool boards. It's early summer, so it shouldn't be sweltering, but the stain is like ice. My fingers almost freeze to it. I draw back my hand, cupping my tingling palm.

Whatever killed this man was not among the living.

A ghost leopard? How is that possible? Naturally, I've heard of the Black Shuck in East Anglia and other black dogs that strike terror into the hearts of men. Never have I heard of this sort of thing in any other country.

I remember the ghost of the woman kneeling over this man. I have only heard of fox spirits that can sometimes turn into beautiful women in China and Japan. They are reputed to have nine tails, which you can sometimes see even when they're in human form. But I have seen no such thing with this ghost.

I must know more about her. I must know why she followed me here. I must know if she knows why the leopard is haunting this ship. Could it be part of an ancient curse?

In my things, there is a book from the Ministry Archives about the proper way to conduct a séance. I brought it knowing that ghosts might be a possibility in the old Imperial palaces, but never guessing I might actually need it to interrogate one about a murder.

I find where they've stowed my trunk and unlock it. Everything is louder in the flickering silence. The thought that I am alone with a murdering ghost-beast possibly watching my every move is small comfort. In the jungles and palaces of China, at least I knew my enemy.

The book is under a folded winter jacket that's oddly heavy. As I lift it, the ginger jar slips out into my fingers. I remember that I meant to find it to begin cataloguing all the things I've collected. The book is beneath the coat. I juggle them both while securing and locking the lid, knowing that at any time the ghost leopard could pounce.

Nothing pounces, though, and I manage to return the lantern to its place and climb the stairs without incident.

In my berth, I lock the door. If I could possibly move the desk in front of it, I would, but the desk is bolted to the floor, like every other bit of furniture. Instead, I place my Wilkinson-Webley by my side on the bed. The light is fretful and my stomach growls, but I'm used to long, hungry nights. This one will be no different. Settling on the bunk with the book, I glimpse something in the flicker of the lantern I hadn't noticed.

On the ginger jar, a classic scene has been rendered in exquisite miniature. The roving mountains, the steadfast pines, and peaceful bamboo of Chinese literature are all present. It seems typical, and I'd not given the scene much thought since picking it up on my way out of the burning hall in the Old Summer Palace. But now I see a tiny, white-robed woman winding her way up the mountain path. On a crag above her, a leopard crouches, his tail sweeping down among the rocks. Her head is tilted as if she's just noticed him, and I can make out the way horror crimps her features in just a brushstroke. Above them on the mountain are the tombs of the dead, where presumably she was headed before she encountered her certain doom. It is a stunning piece of chinoiserie, to be sure.

I turn to the first page of the book. There is much mumbo jumbo about the evolution of the universe, the influence of the planets and so on. Eventually, I find that my eyelids are far too heavy. I put my hand down on the barrel of the Wilkinson-Webley to reassure myself. I don't notice when the lamp gutters and goes out.

Moonlight on water wakes me, and then I realise that I am still in my berth, still abed, with my hand on the gun. The book is heavy on my chest.

I'm trying to get my sleep-crusted eyes fully open when the phantom thrusts her face toward mine. I scrabble for the gun and plaster myself against the wall, while the useless book slides off the bed and crashes onto the floor.

"*Ni shi shei?*" she asks. "Who are you?"

No one, I want to say. I am no one.

"Charles Gordon. *Gordon Zhongwen.*" Chinese Gordon some people have called me because of my help with the Taiping rebels.

She receives this information in silence. The room is freezing. Ice rimes the bedstead and I can see my own laboured breath. Fretful ghostlight flickers through her form. She turns her face away from me and for an instant, I see the spots and whiskers of a leopard.

I gasp and the cold reaches deep into my lungs. I cough and she is looking squarely at me again, her eyes blacker than a starless night.

"*Ni shi bao,*" I say. You are the leopard.

She inclines her head.

"*Weishenme?*" I whisper. Why? How?

"In the Emperor's court, a powerful general named Li Dajun became enamoured with me. He wanted me for himself. *Shi kun rao...*" She shakes her head as if searching for a word she'll never find.

"Obsessed?" I venture. I cannot believe I am having this conversation.

She nods. "What I didn't know was that Li also followed the dark path of *gu.*"

Chinese black magic. *Gu* practitioners were said to be capable of breeding demon worms from which they decanted poisons so subtle and refined as to be almost untraceable. But that didn't seem to be the case here. I had never heard of anyone being able to poison someone into becoming a ghost.

"He waited for me on the mountain when I went to visit the tomb of my old master. He tried to make me break my vow to the Emperor, but I would not. Li used the *gu* to transform into a leopard. And then he devoured me."

I have to remind myself to shut my mouth. My fingers are loose on the cold barrel of the gun.

"But he was not content with this," she continues. "He ground my bones into his inkstone. He painted the jar with that ink and sealed my spirit. He made me into a *guizi*, a demon to serve him. As a leopard, I kill. As a ghost woman, I frighten people with my mourning."

She is very nearly weeping now. "Li's son gave the jar over to the Emperor when Li died. The Emperors have kept the jar as an heirloom and as a weapon. I have begged them for centuries to break it. None of them would."

I can see why. A ghost assassin chained to one's service would indeed be a powerful thing. And such an artefact might be useful at some future date to the Ministry, particularly in unwinding the occult practices of China's dark mages.

Perhaps the Ministry could recruit this spirit and seek her aid against our supernatural foes.

I shake off the idea immediately. Could this ghost truly be controlled? I think about the torture our men suffered in the Imperial Palace and I wonder if not all of it was entirely done by physical means. Wouldn't it be better to free her and spare our agents any potential harm? Recruiting a spirit into the service of the Ministry? Preposterous.

"You want me to break it, don't you?" I ask.

She nods.

"If I do this, you will harm no one else?"

"*Dui.*"

"And if I do not?"

"More will die."

I'm reluctant, I must admit. It's a beautiful, ancient piece of art, a bit of history that can never be recovered. The archivist would be head over heels for it.

The captain had said that something must die to stop the deaths of others. The sacrifice of one ginger jar is both easier and harder than taking a life and making a show of a burial at sea.

"Do it in daylight," she says. "And throw the shards into the sea."

Then, without another word she is gone. The room warms by slow degrees.

I look at the jar. It is a small price to pay, I suppose.

I rise and uncap the ink bottle, dip in the nib, and open my ledger.

I write at the top of the lined page in an unsteady hand.

One Ming Dynasty piece of chinoiserie. Lost at sea.

Panther Nights

Glenn Freund

Taken from the Journal of Edward Riches

May 28th, 1888

    I found another lumberjack killed last night. Upon inspection of the body, large gashes were found on his chest and arms. The wounds appear to be from an extremely large Jaguar or other animal. The odd part is that it looks like he did not die from his wounds but instead drowned. I am not a medical man, but I wonder if he drowned on his own blood. A horrifying thought.

    A loud animal cry was heard right before a man's scream.

May 29ᵗʰ,1888

    It was a rough night last night. Victor, my friend in camp was killed. We went our separate way after dinner, and before I got back to my cabin, I hear him scream. The sound went straight to my bones like an icy fingernail. Running, I got to him, but it was too late. I drew my gun and shot at the black mass that was over him, but it seemed to do no good, the monster just bounded off into the night. I am going to miss Victor. I will have one more drink for him tomorrow, and find this creature, and stop it once and for all.

Belize, Central America
June 15th 1888

After arriving in Belize a little worse for the wear, Agent Flowerdew stepped onto land. Thinking to himself while departing the trade ship, *Pirates. Pirates attacked us. What is this, the bloody 17th century? As if navigating the reef wasn't bad enough…* he met with a familiar heat. After having been a field agent in Jamaica for years, Mathew Flowerdew was no stranger to heat. He dreaded the cold air of London, and tried to go back to the Ministry as little as possible, but he revelled in the heat of Jamaica.

He had been assigned to Belize after Agent Edward Riches had disappeared. Riches had been making reports of men going missing from the lumber camps when the reports suddenly stopped. Never a good sign. Early briefs suspected that it was just the locals making another attempt to rid the coast of the British. After several nights of scouting around the camp, Riches had come up with the conclusion it was a monstrous jaguar. The reports had stopped shortly after.

Flowerdew had not known Riches well. He was a gruff old man with a meticulous hand and a reputation as a crack shot. Riches had saved Flowerdew a couple of times when things got out of hand. He also had a penchant for women a man his age maybe shouldn't have, and that penchant had landed him in trouble a time or two. His box of wedding rings was known all throughout the islands and Central American field agents. But out of respect, the local women didn't. Over all, he was a superlative field agent.

After being assured his cargo would be taken to the lumber camp, Flowerdew grabbed his gun belt, and his vibration blade machete, threw his bag on to the back of a cart, and jumped up to take his seat with the cargo for the journey to the camp. As the cart trundled along the road, the slow rocking and knocking of the cart combined with the gentle breeze coming in from the sea lulled him into a trance-like relaxation. The heady smells of the jungle added to this peaceful, soothing feeling, but the tranquillity was not savoured as he reflected back on his orders from Doctor Sound:

> *Flowerdew,*
> *I need to you go to Belize and check in on Riches. He has been reporting on some disappearances in the area. Riches' weekly reports have stopped however, and I need you to find out what is going on there. Check in on him, make sure he is well, or see if he found himself another ex-wife. If he has, inform him to desist such*

raucous behaviours immediately. There are worse places he can be than Belize. Places with far fewer women.

Be careful, Flowerdew. Bring your full kit. We do not know what happened to him.

Doctor Sound

A hard jostle from the cart snapped Flowerdew out of his reverie, and he found on awakening, the jungle giving way to a clearing. Looking like a giant's muddy footprint in the forest, the sounds of industry came pouring out into the clearing. Saws ripping. Axes chopping, wood cracking. Different languages and accents floating on the air. A strong smell of earth and mud filled the air as he approached the main camp.

Hopping off the cart, Flowerdew sauntered towards the main camp building. As he approached, a mountain of a man emerged from the doorway.

"Hello there! Foreman around?" Flowerdew yelled across the yard as he approached.

He received a gruff reply of "Who wants to know?" surprisingly enough in an accent of the southern United States, as the man looked Flowerdew up and down.

"Mathew Flowerdew. I was sent from Miggins' Antiquities of London," he said as he walked past the block of humanity that was standing next to the door of the main building.

With the sound of the yard fading into the background, Flowerdew entered the main building. Giving himself a second for his eyes to adjust, he surveyed the interior of the room. It had a very modest arrangement with just a few desks and several long benches and tables. On one side there was a large desk covered in maps and piles upon piles of papers.

"Boss ain't in here" the human block replied, walking into the doorway. "He's around back."

The man paused. "The name's Zeke." He extended his hand to Flowerdew, who couldn't help notice it was like hams had been tied together with fingers cut out. Calloused and hard, he had a surprisingly precise hand shake.

"Pleasure to meet you, Zeke."

"Follow me." Without another word, Zeke turned and went back outside.

Walking around the building, Zeke pointed to a fellow who must have been a powerful man in his youth, with a strong square jaw and broad shoulders. However, time had stripped him away, deflating him like a cliff face after decades of ocean battering. He was wearing glasses as he looked over his work. Behind those glasses were eyes that looked like they were prone to smiling, and lines around his face.

"He's got a lot on his mind of late. He feels responsible for the loss of those men. He comes out here to think and take a load off." And with that he walked back around the building, yelling orders to people to unload the cart in the centre of camp.

"Hello, I am Mathew Flowerdew of Miggins' Antiquites," he announced, continuing the cover story that Riches should have established as he walked toward the foreman.

"Oh! Hello. Come over and sit down. What can we do for you, sir?" The man seemed very distracted and slightly nervous.

"I'm sorry, I didn't catch your name," Flowerdew said as he righted a log.

"Bloody hell, I am sorry. Silvester, Silvester Bates," he replied, resting his axe on his shoulder and promptly thrusting a large sturdy hand out. It looked like it had gone around the world and back, but had been back for several years.

"You alright, Mr Bates?"

"You know, when you think you have seen it all, something comes up. I can look a falling tree square in the trunk, laugh in the face of locals with a machete, but...I'm sorry, I did not catch your name?"

"Flowerdew," he offered.

There was a dead space in the conversation as Bates focused on the two hands that were still shaking.

"You know, I wasn't even supposed to be the foreman. Last foreman got killed by it."

Flowerdew stared at the pain that ran across the man's features. He suspected his was a face that must have not been accustomed to sadness. Keeping his face and tone deadpan, he replied, "Well sir, that is why I am here."

Bates' eyebrows wrinkled together. "But you're representing an antiquities boutique, correct? What exactly do antiquities have to do with—"

"I don't know if my associate explained this wholly, when industry reaches untouched communities such as this jungle territory, there can be artefacts disturbed that can provoke retaliation steeped in ancient rituals and folklore. These rituals and folklore, as well as the preservation of these ancient cultures, are our top priority." When Bates gave a slight nod accompanied with a silent *"Ah,"* Flowerdew looked down at their still shaking hands and asked, "Two questions: one, can I have my hand back, and two, what can you tell me about these deaths?"

With a start of realisation, he released Flowerdew's hand and followed it with a sigh so deep it looked like he had deflated. Bates then began to speak. "They started about two months ago, right after we moved the camp to the river. We had made our way far enough from the coast that it was getting hard to move the lumber. This spot in the river was helping a lot with getting the mill up and running. A little while later, some of my men started disappearing. We thought it was the locals at first, but they have not been giving us trouble for a while. Then we thought it might have been some big cat, one of those panthers creeping around at night, making the awful crying sound followed by the horrid screams. But..." His words trailed off. Flowerdew could just make out in the man's eyes a memory bubbling to the surface. "After a few weeks we found the first corpse. He had scratched out his own eyes, and was blue. Blue like he had drowned in the river." Bates reached into his pocket, producing a flask, shaking his head as he opened it and drank several fingers' worth. "A panther does not do that to a man. The disappearances seemed to get a lot worse when we got our shipments in." He took another gulp from his flask, and then slammed his axe into a log. "We can't keep losing men at this rate. I keep having to hire whoever is willing to come all the way down here, not the most top choices if you know what I mean."

As Flowerdew tried to piece together what he knew from Riches' notes, the gears began to turn in his head. "When was the last disappearance?"

"No disappearance this time. Found him dead in the middle of the camp. Blue like he was drowned again," Bates said, his eyes staring into the spirals of the wood.

"Do you still have the body?"

"No sir, we burned it. The men get pretty jumpy about these things. They do not want some cursed dead man around camp, *Obeah*, hoodoo, local lore and the like, you know how it is. Each group has their own reason, but whatever is killing my boys, it just is not right so I do not blame them.

"I am responsible for them, you know. It starts to chip away at your heart, as you are helpless to do anything. I don't know what is killing them, all I know is, my liche yard is getting bigger and bigger. Whenever I close my eyes at night I hear the sound of whatever it is mixing with the screams of ma-boys. It's like nothing I have every heard, it sounds like a monster, grinding metal in its guts, plus the sound of pure terror my boys scream as it gets them..."

"If you can think of anything else that might be helpful, please let me know. I will be staying in Riches' cabin if that is alright," Flowerdew replied as he stood up and passed his hand across to shake.

"That is fine. I will make sure Zeke gets some of the lads to bring your things over."

Flowerdew walked around the building and flagged down Zeke to escort him over to Riches' cabin. Once there, he took out his notebook, and looked around the cabin. At a glance it looked like no one had been in here since Riches' disappearance. It was pretty well-furnished, with all his books kept in a chest to keep the insects out of them. Nice mahogany desk, probably made from one of the rough-cut logs. Taking out the Ministry-issued lock pick set, Flowerdew started at the lock on Riches' Ministry trunk, recognising its make and model. After a few minutes of work and a few choice words best not shared in polite company, he gained access to Riches' life in Belize. The inside of the trunk was for the most part empty: just a small box with a dozen gold rings of different sizes, and a couple of nice suits.

As Flowerdew released the latch to remove the top to the secret compartment, he was shocked to find it just as threadbare as its main compartment. The designated spots for guns, extra munitions, and spectral detection showed they were all missing. Only a stack of Ministry journals and two small, old lodestone communicators—an antiquated piece of technology that had been replaced with wireless communication—remained. While they were effective in their time, they were very limited in their function, and only being able to communicate with each other made them very challenging in the field. Flowerdew checked the stylus and frame on both of them to make sure they were functioning. With the exception of a little rust, they seemed to be in working order.

Sitting down under the mosquito net, Flowerdew began to read through Riches' finely crafted notes on the disappearances. He had suspected some sort of ghost panther at first based off the spectral readings that he was getting. As Flowerdew continued through the notes, he observed that Riches had grown less and less sure of the panther assessment, and began to suspect differently. He mentioned planning a full night's surveillance the day before his disappearance. After that, the notes stopped.

When Flowerdew heard a knocking on the door of the cabin, he looked up from the books. He gave entry to the person at the door, and a large crate was brought in.

He knew right away something was wrong with the crate. At a glance his possessions appeared intact, but the crate was slightly at an angle. Prying it open, he saw all of the trunks had a drunken lean to them.

"No, no, no, no!" he franticly grumbled.

As he opened the trunks one by one, he found all of the seals on the trunks were broken, and all of their contents encrusted with sea-salt. Everything—his delicate tools and intricate arms—were damaged, and without proper tools, there was no way to fix them out here. He would have to send a message to Brazil to get a new kit, which would take weeks.

"Damned bumboclot pirates. The crate must have fallen over when taking all those fucking shots at us." Letting out a large sigh he thought to himself, "*Well*, no use crying over bloody spilt rum."

Flowerdew took stock of what he had with him: a few trunks full of useless equipment, two antiquated lodestone resonators, a few days' worth of clean clothes, and his own weapons: a high frequency vibration blade machete, his own pair of Wilkinson-Webley "Peppershot," a gun similar in design to the confederate La Mat, but with an easier trigger system for the shotgun round, and a few extra boxes of bullets.

And a bag of toffees. Sweets always made travel easier for Flowerdew.

Figuring not much more could be done today, he decided it would be good to get some rest before he went to the mess hall. Lying down, he started to cycle through the information that he knew before he drifted off to sleep.

Flowerdew bolted up right. He looked around to see what had woken him. Night had fallen while he was asleep. A shadow detached itself from the darkness of the doorframe and stepped into the centre of the cabin. "I said it was dinner time, Mr Flowerdew," the shadow said. Striking a match, Flowerdew lit the lamp on the end table. He held it upward to shed some light onto the shadow, revealing a small Mayan boy in an apron. Collecting himself, Flowerdew thanked the boy and asked his name.

"Cookie callz me Cricket," the boy replied.

"Cricket?"

"Yez sir, because I am always jumping to action. When I am not, I am still as stick. Plus Cookie likez me singing. If you can come with me, I'z can take you to the mess hall."

Checking his boots for bugs, he grabbed his gun belt and walked out into the night, the boy staying close to his side.

"Where are you from, Cricket?" Flowerdew asked as they walked across the yard.

"I'm from right here. Well I was right here before I moved, but I come back. This is where I belong."

"Who…uh…. who taught you English, Cricket?" The cross section of different dialects was starting to confuse Flowerdew. Cricket spoke in a form of pigeon English that looked like it took samples from the Queen's English, Jamaican, Southern United States, and who knows where else.

"Whoever wants to talk with me in camp. Cookie been teachin' me most of it, but the men, they help too."

Ahead of them, the sound of plates and knives clashing and raucous merriment filtered softly through the air, then poured out the door like a flash flood. Entering the mess hall, a wave of heat and smells assaulted Flowerdew's nose, painting a picture of daily life. Cricket escorted him to the foreman's table, before disappearing into the crowd.

"Everyone seems so happy, Mr Bates. I wouldn't think people would be this happy out here," Flowerdew yelled to Bates over the roar of the room.

Bates, transformed now to a picture of joviality, guffawed, clapping Flowerdew on his shoulder. "Things are not normally this boisterous, but that ship you came in on had all of our supplies for the next month. The men tend to be a little heavy handed with the rum the first few nights. It's a bit like a celebration," Bates answered.

Nodding, Flowerdew turned back to the table to find Cricket emerging from the crowd. He deposited a plate of food before him, and then vanished again.

"Quick as lightning, that lad is," Flowerdew said before he tucked into the food on the table. A hearty meal, full of spices, something he was used to and made him feel like he was back at home. Eating his meal slowly, Flowerdew was fascinated by the pure sea of humanity that was the mess hall. People laughing, eating, drinking, and generally just so happy with life. It was hard to believe that these were the same people that at any moment could be the next victim. On the other hand, it made sense. If you do not know when your last breath will be, you might as well live life to the fullest. Flowerdew thought it was what he would have done when he was younger.

Having eaten more than his fill, Flowerdew excused himself, traversed the hall, and headed back to his cabin. The trip, he suddenly realised, after his head returned to the pillow, must have left him more exhausted than he had earlier assumed.

With a start, Flowerdew awoke again, but this time it was different. He had heard a scream pierce through his dreams like an arrow through melon. Grabbing his gun belt, he ran out the door while fumbling to get it on. Opening up one of his Peppershots to assure it was loaded and absently touching the handle of his high frequency machete, he snatched up a lantern outside his cabin, brightened the flame inside, and looked about him. The yard was clear. Not a single soul moved. Closing his eyes, he stood there and listened. He heard a gentle breeze through the leaves, the wings of a night bird, the river whispering by...

...and something else.

His eyes flicked open as he drew his pistol. As he closed the distance between himself and the unusual sound, it became clear that he had been hearing someone sucking in a breath, only to blubber without restraint. A second person near him was crying.

As Flowerdew rounded the corner, he spotted a large black mass in front of him. Bringing his light around, a tangle of black hair bolted for the river faster than he could believe. As he raised the lantern higher, the mass of black melted into the water and the sound of crying faded away.

Flowerdew turned around to see a lumberjack lying on the bed of the river.

Running to the still stranger, it was clear that there was no hope for him. His face was blue as a berry, and it looked like he had been clawing at his own throat, his neck was scratched to bloody ribbons. There was, however, blood coming out of the corners of his eyes as well. Filing all this information away, Flowerdew stood up and walked down the riverside, scanning the surface with his lantern, but all held an eerie calm. Nary a ripple in the water. He cast a glance around him, found a large leaf at his feet, and tossed it into the river, watching it drift slowly with its lazy, invisible current.

Following the river downstream, the faint sound of crying returned. In an instant he was dashing down the banks, his three-barrelled Peppershot still out from its holster, pulling the hammer back to a firing position. The sound of crying got louder and louder as he ran, but he saw no sign of that creature. Rounding a bend in the river, something in the distance stirred. This creature, however, was a *white* form. He continued to creep closer, the darkness and shadows eventually revealing what was making the sound this time: a woman. Her shape looked beautiful.

As he approached he yelled to her, "Be careful! There is a monster around here! Get out of here!"

"*¿Que?*" was the choked reply.

He tried again as he got closer to her, but this time in Spanish. As he approached he heard the sound of crying getting louder and slowed his steps.

"*¿Señora, me entiendes?*" *Madam do you understand me?* he asked her.

Getting closer he started to see more of her features. She had long black hair all the way down to the ground that was covering her face. She was dressed in a long white gown made of some fine quality fabric. She was barefoot, but her feet were clean despite being on the muddy riverbed. Flowerdew started to raise his gun when with a cry of pure despair she cried, "I have lost them! I have lost my children. I took them down to the river and they never came back!"

Flowerdew hesitated, stunned to hear her reply in English. He cleared his throat, lowering his weapon. "Madam, you are not going to find them tonight. It is too dark. You should head home." He stopped several yards away. A chill was slowly creeping up his spine, as if it were one of the creatures of the jungle slithering under his garments, searching for warmth.

The crying had stopped, and in its place an unsettling stillness fell over her. With a dark and cold tone emanating from her form, she wailed, "I lost them all for him! I was not pretty enough for him. Why? Why was I not beautiful enough for him? Was it because I was too old?" Turning slowly towards him, she parted her hair and Flowerdew immediately raised his pistol. "Do you think I am beautiful?"

Where her eyes were supposed to be there were only puckered holes. Trails of black tears were dripping from the sockets. Her lips, while rose red, were cracked and bleeding. Her whole face was wrinkled like it had been at the bottom of the river for days.

Flowerdew unloaded the top two barrels. In the blink of an eye the woman was next to him.

"Do you not find me beautiful?" she wailed. *"AM I A MONSTER TO YOU?!"*

Lashing out with her arm, she knocked the Peppershot out of Flowerdew's hand. She released a monstrous scream as he stepped back. Screaming, she charged him. Her hands, that only a moment ago were beautiful, had transformed into frightful long claws. "You are just like the rest of them!" she shrieked.

Drawing his other gun, Flowerdew started again. Cocking the twenty gauges this time, four holes appeared in the creature, but she still came at him. The claws ripped through his shirt even as he ducked backwards. Having trouble with his footing on the muddy riverside, he stumbled. The claws raked his shoulder, sending an icy chill through his arm that forced him to drop the lantern. Pushing against the jungle floor, his heels scrambling for purchase as he scurried away from the monster, he pulled out the high frequency machete. He fumbled at the ripcord trying to get the motor spinning. Finally, he grasped the cord in his teeth and gave it a hard yank. As the motor started to slowly pick up speed he realised how much he was tiring.

His head cracked hard against a thick tree trunk. With the shadows and nightmarish creature closing on him blurring, he focused all his strength to hold on to the machete in his hands. Flowerdew looked up just in time to see her lunge for his throat. She grazed his neck as he lurched out of the way. On hearing the machete finally emit the purr of its engine spinning up to speed, he swung at her, missing the monster's skull, removing a large chunk of hair. The night air filled with a wail of frustration and rage. She leapt over him, bounding over to the water, disappearing into the night.

Breathing heavily, Flowerdew rested himself against the tree. Ripping off his sleeve, he did the best he could to wrap the wound on his shoulder. Using his other sleeve he lightly wrapped his neck. He collected his lantern, the discarded side arms, and what remained of his wits, before making his way back to camp.

As he approached, the sound of running feet and men yelling came from the centre of camp, lanterns and torches spilling from the buildings and coming towards him. All the men circled the body of the dead lumberjack. Flowerdew went to call out to them, when his words and thoughts scattered on seeing and hearing the other men pouring oil over their dead comrade and then lighting him on fire. With a helpless yell, he staggered for the circle, trying to stop the men from destroying evidence. By the time he got to them, it was too late.

"Why would you do that?" he yelled as the corpse smouldered in front of him. Getting a myriad of answers from 'making sure he stays dead' to 'appeasing the gods, ' each group seemed to have their own reasons, but in the end, the result was the same: destroying the body.

Flowerdew's eyes flicked open. He realised that it must be late in the day based on the heat around him. A foggy recollection came to him of wandering over to the mess hall for hot water and maybe some rum to dress his wounds. He remembered taking out his case journal, recording the night's events. Somehow he pulled himself into bed, and passed out.

He redressed his wounds using some of Riches' sheets, then walked around camp asking about this woman in white, but no one would talk to him. Even Riches' notes yielded nothing. Flowerdew screwed his eyes shut, pushing his spectacles up as he rubbed the bridge of his nose. He only needed them for reading, and with all he had done today, his bridge was raw.

There was a light knock at the door. "Sir, dinnerz time is almost done. Mr. Bates said to get you before you miss all the bouffe," Cricket said from the doorway.

"Thank you, Cricket," he said as he stood up and closed his books. Stretching, he grabbed his gun belt and headed for the door. "Cricket, have you ever heard any stories of a woman in white or a weeping woman?"

"La Llorona? I know this story. She killed herself a hundred years ago. My grandpapa tellz me not to walk on riverbank alone at night because of her. She snatchez little children because she drowned her own."

"Why did she drown her children?"

"To be with a gentleman who rejects her because of her family," Cricket said like it was common knowledge.

"A cautionary tale, Cricket, but not sure it fits the bill, as it were. Whatever she is, she has been attacking men, not children," Flowerdew replied with disappointment.

"She takes drunk men too, comes up to them while they are staggering home and asks if she is beautiful." Flowerdew held his breath, and then heard his confirmation. "When they reply, she pulls away hair to reveal gruesome face. Makes men die. Sometimes they don't die, they get very, very sick."

"We noticed the disappearances seemed to get a lot worse when we got our shipments in," Bates had said to him. *"The men tend to be a little heavy handed with the rum the first few nights."*

"Oh no, Cricket, we have to go," Flowerdew said as he secured his belt and gathered up the two lodestone resonators. Dashing out the door with Cricket in tow, he made a break for the mess hall. As he approached, he noticed that for the night, it was pretty quiet. Darting inside, he looked around and saw that the mess hall, with the exception of a few sitting in groups or passed out across tables, was empty. Dinner was already over.

"Cricket, I need your help. Can you summon up your courage for Her Majesty the Queen and the good men here?"

Wide-eyed, the boy nodded.

"Good lad. Come with me down to the river. We will need to wait for La Llorona tonight. Take this." He handed him one of the lodestone resonators. "This is a communications device. Hold down this button and do not touch anything else. It will take your voice right into mine." He held up the other lodestone resonator. "If you see anything, let me know. We have to hurry before another person gets killed."

Grabbing a pair of lamps from the mess hall, they jetted for the river. Once at the bank, Flowerdew pointed further down the river and said to Cricket, "Remember, push the button and I will come running." He put a hand on the lad's shoulder, then lit the flame. "Be brave, lad."

"I will, sir."

In the still of night, Flowerdew closed his eyes and concentrated, listening to the sounds of the night from his hiding place. Snores drifted in from the camp, bats screeched overhead, fish sloshed in the water, but there was no crying. Opening his eyes, he stepped out into the moonlight and began to stalk further down the river. Not even the wind seemed brave enough to blow.

Suddenly, a crack of sound burst from Flowerdew's pocket. "Sir! Sir, it is here, near Zeke's cabin!"

"I am coming. Do not let her see you!" he replied as he dashed up the riverside.

The glow of the camp just came into view, along with two figures in the distance. One of them was dressed in white.

"I ain't got no idea what you saying lady, but you sure look good enough to eat," came drifting across the night.

Pumping his legs harder, Flowerdew shouted out to the two figures, "Zeke! Run! She is the one killing people!"

Zeke slowly turned in his direction, his stance unsteady. "What are you talking about, Flowerpeddles?" he slurred. "This little lady ain't gonna hurt nobody."

Flowerdew could see La Llorona make a motion consistent of pulling back her hair, revealing her face to the inebriated Zeke. The man staggered back as he started screaming in terror. She was on top of him in a blink of an eye, her hands wrapped around his neck. Water started to pour from Zeke's mouth as his body convulsed in her grasp.

Pulling the ripcord on the vibro-blade machete, Flowerdew ran for Zeke, watching him turn darker shades of blue while grasping at the hands of La Llorona. He only managed to tear up his own throat, which was getting bloodier and bloodier as his hands passed through hers with each flail. Hearing the blade idle and ready, Flowerdew swung the blade at La Llorona. She released Zeke, darting away from Flowerdew. Zeke fell to the ground like a sack of bricks, gasping for air as the water spewing out of his mouth vanished. Shattering the night with a wild, primal cry of rage, La Llorona lashed out at Flowerdew in a flurry of strikes. Despite the blade blocking her blows, he found himself pushed further and further back each time. Not wanting a repeat of the previous evening, Flowerdew knocked away one of her swipes, then thrust forward, twisting his weapon to put the blade right in the line of her hand. The machete opened her hand like a clamshell, spraying a thick, black ooze in all directions as she recoiled away.

Crying, she grasped her hand, her disfigured face—in some odd fashion—softening. "Why? Why are you doing this to me?" she pleaded. "He—he is the one to blame! He left me! He left me after I took away the children. Why does he not love me?" she wailed as she wept through her hands.

"This man is not the one you love," Flowerdew said, wielding the machete before him, keeping her at bay. "The man you loved is dead, and has been for a hundred years. You need to stop—"

His own plea was cut off as La Llorona dashed forward and slashed her fingers across his face. Flowerdew managed to turn his head, though La Llorona's fingers cut him from brow to jaw on the right side of his face, and filled his skull with a bizarre prickling. Staggering back, Flowerdew tripped over the uneven ground and stumbled backward.

Catching himself on a cabin, Flowerdew looked up to see La Llorona over Zeke again. "Soon we will be together forever, my love," she whispered as she straddled his chest and reached for his throat.

Pushing off the wall, Flowerdew lunged forward, slashing upward with the blade. La Llorona released another blood-curdling scream as her claws flew away from her body, disappearing into the darkness. Howling like the winds of hell, a pair of black stumps where her hands were, she dashed for Flowerdew so quickly he was unable to react.

The machete was struck from his hand and he felt himself pinned against the cabin behind him. He felt the bloody stumps on either side of his throat, closing like a pair of pincers.

Water started to fill his mouth.

Just as he began to reflect on his life, Flowerdew unceremoniously met with the ground. With his ears ringing, Flowerdew gasped for breath, his eyes coming up to a gruesome macabre sight.

Cricket stood before La Llorona with arms outstretched, begging for her embrace. "Get up, sir," the boy yelled, terror filling his eyes as she walked toward him. "I do not know how long she will be fooled." He then looked back at La Llorona. *"¿Dónde has estado mi madre? Te he echado de menos."*

The monster lumbered forward, weeping once more.

Flowerdew picked up the vibro-blade, but paused. How was this having an effect when the "Crackshots" did not? She felt the pain. That much was obvious on account of her screams.

Just a moment. Screams. Crying during attack from the vibro-blade. She must possess a form responsive to noise.

Reaching into his pocket, he pulled out the lodestone resonator. "Cricket, pull out the communicator and push the button now!" As Cricket pulled out his own resonator, Flowerdew jammed the vibro-blade into the stylus, releasing a high-pitched screech. La Llorona began to whip around to look at Flowerdew, her face wracking with pain as the two resonators amplified each other over the short distance, the sound reaching higher and higher, louder and louder. La Llorona wailed as her body tore apart from the inside out. She lashed at her own body as if there were insects crawling all over her. Her body shredded before them like paper trapped in a heavy water current, different pieces of her drifting away into the night.

The two lodestones shattered in a shower of shards and sparks. Stopping the machete, Flowerdew pulled himself to his feet and stumbled over to Cricket. "What were you thinking? You could have got yourself killed!"

"I figured she kidnaps children because she misses hers. Maybe she would want them back. Felt likez sound tinkin' at dat time," replied Cricket.

"Very astute. Thank you. I do not think she will be bothering us anymore. Let's check on Zeke." Turning around, Flowerdew promptly fell to the ground, the last thought flashing in his mind before smacking the ground being, "Oh bloody hell, this is inconvenient."

Flowerdew awoke to the smell of hot rum and mud. He could tell he was in Riches' cabin, but something was different. He was not able to see as much of the room as when he first arrived. He reached up and found his face covered in bandages. After frantically unwrapping the bandages covering his left eye, he breathed a sigh of relief on being able to see out of both. After that little scare, Flowerdew searched the rest of his body. His arm and chest were properly wrapped with clean dressings. Resting on his chest, hanging from a cord around his neck, he also found a little charm of a white goat-dog looking thing. Curious about it, he filed away his question about it for later.

"You are awake," Cricket chirped. He dashed out of the cabin, returning shortly after with a bowl of stew.

Zeke had probably been too drunk to remember anything clearly, but Cricket knew the truth.

"I am glad you are awake we thought wez gunna looze ya," Cricket said.

"How long was I out?"

"Several dayz. We all tought you were a gonnerz."

"How did I get back here? Did you carry me?"

With a loud laugh, Cricket replied, "Oh no, sir! When your clever machines blew up, it woke up the camp. Camp found you passed out next to Zeke, all cut up. They thought he had gotten a little too rough again. They woke up Doc. Got you in bed."

"Cricket, what is this thing around my neck?"

"It is a *cadejo*. I made it for you to keep the rest of the evil spirits away. I figure it couldn't hurt to help a little."

"Do I need it?" asked Flowerdew.

Cricket looked very uncomfortable. "I think you might, sir. Take a look in mirror."

Flowerdew pulled himself to the edge of his bed, looking at the odd reflection in the mirror. Everywhere La Llorona had cut him, the wounds were surrounded by black skin. Not like frost bite or jungle rot. Something different, as if he had been tattooed with the claw marks.

After giving Cricket a letter to deliver to a trade ship bound for Brazil, Flowerdew spent the next couple of weeks recovering, reading, and recording interviews. When Riches' full time replacement showed up several weeks later, Flowerdew was more than ready to go home. He jumped aboard the first ship toward Jamaica, ready to sail away into the night. He was done with this jungle. Once in his cabin, a private cabin, he removed his jacket, vest and shirt, staring at the scars from La Llorona.

Perhaps he was done with the jungle. The jungle, however, would never be done with him.

New London Calling

Peter Woodworth

New London, CT
United States of America
1894

Bernard stepped off the train and was immediately unimpressed.

Truth be told, he had been in a state of slowly escalating distemper for the entire voyage to the United States. It had been an unusually rough crossing, or so a fellow at his table had told him during one of the rare instances when Bernard had been able to stagger from his cabin for more than an hour at a time. Even the thought of boarding a vessel for the return voyage made him feel a bit queasy, not to mention increased his irritation at the backwards country that demanded his presence.

Bernard fancied himself a cosmopolitan sort, fond of travel and comfortable with all manner of strange customs and exotic locales, though he had never travelled further from London than his uncle's cottage on the Isle of Wight. He did like to think this was just a matter of scheduling, that surely someday the world would catch on to his interest in traveling it, and in the meantime made up for this trifling fact by being as well-read as possible. When Doctor Sound inquired about his eligibility for international assignments, Bernard had positively jumped at the chance, imagining himself carrying out the Ministry's vital work in Parisian salons or the canals of Venice, possibly even an exotic setting the likes of Bombay.

He had most decidedly not foreseen being sent across the heaving ocean to wind up in this backwater territory.

This town of New London, Bernard decided as he looked around the platform, was the cruellest joke so far. Naming this muddy hamlet after the centre of the British Empire seemed a mean-spirited joke gone horribly awry. What about this tiny seaside collection of colonial architecture in any way evoked the majesty of its namesake? It was like naming a harmless terrier "Attila the Hun"—endearing in theory but thoroughly ridiculous in application. A bit of wind whipped across the platform and Bernard closed his coat almost as tightly as his heart, wondering once more what he could possibly have done to deserve this assignment.

Regardless of the assignment, he refused to compromise in his demeanour or fashion. His suit was charcoal grey with the very faintest suggestion of light blue pinstripes, his bow tie a glossy black, his watch chain the very brightest polished silver. His tailor had assured him it was the very essence of modern style, and Bernard liked to think that he kept abreast of the latest fashions. It never hurt to put one's best foot forward when making an impression, after all, especially in a place where sophistication often seemed so utterly lacking.

"Mr Entwhistle! Mr Entwhistle! Is that you?" Bernard started as he saw the young man approaching, an expression of nigh-manic good cheer on his face as he gesticulated frantically to get the older man's attention. He was short and lean, dressed in a dark suit and matching coachman's cap, rather inexplicably paired with a bright blue scarf tied around his neck in a jaunty fashion. Between his stature and his evidently boundless energy, he might easily have been mistaken for a boy if not for his thick red moustache, which Bernard reflected had likely been grown at least in part for that reason. The young man stuck out his hand in an aggressively familiar fashion common to many Americans, at least in Bernard's experience. "So glad you could make it!"

"Yes, well, a pleasure," Bernard managed, taking the offered hand and nearly losing his arm at the shoulder as the young man shook it. "And you are…?"

"Oh! So sorry! Where are my manners?" The young man doffed his cap. "Arthur Kraft. Archivist, New London field office."

"Charmed," Bernard said, anything but. Since arriving in New York he had become increasingly accustomed with Americans and their awkward etiquette. It worsened steadily the further he travelled away from the city. "Bernard Entwhistle. I've come from the home office regarding—" He glanced around the platform a touch theatrically, especially considering it seemed he was the only passenger to disembark at this stop, but he was determined to salvage some sense of adventure from this farce if he could. "—the business you wrote about. Is there perhaps somewhere private to which we could retire?"

"Of course," Arthur said brightly, replacing his cap and gesturing toward Bernard's trunk. "May I?" A bit taken aback, Bernard simply nodded, and Arthur took the trunk up with an easy strength that belied his small stature. "It's only a few blocks to the field office, so I hope you don't mind if we simply walk?" Arthur gave a little laugh. "A little more time to take in the town, am I right?"

"What a lovely idea," Bernard said as a carriage splashed past, wheels clattering on the uneven stones, narrowly avoiding showering him with dirty water in the process. He saw Arthur looking back at him a bit quizzically and fixed a smile on his face. It would not do to have an actual Ministry representative be ungracious to what passed for its local operatives, even in this colonial backwater. He smoothed the front of his coat, tugged once at his collar and extended a hand in the direction that Arthur was indicating. "Lead on! There is much to do, after all."

"I apologise for the state of the place," Arthur said as he put the trunk down and fumbled in his pockets a moment before producing a heavy brass key. "I must admit I have been positively frantic in my preparations for your arrival, and I fear it has left the place in quite a state."

"Think nothing of it," Bernard replied.

Despite the walk being largely uphill—a detail Arthur had neglected to mention, though Bernard's aching shoulder would not soon forget—the house itself was quite lovely. It was set on a quiet lane of stately houses with small but well-maintained lawns, and even with the chill of the departing winter heavy in the air the street was bright and cheerful in the late afternoon light. The building was a design that seemed quite common to the area, slightly more narrow than most free-standing houses but three stories tall, with a peaked roof that spoke to heavy snowfalls during the year. Bernard was a bit taken aback when he realised that the paint on the house matched Arthur's scarf almost exactly, but then again, one who works for the Ministry becomes accustomed to certain eccentricities.

As it happened, Arthur had not been exaggerating at the state of the house —upon crossing the threshold Bernard could see the sitting room was coated in a layer of loose papers, all strewn about like autumn leaves. If there was an organisation to the material, it eluded his inspection, though as his eyes adjusted he could see that many of the papers had handwritten notes scrawled in the margins. Newspaper clippings were liberally dusted atop the mess, along with what appeared to be nautical charts with lines added in heavy, excited strokes. On the whole, though, it was a scene out of a circle of Hell constructed solely for the bedevilment of archivists.

Fortunately, Bernard was no archivist.

"Looks like you've been busy in the time since your last communiqué," Bernard said with measured understatement, setting his valise and traveling cane down to remove his heavy fur-lined top coat. "These charts look promising."

"Ah! Yes! Let me explain those." Arthur hurried over to the table, carefully set aside a stack of papers from a nearby chair and sat down. Bernard was left to hang his own coat with a faint sigh and find his own seat as the young researcher pushed papers into what was apparently some semblance of order to his eager eyes. Arthur opened his mouth to speak, then closed it with a look as though suddenly remembering something, and met Bernard's gaze across the table. "Not that I don't think you were fully briefed before departure, but—"

"No, no," Bernard put up a reassuring hand. "It's always best to make sure there are no missing pieces or inaccurate assumptions. I studied the briefing documents on the voyage over, though I must confess that it seemed there were a number of…" His words trailed off for a moment as he thought of the most tactful way to put it. "…missing pieces, shall we say."

"Yes, well, I think I can fill those in now," Arthur hurried to reply.

"Then I will begin, and you fill me in as needed." Bernard took off his spectacles and cleaned them with his pocket square in a series of neat, efficient motions. "According to the dossier, you have been working on a connection linking a number of suspicious fires and collapses for, what, three years now?" Arthur nodded. "And you believe that some sort of experimental device is behind it?"

"Most certainly." Arthur fished through the stacks of paper, pulled out a small leather bound journal, strained at the bindings and bulging with what appeared to be newspaper clippings, pages from academic journals and other scholarly miscellanea, and opened it up to a specific section marked by a wide elastic band. The young researcher presented the open pages to Bernard, revealing what appeared to be a patent from just over four years ago. The specifics of the engineering were quite out of Bernard's depth, even just at a glance, but the name of the device was plain enough: Maritime Resonant Frequency Amplifier.

"And what does this invention do, exactly?" Bernard asked.

"In brief? It purports to be able to amplify aural waves and other forms of vibration. You create these vibrations in a specially designed chamber wherein they are captured by this device, then transmitted via a transatlantic cable—"

"I say!" Bernard exclaimed.

"—but far more advanced than Atlantic Telegraph's. An all original design." Arthur searched through what seemed to Bernard as random piles. "Let's see, I had that patent here too. Blast!" On a pile situated behind him, Arthur gave a barely audible *"Ah!"* and then handed the paper to Bernard. "This proprietary transatlantic cable connects to a network of similarly designed receivers."

"A network?" Bernard tensed. A network implied that this investigation was going to be a bit more complex than anticipated. He had an aversion to complexity, at least of a kind that couldn't be resolved in a suitably Gordian fashion. "I don't recall anything about a network."

"It wouldn't be in the file. I just learned of it myself, not four days ago." Arthur shifted in his seat. "After learning the identity of one of the figures involved, I may have, ah, employed a fellow at the telegraph office to alert me when said individual receives any new correspondence." He shrugged, motioning to the clutter around them. "With my limited funds from the Crown, I chose to invest in informants rather than filing cabinets."

"Good show!" Bernard said, with genuine warmth. Anything that got them away from reams of paper and out into the field was fine by his standards. "We'll discuss a proper introduction with him presently. But first, this network?"

"According to the correspondence that I—uhm—*witnessed*, there was mention made of several connected stations of identical design." From another seemingly random stack, this time to the right of Bernard, Arthur dug up another page of scribbled notations. "Here we are. London, Leeds, Glasgow, Exeter, Dublin, and Limerick."

Bernard raised an eyebrow. "Quite a diverse array of locations."

"Indeed. And that's not the strangest part of this technology." Arthur produced a map, laid it across the top layer of papers and smoothed it with the side of his hand. "As I'm sure you know, the current transatlantic lines run from Canada on this side of the Atlantic. It's simply the most cost effective for crossing the distance required. This project, however, rejected running cable from the conventional locations and chose instead to set up a base of operations out on Block Island, of all places. The costs involved must have been staggering, simply staggering."

"Block Island?" Bernard peered at the map but couldn't find the location until Arthur indicated a tiny speck off the coast.

"An extremely small island off the coast of Rhode Island, home to just over two hundred souls. A resort community with some fishing activity, nice enough I suppose but not exactly a bustling centre of transatlantic commerce."

"I see. How best to arrange a visit?" Bernard smiled, though as with most of his smiles the gesture had more in common with an animal baring its teeth than a display of affection. He sensed his sort of work in the near future, and it was the first good news he'd had this whole trip so far. "I suddenly find I've a mind to knock on their door and inquire about their business. Don't you?"

"I do. There's a ferry that runs to the island daily," Arthur said. "Should be no difficulty."

"Excellent. Now, about the device itself–to what end would they incur such massive additional costs, with less expensive alternatives readily available?" Bernard frowned. "That is, secrecy seems the goal, certainly, but that still does not speak to its function. Something to do with telephonics, perhaps?"

"That was my assumption at first," Arthur said. "But on closer inspection of the device's design, its primary function is not to gather vibrations, but amplify and *project* them."

"Project them? As a weapon? Some sort of, I don't know, aural cannon, perhaps?"

"Possibly," Arthur allowed, though his tone indicated the contrary. "I didn't see anything that looked like it might be used for that purpose, but then, I'm not confident I really understand its purpose at all, so I'm afraid I may not be the best expert to consult in this circumstance."

"Hmm." Bernard mused for a moment, still turning his spectacles over in his hands. "I have a feeling we know exactly the expert we might consult, but until then, it might be best to focus our efforts elsewhere." He set aside the documents and journal, and turned back to Arthur to ask, "Your report mentioned a conspiracy behind these actions? These so-called True Sons of Henry?"

"Took a bit of digging to uncover that connection, let me tell you." He leafed through one of the nearby stacks, took out a thick sheaf of yellowed papers that looked about ready to turn to dust with little more than a hard look. He carefully handed them across to Bernard, who replaced his spectacles and peered down at the neat columns and their shaky, spidery script. "I started with the inventor, Richard Henry, the reason I brought you to New London. Given the expenses involved in this project, I started looking into his family, just to see where the money was coming from. Can you imagine what I found?"

"I'd rather hear it," Bernard said, trying not to be too harsh but also wary of over-indulging Arthur's evident excitable streak when it came to research. That was the trouble with archivists. Sometimes they tended to enjoy the digging so much they forgot other people often didn't share their love of riddles and guesswork.

"Right," Arthur said, his face reddening. "As far as the funding of this endeavour, I couldn't find a damn thing. I mean, family money, clearly, but it must be the most conservatively managed fortune I've ever seen. Up until this new venture, anyway. What did catch my attention was the fact that the same partners kept showing up in those ventures they did back, so I looked into those names. All with the Henry surname. I deduced it must have been an extended family, but then I discovered these family trees never connected. Now while you may think Henry is a common name like Smith, Jones, or Morris, it is not as unexceptional as one might—"

"Arthur…" Bernard warned.

"Right. Sorry." With a nod, he continued. "Look at this. Census records from Boston, 1631. Take note of this curious stretch on this page here–see all those men, surname Henry? All approximately the same age? That's where it started, at least in this country."

"Not exactly a subtle lot as conspirators go," Bernard said, decidedly unimpressed. "I remember the rest. This is when you started writing the home office, correct?" He smiled almost despite himself. "As I recall from my departure briefing, you made quite a pest of yourself for some time, asking after those records. No, don't apologise. It's a good trait in an investigator, to be sure."

"Thank you," Arthur said, clearly pleased at the compliment and recovering a bit of his poise in the process. "As it turns out, this group of young men—all younger sons of old but lesser families in the peerage—met at university and somehow got it in their heads that they could trace common ancestry to a heretofore unknown legitimate son of Henry I. No idea what brought on this delusion—"

Bernard scoffed. "I blame university," he interjected. "Too much time for idle speculation. Leads to foolishness, particularly in groups."

"You didn't attend?" Arthur said, looking surprised.

"Oh, I did." Bernard made a show of inspecting his nails. "I was simply asked to leave not long after matriculating. Some hurt feelings, and a bit of broken furniture. Best for everyone, really."

"I see." Arthur coughed politely. "In any event, however silly their notion of their ancestry, it seems the authorities were obliged to investigate after they made public some of their 'ancient and viable' claims, and the boys fled to

Boston soon after. It doesn't look like any serious effort was made to track them down, however."

"'The wicked man flees though no one pursues,'" Bernard said with a shrug. "It's a lot more likely these lads heard someone was coming around to put them to the question or, more likely, give them a slap for talking nonsense. They let their imaginations get carried away to the point where the Star Chamber was convening a whole session especially for them. I've seen their type before. This lot was just rich enough to make a real go of it."

"It seems as though they've been stewing here ever since," Arthur said. "When you know what to look for, it's not terribly difficult to find the connections. They stayed close, and—I must admit—aside from the ridiculous surname business, well, they have certainly kept collars up and brims down, as my father used to say."

"So it would seem," Bernard agreed, opting against re-iterating that hiding was simple when no one sought to find you. "First class work, Arthur. You certainly put in your due diligence."

"You really think so?" Arthur said. "I actually put in a request to join the Research and Development division not too long ago, see if I can't do some field testing. I've a knack for mechanical improvisation, and I've been working on a couple of gadgets—"

"Arthur. One matter at a time, yes?"

Arthur bowed his head, but added, "I wish I wasn't still left with quite so many questions. Why have they been present at six of the last eight significant landslides and avalanches in New England in the past four years? What's the connection?"

"Precisely what headquarters felt worth investigating, combined with your exhaustive reports and their own bizarre family history, of course," Bernard said, standing and doing his best to stretch a bit. Stiff muscles were of little use to anyone, him most of all. "Don't be too hard on yourself—you've done brilliant work, but you can't be expected to do it all."

"So what do we do now?" Arthur asked, also rising.

"Why, dinner of course. Somewhere with a decent menu, if there is such a place in New London?" Bernard could hardly contain another predatory grin, which he hoped Arthur took in its intended spirit of good humour. Despite the miserable voyage, the deplorable manners of the Americans, and the overall stifling lack of importance that pervaded this shadow of a country, he had still come to work. And that he truly adored. "In the morning, we head to Block Island and see this Richard Henry. I'm quite confident he'll be happy to answer our remaining questions."

"He will?" Arthur asked, a bit dubious but clearly not eager to contradict him.

"He will," Bernard concurred, taking up his cane with a flourish. "As it happens, I am excellent at asking questions. A very *specific* kind."

Dinner was pleasant enough, though as the meal went on Arthur noticed a rather sour expression crossed Bernard's face whenever he wasn't expressly guarding it, as though everything in front of him of was simply failing to meet his expectations. Nevertheless he was a capable enough conversationalist, and before turning in the agent even regaled Arthur with a few redacted but engaging tales of pursuing malefactors through the streets of London. Truth be told, it was still difficult to get a read on the Englishman—it was plain he was not fond of America, but the next morning as the time came closer to depart for the island, the agent became more and more excited.

He also seemed easily distracted, glancing out the window often, both during dinner and afterwards on returning to the field office.

Foul weather delayed their departure, causing Bernard to pace like a dog following a stranger on the other side of a fence. By the time the ferry arrived on Block Island, however, the last of the rain had retreated and the afternoon sun was at its peak, nearly taking the edge off the chill in the air, save for the breeze still coming off the water. Asking directions in the tiny harbour town proved easier than expected, though the walk took them out of town and down a road that was little more than packed earth and lonely stands of trees by the seaside.

Richard Henry's house stood by itself at a bend in the road on a little bluff overlooking a narrow strip of beach, with the dark blue expanse of the ocean beyond. A small dock jutted out into the sea, a rowboat tethered to the solitary post. The house itself was a simple affair done on the slightly grander scale that money tends to lend things, weathered white paint with dark trim and surrounded by a low stone wall with a disproportionately large iron gate, currently standing slightly ajar. Bernard approached the gate without hesitation, peering through curiously, though Arthur hung back.

"Something wrong?" Bernard asked.

"Are you sure that's wise?" Arthur said.

"Oh, absolutely," Bernard replied airily. "They're expecting us."

"How is that possible?" Arthur said with a start. Suddenly the house seemed far more sinister.

"A gentleman was shadowing us last night. He showed potential, but he needed a bit more coaching on remaining in shadows when close to streetlamps and open windows. His bowler brim was the tell. I suspect he might have been at the train station as well." He pushed open the gate and gestured for Arthur to follow. "Shall we?"

"Right into a trap?" Arthur tried to keep the squeak out of his voice.

"Sometimes the best way," Bernard said. His smile was back, as wolfish as ever and not at all comforting in context. Together the two men crossed a small courtyard and stopped at the heavy wooden door. Bernard raised his cane and rapped at it twice, a pair of robust knocks that must have sounded like thunder inside the house. A bell sounded somewhere within, and through the frosted glass panel next to the door proper Arthur could see a shape coming toward them. There was the sound of a heavy bolt sliding back, and then it happened. Quickly.

In fact, Arthur had never seen anything happen so fast in his life.

When the door opened, Arthur had no sooner opened his mouth to speak to the elderly gentleman in the servant's livery than Bernard shouldered the young researcher aside, sending him sprawling in the shrubs next to the door. Light glinted off the silver ball atop Bernard's cane as it flashed down in a tight arc, striking the servant's wrist in mid-draw. A revolver the doorman was sliding from his jacket clattered against the stones of the stoop. Bernard was already moving in behind his strike, grabbing the man's injured wrist with his left hand and pulling forward while pivoting his body so that the man collided with him right at the hip. The servant yelped as he was hip-tossed and went sprawling, landing on his back with a heavy thud. Bernard knelt down, following the man to the ground, and administered a single, savage punch to the man's temple that left him limp.

"My-My God!" Arthur stammered, struggling with the shrubbery as he clumsily regained his feet. "Did you—"

"No," Bernard said simply. He rose to his feet and took off his spectacles with a casual gesture. He looked as if he was going to place them in his coat pocket, then seemed to think better of it and offered them to Arthur instead. "Mind holding these? I'd hate to have them broken. Step lively, there's a fellow. Likely to be another one or two of those about before we can meet our mysterious Mr Henry."

"Certainly," Arthur mumbled, feeling a little numb, taking the spectacles and hurrying after Bernard. The agent had turned on his heel and started off into the house like a man out for a brisk constitutional.

In the space it took Arthur to glance over his shoulder at the man they left in the doorway, he heard a shout cut off with two swift thuds and turned back to see Bernard stepping over another servant. The man had evidently lunged from a side room, knife in hand, but the attempted ambush had earned him a trip into unconsciousness. Good Lord, but this English gentleman was *fast*.

The house seemed a bit of a blur to Arthur, the details growing less distinct with each beat of his pounding heart, though later he would recall a collection of antique furniture and shelves heavy with leather bound books. From somewhere upstairs Arthur heard muffled voices and what sounded like heavy furniture being dragged across the floor.

When they finally stopped at the base of a grand stairwell, Arthur whispered, "Where did you learn to fight like that?"

"A good friend and advisor for the Ministry," Bernard said. "Spent some time learning to fight in the Orient, something called Bartitsu."

"Never heard of it. Remarkable!"

"Isn't it, though? Our little secret, at least for now. But mark my words, when it gets out it'll be all the rage in a few years."

"I can see why," Arthur replied, looking at Bernard in a seemingly whole new light. "What now?"

"They always go up," Bernard said in a conversational tone as he mounted the staircase. That satisfied smile had grown even wider, and though Arthur felt as though he struggled to breathe from all the excitement, Bernard sounded no more impaired than if he was remarking on the weather to an acquaintance he chanced to meet in the park. "Never understood that."

"What's that?" Arthur asked, his eyes darting to the upper level. Wasn't Bernard worried about being discovered?

"Cornered men," Bernard said. He reached the top of the stairs, paused, held out a hand to indicate Arthur should stop as well. "They always go up, when they should go out," Bernard said, too loudly, obviously baiting those others who might be listening. Bernard leaned out for a peek around the corner and ducked back with lightning speed—just as well, too, as there was a thunderous blast as some sort of rifle or shotgun was discharged. The bullet ripped a chunk out of the corner and sprayed Bernard with plaster, making it look as though he had been dusted with flour.

"Oh, come now," the agent said, face positively twisted with disgust as he looked at the mess. "Is there really any call for this?" Bernard reached into his coat pocket and threw something around the corner out of sight. "Best to close your eyes," he added, not quite in time for Arthur to take action. There was a tremendous flash, not quite equal to a lightning strike but certainly cousin to one, followed by a man's pained shout and another blast. "Just be a moment," Bernard said, vanishing around the corner. There was a cry of pain, the scuffing of shoes on the floorboards, then another heavy crash.

"You can come out now," Bernard's voice called from the corridor.

"Thank you," Arthur rubbed at his dazzled eyes, shaking his head instinctively to try to chase away the patches of colour lingering in his eyes. Arriving in the upstairs hallway, he looked past the open doors to more rooms of tasteful opulence and focused instead on Bernard. The agent was standing over the unconscious form of a heavyset man slumped against the only closed door in the hallway. A shotgun had been kicked away from his grasp, though judging by the nob already rising on his temple he was unlikely to wake any time soon. Bernard was rapping on the door with the head of his cane impatiently; his good humour apparently another casualty of the plaster dust.

"Richard? Mr Richard Henry? Open the door, please." Bernard huffed before knocking again. "We haven't come to hurt you. Open the door and let us discuss matters like gentlemen. There's nothing to be gained by acting the petulant child now, I assure you."

"I have a gun! If you come in I'll shoot!" The voice was high with fear and tension but unmistakably still quite young. "I swear I will!"

"No, you won't," Bernard said, resisting the urge to roll his eyes. "If you'd had a weapon you'd have used it by now, and we both know it. Come now. Don't make matters any more difficult than they have to be. I promise, no harm will come to you."

There was a long silence, then the sound of the door unlocking. It swung open to reveal a nervous-looking young man with thinning brown hair. He stepped back immediately as Bernard entered, Arthur following, and all but tripped over himself in his haste. "You're British agents, aren't you?"

"I am," Bernard said simply.

"Well, on paper, I'm an archivist," Arthur stammered. Bernard glared at him. "But, ah, close enough."

"Well then," Richard Henry said, drawing himself up a bit, "I'd say that you have no authority here, but I doubt that would stop you so I won't waste my breath. We always knew you'd find us eventually. But you'll never find the device. Not in time, at any rate."

"We already—" Arthur began, but Bernard cut him off with another venomous look and pulled him a few steps away. "What?"

"Don't say anything you don't have to," the agent hissed, watching Richard carefully.

"But, the location of the transatlantic cable is a matter of record," Arthur whispered. "Surely he's aware of that?"

"Do rational men plot conspiracies?" Bernard replied, perhaps a touch too sharply. He collected himself, stepped back to Richard. "Of course, Richard. We are doomed, all of us, I'm sure. Speaking of our untimely demise, where is the rest of your intrepid band also bringing forth the end of days?" Bernard asked. "Seems a bit rude of them to leave you here to face us by yourself."

"And let you potentially capture all of us at one go? I think not." Richard swallowed heavily, beads of sweat standing out on his forehead. "I volunteered. It is my solemn duty to resist the forces of the Illegitimate Monarchy—"

"Yes, yes, I applaud your martyrdom, now about this technological terror of yours," Bernard interjected, "exactly what does it do?"

Richard simply stared at him, trying for noble defiance and managing a passable semblance of it. Right up until the point where Bernard stepped toward him and brought the end of the cane up under his chin, anyway, at which point his stony demeanour crumbled.

"It's a resonant frequency generator," Richard said quickly. "It generates very specific wavelengths that destroy particular kinds of matter attuned to the device. Our first field trials proved successful beyond our wildest dreams— avalanches, rockslides, and tremors. And our most recent project, for instance? British bedrock." He managed a weak smile. "Might not be enough to sink the wretched island, but it should do enough damage that there will be no recourse but to recognise us as the legitimate heirs."

"You're joking," Bernard said flatly. "Actually, no, strike that. You're mad."

"I don't believe he is," Arthur said, studying Richard's face carefully. He was flushed and still sweating profusely, and swallowing every few moments. "Joking. I do not believe he is joking. I think he's telling us the truth." He leaned in an inch closer to Richard, and nodded. "And yes, he is quite mad."

"Oh?" Bernard asked, not turning away from Richard. "How do you know?"

"Because dying men rarely lie," Arthur said. "Look at him. He must have taken something before we came in. Some sort of poisonous failsafe."

"Richard? Is this true?" In response, Richard simply pitched forward, a slight trickle of foam issuing from his lips as Bernard and Arthur caught him by his armpits. The agent lowered Richard to the floor, his face screwed up in even more peevish displeasure, as though Richard's impending suicide were somehow an insult to his person. "Why'd you build it? Tell me, you sorry sod!"

"Wanted…" Richard coughed thickly, further ruining Bernard's suit. "Wanted to show…the full extent …of our…" But his last words were gurgled more than uttered, and after a sudden, shuddering spasm, Richard laid his head back and breathed his last.

"It simply astounds me how self-centred lunatics are. Truly. Quite selfish." Bernard stood up, the look of disdain never faltering. "As though anyone even knew enough about them to question their resolve until they took up this lunatic endeavour."

"At least we know what the device is supposed to do," Arthur said, trying not to look at the body. He didn't desire to experience his breakfast in reverse. "That's something. It explains the rock slides too. They must have been testing it locally before they moved forward with this insane scheme."

"That makes sense," Bernard acknowledged tersely. He gripped his cane so tightly that his knuckles cracked. "At least to lunatic minds such as these. Best we head to the cable facility then, I imagine. If they were prepared to receive us here, I've no doubt they have more waiting."

"I have an idea about that," Arthur offered. "Something that might not involve something quite so dramatic as storming a facility of armed men, but perhaps a bit more effective. We should get underway, then, before we've lost the light entirely. I'll fill you in on the way."

"Certainly," Bernard said. "I will tell you something, though." He stared the young researcher right in the eye, deadly serious. "If I ever find the penny dreadful author responsible for popularising these damned poison pills, I will give that man a thorough thrashing. Never give the silly blighters ideas."

The agent shook his head, daring to glance down at Richard. "Ideas just lead to trouble, really."

"I can't believe I'm doing this," Bernard muttered, staring at the building down the road where Richard Henry's device was contained. Whoever was inside had certainly noticed him—he made no particular effort to hide, not that there was much he could have done on with the sandy scrub and nearly full moon in a cloudless sky overhead. For their part, their light discipline was terribly shoddy, and he kept seeing dark shapes crossing in front of the windows. Had he been a marksman, things might have been very different, but he wasn't, and so this would be resolved another way.

A loud hum began emanating from the building, the vibration strong enough that it was starting to make his teeth hurt. Evidently they were making ready to use the device, which meant it was time to put Arthur's plan in motion.

Bernard raised his pistol and fired at the ground floor windows. His shooting skills were a bit rusty, so he was pleasantly surprised to find that all three shots struck home, shattering glass and eliciting distant shouts of surprise from within.

"I don't suppose you'd consider surrender?" Bernard shouted, still annoyed that he was forced to use a pistol for this stage of the plan but seeing it through regardless.

"Imperialist dog!" The speaker was trying for furious outrage but an edge of panic ruined the effect. "We've been waiting for you! You're about to witness our moment of triumph!"

"Well, I daresay that's a problem right there," Bernard said, taking a lazy shot at the sill where a head was slowly poking up and sending it back out of sight. "Never wait for your enemy to start going about your business, old son. Just gives them time to manoeuvre. You should've taken care of things while we were meeting with poor Richard."

"You'll pay for what you've done, you royalist swine!"

Bernard winced at the melodramatic retort, absently wondering if they had stolen more than just their penchant for poison pills from the penny dreadfuls. He allowed himself the consolation of replying with another bullet, sending the silhouettes away from the windows again.

Bernard fired his remaining shot just to discourage anyone from sticking their head up for a moment, and pulled out the bulky canister that Arthur had given him. Supposedly all he had to do was shake the contents and throw it; that seemed a bit simple for Bernard, but then, he wasn't the expert in such matters. Arthur might just be an archivist and not a full Ministry scientist yet, but he was as close as Bernard was going to get in these circumstances. So he shook it twice, hearing the rattling of the metal and the shifting of the powder, and threw it as hard as he could.

The canister hit the side of the building and exploded with a loud cracking bang, pushing back the darkness with a bright flash and coating the wall with flame. Bernard stepped back and reloaded his revolver as smoke billowed from the point of impact. He could hear shouting from inside the structure as the flames spread; it certainly seemed as though Arthur knew his stuff. Research and Development might soon have a new addition after all. Bernard's portion of the plan was just about concluded, save for rounding up the members fleeing the burning building.

After a minute passed, however, and then another, with still no break in the humming sound of the device or the emergence of any of the society members, Bernard grew concerned. Why weren't they trying to escape? Perhaps they were trying to complete their work on the device, but there was also the chance that these rapscallions were eager to martyr themselves as Richard had and relishing the thought of leaving charred remains behind. Idly, Bernard wondered if the device was even vulnerable to fire, or if burning it might have some catastrophic effect, but supposed it was too late now.

Another long moment passed, the whole side of the building and part of the roof now on fire.

Bernard let out a long sigh as the front door of the manor suddenly flew open, loosing a veritable pillar of smoke in the process, and coughing, ash-covered men, all of them staggering to safety before collapsing on the sandy ground. A half dozen of them, apparently well-dressed before the fire ruined their clothes. Bernard walked over and pulled the nearest of them away from the fire, keeping the rest of the group covered with his revolver all the while. The building burned merrily, but it was not until the roof collapsed a bit later that the hum finally stopped.

Around the same time, a shivering, bedraggled Arthur walked up from the direction of the surf. He surveyed the prisoners, now ringed in a sullen half-circle as they watched their ambitions drift away on the smoke, his teeth chattering so loudly it sounded like dice clattering inside a cup. "D-D-Did we stop it?" he asked.

"Judging by the state of things here?" Bernard removed his topcoat and suit jacket, and placed them around the young man's shoulders. "I'd certainly say so."

"A-A-Are you s-s-sure? I'm s-s-soaked. D-D-Damn b-boat cuh-cuh-capsized on me."

"Of course," Bernard said, casually pointing his pistol at a man attempting to scoot a few more feet away. He left it pointed until the conspirator sulkily moved back to his original spot. "Just look at the place. No, keep it on. Jacket's already ruined anyway. Might as well ensure you are not ruined either." The agent gave the young researcher the barest of nods, and yet Arthur felt as though he had been granted a tremendous sort of honour along with the suit jacket.

"So what happens now?" Arthur asked, letting the heat of the blaze wash over him.

"I expect the local authorities are already on their way, so it will be time for me to use the identification the Ministry arranged just to smooth things over a bit, put this lot in custody, and arrange for proper transportation back to Britain. I expect this lot have an interesting trial in their future."

"I see," Arthur said. A long moment passed as they watched another timber collapse into the inferno. "You weren't supposed to burn the building down, you know."

"Oh, I do." Bernard replied, a pleasant, slightly faraway smile on his face, the blaze reflecting on his spectacles so that it looked as though his eyes were aflame.

"Yes, well, that device I gave you? I designed it to be a smoke bomb for misdirection while I rowed out to deliver the counter-insulator to the cables. In a matter of moments the device would have been useless anyway, without further property damage."

"Oh, I know. And you did instruct me not to throw it at the building directly." Bernard shrugged. "I decided we needed a contingency."

"And your contingency is to burn down the whole building? Device inside?"

"The world is better without that monstrosity in it," the agent answered.

Arthur didn't protest. Bernard chose to omit his suspicion a search of Richard's house might provide plenty of material to reconstruct one. That would be for his higher-ups to determine.

"I see." Arthur heard a whistle, turned and saw a party of men bearing lanterns heading their way from back in the direction of town. The two Ministry agents waved cheerfully. "It's been a pleasure working with you, Agent Entwhistle."

"You too, Mr Kraft." Bernard furrowed his brows, clearly thinking something over. "Oh, and regarding that application you mentioned before? I think I'll be putting in a word when I return. I do believe you might be put to better use closer to the home office. We could always use more men with your eye for detail and quick hands in the lab." He cracked the barest of smiles. "Or a new strong back for the office rowing team, at least."

"The home office? Are you serious?" Arthur's eyes went wide with almost childlike surprise. "Of course. I'd be delighted!"

"Good," said Bernard, removing his identification from his pocket. He glanced over his shoulder as the far wall pitched forward into the flames, sending a shower of sparks skyward. "Because it would be delightful working together, and…" His sentence was punctuated by a roar as the last of the building collapsed behind them. Yes, Doctor Sound would have a few words with him about *clandestine* operations overseas. "… and I have a feeling I may not be leaving Britain again for some time."

Where the River Shines

Dan Rabarts
based on characters created by Grant Stone

Tarawera Ranges
North Island, New Zealand
1896

With a sick gasp and the stink of burning metal, the tractor's propane motor rattled to a halt.

"Uh-oh." Barry Ferguson's voice filtered into the hansom. Lachlan King heard the young man hop down from the cab with a squelch of mud, probably sinking up to his knees in the quagmire that had once been the track they had been following.

Lachlan popped open the hatch of the covered hansom, and peered out into the downpour. "Ferguson? What's the hold-up? We have a thief to catch, remember?"

"Well," Barry called over the rain hammering against his oilskin coat and soaking his hair, "see that smoke there?"

Lachlan squinted. "What about it?"

"That's meant to be steam."

"That's bad, I trust."

"I'd say so, sir, yes."

"Not a good place to break down, lad." He cast his eye over the ranges, shrouded in mists that were older than the hills, older than time. The primordial long white cloud.

"Leave it with me." Barry threw Lachlan what could, under the circumstances, only be described as a jaunty wave. "You know where the lever is if you need it."

As the clankerton trudged around the tractor with his toolbox in hand, Lachlan tugged the hatch shut, comforted only slightly by its hollow metal clang. He might have been encased in iron, but that didn't mean to say the warriors of Ngai Tohai couldn't drag him out into the mud and carve out his heart, or whatever it was they did to their prisoners.

But he needed the Ngai Tohai, however absurd an idea that was, to help him track down Frances Ascot and bring back what he had stolen. It would not serve him well to continue thinking of them as the enemy.

He listened to Barry, clanging and whistling away in the mud, a colonial farm boy as happy as a pig in muck. Lachlan could think of nowhere worse to be.

Other than his father's house, he groused silently. But how long before the old man was no longer around?

Unconsciously, he patted his breast pocket. He had read the letter from London so many times he knew every word by heart, yet still he wondered if it could be real. So the old man's sickness had finally caught up with him, and he probably wouldn't last out the London winter. Meanwhile, the Ministry had a position free for Lachlan King in the office when he was ready to return. England, her cool rains in the summer and the comfort of soft snows blanketing the hedgerows in winter. How he missed her white cliffs, her lilting songs. England, a world away, where he belonged.

Nevertheless, it was somewhat disturbing to have people in high places keen on your every dark blasted secret. If the Ministry knew of the schism within the King family, what else did they know? *Maybe,* he thought ruefully, *it's not that I belong in England. Maybe it's that I belong to England, or to her eyes and ears, at the very least.*

A sudden rapping on the hansom startled Lachlan, and he cranked open the hatch. "All done, Ferguson?"

"Ah, that might have to wait," Barry said. "If you'd be so good as to pull the lever, sir..."

Dark indistinct figures were emerging from the *punga* trees, weapons of carved wood and stone held low. "Oh," Lachlan said. "I see." He wrenched the lever.

"There's a good chap," Barry quipped as he hauled himself up and began tugging on handles and dials.

Metal slid and slammed around them as air lines hissed. The hansom walls shifted, opening slits wide enough for a pistol, while a set of gears on the back of the hansom cranked and a telescopic handle-set and eyepiece dropped in front of Lachlan. Polished brass grips and guards fitted smoothly into his palms, his fingertips resting lightly on triggers. He peered into the periscope as his chair craned up, allowing him to swing the entire contraption and look, as it were, down the barrels of the twin machine-cannons now bristling from the top of their battle-tractor.

However, he was not here to start a war. There was plenty of that going on already. He was a gentleman, and would not fire the first shot. He would not use the Empire's hot lead to cut down men armed only with sticks and stones unless he had absolutely no other choice. His family had been knights, not so very long ago. Lachlan King knew a thing or two about honour. He swung left and right, searching. Bodies slipped between the trees, coming ever closer.

"Dammit! Stupid army clankerton hardware!"

Barry's words were followed by the sudden heavy squelching of his boots slurping through mud.

"Ferguson? Get back in the tractor, lad! They'll tear you to shreds!"

Lachlan swung the cannon mechanism in wild arcs, trying to get a view of the track, but the machine did not swing that low. It would be folly to think he could wait for the enemy to come to him. By the time they reached the tractor, the guns wouldn't be able to turn to face them.

Then he saw Barry. Like a farm boy who has never seen war, the lad was trudging out through the mud towards the enemy, nary a weapon upon his person, waving his hands over his head, and shouting.

"Ferguson?" Lachlan muttered. "What the blazes are you doing?"

This became clear moments later, as Ngai Tohai warriors flowed from the trees and pushed the boy to the ground.

Barry Ferguson was surrendering.

With his hands over his head, and with consequent awkwardness, Lachlan pushed open the hansom door and climbed down. His feet sank into the muck, sucking at his boots as he stepped away from the battle-tractor.

Around him, several wide-eyed Maori warriors stalked closer, knees extended, tongues tasting the air, weapons shivering in their hands—long heartwood *taiaha* and carved stone *patu*. More men knelt among the trees, black iron muskets poised. Barry was being hustled back towards him, the lad's grimy hands held above his head, that indefatigable grin plastering his muddy features.

"Surrendering to the enemy isn't exactly Ministry protocol, lad."

"Better this way, sir. It's not the Maori way to kill non-combatants out of hand. Mind you, if we'd tried fighting them we might be dead by now."

"So, you just saved my life?"

Barry shrugged. "Sorry, sir. I'll try not to make a habit of it."

"Never mind." He sighed, his attention turning from the circling warriors to a figure approaching from the treeline. "Good day!" Lachlan called, trying to coax some good humour to his voice. If they were to be prisoners, they may as well try to get off to a friendly start with their captors.

The approaching man paused, inspecting the *pakeha*. White hair sprang from beneath his battered bowler hat, his face a pitted landscape lined with the dark tracing of many *moko*. He might be fifty years old or ninety, for all Lachlan could tell. He walked with care, as if he fancied the preponderance of making the prisoners wait. Only a mischievous twitching at the edges of his thin lips hinted that the old man might be making a game of what was, in Lachlan's view, a most serious business.

However, Lachlan was not here to dally. He was on the trail of a dangerous criminal. In all the flurry of failing engines and enemy advances, he had not lost sight of his mission. Stopping short of the muddy track the old man looked them over, his eyes twinkling. The rain streamed in small, shifting cascades off the rim of his hat, and rolled away down his feather cloak. Lachlan resisted the urge to wipe streaming rivulets from his own face.

"Aue," said the old man, eyes roving over the battle tractor, its twin machine-cannons hanging limp over the hansom. "What do you call this, then?"

"It's a Massey York-Class tractor, modified by the British Army for all-terrain field operations," Barry jumped in, complete with predictable enthusiasm, an equally predictable lack of tact, and a complete absence of understanding over the imminent danger. "But put me in a room with the guy who designed this piece of junk and I'll teach him a thing or two about how to build a tractor. Needs a secondary low torque gearset for starters, and maybe a cooler fuel source, or else the propane regulator overheats when you lose traction. Especially with all that extra weight on the back." Ferguson jerked a thumb at the cannons and their steel-plated armatures while the old man stared at him intently. "Mind you, firing the boiler with propane has its advantages—saves us hauling a trailer of coal around, you know."

"Thank, you Mister Ferguson," Lachlan forced through gritted teeth. "'It's a tractor' would have sufficed."

The elder glanced to Lachlan, then back to Barry. "So you can make it go?"

"I've got some ideas," returned Barry.

Lachlan huffed. "But without tools and a workshop—"

"Actually sir—"

The elder held up a hand for silence. "You, your name?"

Lachlan straightened. "I am Lachlan King, here on the Queen's business—"

"You are a king?"

"What?" Lachlan shook his head. "No, you misunderstand."

The elder grinned, showing that he did not in the least bit misunderstand. "Then you must come meet our *rangatira*, our king, certainly? Whoever thought a king of the pakeha would come to our humble forests, riding a tractor?"

"No, no I—"

"*He* will stay here and fix the machine. It is a suitable gift, from one king to another." Without another word, the *tohunga* turned towards the trees. Before Lachlan could protest, two men grappled his arms and propelled him after the elder.

"Ferguson!"

"Don't mind me, sir," Barry replied, "I've got this covered!"

Lachlan twisted around, trying his best to express to the boy by eye contact alone that he needed to escape and get help, even though he knew that help would never arrive in time to save him from the Ngai Tohai.

But just before he was spun about and forced into the bush, Lachlan was most certain that the lad winked.

"You ought to know that this will not be viewed well by the Governor," Lachlan said over the old man's shoulder as bristly punga trunks gave way to lean *rimu* and mighty *totara*. Somewhere ahead, Lachlan could hear a dull roar, as of a waterfall. "I am the Queen's servant, and your people have signed a treaty."

The elder chortled. "Not all of us signed that treaty of yours. We are not all like fish to the hook. We read both papers, the English *and* the Maori. We saw that they don't say the same thing. I think there's a word for that."

Lachlan bit his lip. "We have not come here to dispute treaties. We are on the trail of a dangerous criminal, a thief, who has stolen something very important and valuable from the government. He fled this way. We have come to Ngai Tohai not as enemies but seeking your aid, as you are most certainly the ones who will know the area, and can maybe help us locate where he is hiding."

It wasn't the whole truth, but it would serve well enough. "He ought not be hard to find. He is pakeha, like me, only younger and his hair is different, red with grey through it. So he will certainly have been noticed if he came this way."

"His name, *e hoa*, what's his name?"

"Frances Ascot, but he is known as Frankie, the rare times he is seen in the city."

The old man stopped and turned back to Lachlan. "Frankie?" He grinned, a grin of secrets. "*Kapai.*" For the first time, he seemed to study Lachlan, up and down. "This is no way for a king to dress. Here, we make a trade, *ae?*" He gestured at the agent's oilskin coat as he untied the feather cloak from his shoulders.

Lachlan wasn't holding any cards, so if playing up to the old man's eccentricity was what it was going to take to survive, then he'd go along with it. He shed his coat and assented to one of the warriors tying the feather cloak at his neck.

The old man slipped Lachlan's coat on and held out his arms, apparently amused by how it felt on his thin shoulders. He caught Lachlan's eye and nodded at the cloak. "This is a great honour, you know. Worthy of a king."

"Can you help me find Frank?"

The elder turned and continued into the bush.

"This Frank must have stolen something very precious that the Queen would send two white men in a tractor after him. What was it?"

"It doesn't matter. It was to be sent to London, and the Queen will be most displeased if it is not delivered to her."

"Mister King, I think you think you know a lot about people, about *our* people, but I think you actually know very little. Do you know our legends? What do you know of Maui?"

"Maui was a hero, one of the greatest—"

"Maui was a thief, Mister King. *And* a hero, but first a thief. Maui stole fire from the underworld, among other things. Do you understand?"

"I—" Lachlan was finding himself at a loss for words far too often today. Why could they not have sent an Æthnographer with him on this mission? "You may need to explain."

His pride when he swallowed it was rather more bitter than expected.

The old man shrugged. "Maui wove ropes of flax to slow the sun as it raced across the sky. He carved a hook and with it he pulled this land from the sea. It was a fish, *Te Ika a Maui*. He and his brothers roamed across its mighty sides and cut it with their *patu*, carving rivers and lakes."

"No man could bring in a fish as vast as this entire island," Lachlan scoffed. "Even for a creation myth, that's simply not logical. There wouldn't be line enough, or strength enough, or a fishhook big enough..."

Then the bush opened up, revealing a lush river valley wreathed in mist. Lachlan forgot the conversation as his eyes turned up towards the bright lance of water that streamed from a hole in the cliff-face far above. It was high, higher than the cloud and the clinging mists, a wound in the ramparts of the mountain, upon slopes where the sun yet burned, up above the mist that rolled around them and the shadows between the trees, in a place where the river shone in the sky.

"In some places," the elder said softly, "we can still see the fish bleed."

Lachlan King was a practical man, but for a moment the sight of the mighty cataract overawed his habitual urge to scorn the myths of savages.

"Things are what they need to be," the elder said. "Sometimes, men must be bigger than they know, to do what must be done. It is only the world's rules which try to tell us otherwise. Maui had no care for such rules. Maui did not belong to this world."

Then the old man stepped down into the mist, and was gone.

Barry Ferguson had long since given up on the prospect of making small talk with the Maori warriors guarding over him. He worked quickly and carefully, resting tools and pipes and valves and bolts and gaskets on the metal wheels and running boards as he went, careful not to let his equipment get too dirty. The rain had eased but the mud would be an issue for days.

Too much weight and not enough torque was the problem. Barry didn't have the machinery on hand to rebuild the burnt-out gearbox, but he hoped he knew enough about basic physics to get around the pesky mechanics of gravity and friction. It was, he reflected, rather fortunate that those army boys insisted on hauling so much useless junk about the place with them in the lockers at the back of the tractor.

Redistributing the gas lines would be easy enough, but he was not looking forward to stitching all that tent canvas together. He hated sewing.

Lachlan edged forward, finding in the fog a surface of timber beneath his feet, and taut ropes in his hands, stretching out to either side of the narrow swing-bridge hidden in the waterfall's spray. Lachlan stepped onto the bridge as it swayed slick beneath him, the flax ropes' smooth weave slippery in his grasp.

He considered what he had established so far which was, he deduced, that the old man knew Frank Ascot—knew him well indeed—and that the elder had either guessed or already knew exactly what the navy deserter had taken from the safety of Auckland's Bankhouse, and that he was quite pleased with how things were developing. Ascot was a bushman, a British Navy deserter who had fled his vessel for the forests and *kainga* of the Maori, adopting the culture of any tribe willing to take him in. In return for this sanctuary, a pakeha among the Maori might sometimes return to the city streets where he could blend in, do things and go places that the Maori could not; though why anyone would want to live like this, in the cold and the damp and the mud, not a teapot in sight, was quite beyond Lachlan King.

It stood to reason, then, that the tohunga would be Ascot's ally in the Bankhouse theft, and would be unwilling to give him up. Lachlan's options were running thin, and demanded another tactic. If the old man wished to play games, then Lachlan could play games too. He had been playing them for a long time.

Yet, despite himself, Lachlan could not help but feel a grudging and somewhat ironic respect for his quarry. Ascot had found a place where he could fit in. A place where he was respected. Lachlan had run too, long ago, but had never found that place where he could simply be, could just *belong*. He may have fled his father's rod, but Lachlan was a man like any other, made of little more than blood and fog, and was not so difficult to bend with words, be they threats or orders. Frances Ascot was a free man, in ways Lachlan King had never been, *could* never be.

Across the river and its mists the tohunga waited, an unfathomable, secret smile on his lips. "*Haere mai.* Best we don't keep the rangatira waiting all day."

The track began to climb steeply up the side of the cliff and they ascended, up and up, as the waterfall came down, the mists embracing them as Papatuanuku would take her powerful children into her arms.

Dusk was settling over the riverbank by the time Barry had everything in place. It was by no means perfect; in fact it was downright rough, but with any luck it ought to work. Maybe not well, but hopefully well enough.

The warriors milled about, keeping a safe distance from "*te pakeha porangi*" —the crazy pakeha—as he had heard some of them mutter. Clambering over discarded metal plates and pipes, he pulled himself into the gunner's seat, which now hung over the control gears, the driver's seat tossed aside. The machine-cannons swung behind him on the denuded platform that had once been their hansom. To either side pipes bent upwards past his shoulders from the air- and gas-tanks bolted underneath, thrusting into the mouth of a huge canvas bladder which looked suspiciously like several army-issue field tents all sewn together with thick hemp. Four tent-poles held the bladder's mouth aloft while its remaining bulk lay spread out across the mud, draped up on the scrubby *manuka* bushes alongside the track.

"Righto," Barry muttered. "Time to kick it in the guts."

Thumping the propane pedal, he cranked the ignitor. With a geyser's hiss, a white flame burst from the overhead pipes, billowing hot air into the bladder's mouth.

Barry figured that these warriors must have seen Army airships during one of the three attempts that British forces had made to invade the Ngai Tohai stronghold in the eastern North Island, but Barry, on pumping the pedal to coax more heat from the burner, was gambling they would be sceptical that a makeshift balloon would ever lift the tractor high enough to get it free of the mud. Not even the detritus of metal plates and bolts and other junk strewn beside the track could possibly make the critical difference. Surely not.

"Come on, girl," he urged the extremely unlikely dirigible, "you can do it."

Others' scepticism was why Barry Ferguson preferred to work alone. While his wardens japed at his folly, Barry watched the balloon swell and lift. His fingers grazed the lever by his seat as his eyes glanced down at the iron plates he had slipped inside his coat. Another gamble, but they would have to be protection enough if the snipers were still paying close attention.

Because when it happened, it was going to be a very close thing indeed.

By the time Lachlan crested the incline, he was sweating like he hadn't in years. Several hundred feet above the river, here was an alpine lake, a sheet of glass set afire by the dropping sun. The mist glowed like embers in the sun's dying rays, swirling up from some unseen place where the lake escaped through a hole in the mountainside. Rainbows arced above the valley, sparkling like lost jewels.

But Lachlan had no time to appreciate the view, as the tohunga's bodyguards hustled him into the lakeshore village past smoking cooking pits and flax-roofed *whare*.

"Remember." The tohunga winked, glancing over his shoulder. "Remember *Maui*. Remember that we're all just fish, snapping at dark things that move in the water and hoping the next thing we bite into isn't a hook."

"Thank you kindly," Lachlan grimaced. "I needed to be reminded of that." He had bitten quite enough hooks already for one day.

They passed the *wharenui*, a looming structure that Lachlan knew to be the tribe's meeting house, bedecked in twisting carvings of red-faced warriors thrusting out their piercing black tongues. Lachlan met their fierce *paua*-shell gazes, convinced for a moment before he entered the adjacent eating house that those eyes were somehow staring back at him.

Inside, several long low tables stacked with food ran across the room, while people moved about or sat and ate and talked. The smell of hot pork, kumara and *rewa* bread hit Lachlan, making his mouth water and his head...dizzy? In the aftermath of their climb, he suddenly became aware of how long ago he'd eaten lunch, and how hungry he was.

But food was just bait on the hook. He was among enemies, he had to remember. Better hungry than dead.

All eyes were turning his way as the Ngai Tohai realised there was a white man in their midst, the rising hubbub overlaid with a note of confusion: who was this pakeha who walked among them, he led by the tribe's wise elder, and wearing a cloak befitting a man of *mana*?

Lachlan was being led to a table near the top of the room where a warrior wearing his own fine cloak of feathers watched them approach, his jaw set in a hard line. From the moko tattooed in kohl on his face, Lachlan guessed that this was the rangatira, the tribal chief.

Then his eyes snapped to the man sitting beside the chief, his grey-flecked red hair completely out of place here among the Ngai Tohai. An urge to dive across the table swept through Lachlan but he quashed that desire, remaining stock still. The bushman was handing a piece of polished greenstone large as a man's forearm and carved in the shape of a fishhook to the rangatira. From it dangled a length of flax rope. Frankie Ascot smirked at Lachlan, the face of a man who knew he was guilty yet untouchable.

Bait, Lachlan thought again. *Don't be baited.* He wouldn't allow himself to become a fish on a line.

The tohunga addressed the men at the table in his rolling tongue, gesturing at Lachlan and finally ushering him forward. "Rangatira Kahanui will speak with you now, honoured king," he smiled, thoroughly enjoying his little joke.

The warrior-chief glowered at Lachlan, cradling the hook to his chest. "Te Korunga tells me that you are a king of the Pakeha, and were he not *tapu* I would call him a liar. The kings of our people are warriors, as were yours, in days past. You look to me like neither warrior nor king. You come for this," he raised the hook, "yet you have no claim to it. Do you even know what it is? What it means to us? *Korero mai.* Speak."

Lachlan swallowed hard, looking from the *rangatira* to the *pounamu* hook, to Ascot, and back to the hook. Torchlight shivered across its dark green surface, shadows flickering within its carved whorls. For something so big—something only meant to be an ornament, for how could any man ever throw such a hook or haul anything it might catch?—its point sported a sinister sharpness, its shape elegant and simplistic, rolling like waves. In the world Lachlan knew, a place of airships, telegraphs, and battle-tractors, he had never known a thing of such terrible and unexpected beauty. Suddenly all his arguments seemed fleeting and pointless. He claimed to be chasing a thief, an insidious deceiver who had crept among his own kind and betrayed them for the sake of pleasing his savage masters, yet nothing of such fine craftsmanship could possibly have sprung from the mills and factories of Old Blighty. Nothing so wondrous could *belong* to the British Empire.

Frankie Ascot had not stolen the fishhook. The bushman had simply honoured its legacy, in the manner of its maker. Frankie Ascot had stolen it *back* from those who had stolen it from the Maori.

"The piece," Lachlan began, his voice faltering, though whether from the anxiety or the hunger or the sudden flood of self-loathing, he wasn't certain, "was gifted to the New Zealand Government by the Ngati Hareke people—"

"*Hei Matau a Maui* was not *Ngati Hareke's* to give!" Kahanui snapped, slamming a fist on the table top. The hook floated, dark and deadly, in his other hand.

Lachlan imagined that tip lashing out, tearing his throat open in a single fine shred. Whether it was the fear or the sun casting its final rays through the thin gaps in the walls, Lachlan thought he saw the hook shift, as if it pulsed or breathed, and in that moment things became clear, snapping into focus in ways they had not been since he had entered this land of rain and mud and mist.

In this place the hard edges of the world blurred, where ropes of flax might stretch out and drag down an errant sun that sleeks too swiftly across the sky, where a hook carved of stone and blood and magic might pull forth a fish from the sea so vast it becomes a land all its own. A place where the rules became misty, where a man might be bigger than he ever knew.

Had the Governor thought they could retrieve the artefact by brute force alone he would have sent constables and militia, but he had not. He had sent Lachlan King and Barry Ferguson, investigators of the peculiar and the inexplicable, because this place defied reason, its people the children of the mist, shadows against the hills, ghosts and giants.

"Got anything else to say, Guv'nor?" Frankie Ascot jeered. "Or shall we just get on with making an example of you?"

Lachlan eased his arms out from under the feather cloak and raised them in what may have been a command for silence, or a gesture of surrender. "Rangatira Kahanui," he intoned, blood pounding in his temples, "in the name of the Queen, I wish nothing but goodwill to you and your *iwi,*" he nodded at the gathered tribe. "I would be a fool to disbelieve that it is too late for such words, and that it is too late for me. I know your mana is worth more than my meagre life, and that allowing me to live through my transgression of your honour would be insufferable. I come from a long line of knights. I understand honour, even among thieves which, it appears, I must now consider myself, in your eyes at least. For a long time, *Hei Matau a Maui* was but a few streets away from where I worked, and though I knew its legend never did I take the time to look upon it because I, for one, believe it merely a trinket, however beautiful; a token, a symbol, nothing more. It is like so much in life, these things of beauty which we do not appreciate until they are taken from us. I have come a long way to find this treasure, this *taonga* you hold. Would that I might hold it, and know what it is for which I shall die?"

Kahanui snatched the hook away. "It is *tapu!*"

Lachlan nodded. "Of course, it is sacred, and precious. That is why you would risk another invasion to keep it out of British hands. But I am an old man, surrounded by your finest warriors. What harm can I possibly do? Surely, you know our tradition of the dying man's last request?"

The rangatira flicked a glance at the tohunga, and though Lachlan dared not follow his gaze, he was relieved when Kahanui reluctantly passed him the sleek pounamu.

It was heavier than he had anticipated, for it came with the weight of expectation, the promise of mortality. Lachlan King felt its weight in his bones, in his aging joints, felt it drag against his tired muscles. He felt it resist him, dare him, just as the old man had dared him, *baited* him.

But Doctor Sound had sent very explicit orders that *Hei Matau a Maui* be returned to London so that rumours of its mysterious powers could be investigated fully. Lachlan King wasn't here to philosophise on what it meant to be a thief among thieves, or to cast judgements on his distant masters' colonial politics. He was a pawn, sent to do their bidding.

A fish on a hook.

Yet somehow Lachlan King knew that, right at this moment, holding *Hei Matau*, he was more than he had ever been. His father had not lived up to his knightly blood. Lachlan would not make the same mistake. He would prove, if only to himself, that he was indeed a king among men; that the sun would shine through him and cast his shadow like a giant upon the mist.

For Queen and Country, he thought ruefully, in the same instant as he wrapped the rope around his hand, took a deep breath, and whirled the hook over his head.

The balloon, now fully inflated, struggled to take flight. Barry's bodyguards watched, chortling amongst themselves, while the tractor remained firmly settled in the mud.

"Here we go," Barry muttered, then jammed the lever forward.

Dozens of wires, roughly arc-welded to bolts buried in the mud, tore free, whipping dangerously around the tractor. Barry's armoured balloon leapt skyward, taking only what was needed: the gunner's chair, the cannons, the propane and air tanks and their respective lines and the tractor radiator, all bolted or hastily welded to the underside of the hansom.

And, of course, Barry Ferguson.

Ignoring the flurry of shouts from below, Barry swung the cannons and fired several rounds into the trees to cover his escape. With his feet driving the gas and air pedals, he released a jet of air over the radiator fan-blades, spinning them with a banshee's wail and propelling the impromptu airborne gun-platform away in a mad arc amidst the crack of musket-fire.

After a few moments of acclimating to the dirigible—far different to steer than an all-terrain hansom—Barry yawed towards the glow of firelight in the ranges, where he was fairly sure he would find Mister King.

See, he would say when he arrived, *I really did have it under control, sir. Shame about poor Mister Massey's tractor, mind you.*

Lachlan King wasn't sure at what point the real world fell away and what could only possibly be a waking hallucination born of exhaustion and terror settled upon him. A guttural roar plucked from some dark and hungry creature of the mists erupted from him. He imagined the rope in his hand growing longer, the pounamu lighter, perhaps even sharper. This allowed him to swing the short rope with its sharp, heavy load harder, faster, sending bodies both unmarred and sliced open by his emerald blade scrambling around him. The walls and roof of the *wharekai* ripped open, sending shreds of timber and thatch in all directions. Through this maelstrom of madness, Lachlan knew the power of *Hei Matau*, the hook that had pulled a nation from the sea, a tool fashioned of the same ancient magics that Maui had used to weave ropes to slow the very sun in its race across the sky.

In that moment he was, he knew, quite lost in a safe and convenient insanity wherein the rules of the world no longer applied, lost where myth and legend replaced the rational and the real. The hook dipped, carving a line in the dirt floor as it howled about its deadly arc, and Lachlan wondered in passing if he spied thin liquid, bright red and bubbling, seeping up from the flesh-pale gouge it left in the earth.

Then he was running, the hook still whirling overhead, his voice a harsh cry echoing off the mountainside as he pelted past the furious eyes of the *tekoteko* that overlooked the wharenui, legs pounding as he reached the lake shore.

A quick look over his shoulder told him that he was not alone. Pulling himself from the wreckage, Frank Ascot was hot on his heels, his face a livid mask of blood.

Lachlan ran. The mist hung thick in the air where the waterfall spilled free, near the few small trees that clung to the cliff-edge. Lachlan envisioned himself swinging the hook on its rope, wrapping around one of those stunted trees, and swinging through hundreds of feet of shadow, his fine feather cloak spread out behind him like the wings of some nightbird, like the great eagle *Hokioi* in his rage. With a quick tug he would shear through his anchor tree, reel the hook back to himself, and ride the Pacific winds all the way back to England.

He was Maui, a legend of flesh who could break the rules of the world, the laws of the Empire, spit in his father's face.

It seemed so perfect, so unpredictable.

Then he saw it; a great, looming brown eye with its pupil of blazing white as it swelled up from the glowing fog.

"Away with you, *taniwha!*" he barked, a mad sound, and swung the hook out and over his head. "Fear me!"

"Sir? Is that you?" came an uncertain call from the fog.

Reality slammed home, but already it was too late. The hook flew true and deadly, slicing a thin tear in Barry's bizarre construct and wrapping itself around the poles that held his would-be escape vessel aloft.

Hot air shrieked from the balloon, sending the dirigible spiralling out over the void. It was all Lachlan could do to wrap both hands around the rope before he was lifted from his feet and pulled over the cliff face, leaving Ascot's furious screams behind as momentum and gravity whipped him around in dizzying circles. Above him, Lachlan could hear Barry swearing over the hissing and whining of the slap-dash airship.

"Hold on sir," Barry yelled. "I'll have this sorted in a two shakes of a dog's hind leg."

Lachlan couldn't answer. It was taking all his strength just to hold on as they plunged from the hole in the world where the river shone, down into the well of shadows.

"Sir, I'm going to put her down, nice and easy," Barry called with impossible optimism, as the craft fell sideways in sickening arcs across the sky.

The bush-clad valley spiralled nearer. When they hit the ground and the propane tank sheared open in a flurry of sparks, it would all be over, and for nothing. Lachlan looked up to where the gash in the canvas fluttered and snapped.

Sometimes, we must be bigger than we really are.

They dropped into the mists.

Summoning what was left of his flagging strength, Lachlan reached over his head and stretched, pulling himself up the rope one aching foot at a time, feathers billowing behind him like dark wings. The rope was wrapped right around the balloon's metal poles, pinching it in the middle so that it appeared like a bloated figure-of-eight. The hook dangled in a loop of its own making an arm's reach from the tear. His focus intent on the artefact, Lachlan climbed past the tractor cab, refusing to contemplate the empty space below him. Wrapping a leg hard around the nearest pole, daring to let go of the rope with one raw, blistered hand, Lachlan lunged out and grabbed the hook's smooth edge.

Maui did not care for the rules of the world. Maui had cast a rope to catch *te Ra*, the sun; had thrown a hook which pulled a land of plenty from the sea. Lachlan King was not Maui, was not made of the same stuff as that ancient hero, but he was the son of knights long dead, and he could be more than his father had ever dreamed he might be.

Lachlan tugged the hook towards him and began to haul in the rope, drawing its length through its own loops, his eyes straying to the high glow of sunlight that slid, breath by breath, towards darkness.

Perhaps a little insanity lingered. Time for *te Ra* to catch itself a fish.

Lachlan hooked the coil over his shoulder and slid down the pole, ignoring the pain in his palms, hitting the hansom platform with a grunt. The roar of water was loud in his ears now, the mist shadow-shrouded except for the propane's glow. The unseen earth rushed ever closer.

Lachlan lashed a hasty knot through the base of the cannon-armature, wrapped one arm around a gun-barrel and hurled the rope up and out, towards the disappearing sun. He braced himself and hoped that, in this modern world, there was still room for the making of legends.

"Sir?" Barry's concerned voice seemed very distant, lost in the mist, as the rope flew away from him.

The dirigible jerked suddenly and snapped backwards, nearly tossing both agents into the mists as its descent was violently interrupted. Both men clutched onto the gun platform for dear life as it swung pendulously to and fro. Between the roar of the waterfall and the swallowing mists, Lachlan and Barry were blind and deaf, bobbing in the fog, hanging with no visible means of support, the propane flame illuminating nothing but white all around.

"For goodness' sake lad, turn off that light before they find us," Lachlan chided.

"Sir, what just happened?" Barry asked, struggling to secure a foothold.

Lachlan closed his eyes and let a smile wrinkle his exhausted features. "I believe that we just caught the sun."

Barry squinted over his head. "Are you sure? Because I think that looks like some sort of swing-bridge up there. I don't suspect it's likely to hold this weight for long."

Lachlan took a deep breath, feeling the strain in his shoulders. This night wasn't over yet. "Let's get out of here with what we came for, lad. I'll tell you what I can on the way."

"Righto," Barry agreed, hauling himself up the hansom to grasp the rope in one hand, and reaching out to Lachlan with the other. "If we can make it back to where the tractor was, sir, I believe I left the billy there. We might have time for a nice cup of tea."

"That," Lachlan breathed, "would be quite divine."

時計仕掛けの神輿事件

The Incident
of the Clockwork Mikoshi

Lauren Harris

Kyoto, Japan
July 15, 1864
京王元年 — *First Year of Emperor Keio*

People always gave Ministry Agent Lawrence P. Dagenhart the kind of wide berth reserved for night men, mug-hunters, and sooty chavies of the light-fingered sort. He usually had his reputation to thank, but now people scattered to either side of the Kamo River bridge because he was exactly what the Emperor's woodblock-prints taught them to fear—a foreigner.

He had no quarrel with the people of Kyoto, not yet in any case. They weren't as used to Europeans as the population at his post in Nagasaki, so the sight of a five-foot-eleven bodyguard with a prosthetic brass arm and a massive horse was bound to cause distress. The bridge was packed with people headed toward the main city for the parade. Of course, the Aizu Lord would choose the busiest day of the biggest festival in Kyoto to ask his help in solving a murder. At least he was heading into the smaller, quieter district of Gion. Planks trembled under Brutus's hooves, and Law, ever late to the party of discretion, dismounted.

He rolled both shoulders—one flesh, one fiction—and attributed the fear to fox mentality. The Emperor's subjects, he had deduced during his time on assignment, were either the scattering sort or the fighting sort, startled foxes or startled hounds, and it was only the latter Law was bothered about.

He was a hound when it came to fights, but Law reckoned he was a fox with everything else. He'd been running since the day he learned to walk. Running from a home overrun with cholera to beg on Artillerie lane, from begging to bare-knuckle boxing in the East End rings and from that to play personal guard for a clankerton on the edge of London. Then, when the man realised there was a brain beneath his bowler, to Oxford. After that... well, he tried not to think much about what happened after that.

Over the hump of the bridge, Law spied the turquoise uniform coat of a Shinsengumi patrol officer. He squinted, trying to decide if it was Investigator Ogawa or a page sent to bring the *gaijin* to the murder site. Law might solve mysteries for a living, but determining anyone's age in Japan was like shooting a river scamp halfway across the Thames with a Colt—mostly luck and likely to backfire. He brought Brutus to a halt, took in a slow breath to clear his head, then drew his Remington 44 and snapped out the cylinder, finding it full. They'd called him to shoot. Might as well make sure he was prepared.

He holstered the revolver and extended his mechanical left arm, sliding his right hand down to flip open a compartment of loaded magazines on his metallic bicep. With all the steam his arm generated, he'd been afraid the black powder would dampen to uselessness, but the clankertons had assured him it was quite waterproof. That had remained true, but Law still had a hard time putting away the instincts of an East Ender. Water plus black powder equaled a ball in the backside.

Or the shoulder, as it happened.

He loaded a magazine of rifle bullets into the cavity on his bronze forearm and finessed it into place, keeping the hammer locked inside his wrist lest he shoot off a leg as well.

The lad spotted him just as he finished loading and approached. He executed a graceful bow, half-cat and half-clockwork. Investigators—or *shinobi*, as the Japanese called them—were more spy than samurai. By all accounts they blurred the line of supernatural, and by the time Law reached the end of the bridge, he'd decided.

"Investigator Ogawa." He tipped his bowler and the suggestion of a smile tensed the youth's black eyes.

"I am honoured to meet you, Agent Dagenhart," a sweet alto voice returned in English, much better pronounced than his own.

He took a step back, eyes flicking to the Investigator's throat, then back up at the childlike face. His left arm hissed, articulated joints venting steam into the muggy summer air as he reached up to remove his headwear properly. "Beggin' yer pardon, miss," he said. "I was expecting... well, beggin' yer pardon, miss..."

The woman in the Shinsengumi uniform gave her strange, not-quite smile again. "I am often Investigator Ogawa," she said. "But you may call me Tokiko Hanamura. Come with me—our victim is a *tokeiya-san*."

A clock-maker? Law replaced his bowler and forced himself back into a business frame of mind. Well, as business went in this Land of the Rising Sun. It would have been nice if someone had told him he would be partnered with a woman. Just when he thought he understood the way this country worked...

The Shirakawa district's tea houses and specialty shops were set close to narrow stone roads, as if corralling the small river between them. Cherry trees fringed the embankments and cast a lace of shadows onto the green water. There was so much colour here, so much life, all carefully tended. Back in Whitechapel, the only green Law ever saw was in half-healed bruises and the coat of slime at the base of the buildings. You wanted green growing things? You left London.

Law ducked through the doorway of the *tokei-ya* and banged his head on the lintel, toppling his bowler to the floor.

"Bloody end to you too," he muttered, remembering too late his companion was both an English-speaker and a lady. As Law bent to retrieve his nab, the pneumatic hiss and clicks of his prosthetic left arm blended with the shop's clockwork ticks and sighs. Most tokei-ya, the Japanese clock-shops, belonged to one side of the country's civil conflict or the other. Harassment of the shop owners was not uncommon as Bakufu supporters like the Shinsengumi warred with Imperialists, who harnessed the infernal technology for the sole purpose of kicking those same foreigners out boots over bowlers.

This time, though, the Imperialist's xenophobia didn't seem to be at fault. That was why the Aizu Lord had called Law all the way from Nagasaki, requesting he bring his "unique Ministry skills to bear on a problem requiring supernatural expertise." Law wagered that was the honorific version of "We've no idea what's got us in the suds, so if swords don't work, could he try shooting it?"

Unwilling to alienate a powerful member of the Bakufu, Law shelved his Tengu investigation, saddled Brutus, and made the long, humid trip to Kyoto. If he happened to have liquored his boots before he left, well... he was from Whitechapel.

He swatted aside the curtains and squinted into the dark shop. The rich stink of blood hit him first, followed by the descant buzzing of flies. Like all buildings in Japan, the entrance had a step where folk removed their footwear before entering the shop. But a glimmer of dark liquid pooled at the edge of the *tatami* mats, stopping Law in his boots.

A striation of light shone past his shoulder, and the dark liquid flashed scarlet. He glanced past the blade of light into the darkened shop, where Tokiko stood in woven sandals on the shop's ruined tatami. Behind her, tiny clockwork mechanisms glimmered and clicked, pulsing together as if they stood inside a breathing, sleeping beast.

He stepped up into the shop and navigated around a smashed grandfather clock and peered at the clock-maker's body, sprawled across two tatami mats, his arms outstretched. A large scarlet stain spread around the chap's top half, though Law couldn't see where it came from. More blood glinted on the wall between the show room and the workshop. Law followed the spray pattern up the rice-paper all the way to the ceiling, and back down again. Irregular as a Parliament convening in a dollhouse.

He scraped his knuckles across his stubble and glanced back down at the dead tokeiya-san. "Well, well, well. What in 'ell."

"More precisely," Tokiko said, "what in Heaven." She pointed in front of the dead chap's hand. The tokeiya-san stared, as if he, too, gazed in the direction of his extended right arm. Law squinted. Judging by the streaked liquid, the clockmaker had dragged himself across the mat toward the workshop and, failing to reach it, wrote something on the woven surface of the next tatami in the only ink he could find—his own blood.

It took Law a moment to recognise the character. He knew few enough, and the easiest to remember was *sake*, since whoever first wrote it had the good sense to draw a liquor bottle and have done with it. This one, however, was less familiar.

"Kami," he said at last. "God?"

Tokiko nodded. "According to the Emperor, the god of war will punish those using foreign technologies." She looked serene as she crouched, pointing to a smear next to the symbol, where blood seeped between the woven bamboo threads. "Something else was written here, but whatever came after him—god or otherwise—did not want it to be read."

Law crouched, mind clicking and whirring in time with his arm. "'Ow long's the chap been backed?"

Her eyebrows drew together. Law clicked his tongue and shook his head. Old habits.

"Dead." He clarified. "'Ow long's 'e been dead?"

"Ah. Since this morning. The tea shops on either side were open late, and Shirakawa is quiet compared to the rest of Gion." She stood, adjusting her white headband with fingers that looked too delicate to wield the katana through her belt. "I will check his records. Perhaps it was a client."

He quirked an eyebrow, watched her glide across the floor, past the stairs, and into the syncopated commotion of the workshop. He'd not been comfortable with women since Phoebe's death, but Tokiko possessed a natural gift at making him quite unsettled. It was as if she didn't notice the ground. She didn't move like other samurai, with their erect posture and sure footing, their strict economy of movement. Rather, she seemed to flicker, to bend like flame and catch again in a place where there'd been only shadow before.

"You don't think 'e was killed by the god of war then?" he asked, gazing back down to the corpse at his shoes. He leaned to either side, noting a greater amount of blood soaking the man's *yukata* on his left.

"Of course not," Tokiko said with a slight laugh. "Until now, every murder attributed to the god of war was of a Bakufu supporter. The Choushuu clan insists they are being punished for allowing foreign technology into Japan, and the Emperor supports them. This man was a Choushuu retainer."

Law pushed the aged clock-maker's body onto its back, careful not to get blood in any of his brass joints. The man's long, thin mustache dragged gummy streaks of blood across his waxy face. He looked rich, pale and paunched like any chap with poppy to spare. But nothing set him apart as an Imperialist—no Choushuu or Satsuma clan crests, which Law had learned to recognise and avoid well enough in Nagasaki.

"This bloke was an Imperialist?"

"Yes. All the others were as described in the Daimyo's letter to you: Bakufu supporters, most of them victims of *oni*."

Law grimaced. Oni were no chavy game, but he'd expected some such creature here in Kyoto. "It's not consistent with the murders what's already 'appened," he said. "Why add it to the case?"

"The writing."

"Kami? Anyone 'oo heard the Emperor's warnings might 'ave writ that to shift blame. You sure it wasn't one of yours? As I understand, it wouldn't be the first time a Shinsengumi officer got 'is back up and snuffed some chap what 'e shouldn't."

That earned him a dark look from his contact. "All our members were accounted for at the *bansho*."

Law touched his brim with the barest of bows and looked back to the dead clock-maker. The wound wasn't hard to find—a single puncture to the throat, as wide as Law's thumbnail. Its placement accounted for the spray radius, but the skin was pushed in, made with a flat blade rather than a sharp one. Even stranger, one side of the wound had a slight bow to the shape, as though there were a groove down the back of the instrument.

"I've never seen a weapon what made this kind of mark," he spoke over his shoulder. "And unless your god 'as powerfully abnormal fingernails, I'm guessing it'll be a trade instrument."

Tokiko neither looked up nor changed her expression. "If he punishes me for my support of the Bakufu, I shall be certain to check."

Law snorted. So she did have a sense of humour.

Tokiko rifled through what Law assumed were receipts as, for the next half hour, he checked every corner of the shop for a tool that might have made the puncture wound. It wasn't until he scanned the work-benches at the rear that he noticed something irregular. Though most of the shop was impeccable, an oil flask lay on its side, contents seeping into the wooden bench.

He crouched by the bench to get a closer look. A cloth lay crumpled beside the work area, no longer covering whatever device the clock-maker had been working on. Mechanisms whirred as he closed his fingers around the cloth and shook it out.

A fist-sized clockwork *thing* sprang out, rebounded off Law's chest, and went scampering toward the door. Law stumbled backwards, drawing his revolver as the thing flashed, all copper and gears, here and there across the shop. It was no bigger than a rat, tails buzzing like airship propellers behind it, but damned if he wouldn't shoot it before it could do any damage.

He drew back the hammer but just as his finger tightened on the trigger, Tokiko's sword flickered from its sheath. She flipped the clockwork creature into the air where it spun, heavy and glinting, back toward Law, too close to shoot.

He swung, smashing the back of his mechanical wrist into the clockwork thing and sent it into one of the gear-laden tables with a crunch of delicate mechanics. One slender leg continued to churn with a steady *tick-tick-tick-tick*, but otherwise the little clockwork creature was still.

In the echoing absence of frantic mechanicals, Tokiko blinked at him, both hands still on her raised sword. She glanced at the creature, then back at Law in apparent incomprehension.

"I thought you would catch it," she said.

"I just did." Law holstered his gun. "If you knew Whitechapel, you'd understand."

The creature turned out to be a small copper fox, still recognisable despite its dented casing. It had three tails, and odder still was the tiny slip of paper unfurling like a dragon's tongue from the creature's open jaws. Tokiko sheathed her katana and stooped, withdrawing the paper.

"It is a *myoubu*," she said. "A messenger to the god Inari." Her brow knotted as she peered at the minute characters. How she could differentiate strokes the size of fly shit was beyond him. Law lifted the twitching clockwork fox by its tails and peered at the damage he'd caused. There was a sizable dent in its side. That belonged to him. The scratches running along its belly and head, though, didn't come from his arm-attack. He looked closer, noting its tiny copper teeth bent outward as though something had been pried from its jaws. Whoever had stolen it either missed or hadn't cared about the message.

"This note is addressed to one of the Shinsengumi captains," Tokiko said. "A meeting place and time, and the clock-maker's name-stamp. He's promised important information regarding the events of the Ikedaya incident."

"Sorry? The Ikedaya incident?"

Tokiko's dark eyes did not soften, but her gaze cut back down to the slender note in her hand. "The events that unfolded at the Ikeda Inn a few weeks ago involved a disturbing conspiracy. The Choushuu clan intended to kidnap the emperor and force him into open war with the Bakufu."

Law nodded to the corpse. "And this bloke knew somewhat he oughtn't? And it made 'im want to spill the tale to the Shinsengumi?" He studied the clock-maker's rigid face, the puncture in his throat, and sucked his teeth. "Why wouldn't the Choushuu send oni and make it look like the others?"

"Oni are not discreet. If the clock-maker had information, they would not have wanted to attract the attention of the Shinsengumi before they could be sure he was dead. Better to assassinate him."

Law grunted agreement and glanced around the shop, imagining what havoc the enormous goblins would have done to such delicate contraptions. His gaze landed on the toppled oil and the empty workbench where he'd found the fox. They wouldn't have left it behind if that's what they'd come for.

"What if this Choushuu clan 'ad 'im make something? Some kind of weapon?"

Tokiko glanced back toward the stack of receipts and shook her head. "Neither the Choushuu nor the Satsuma clans had anything under commission."

"Yes, of course," Law snorted, "because if I were under duress, I would naturally track my time and keep detailed books on this secret commission, right?"

She tilted her head, crooking a single eyebrow at him. "Perhaps that would be too obvious." She slipped past Law, stepping close as she avoided the outskirts of the blood-stain. Her dark hair smelled of trapped incense smoke, blotting out the iron tang of blood for just a moment. He glanced down at her slender hand perched like a bird on her katana. Suddenly, he felt like the oni in this fragile eco-system of ticking life—large and destructive. He decided not to follow her into the workshop.

"Could be the old chap changed 'is mind at the last minute," he suggested. "Didn't want to start sliding down that particular slope?"

"Perhaps," she said. "It is also likely he did not know how his work would be used."

"You think he refused to 'and it over?"

Tokiko pulled out a receipt and squinted at it. "I do not think he is so noble he would refuse a group of Choushuu ronin. Decisions are remarkably simple with a sword to your throat."

"Not if you 'ave a pistol," he said, just to have a response.

"This was for a parade float," Tokiko said, and the confusion in her tone made Law look up from the dead clockmaker. He thought of the enormous wagons with their colourful paper and fabric, loaded down with folk in resplendent kimono like the queen herself was on parade. Was it so strange to include clockwork in one of those posh floats?

"If the gods don't approve of western mechanicals, might one find it insulting to use 'em in a float?" he asked.

Tokiko nodded. "Insulting enough to punish the city. Whether by their own hand, or through the Choushuu."

"Using the gods as a scapegoat for political balderdash," Law growled, feeling his nostrils flare as he inhaled the scents of dust, oil, and blood. And the faint reminder of incense. He flexed his hands, the stretch of muscle in his right hand, the whirr and tick of clockwork in his left. "I 'spect we 'ave a float to catch."

Tokiko Hanamura pressed her hand against her *katana* and *wakazashi's* grips to keep them out of her way, walking fast enough to scandalise her *Nee-san*. Luckily, without a Maiko's face paint, elaborate hair, and cumbersome costume, no one recognised O-Tokiko the Geisha-in-training, and no one would blink at a Shinsengumi Investigator hurrying through Gion on a festival day.

The *taiko* drums pounded several streets ahead and she picked up her pace, determined to catch the floats before any could make it across the Kamo River. Whatever the Choushuu had planned, it couldn't be good. Her skin crawled as she recalled the Imperialist's screaming confession the night of the Ikedaya Incident, how he'd said the Choushuu dogs planned to set her beloved city ablaze. Tokiko's feet struck the stone faster as she imagined the beautiful city her brother had died for burning to ashes. She would never allow it.

The Englishman's horse made a steady clicking sound behind her, and from the corner of her eyes she could see people press toward the shop fronts to avoid him. Even walking beside his horse, few Kyoto-jin were taller than Agent Dagenhardt's shoulder. He proved many of her father's observations about westerners—ostentatious, outspoken, and bellicose—but diverged from them in others, most pointedly in that he'd neither threatened nor shot anyone since arriving in Kyoto.

Agent Dagenhardt sped up, drawing level with her own shoulder. She tried not to stare as he swept off his bowler with a ticking left hand, dragging his real fingers through sweaty, barley-coloured hair. His face was strange with its deep-set features, his emotions easy to read as a *Noh* mask. Now he was the aspect of anger, his brow drawn in a scowl as he jerked his stubbled chin toward the roadside. She craned her neck as they sped past, noting the red lacquered columns and wheat sheaves decorating a small shrine wedged between two buildings.

"There are fox statues," Agent Dagenhardt said. "They've got some kind of ball in their mouths."

"*Tama*—a jewel," she said. "They are said to grant wishes—all the *myoubu* have them."

"Excepting ours. The clockwork fox 'ad its teeth bent out. I 'spect the same folk what done the clock-maker pinched it."

Tokiko glanced up at him in surprise. She had been so intent on the message, she'd missed the state of the clockwork myoubu's teeth, but it could have been carrying a tama. She nodded, matching her footfalls to her racing heartbeat.

They skirted Yasaka shrine's north side, murmuring cursory apologies as they shouldered past the throngs preparing the festival. Heart thumping, Tokiko scanned the courtyard for the enormous *yamaboko* floats, but they were already gone. All that was left were the *mikoshi*, the Shinto Pantheon's portable shrines. The taiko drums grew louder as gathered men lifted the gold-leafed shrines on long poles and settled them on their shoulders. The hair on her neck rose and stray thoughts attempted and failed to converge. A sinking feeling in her stomach made her hand tighten on her sword. The first float would already be halfway across the bridge.

Agent Dagenhardt growled something crude. "We don't know which wagon we're looking for do we?"

"No," she said, meeting his bright eyes, which seemed to have trapped all the shades of the summer sky. His strange, foreign eyes.

Now that was an idea.

She glanced at the enormous horse who stamped and tossed his head in impatience, and looked back at Agent Dagenhardt. Her lips curled into a smile. "But I think I know how we can make them reveal themselves."

Agent Dagenhardt, who had tracked her gaze, twitched his lips. "I believe I take your meaning, miss. Allow me to take a butcher's."

And before she could remind him to address her as Investigator Ogawa, he put one enormous boot in his stirrup and swung into the saddle, sinking deep into his seat like a man returning home. He shed the awkwardness of his size and bearing, emerging still and calm and strangely graceful. He made a thousand times more sense in the saddle. He clenched the reins in his brass hand and touched two fingers to his hat.

He whipped his pistol from its holster and fired three rounds in quick succession, letting out a loud, high-pitched howl like an enraged oni. The multitude scattered and Brutus exploded forward. They plunged toward the Kamo River.

She had met Englishmen before, but this one from Whitechapel was very different. Most apt that he represented an organisation dealing with the peculiar.

Tokiko coiled her muscles and sprinted through the startled throng, which sucked back into shops like a retreating wave. They saw her Shinsengumi *haori* and pointed toward the crazed foreigner shouting, shooting, and trailing steam and gun smoke. The road was straight as a sword from Yasaka shrine to the bridge over the Kamo River, and with the crowd cleared to let Agent Dagenhardt pass, she had an unobstructed view of what happened next.

The rear float—an enormous, gilded thing hung with rich tapestries and lanterns, capped with a roof like a miniature shrine, stopped before it reached the bridge, and men boiled from the float like bees, their steel katana appearing as glittering stings. A familiar white crest emblazoned their jackets: the number one above a trio of pearls—the Choushuu clan's sigil.

The first Choushuu ronin reached Agent Dagenhardt just as Tokiko passed the last building. The Englishman leaned hard to the right, his horse made a nimble turn, and Agent Dagenhardt caught the first katana across his prosthetic arm. A loud ring shivered through the air, heralding battle. He kicked out, boot connecting with the man's face and sending him back into the man behind him. Two more replaced them, and the swarm of swords drove Agent Dagenhardt further up the riverbank, away from the bridge. It was possible they intended to protect the parade from the mad Englishman, but they split into groups, some going after Agent Dagenhardt, the rest creating a perimeter around the float, with no apparent communication. As if they'd had a plan for being attacked, and that plan was protecting whatever destructive force waited inside the float.

Tokiko surged straight toward the perimeter, drawing her sword in one liquid motion. Their muscles coiled, and they sank low into fighting stances, teeth bared like dogs, bristling with steel. She held her sword out forward and the flash of her turquoise haori sent pride spiking straight to her heart. They may call her an Aizu wolf, but they were nothing but mongrels, destroying what they could not rule. She was a Shinsengumi warrior, tasked with protecting her beloved city be it from man, monster, or god.

Five feet away, she leapt. The world stilled a moment, like the instant before the curl of a wave, and she broke against the black rocks of the Choushuu ronin. Her gaze narrowed to throats, armpits, knees, striking vulnerabilities with blade, pommel, and feet too fast for the lead-footed *ronin* to follow. She blocked a downward cut and twisted aside, sweeping her blade up into one man's groin.

A crack sounded, echoing off the river, and Agent Dagenhardt shouted something unintelligible. Then she saw her opening. Tokiko drew her sword back and pivoted, catching the blade of a man with his face contorted into a murderous, wolf like snarl. She twisted her grip, directing his sword toward the ground, and released her katana. The unexpected manoeuvre left him staggering forward. Then her foot slammed his shoulder and she launched herself up, twisted mid-air, caught the float's protruding roof with both hands, and swung up.

The roof beneath her moved, the same noises as Agent Dagenhardt's arm and the dead tokeiya-san's shop emanating from under her. Sunlight glinted off the little door and track where, at a specific time, a tiny clockwork bird would emerge to announce the time. A cuckoo clock. Clocks that were designed to start and stop with a special key.

This was the right float. Unquestionably.

She crossed the roof in a crouch, drew and swung down, wakazashi drawn—

—and caught a gleam off a tall man's katana, threatening to skewer her.

Tokiko changed her direction at the last moment and slapped the blade aside, but the movement sent her off balance and her fingers twisted free. She slammed into the floor, rolled, and came up in a defensive crouch, bringing up her blade. Her adversary was a long-faced ronin, his dark haori blending in with the shadows. The light shining in from the wagon's front cast his eyes into shadow, giving his grinning face a skullish appearance. She clenched her jaw, and he ducked his head, the grin turning into a snarl. Something glittered at his chest, catching the light from the folds of his *kosode*. It was a small golden orb, the gears between the two hemispheres visibly working as the two pieces ticked in opposite directions.

Of course. Time-wired black powder kegs.

This must be the key the clockmaker had designed and tried to send the Shinsengumi for safekeeping, which meant above her, packed into the roof's delicate mechanisms, was a battery of black powder. Her eyes returned to the ronin's face, and Tokiko favoured him with a cold smile.

"Aizu wolf!" He pointed his sword straight at her collarbone and drove it down. Tokiko jerked sideways, but he was fast, pivoting on one foot and redirecting his cut much quicker than she'd anticipated. She brought up her wakazashi, and the clash of steel sent a shudder down her arm. He withdrew his blade, slashing her across the arm. It opened up her sleeve, and blood welled to the surface, staining the turquoise fabric. She sprang from her crouch to drive him back, but he was too fast, catching her blade and redirecting her into another warrior climbing into the float.

Several more sharp cracks sounded and Law gave another unearthly scream, startling the men reaching for her. Tokiko dropped her weight before the first man could grab her, reaching around to slash open the meat of his calf. She jammed the heel of her hand into his groin and he staggered, falling from the wagon and taking down the two other ronin climbing in. Movement stirred the air behind her and Tokiko rolled backwards just as the Choushuu leader brought his katana in a powerful downward strike that would have split her skull in two. Her shoulders slammed into his toes at the exact moment his katana buried itself in the wagon's floor, giving her scant seconds to react.

She surrendered to instinct and training. Tokiko dropped her wakazashi, grabbed his ankles, and kicked both feet straight up. Her wooden sandals slammed into his chin and his head snapped backwards. It was not the fighting style in keeping with the *bushido*. Most fortunate Tokiko was no samurai.

The Choushuu ronin went boneless, dropping hard to the float's floor. She hadn't had the leverage to snap his neck with that kick, but it had done the job well enough. She pressed her hands behind her shoulders and leapt up from the ground, jerking the man's katana from the floor. She swooped down and hunted in his kosode for the key, the sudden absence of immediate danger reminding her of the clock ticking overhead. How long did they have? When was the float meant to go off? Cold sweat slid down her back, but she forced stillness into her soul as she hunted for the tama. The instant her hand closed around the cool sphere, clicking and fluttering in her hand like a metal cricket, a cold hand snapped up and clenched her wrist.

She jerked back, but the man held fast, strong despite his injuries. Blood trickled from his mouth, seeping between his teeth as he grinned up at her.

"It is too late, Aizu wolf," the man slurred. He laughed, sucked in a rattling breath and coughed on the blood seeping into his throat.

The battle outside now grew louder, this time with the familiar voices of Captain Hijikata and his forces. People streamed past the immobilized float, the mikoshi-bearers ushered onto the bridge despite the danger, to complete the parade so the gods would spare them another year's strife.

"Susano'o, god of sea and storms, will visit his wrath upon you! The city will blaze in the wake of his chariot," he pronounced, his dying breath dripping with victory and his own blood, "and judgement will fall on the Aizu wolves! He will vanquish the foreign pestilence the Bakufu have allowed to plague Japan."

"His chariot?" she said, her brain whirring, spinning backwards, flashing like the pop of those infernal cameras. Her mind produced a snapshot of memory, words painted in blood. The word *kami* beside a red smear actually resolved into the word *chariot*.

No, not a chariot. A palanquin. A divine palanquin, to carry the gods.

She looked up, her eyes tracking the parade across the bridge, on the heels of men bearing portable shrines, ignorant of the danger they carried.

"The mikoshi," she whispered, and surged to her feet. She leaned out the float's rear and surveyed the carnage—six Shinsengumi officers fought a dozen Choushuu, half wearing hair-covered oni masks. Agent Dagenhardt rode like a wild man between them, herding them toward the Shinsengumi. She watched him straighten his arm at one point, shifting back the entire top plate of his brass forearm with an audible clunk, to aim it at the ronin sneaking up behind one of her engaged cohorts. A small explosion roared from his arm, recoiling his shoulder, tightening the straps across his chest. A cloud of black smoke obscured Dagenhardt as the dishonourable ronin fell.

Then Tokiko did something that would have made her Nee-san faint outright. When she was nine, Tokiko's father had translated for an American ambassador, whose son had spent the day teaching Tokiko and her brother shocking western customs. She put her thumb and forefinger in her mouth, curled her tongue, and whistled.

Agent Dagenhardt's head jerked around, and his horse's body followed the direction. She held out the orb for him to see, and swung her arm toward the bridge, pointing after the mikoshi. The Englishman's summer-sky eyes widened in a face coated with gritty gun smoke. He kicked Brutus, which, despite his cumbersome size, cut deftly around knots of warring samurai.

Agent Dagenhardt lifted his hand, shouting something she couldn't hear over the whirr of clockwork above her. She leapt into the scalding sunlight just as a battering ram of bronze slammed into her back.

Law's shouted warning came a second too late. The enormous mechanical beast slammed full force into Tokiko, sending her sprawling onto the stones. He watched, trapped in horror, as the glittering orb shot into the air and made a long, graceful arc straight into the Kamo River. The shinobi woman lay still.

When she rolled onto her back and lay there, head tipped back, fingers twitching toward her dropped weapon, Law saw Phoebe—half crushed beneath the hansom she'd tried to escape, smuggling her father's newest invention away from Tsar Nicholas I's assassins. Her fingers had twitched like that, reaching for the weapon even as she died.

He reigned in Brutus as memory muffled the sound of battle. His face was cold, gaze narrowing to the stretch of stone between the monster and himself. He straightened his arm and conjured a wild firestorm from the gates of Hell.

The thing that had slammed into her hissed steam from every joint as the pneumatics in its legs settled. Law knew that noise, and his lip curled at the full-bodied version of his own simulacrum. A suit of clockwork armour had dropped from the float's ceiling. The masked samurai within piloted a sword-wielding oni golem. The ronin lifted his leg, and the clockwork oni started its inexorable forward march.

Law tugged out a fresh magazine from his saddlebag, snapped it into his Remington 44, and drew back the hammer. He felt calm, transcendent, as if this were a terrible nightmare he'd gone through a thousand times and grown bored of enduring. In a way, it was. The high-pitched buzzing in his ears was exactly like it had been that day, and even the lantern-light flashing off street windows replayed in the Kamo River's glimmering water. In his dream, he always missed his shot and staggered to Phoebe's side with her blood still warm and her eyes gone cold.

He buried her, in the ground, and in his heart, then ran away.

The hammer's satisfying click shifted something inside him, and he clenched his nerveless left arm, sending the clockwork spinning even as gears in his heart and mind ticked into place. In the glare off the clockwork oni's massive blade, Law squinted. No more running. Not this time.

He let up on the reins, settled his feet heavy in the stirrups, and wrenched a harsh *"Yahh!"* from his throat. Brutus surged forward like a warhorse and Law levelled his pistol at the man inside the clockwork suit, who raised his sword high over Tokiko.

Horse and rider thundered toward the oni, and Law squinted, aiming for the centre of the masked forehead through the vision pane in the golem's brass plates. He sucked in a breath, felt a calm wash over him as he exhaled, and fired.

The blade came down, and Tokiko rolled aside, coming up on one knee as steel sparked off the stone where she'd been seconds before. She clutched her shoulder, which hung low, and blood poured from her nose and seeped from a scrape on her cheek, but she was alive. His heart rammed into his throat.

Lawrence steered Brutus with his knees, bending the horse around behind the clockwork-oni like he had the spies' carriage. The oni settled and hissed, overbalanced forward on its large sword, which skidded, drawing a slow, deep gash through the stone. Dark blood oozed from the opening at its metal head.

"Agent Dagenhardt!" Tokiko called. Her voice sounded pained. Brutus skidded to a halt, hooves sparking on the stones, and Law leapt down. Tokiko's strong, delicate hand was covered in blood.

"The bomb," she wheezed. "It isn't in the float. It's in the mikoshi—Susano'o's. There is a phoenix on top. The tama was a key to halt the mechanics." She struggled to her feet, and though Law was tempted to give her his arm for support, something hot and fierce in her eyes stopped him. This woman was neither delicate flower, nor the ethereal, supernatural thing he had imagined. She was just a woman, hot-blooded and burning with a fiercer fire than he'd ever possessed.

But, as fire was like to do, it caught. First a spark, lighting something long-dormant inside him, limning the edges to a hot orange glow. Then it flickered to life in his chest, a soft candle illuminating an empty, disused chamber, sealed tight as a tomb. He stretched out his left arm and checked the watertight compartment for a new cartridge, waving away the steam before he pulled it out.

Watertight.

He glanced up, seeing the first mikoshi already reaching the far shore, where thousands of unsuspecting men and women waited for the parade. Without the tama to turn off the bomb, they would have to stop it another way.

"I've either a plan or a death wish," he said. He snapped the magazine into place, tugged the loading lever back, and swung himself in the saddle. "Time to find out which."

Tokiko nodded and drew her wakazashi, turning back to the skirmish now leaning in the Shinsengumi's favor. "Forgive me if I do not wish you Godspeed."

Law tipped his bowler and spurred Brutus. The groups carrying mikoshi moved slowly, their walk a rhythmic dipping gate, bouncing the shrine up and down like a stagecoach over uneven ground. Law and Brutus drummed the planks toward them, and caught up just as the final mikoshi reached the bridge's centre. The men were turning around, scrambling and staggering to clear a path on the bridge without dropping the elaborate shrines.

Where was the phoenix mikoshi? Law stood in his stirrups, hot wind whipped past his face as Brutus surged down the line. Then he saw it—the intricate carving atop the second-to-last mikoshi. It was burnished to a high sheen, but the lid's wood was newer, brighter than the rest. He whistled, sending Brutus into an immediate lunge to the right, heading off the mikoshi.

He drove the bearers sideways on the bridge, and the men holding the two rear mikoshi seemed to think better of trying to cross the mad Englishman armed with the horse and gun, turned to flee back the way they had come. These were normal tradesmen, not samurai. He drove them back, cursing his poor Japanese as he shouted vague orders they didn't seem to understand. He wasn't sure how to tell them there was a bomb, couldn't impress on them his desire to save them, not hurt them. Treating these people like sheep wouldn't do much for peaceful relations, but the only way to get them where he wanted was to herd them.

They reached the centre of the bridge just as the mikoshi began to smoke. The bearers shouted in alarm, half letting go and scrambling away from the shrine, which now ticked loud enough to hear over the drums and shouts. He dismounted and swatted Brutus. As hoof beats retreated, he grabbed a pole, tugging it toward the railing.

"In the bleedin' water!" he shouted. The men resisted him, shouting and arguing at each other in Japanese, their dialect so thick his limited grasp of language failed to help. He caught the nearest man's gaze and paused, wishing he could explain that he was trying to help. They looked at each other for a beat, and the man stopped struggling away from him. Something in the man's dark eyes shifted, opened, and Law was looking at a person. Not just a part of the crowd, but another human being with as long a history as his own. Perhaps not so much spent running away.

Sunlight flashed off the mikoshi then, blinding him. Suddenly, he knew what to say. Words appeared unbidden in Law's mind and with them came recognition. A chill shuddered through him, seeming to take hold of his jaw and force out the words. *"Mizu ni ire!"*

The old man's eyes widened, and together they heaved the clockwork mikoshi skyward. The muscles in Law's back strained and the wooden box knocked off his hat. The ticking, smoking mechanism was right next to his ear when he heard the familiar zip-hiss of flame catching fuse. His heart leapt into his throat.

Law shoved into the mikoshi's underside, feeling the clockwork in his shoulder screech to a halt as the last heave sent the heavy shrine over the red-lacquered railing.

An instant before the mikoshi hit the water, it erupted. The concussion sent a watery jet into the air and Law was slammed up and out, soaring over the Kamo River's rushing green current.

The last thing he thought of was Tokiko's burning eyes.

When Agent Lawrence P. Dagenhardt opened his eyes, he expected to see angels, not ragged samurai silhouetted against the sky, their coats painted with various stages of gore. The Shinsengumi officer nearest prodded him with his katana's sheath, saying something like *"Is it still alive?"*

Law tried to explain that yes, against all odds, he was alive but unless they found him a stiff drink in the next hour or so, he might change his mind. Hacking coughs came out instead. Then she was there, leaning over him with her scraped cheek, her long, dark ponytail swinging over his brass shoulder.

"I am glad to see you in more or less one piece, Agent Dagenhardt," she said.

He coughed, tilting his head left and right, scanning between *hakama*-clad legs for Brutus's fetlocks. He attempted to sit up, but Tokiko pressed a hand to his chest, where the straps holding his arm in place intersected over his breastbone.

"Your horse is well. He is waiting on the other side of the river." Her hand let up. "While you were busy destroying the bridge, I located our murderer."

Law raised his eyebrows. "'Ow'd you manage that?"

"Trade tools." She smiled. "Susano'o's mikoshi had a new lid, and the festival preparations are public. It was not difficult to discover which wood-carver replaced the mikoshi's roof. Our culprit confessed: he went to the clock-maker's shop to retrieve the bomb and discovered him sending a message to the Shinsengumi. He killed him with this." She brandished a small, flat blade. Sure enough, there was an arched groove up the back of the tool. "A carving instrument."

Law reached for the tool. Or, tried to. The mechanisms in his arm protested, grinding as he tried to move. He clenched his teeth, immediately feeling the shackles of his handicap tightening on him. No left arm meant less balance, less mobility, less agency. It would take him an hour to saddle Brutus.

Tokiko's small, strong hand gripped him behind the neck and pulled him upright. Dizziness took effect, and it was a marker of personal control that Law didn't heave up half the Kamo River on her Patrol Captain's sandals. She gave him a sympathetic smile and he couldn't help but feel a slight tremble in his stomach that had nothing to do with how much river-water he'd swallowed. He looked toward the bridge instead.

There was a great chunk blasted out, planks dangling in charred tendrils from the crater. Only a smouldering lattice of the hardest, blackest wood remained around the middle. He sighed, looking down at his bashed up brass shoulder. It wasn't in much better condition.

"I am sorry about your arm, Agent Dagenhardt," Tokiko said, following his gaze. "At least the Choushuu have provided parts for its repair." She nodded at the clockwork oni. Her hand moved from his shoulder to his forearm and squeezed until he met her gaze. "I suppose we cannot let you run away to Nagasaki until it is repaired."

Why she'd chosen those specific words he didn't know, but Law glanced up at her, squinting without a gentleman's bowler to shield him from the sunlight. She was giving him her not-quite smile again, fanning the embers in his chest. As if to give those embers evidence, his throat opened like a flue, sending up words like smoke.

"Miss 'Anamura, begging your pardon, I'd very much like to stay a while, if it pleases you."

The flicker in her dark eyes told him it did.

The Trouble with Phoenixes

Jared Axelrod

Ministry Headquarters
London, England
Spring, 1895

Within Research & Design, deep in the bowels of the Ministry of Peculiar Occurrences, The Future was already taking place. Science was being done there, Science with a capital "S," which meant that Director Sound had often referred to R&D as a phoenix egg, from which The Future—you could hear the capital letters in his voice when he said this, there was no mistaking it—would arise, bright and brilliant, a beacon of the shining world to come.

"The trouble with phoenixes," Wellington Books muttered out loud as he trudged down into the R&D Department, "is that they often burn the house down when they hatch."

Wellington kept his interaction with R&D to minimum. He preferred to use gadgets of his own design whenever possible, and when a visit to "the catacombs of horror and depravity" as he liked to call it was required, he tried to time it so that Agent Axelrod was not there when he arrived. He would knock on the door during lunch breaks, tea times, football matches, or deep in the dead of night. This normally worked well, with Wellington having to interact only with a young trainee or be temporarily befuddled by Agent Blackwell's particular blend of sarcasm, innuendo and nonsense. But he found

125

that Axelrod was keeping more and more peculiar hours, and that the usual tactics were no longer working.

This was the very position he found himself. He had thought, with the Sand's American Circus opening its tent that afternoon, Axelrod would have taken the day off. Axelrod was a fanatic about Sand's "ceiling walker" routine, and never missed a chance to see it. But instead of a bustling laboratory sans Axelrod, Wellington found a laboratory empty of everyone *but* Axelrod. Professor Hephaestus Axelrod was sitting in the centre of the lab, heavy goggles over his eyes, his coat off, his shirtsleeves, trousers and waistcoat all but covered with a mélange of motor oil, sweat and some sort of...green stain Wellington was uncomfortable identifying. Axelrod was perched upon a massive device, an enormous æther tank festooned with Telsa Coils like a peacock's tail, his hands trying to make sense of the tangle of wires that spilled out of an open panel.

"Ah, um, Axelrod," Wellington said. "I'm surprised to see you here."

"I work here, Books," Axelrod said. He did not look up.

Wellington tugged at his shirtcuffs. "The circus is in town."

"I know. That's where everyone else is."

"Yes, well, what I mean is, I thought you would be at the circus. It is Sand's, after all, and I thought you'd be, well, you'd be first in line."

"You thought wrong."

"Yes. Of course. Well. I see." This was extremely odd behaviour from Axelrod, as verbosity was akin to breathing. Such terseness seemed completely out of character.

"Do you need anything, Books?" Axelrod's eyes were still intent on the wires in his hands.

"Ah, yes, an electrorifle, please. The current specifications on record are woefully out of date."

"They aren't. I updated the files myself." Axelrod's head finally turned, the swirling green glow of his goggles made Wellington feel queasy. It was making it difficult for Wellington to keep looking at him. "Pests in the Archives, perhaps?"

Bugger. Wellington was hoping to avoid questions in order to get a closer look at an electrorifle. Regardless of its reputation in the field, the electrorifle's mini-generator was quite the design.

"Qualifications are coming up, and while I am not in the field, I still need to keep up on the bas—"

"Swift or Cover model?"

Wellington arched an eyebrow. "Cover, if you don't mind. The swifts are so...noisy."

"You know where they are." He motioned absent-mindedly to the cupboard where the rifles were kept. "Sign the docket before you go."

"You sure you don't want to..." Wellington didn't know what to make of this. Resignedly following procedure was not Axelrod at all. "I mean, you've usually watched me like a hawk in here, and wouldn't let me touch any—"

"If you want the rifle, get the sodding rifle!" Axelrod cut him off with a shout, as sparks crackled about his goggles. Wellington was aghast. Axelrod collected himself and removed the goggles from his eyes. Once he had completed rubbing his grubby hands over his filthy face, Wellington could see that the poor chap had not slept in some time. "Please excuse me for raising my voice, Wellington. I've got a great deal on my mind right now."

"Yes, of course," Wellington said, taken aback by Axelrod addressing him by his first name, as if he were an equal or chum. He selected a Cover, checked its stock and barrel, adjusted the sight, and signed the docket with his usually florid script. That odd shout aside, this was how he always wished his visits to R&D would be. Breeze in, select the device that he wanted, waltz out. And Wellington was about to waltz out, too, when he stopped.

That shout. Try as he might, he could not overlook that shout.

There is a devil on Wellington's shoulder. It is a devil that whispers things into his ear that he'd rather not hear. Things that he knows will cause him to make irrational, emotional decisions. *Just leave,* the devil whispered. *You've got what you want, now leave. You're going to regret whatever concern you are about to—*

"I say," Wellington said. The devil was now quite loud, rumbling with the low gravity of his father's commands. *Leave! Don't take one step further, you soft-hearted git.* Nevertheless, he wandered closer to the monstrosity Axelrod was working on. "This configuration, this isn't a Stratus Manipulator? I remember reading a case concerning a smaller one to control the fog in Whitechapel."

"That's the basic configuration, yes."

"But one of this size," Wellington mused, his finger on his chin. "Why, I imagine you could control entire weather patterns with this."

"That *is* the idea."

"Yes, yes, well, I was just thinking, since I'm familiar with this design..."

"Since you've *read* about this design, you mean."

"Yes. I'm just—" Wellington took a breath and swallowed back the lump of pride that was lodged in his throat. "I'm just saying, well, I could help you."

"No."

"Now, Axelrod, I am perfectly capable— "

"I know you are," Axelrod said, cutting him off again.

Now *that* was a surprise. Axelrod had treated him like bumbling idiot so often, he could not believe what he was hearing. "You know...?"

"I am entirely aware of your capabilities. You've got quite a mind on those shoulders."

"So you admit I could be of some help?"

"No, Books, nothing of the sort. It is fundamentally impossible for you to be any less help to me."

Told you, the devil whispered.

"Well. I never!" Wellington huffed, and turned on his heel. *This—this—is why I try to avoid coming down to R&D.*

"Wait," Axelrod said. Wellington turned around to see the engineer had fixed him with a gaze that was almost pleading. "There is a way you can help. You...you spent a lot of time with Eliza, don't you?"

"Agent Braun, you mean?"

His new charge. He was on his fifth day with the Ministry's new Junior Archivist in his Archives.

144 hours.

8640 minutes.

518,400 seconds.

Five of the longest days of his life.

"Well, the assignment is still new to us both. But yes, we are adjusting quite well if that is what you mean."

"Yes, well, Eliza and I have another outing coming up...."

"What did she take?" Wellington asked, his arms folded.

"An experimental jet belt. Don't worry, I'm sure she'll bring it back before anyone notices it is gone. It's just, well, our last evening together went abysmally, and I didn't want the same thing to happen this time, so since you know her probably better than anyone else—no, scratch that, *without a doubt* better than anyone else, you're almost like brother and sister you two—since you know so much about her, well, you would know exactly what kind of evening she would enjoy the most."

At that very moment the devil on Wellington's shoulder was whispering, filling his ears with gravel. *"Brother and sister, brother and sister. He thinks you two are like brother and sister. How'd you like that, Wellington? How'd you like to be Eliza Braun's brother, nothing more, nothing less. Might as well be, might ya? That's what they all think."*

Wellington Books was not a man to be ruled by his emotions. But sometimes, sometimes the devil's hot tongue is very convincing.

"You know what Eliza likes? She would never admit this to anyone, but what she loves most of all is music halls. Quiet, soothing, music halls." Axelrod cocked an eyebrow in disbelief, but Wellington continued, a devilish grin forming over his normally collected features. "She sees so much excitement in her job, you see, that all she wants to do is sit down, and relax to an old ballad."

Axelrod sat back. "I would not have expected that."

"She's a woman of contradictions. Take her to Weston's on High Holbron in Camden. She'll love it. Now if you'll excuse me, I have to take this rifle apart..." Axelrod gave Wellington a quizzical look. "Errr...on the firing range! Take apart...with my...skill? At shooting! Yes. I'm going to go fire now. Well, cheers."

Wellington waltzed out of R&D as he had intended, confident in the forthcoming disaster. It was a dirty trick, perhaps, but when dealing with phoenixes, sometimes you had to fight fire with fire.

"I just don't understand why you would ever think I would enjoy that," Eliza D. Braun said, as she angrily left the theatre. She fussed with the layers of satin ruffles on her skirt, and mentally cursed the fact that she had decided not to bring a weapon with her this evening. If anyone deserved a gutting, it was that last soprano. "It was worse than the opera!"

"I am dreadfully sorry, Eliza," Axelrod said. He worried the brim of his hat before carefully placing it on his head. "I was told—"

Eliza whirled around. "What? You were told what, Axelrod? Tell me what you were told, and who told you!"

Axelrod adjusted his lapels. "I was told that the lady is always correct. You are completely and totally right. That was an utter waste of a wonderful evening. And please, would you call me Hephaestus?"

Eliza gave a snort in response. "Must be a pub around here somewhere," she muttered under her breath.

What caught Eliza's eye, though, was not a pub but rather a large group of people milling about what appeared to be an abandoned stable. There was a large amount of noise coming from the inside, the outside gave no information about what was going on.

"What is it?" Axelrod asked. "Is it a fire?"

"Most often people run away from a fire, do they not? Sane ones, leastways," Eliza said. She motioned to a young boy leaning against the stable. "Oi. You lad. What's going on?"

The boy looked her, and her satin ruffles, up and down. "Nothing for posh toddies, I can say that."

Eliza gave the boy a glare and flipped him a shilling. "You'd be surprised what a posh toddy could get into."

"Fair enough," the boy slipped the shilling into a patchwork pocket. "You're a bit late, though. Mad Dog's tearing through all comers like a scythe through wheat. No one's gonna jump now."

"Tearing through all comers?" Axelrod said. "What could that possibly mean?"

"Only the best of all possibilities," Eliza said with a grin that could curdle cream. "It's a fight!"

Eliza and Axelrod moved through the greasy, unkempt crowd with some difficulty, until they came dead centre to the ring. A pit had been dug in the earthen floor, some four feet lower than where the crowd stood. A chest-high fence of scavenged wood lined the pit, and kept the crowd from tumbling in. Within the pit, Axelrod could see that one man stood, his arms outraised. Next to him was something that perhaps was a man at some point, but was so battered and bloody it was impossible to tell.

A third figure, a scruffy little man in a colourful coat and ill-used top hat, leapt into the pit, and shouted with a volume many times the size of his body. "Here he is, here he is, Mad Dog Maquire! Undefeated! He'll take all comers! Who wants to fight? Who wants to fight? Who wants to make Mad Dog heel? Come on now, the night is young, the night is young! Let's get some fresh meat in the pit, eh?"

"He'll fight him!" Eliza said, pointing at Axelrod.

"Looks like we've got a challenger!" the announcer said, heralding a wild roar from the crowd. "This one might even last longer than the last one!" The spectators erupted in the delight at the idea that more blood would be spilled.

"Now, Eliza, all I wanted to do was show you a good time..." Axelrod began.

"You know what would be a good time, Hephaestus?" It was the first time she had said his first name all night, but she drew out every syllable like a teasing child. "You know what I would really enjoy seeing? You. In the ring. Fighting."

He looked at the sweaty, bald monster in the ring. "You cannot be serious."

"Oh, but I am. Any beau of mine should feel entirely comfortable in such surroundings. Go on then. I'll hold your coat."

"Miss Braun, I have an increasing suspicion that you are attempting to punish me," Axelrod said. But he resignedly doffed his topper and removed his coat.

"My dear Professor Axelrod, I have spent what seemed to be an eternity trapped inside the confines of a music hall. I believe that no matter what happens to you in the ring, I will still have carried the lion share of suffering for the two of us."

Axelrod regarded his presumptive opponent, a towering hulk of equal parts simian and canine, with arms powerful enough to drive a locomotive's piston all on their own. "I'm not certain of that. But far be it from me to deny a request from a beautiful lady. Careful with that hat."

"Oh, is it expensive?"

"In a sense. It's filled with rocket fuel."

"What?!?" Braun shouted, but Axelrod had already hopped down into fighting pit, rolling up his shirtsleeves.

"You look a right sort, a right sort indeed," the announcer spat through a mouthful of rotting breath and absent teeth. "You're sure you're prepared for this, Squire?"

"Without a doubt," Axelrod flashed a grin and a wink to Braun, who was now beginning to look quite white. "I did a bit of the sweet science back at Eton."

"Oh, I say. Got a learned one here, do we?" The announcer gripped Axelrod's wrist and held it high, his mouldy fingernails digging into Axelrod's soft wrist. "Bets on, bets on! Who's got a coin for the brain, here? Who's got a coin for public school lad? Could this be the bloke who finally takes down Mad Dog Maguire? Bets on, bets on! Grease my cockney palm!"

"Hephaestus!" Eliza leaned forward over the ring's wooden wall, and Hephaestus felt his breath catch in his throat on sight of her lovely bosom. She was having trouble shouting over the din of excited and anxious bidding. "I've changed my mind. You don't have to do this."

"Not to worry," Axelrod said. He threw a few practice jabs in the air and scuttled back and forth on his feet. "I am entirely comfortable in these surroundings, as befits your beau."

"Stop," Eliza said. "Just stop. I just wanted to embarrass you a bit. Have a right laugh? I don't want you to get hurt."

"This might embarrass another man," Axelrod said, his fists up. "Fortunately, I am an adept at Queensbury Rules."

It was at that moment Axelrod was clocked by the back of a fist harder than a blacksmith's anvil. The man of Science, of the Future, of things that would not involve people named "Mad Dog," staggered to the packed earth, only to catch the steel toe of his opponent's boot right in the stomach, sending him back to the wall where Eliza watched from.

"I'm not…sure…those…are Queensbury…rules," he wheezed out.

"This is a bareknuckle match in Camden Row!" Eliza shouted over the din. *There are no rules!*

"No rules, eh?" Axelrod managed to straighten up, regardless of his body's protests. "That changes everything."

Axelrod yanked hard on the pocket flaps of his waist-coat. As one, all five of the waistcoat buttons exploded from his torso, flying forward into the face and chest of Mad Dog. The impact startled the brute, but it did not quite have the subduing effect Axelrod was hoping for. Quite the opposite, in fact, as Mad Dog's confusion quickly melted into all-consuming rage.

"*Yawwwwrrrrr!!!!!*" Mad Dog bellowed.

"*Yaaaaaahhhhh!!!!*" Axelrod screamed in response.

Mad Dog charged at him, both arms outstretched. His meaty, grasping hands found Axelrod's waistcoat, and proceeded to lift the much-smaller man up on his toes. Axelrod managed to twist out of his waistcoat—not a difficult manoeuvre, as it had shot off its buttons. Axelrod contorted his body and arms in such way that it left the waistcoat tangled around Mad Dog's wrists. The large man tried to yank his fists free, but they were locked just as surely as if clasped in irons.

"You're not going to get out of that any time soon," Axelrod said, thumbs hooked in his bracers. "That's one hundred per cent steel-bonded silk. It is supposed to stop a bullet dead in its tracks, so I imagine it'll hold you for a piece."

Not about to let the binding of his fists stop him from winning the fight, Mad Dog slammed a ham-hand into Axelrod's face; but it was without the power of his first swing. The waistcoat had forced Mad Dog to adopt a clumsy parody of Axelrod's original stance.

"Ah, so we are doing Queensbury Rules, are we?" Axelrod was winded by that last blow, but the sight of Mad Dog with his fists awkwardly upraised brought a smile to his face. Axelrod resumed his original fighting posture. He gave Mad Dog two quick jabs to the face before the massive man could react. Mad Dog swung again, but the slow punch was easily dodged. Axelrod made contact with another jab before giving a powerful punch to Mad Dog's bread-basket, causing him to stagger away.

Axelrod turned, grinning, in a hope to catch Eliza's eye. She returned his smile, only to immediately show an expression of horror. He gave her a look of confusion, only to turn and see Mad Dog swinging his bound fists together like a club. The sledgehammer of meat and bone made contact with Axelrod's head, and he swore later that he could feel his brain smack into the inside of his skull as he tumbled to the ground.

Axelrod was on his hands and knees. His right eye was swelling shut, and the blood rushing through his ears all but drowned out the crowd's cries of *"Get up! Get up!"* If he had raised his head, there is a possibility that through the growing blur he might have seen Eliza mouth the words *"Stay down,"* though there was no way he could have heard her over the commotion.

Shaky as a hog on ice, Axelrod got to his feet and rolled his shoulders. He undid his bracers, keeping them in a knot in his fist. Once again, he raised his hands the closest approximation he could come to a proper stance. Mad Dog was ready, swinging his bound arms like an executioner's axe.

Axelrod dropped to his knees, allowing Mad Dog's blow to sail over him. As it passed, he looped his bracers around Mad Dog's forearms, and fired the miniature grappling pinions and cables that were hidden with the clasps. The pinions lodged firmly into the packed earth. Axelrod had just enough time to activate the mighty miniature winch, which wound the cables up with astonishing speed. Mad Dog was pulled to the ground, his destructive fists tied to the very earth.

"This is far from sporting, I know," Axelrod said, coming up onto the trapped fighter. "But you have to understand. I'm trying to impress a woman." With that, Axelrod gave Mad Dog a mighty kick to the head, sending the fighter down for the count.

"Impressive, squire," the announcer said, clamouring over the fence. "Didn't know you had that in you."

"I have a tendency of rising from the ashes," Axelrod said, as he shook his smarting foot. "After all, proper kick is not about power, but about aim. I also played football at Eton."

Eliza muscled her way through the crowd, and vaulted over the wooden wall to land expertly on her feet, as if the bustle and yards of satin she was wearing meant nothing at all. Axelrod, even in his unsteady, punch-drunk state, was reminded of why he found her so fetching in the first place.

"You've got to get out of here," Eliza said.

"Eliza, darling, you don't understand. It is perfectly fine," Axelrod tried hard to enunciate, but his rapidly swelling right cheek was making polished conversation very difficult. "I won. I don't have to leave. I won."

"That's exactly *why* you have to leave," she insisted. "All the people here? They bet *against* you. And they don't take kindly to losing."

Axelrod turned his dwindling focus on the crowd. What he had once assumed were cheers celebrating his victory were now clearly yells of anger and discontent. He could just make out makeshift weapons in the hands of the angry mob. The wooden wall that kept individuals lacking Eliza's athletic capabilities was now on the verge of collapsing.

"Riiiiight," Axelrod drawled. He could not shake his eyes from the wave of oncoming people. Without looking away, he pulled a white handkerchief out of his back pocket and tied it around his head like a pirate. Axelrod fingered the handkerchief's tag only to yank it off. The chemical reaction in the fabric hissed and the material blackened. Axelrod rubbed his hands over the now-hard shell on his head, never taking his eyes from the crowd. "Should be sufficient. Could you hand me my hat? There's a love, thank you."

"Hephaestus? Are you all right?"

"I am perfectly fine," Axelrod said, as he spit out a tooth. He flipped down one side of the hat's brim, making it flush with the crown. Axelrod ran another finger up the crown, loosing two vertical straps that previously had been unnoticeable. "Right then, a few moments from now, I am going to have to be unmistakably forward. Please find it in your heart to forgive me."

"What are you going on about?"

Axelrod slid his arms through the top hat's straps, adjusting it so that the hat was now strapped between his shoulder blades. "Remember when I said this hat was full of rocket fuel?"

"I thought you were joking." Eliza had balled her hands into tight fists, her cold gaze turned toward the oncoming throng of disgruntled boxing enthusiasts.

"I never joke about rocket fuel. It's just not safe. Forgive me." Axelrod enveloped Eliza's frame in a powerful bear hug. Before she could protest, flames erupted from the hat on his back, rocketing the two of them up into the air. The force of the hat sent them crashing through the roof of the stable.

Up, up, and up they went into the night sky, tight in each other's arms, a trail of fire in their wake.

Wellington could not help himself. He had to know.

Despite his usual discomfort at going down to Research & Design, and his new discomfort in leaving his charge alone in the Archives, Wellington had to see the condition of Professor Axelrod. Based on the tension Eliza nurtured this morning, he had known just how disastrous the previous evening had gone. How miserable had Eliza been? Had she made a scene? Did Eliza slap him?

Had Eliza punched him? Oh, he hoped so. The prospect made Books absolutely giddy.

He walked in without knocking or announcement. "Good afternoon, Profes—*OH MY GOD!*"

"If you like. I'm not a religious man, but appreciate some worship as much as the next deity." Axelrod managed to smirk through puffy lips and cheek. "And good afternoon to you, sir."

Whatever situation Wellington expected to find when he walked into the lab, it paled in comparison to what he actually saw. Professor Axelrod was there, all right, but he was singed and swollen, his face a mess of bruises, cuts and burns, his hands similarly scarred. He was sitting in a chair that looked like a half-finished torture instrument—*which is probably exactly what it was,* Wellington thought upon reflection—as Doctor Blackwell fussed over him with bandages and foul-smelling ointments.

"I say, Professor," Wellington said. "Are you quite all right?"

"Splendid!" Axelrod said, forcing a smile that made Wellington wince. "Just, ah…a bit sore from last night. You know how an evening on the town with Eliza can get, eh? Fortunately, I've got Doctor Blackwell here, who has volunteered to play nursemaid. She swears this poultice will have me right as rain in no time."

"It smells revolting," Wellington said, covering his nose.

"It's an old family recipe," Blackwell said. "Would you believe some of the ingredients aren't even available in this country? What people choose to make illegal always confounds me."

"I appreciate you making the sacrifice of your personal store," Axelrod said, gingerly placing a burnt hand on Blackwell's pale fingers.

"Well, I couldn't have you suffer, now could I?"

As if this tableau could not descend deeper into madness, Wellington watched as Blackwell *blushed.* He thought the very action impossible.

"So, I... Ahem…I take it the evening went poorly?"

"Oh, no," Axelrod said. "It went quite well. It's just…I'm not sure Eliza is the woman for me."

"Oh?" Despite the fact that it meant being closer to the horrid smell, Wellington inched toward Axelrod.

"It was something she said. She was incredibly irate about her singed dress."

"That doesn't sound like her at all," Wellington said.

"Ah, well, she may have also been on fire at the time. And cursing."

He nodded. "That sounds like her."

"You know," Blackwell said, examining Axelrod's mouth. "I think I have something that will regrow those teeth. They just might be…sharper than they were before."

"I can't see how that would be a problem," Axelrod said.

"Splendid," Blackwell said.

Wellington blinked. How did the discussion turn to teeth? "Forgive me for interrupting, but why were you and Agent Braun on fire?"

"Because of my hat," Axelrod stated matter-of-factly.

"Your…hat?"

"Yes, see after I subdued the Mad Dog with my waistcoat and braces—"

"Stop." Wellington held up a hand. "Stop right there. Mad dogs? Flaming hats? Fighting with waistcoats and braces? It is clear you are under the influence of these fumes that Doctor Blackwell's concoction is creating, and I refuse to converse with you when you are out of your right mind. Therefore, I bid you both good day, before I succumb to utter madness myself. I must return to the Archives. My Junior Archivist has already shattered an irreplaceable vase that revealed the location of El Dorado, and I just left her alone with a collection of unsolved cases. No telling what disarray she has caused."

With that, Wellington Books gave a tight smile to Axelrod and Blackwell, turned on his heels, and left R&D, trying to process everything he had just been told.

He had almost made it out the door when the voice of Doctor Blackwell caught his ear. "What did she say?"

Books turned to see Blackwell applying more of the foul ointment to Axelrod's face. She was looking deep in his eyes as she asked, "When you knew it wasn't going to work out with Agent Braun. What did she say?"

"Honestly, I can't remember much after my head hit the roof. Fossillinen will need a few more refinements before it will ever be an adequate crash helmet. I think it was mainly her attitude. So put out over a little flame!"

"You know," Blackwell said, delicately running her finger around the burns on Axelrod's face and neck. "I'm not afraid of a little flame."

"No," Axelrod purred, giving the closest thing to a smile his maligned face could muster. "I imagine you are not."

Those lunatics are going to burn this place to the ground, the devil on Wellington's shoulder whispered.

For once, Wellington found that voice sensible.

The Boy, the Bomb, and the Witch Who Returned

Alex White

Whitechapel, East London
England
Winter, 1876

Snow whipped Vasily's face as the witch threw him to the ground. "Hag," they called her. "Old Bones," he'd heard her named. She'd arrived in the night and stolen him, just as his mother warned. His heart pounded to look at the crone, but he could not turn away: crooked nose and spiteful eyes, long white hair, glowing blue in the moonlight. Baba Yaga had stood over him, a nasty smile withering on her lips.

Now, the icy cobblestones scraped Vasily's hands and knees. Clanking factories and bells in the mist rattled in his ears like bones. He begged in his native Russian for her to take him home. He cried, tears streaming down his face in the winter air. He wet his pyjamas. She laughed, her shrill cackle echoing through the alleyway. Vasily clenched his eyes tightly, certain the hag would eat him soon.

He waited for the death stroke, his skin electrified with fear. It never came.

He sensed light behind his eyelids and opened them to a roaring green bonfire. Baba Yaga sneered as she backed away into the flames, and they consumed her before vanishing with a sucking pop. The wet cobblestones where she'd been standing hissed and steamed with her passage.

Vasily was now alone.

The little Russian peasant boy whimpered and stood, his hot urine now frigid on his legs. The foreign city echoed around him, and he smelled a river nearby. He dared to look beyond where the witch had stood and saw something of which he'd only heard tales—a tremendous clock tower watching over the city like a second moon. And in the same way he'd recognised the legendary witch on sight, he recognised the legendary clock, as well—Big Ben. Surely, this was London, which meant Baba Yaga had taken him quite far from home, indeed.

When he turned to see the rest of the alleyway, he spied a fat man in a bowler hat, making steady progress toward him with the aid of a cane. The fellow called out to him in English, but the young boy had no knowledge of the language.

"I can't understand you," Vasily sobbed.

"I said," came the fat man in perfect Russian, "it looks as though you're having quite the extraordinary evening."

"Who are you, sir?"

The man smiled and doffed his hat, his nose chapped red. "My name is St. John Fount. I'm a scientist and a servant of Her Majesty's government. I'll give you a hot meal in exchange for a good story."

13 Years Later
Outside Chudovo, Russia

Field Agent Vasily Zinchenko dropped onto the snow bank, splashing little flurries into the air as he readied his rifle. He'd trekked in through the quiet countryside, past burning cottages and ruined farmsteads, the night sky the only other witness to their fate. Vasily had been tracking the movements of a battalion of Lev soldiers for two weeks, and they'd led him to the mother lode. From his perch at the pine thicket's edge, he could see a hive of men centered about a place his map called "Bugorski Hill".

Whatever the Lev were planning, they'd set up camp on the long railway that ran from Moscow to Saint Petersburg. Vasily looked over the tall, windowless wooden structure they'd built alongside the rails. It looked to be about the size of three large barns stacked on top of one another, and it was packed with men coming and going at all hours. He shuddered to think what was in that wooden fortress. The agent wondered if the newly-coroneted Tsar Nikolas knew the Lev were about to wrap his favourite railroad around his country's neck like a silvery noose. The only thing between the colossal structure and Saint Petersburg was two Imperial Army detachments, and Vasily wondered if that would be enough.

He peered through his rifle's scope, a gift from the Ministry clankertons. He sighted on a distant pair of men and clicked a button on the side. Twisting a few dials locked a light green lens over the hood, and night became day. A subtle whirring from the tally counter told him the range was locked in at three-hundred yards. And to top the whole thing off, a little spinner popped up and measured the crosswind. Vasily had once played golf in Scotland, and the caddy was ever so helpful with advice. He liked to think of the scope in very much the same way as his caddy, but with more killing involved.

Ten men patrolled the perimeter, but the pair in his sights had just opened a flask and lit cigarettes. The others would leave, but the two in his sights would stay, and they would die. Then, Vasily could sneak in, ascertain the contents of the building, and move from there.

He remembered Doctor Sound's assignment:

> *Our man on the inside only got us one message—Koschei the Immortal is coming to destroy the capital. Find out what the Lev are up to and cripple them if you can. The Queen rather dislikes the Russians, but she likes the Lev even less.*

A normal man would have scoffed at the idea of Koschei the Immortal—a god, whose soul is locked inside a chest, inside a hare, inside a duck, inside an egg, inside a needle. Open the chest, and you must catch the hare. Kill the hare, and the duck flies away. Only by smashing the egg, can Koschei be killed.

Of course, a normal man had never met Baba Yaga, either.

The agent was about to screw a sound dampener onto his barrel when he spied a figure creeping toward the structure from the east. Closer inspection revealed a woman in a strange uniform with locks of wavy blonde hair spilling down her back. Vasily watched her unholster a strange pistol as she moved toward his targets, and she took careful aim at one of them.

His eyes darted to the patrols, still in the area. "You can't be that stupid," he whispered to no one.

When she fired, a soundless heat wave swept across the sentries, felling them instantly. She set upon their pockets like a vulture, tugging at them for some keys. The gun was a very cute toy, to be certain. Vasily cocked an eyebrow, watching the scene unfold through his scope. What was she thinking? She hadn't given the other patrols enough space.

No sooner had she come up with her prize than another Lev guard rounded the corner right in front of her. The guard brought up his rifle to gun her down, but Vasily put a shot through the man's head before the sentry could even take aim. A thunderous crack rolled through the valley, and the pines over Vasily rained snow with the force of the shot. The field agent's eyes drifted to the sound dampener at his side, the one his clankerton friends had worked so hard to make. They would be angry, if he lived to tell them.

"Oh, no," grumbled the field agent as klaxons spun up all over the camp.

Men emerged from the building at all angles as searchlight spots spilled over the ground like a bag of marbles. The structure lit up with a crackle of gunfire, spattering the ground all around Vasily. If his cover hadn't been so good, he would have been Swiss cheese right then. He had just enough time to see the blonde hunker down behind a couple of crates before he had to duck, as well.

He dashed along the snow bank, hidden by the forest, before dropping back down and firing another two shots into the closest Lev soldiers. Both men fell as the remaining guards re-centered their fire on his new position. Not to be outdone, the blonde jumped from her hiding position, spraying the men nearest her with her queer pistol. She took out another three. Between the two of them, Vasily optimistically wondered if they could take this base alone.

No sooner had he completed that thought than the top of the wooden building lit up with cannon fire, shredding his cover. The field agent sprinted from his shrapnel-filled nest, near certain that he'd feel the killing shot any second. He chanced a look back to his hiding spot, only to see a fountain of dirt, fire and splinters. He could see great gouts of flame blasting out of the structure's roof and ripping into the countryside. What the devil sort of gun did they have? He ducked back into the tree line, trying to stay hidden.

The klaxons ceased abruptly, and over a loudspeaker came a deep, Russian voice, "Prepare for launch."

Explosive bolts tattooed the sides of the building, and the wooden planks fell away, revealing an iron fortress on tank treads, bristling with guns. Her Majesty's dreadnaught fleet inspired less fear than the Lev monstrosity. Vasily's eyes bulged when he saw just how many of those guns were trained on him. He shouted every curse the Russians knew as he sprinted along the forest edge.

The firing stopped, and the gargantuan contraption rolled out over the tracks. Interlocking sections disengaged, and the massive tank sprawled forward across the tracks like a cat stretching in the sun. They didn't need to waste any more ammunition on Vasily when they were about to make their move on Peter. He'd never catch up to them again.

The beastly machine rumbled away as Vasily emerged from his concealment and killed the last of the remaining guards with several well-placed shots. He'd have to find a horse if he wanted to run the tank down. What had become of the blonde woman who'd blown his surprise? When he scanned the surrounding countryside for her, she was nearly on top of him. She levelled her pistol and shouted for him to put down his own weapon. He lowered the muzzle.

"All the way down," she said.

"I saved your life," he snapped, complying with her command.

"That you did," she said, stepping closer. From this distance, he could see her full lips, her bright eyes. She had a flowing voice, like Lavrovskaya, and a little shiver ran up Vasily's spine. He hadn't expected to find a flower on a battlefield. "What's your name?" she asked.

"Do you mind, miss? I believe the Lev are escaping."

"Yeah. Looks like you scared the shit out of them."

He balked. "Who taught you to speak in such unladylike fashion?"

"You get to ask questions when you're the one pointing the gun." She craned her head and smiled, the beautiful façade giving way to the cruel turn of her mouth. "Who do you work for?"

Something about her expression unnerved Vasily. He'd seen his share of rogues in his tenure at the Ministry, but none of them set him on edge quite like the wolfish grin of the woman before him.

A twitch in her eye told him she sensed his discomfort, and she flicked a switch on her gun. "Are you going to tell me or not?"

"I was shooting the Lev. Isn't that enough for you?" He nodded in the direction of the tracks. "Now, if you please, they're getting away, and we've need of horses, or motorcycles or...something."

"Didn't bring your own?"

"I travelled light, to avoid announcing my presence." He looked her over, head to toe, and grumbled, "I wish you'd done the same."

She lowered her pistol. "Don't worry. I live nearby."

With that, she took off into the woods, away from the rolling fortress. So this was to be it: either try to run to some peasant's house so he could steal transport, or follow a strange woman into the woods. With a sigh, Vasily slung his rifle across his back and trailed behind her. They dashed between the trees by moonlight, and he tripped over the odd root or hidden rock more than once. When he was finally sure they were truly lost, she stopped. He looked around; unless their destination was an unremarkable clearing in the middle of nowhere, she'd led them astray.

"Great," he said. "Now the Lev can march on Peter while I play in the woods."

"Shut up, you inbred farmboy," she spat.

"Excuse me, but I am not—"

She silenced him by whistling a shrill melody. They stood without speaking while trees creaked overhead, their crowns bowed with frost. Vasily was about to leave when a cabin materialised out of thin air before him, stray reflections peeling from its walls like old paint.

The structure wasn't any ordinary hut. Dozens of bleached bones dangled from the eaves of the roof, macabre icicles with bits of fur and leather tied to them. The windows glowed with an eerie, green firelight, and the stench of rotting meat permeated the clearing.

"Sweet Mary, Mother of Christ!" he shouted, drawing his revolver.

"I told you not to worry," she said, making her way toward the door. It opened by itself as she stepped onto the porch. "I said I lived nearby. You coming or what?"

"What did you say your name was?"

"Yevgeniya Babikov. Zhenya for short. Now, I'm tired of you wasting time. Get in here, or I'm leaving without you."

"Leaving?" Vasily lowered his weapon and followed her to the door. He saw no horses, but then again, anyone who lived in a hut like this would probably eat their horses. He stopped at the threshold. "Where are we going?"

"After the Lev! You're a thick one, aren't you, farmboy?" She jerked him inside by his collar.

The interior of the hut was far less pleasant than the outside, sporting thousands of dried bundles of herbs lining the walls. Dusty shelves of greasy jars contained a menagerie of grim trophies, from eyeballs to human hands. Hooks, crusted with blood, hung from the ceiling, and Vasily eyed them nervously. Pale, pink skins lay stretched across the ceiling, nailed to planks, while a spiked, iron candelabra illuminated them from below.

While Vasily's fellow agents may have been sceptical folks, he had personally met Baba Yaga. This woman was a witch.

"Don't go fainting on me," said Zhenya.

"Who the Devil are you?" Vasily asked. He fumbled the cross from under his shirt and rubbed over it with his thumb.

Zhenya chuckled, rolled her eyes and strode to the corner of the room. She banged on a board and it flung open, revealing a recess containing a long, brass lever. "The saviour of Mother Russia," she laughed, throwing the huge switch.

The stench disappeared with a hum, and the room grew a little brighter. With a tremendous clank, the ceiling overhead flipped over, hiding the skins and hooks as it became a brass sheet. Dozens of hidden panels reversed across the walls, showing gauges, levers, switches and other indicators. Vacuum tubes jutted out from hundreds of hidden compartments, coruscating with incandescent light. The cauldron folded down on one side, revealing a leather-upholstered seat, bristling with all manner of control apparatuses.

Vasily suddenly became conscious of his bulging eyes. "I say again, woman, who the Devil are you?"

She vaulted into the seat, her deft hands wrapping around the two largest levers. "Try to hang onto something."

The house bucked, the floorboards rushing up to meet Vasily as he was thrown from his feet, barely managing to keep hold of his pistol. He rolled to one side and watched in astonishment while the trees rustled past the window. The house rose fifteen feet into the air. Then it lurched forward, lunging ten feet with a resounding crash. It lurched again and again, until Vasily understood the motions—a steady gait. The house was walking. He knew what he'd find if he could see it from the outside; it would be a witch's hut, running on a pair of chicken legs.

He managed to get his knees under him. "My God. You're Baba Yaga."

"What was your first clue?" She cackled over the clanking of her mechanised house.

His fear became anger as it churned in his stomach. He raised his pistol to her, pulling the hammer back. "All these years. All these years I've thought of my parents. Of my childhood. You stole me away from them!"

Her expression changed. "Oh," she said. "You're one of the children." She sighed and flipped a stray lock of blonde hair from her eyes. "I kidnapped you, did I?"

"You left me in London, thousands of miles from my home! By the time I got back, I learned my parents had died in the famine!"

She cocked an eyebrow. "Sounds like I did you a favour, then."

"The choice wasn't yours to make!"

"You did all right, didn't you? Found someone to take care of you?"

One twitch would erase that smile from her face. Four pounds of trigger pull. He tensed, his leather glove creaking in the frozen air.

Professor Fount had seen fit to send him away to the finest boarding schools and personally taken charge of his education. Even though the previous head of the Ministry of Peculiar Occurrences had always maintained his distance, he groomed Vasily to be their best Russian operator. If not for Baba Yaga, he would have died in the famine, too.

But it had not been her choice to make.

Zhenya's voice snapped him back to the present. "Go ahead, then. Shoot me and go back to being a farmboy. You can do that, can't you?"

"How will shooting you return me to my parents?"

"What did I look like when you met me?"

Old.

Frightful.

The same smile, though.

Vasily looked her over. He could imagine her hands growing into the talons of the crone, her now-beautiful nose crooked in age, her pert lips withering like rotten fruit.

She smiled. "I haven't kidnapped you yet, but I will. One day, when I grow old, I'll go back and take you from your parents. I'll travel through time, because that's what I do."

His fury renewed, and he grit his teeth. He knew it was unreasoning. He had to think of his training, but he had lost his childhood. The trigger itched under his grip. "I never got to see them again, you know. What a perfect reason to kill you."

Her expression softened. "Yes, and if you do, I won't be here—in our present time— to save Saint Petersburg. Neither will you. There will be no Agent Vasily Zinchenko of the Ministry of Peculiar Occurrences. There will be a young boy whose name will go forgotten, just another death in the all-too-common famine of the Russian wilderness. And the Lev will gain control of the country, and eventually all of Asia. You weren't kidnapped. You were recruited."

He shook his head. He didn't want her to make sense.

"I'm sorry. I wish there was another way for you, but this is what fate has written. Do you think it was an accident that you found your way to me?"

He lowered his weapon and dropped to his knees. She joined him, and took his face into her hands. She was so beautiful. The most incredible eyes he had ever seen…

"Tell me of the day we met so we can get on with the task at hand."

As they travelled, he told her every last thing in exacting detail: where he was from, how she'd lured him into the woods, of his meeting with Doctor Fount in the early hours of the London morning. He left out as much sensitive Ministry information as he could, but if he wanted to make it to this exact moment, she would have to know as much as possible.

"And where are you from?" he asked

"About thirty-one years in the future. Other than that, I can't tell you," she said with a wink. "I'd hate it if you decided to return the favour and kidnap a little girl."

"So you grew up and built a time machine? What are you, some kind of genius?"

"I stole it from the Americans. Great at baseball. Bad at guarding Air Force bases."

When they crested the next hill, a war zone greeted their eyes. Explosions, cannon fire and the crackle of rifles filled the air. A regiment of the Tsar's men had engaged the behemoth, to absolutely no avail. The Lev tank laid waste to all before it with dozens of guns. As Zhenya's hut raced down the hill toward the action, Vasily knew it would be too late for the Tsar's soldiers. He saw them torn apart as they tried to flee on horseback, and he said a silent prayer for their souls.

"If you can move through time, why can't we go back and stop the Lev from gaining that monster?" asked Vasily.

"I would if I could, but the old witch went back and locked the time jumps into the system when I stole the stupid thing. The horrible bitch also made it look like this house."

"You're talking about yourself?"

Zhenya shot him a sidelong glance. "She thought I'd use it to make money."

"And would you?"

"What can I say? She knows me pretty well."

"When are you headed to next?"

"Fourteen years from today. I'll land somewhere near the Podkammenaya Tunguska River."

He frowned. "There's nothing there."

"Then I'll take a vacation. Maybe bed one of the Tungus. I bet some of those hunters are great fun."

Vasily blushed. This woman reminded him of a Ministry operative from New Zealand, Agent Eliza Braun. When she would be partnered up with him, he lacked any idea how to speak with her, and he often pretended his English was bad so he could avoid conversation. While Braun enjoyed a bit of fun in her work, Vasily was all business.

With a half dozen leaps, their hut had closed the distance to the tank. Up close, Vasily already regretted tagging along for the ride. There was nothing his rifle could do against its iron sides, and the plethora of guns bulging from the beast did nothing to calm his nerves. He saw several of the cannons swing in his direction. He hit the deck as the house took a flying leap to its left, sending him rolling into the far wall. Explosions turned the night orange as shells peppered the trees around them.

"You're going to have to board it!" shouted Zhenya.

"I'm sorry, I'm going to have to *what?*"

"This thing doesn't have any weapons! You're going to have to jump aboard! And do, you know—" she said, gesturing wildly with one hand while driving her time-traveling hut with the other, "Secret agent...stuff."

Vasily staggered to the front door and whipped it open, watching as the black pines blew past. His stomach flipped—fifteen feet to the ground seemed a lot further when the ground went shooting by like that. He took a long swallow and calculated the distance to the upper deck of the monstrosity. Ten deadly feet hung between him and the freezing iron tank.

Cannon fire streaked across their eaves, and Vasily was forced to grab hold of the door frame as Zhenya executed a swift dodge.

"Step on it!" she screamed at him.

"Step on what?" He shook his head. He couldn't feel more mortal in that moment: cannons on one side, a death-defying leap on the other. Now he was supposed to step on something?

"It's an expression. From my time, not yours! Now get over there, farmboy!"

The cannons were reloading. This would be his only chance. He was a secret agent, damn it, and this was for the Queen. They'd trained him for this sort of thing—

Well, not *this* sort of thing, but close combat.

He backed up against the far wall, slung his rifle and looked to Zhenya. "If you could get me a bit closer, that would be just ducky!"

"Just what?"

"An expression from my time!" he snapped, holstering his pistol and rifling through his shoulder bag. He finally grasped what he sought—the Mountaineer: a fierce-looking pistol with a barrel the size of his forearm. He just hoped the clankerton Blackwell's work was as fine as her smile. *"Just get me closer to the damn tank!"*

The house lurched to the right as Zehnya shouted, "Now *that* I understood!"

She lined them up for his leap, and sprinting over the unsteady floor of the cabin, he launched himself into the blistering Russian winter. The explosions, the gunfire, the screech of the train, all of it melted away, leaving Vasily with the distant edge. So close... he reached out.

And he missed.

As he fell, Vasily took aim on the hull and fired the Mountaineer, its magnetic cylinder slamming into the hull of the tank. The cable running from it back to the gun went taut, and he kicked, the sudden momentum lifting him back up in the air. His fingers found purchase on the rim of an iron hatch. He hoisted himself up to the tank just as a pistol-sporting soldier popped open the hatch next to him. Vasily caught the man's wrist before twisting the weapon from his grip. The Ministry agent blasted his attacker through the cheek with his own pistol, leaving the Lev scum to prop the door for him. Vasily then drew a grenade from his belt, counted down, and chucked it into the hole. Several screams were silenced by the sharp pop of small ordinance. He clambered inside, shoving his shrapnel-shredded acquaintance out of the way.

The metallic interior reeked of blood, organs and gunpowder—two more fellows downed from the blast at the base of the ladder. From the hallway stretching before him came the clamour of troops. Oddly enough, he felt safer here, surrounded by enemies, than he did back in Baba Yaga's house.

From inside the tank, Vasily heard engagement with dozens of enemies. The Tsar's men would not surrender without a fight. How far had they travelled? For that matter, how fast had they been going? Could they already be at the first military post before Peter? The combined forces of the Tsar would be no match for this monstrosity and its ability to punch right through any blockade.

A klaxon sounded and throughout the corridor echoed, "Make ready the Hare."

It couldn't be! This whole blasted contraption was what the Ministry's mole inside the Lev had meant by "Koschei." They'd be launching some sort of secondary craft soon, and that was where he'd find the deadly payload that would destroy the city. He checked the ammo on his newly-acquired pistol and dashed down the hallway.

Evading the guards was a simple matter. As long as he avoided the sounds of cannon fire, the rolling castle was sparsely populated. He made his way toward the front as best he could figure, eventually coming upon a cavernous, central chamber. What he saw in the centre took his breath away—perched above the train tracks was a sleek set of train cars with a strange nozzle protruding from the back. The contraption was at least as long as three passenger cars, but lower to the ground. A control room glowed orange in the front through porthole windows. The small train had to be the Hare, poised to take off. The tank had only been a shell. The true payload was a bomb whose infernal origins Vasily could only guess.

The place swarmed with hard-looking men, and Vasily knew it would be death to show his face. He ducked back into the shadows and watched the scene unfold. A man in regalia, his chest scaled with shining medals and insignias, descended a distant staircase, his men bowing before him as he passed. His violet cape fluttered behind him, as though he already thought himself Tsar. He must have been the ring leader. Vasily thought back to his orders: *"Cripple the Lev."*

Killing their show-off leader would do it. He unslung his rifle and took cursory aim from the hallway. His heart thundered, but he slowed his breathing. In... out... in... out... Do not open the scope until ready.

Another klaxon screamed, and the front doors to the chamber slowly opened to the outside with the chugging of two powerful engines on either side. Snow twisted into the chamber, and the men shielded their eyes from the oncoming wind. Their leader, however, did not, his cape whipping about his shoulders. Vasily popped open the scope, the dry, frosty air tickling his face around the eyepiece. He exhaled and wrapped his finger around the trigger. One shot, for Queen and Country.

"Intruder!" came a shout from in front of him.

Vasily brought the rifle up to the opposite gangway to find a guard pointing his rifle at him. "Bloody Hell!" he grunted, using his one shot on this immediate threat.

Vasily ducked back behind his column and panic erupted throughout the room as every Lev soldier decided to empty his rifle in whatever direction he was facing. No doubt, the Lev Tsar would be boarding his warship that very moment. If the Hare launched, the mission was over. Vasily yanked his remaining two grenades from his belt and steeled himself.

He tossed the first around the corner, where it clanked down some metal stairs before blasting some poor chap. He then ran into the room and hurled the remaining grenade as far as he could toward the opposite wall. Screams, alarms, and gunfire followed in the explosions' wake, and Vasily leapt over the railing into the madness. A dozen Lev soldiers confusedly attacked their surroundings, but Vasily only cared about one man—the fellow boarding the Hare. The man in regalia smiled, slamming shut the hatch. Arclight struck the engine from an ignition system in the back of the train, and the nozzle burst to life with a blue peak of fire.

Throwing his rifle back over his shoulder, Vasily bounded toward the Hare. Already, the contraption had begun to lurch forward, and automated winches released it onto the tracks. He ran as fast as his legs would allow before taking a flying leap onto the back of the slick train cars. He scrambled to right himself on the roof of the rear car.

The engine blast became a beastly roar, deafening him.

"Oh, no," Vasily said, but he couldn't hear himself as the vehicle rocketed from its well-armed cradle and down the tracks. The launch attempted to shake him free, but all it did was cause him to lose his hold on the pistol Vasily liberated from the Lev soldier. His lips flapped about his clenched teeth as the god-awful engine reached full speed, and it took all of the strength in his fingers and arms to hold on. He looked behind him, seeing the Chest, along with Baba Yaga's hut, fading into the distance. The Lev's plan to launch a manned bomb into the heart of Saint Petersburg seemed like a very smart one in that moment.

Vasily tried to pull forward, but found the force of the wind far too strong to assault. However, the vehicle slowed as the speed evened out, and the agent found he could almost stand. He made little progress forward as the trees tore past, and he knew they would see Peter soon. He had to get to the front car before that happened.

The hatch on the lead car swung open, and the soldier-king leaned out with a long-barrelled pistol. He happily blasted away as Vasily took cover by hanging off the other side of the train. As the ground dashed past Vasily's feet, he questioned his choice of hiding spot.

"Tell me your name!" called the soldier-king. "So we can remember the man who dared to stand against the Lev."

"I'd rather shoot you, if it's all the same!" Vasily shouted back, drawing his own Ministry-issued pistol. He flipped the compressor on the Wilkinson-Webley "Crackshot" and tightened his grip on the weapon.

"It would do you no good. Koshchei's wrath has been incurred, whether you kill me or not! Were you to stop the bomb right here, it would kill a thousand peasants."

"Better a thousand, than a million!" he grunted, pulling himself back up onto the roof. He popped off two shots in the direction of the soldier-king, missing both.

"Oh, so I should detonate it this instant!" The Lev returned fire.

"Would you be so kind?" Vasily flattened against the icy roof. "I'm finding this mission rather tedious now."

The soldier-king emptied his pistol clip, forcing Vasily back to his hanging cover on the opposite side of the train. The Lev mock-saluted. "This has been most diverting, but I'm afraid I must depart now!" Then he shut the hatch.

Vasily knew if he could get to the front, he could shoot the man through the portholes, provided the Lev didn't shoot back. But then, the portholes were so small, and how could he get inside once he'd killed the soldier-king? It was a bad plan—and a sure ticket to a bullet in the head. Vasily pulled himself up, his tired muscles complaining, and laid against the icy armour of the train. His thoughts raced along with the Hare, and he saw a dim illumination in the distance. The beautiful spires of Peter drew closer.

His eyes scoured the infernal mechanical carapace, but he saw no weakness. Surely there was some way to destroy the thing. Then his mind settled on the soldier-king's parting words: *"I must depart now."* Hadn't they already departed?

A dozen loud pops sounded, and the plating underneath Vasily's hands lifted up like a kite on the wind. For a moment, he felt weightless as he watched armour fly from the craft on all sides, including the piece on which he was perched, twisting in the wind. He held on for dear life until the plate crashed into the snow, sending him tumbling head over heels. Miraculous luck brought him back onto the armour plate as it bounced like a Hellish sled ride through a field... headed straight toward a copse of oaks. The Ministry agent braced himself for the inevitable.

The plate wedged against a root, catapulting him into the air. The ensuing assault of tree branches was far worse than any beating Agent Campbell had ever given him in their Bartitsu training. A particularly sharp smash against his face left him reeling, and when Vasily came to rest on the frost, the stars still hadn't settled. He blinked hard, and looked in the direction of the Hare.

Wings ejected from its sides, and it rocketed into the sky. The Duck had launched. Vasily had failed.

He felt for his limbs. He still had the required number, but they moved lazily, like a drunk man's. He wiggled his fingers, surprised to find nothing broken. Salty copper filled his mouth, though, and he sat upright to spit out one of his front teeth into his hand. Hot pain seared his guts as he did, and he swore before falling into a coughing fit. Slowly, he got his feet under him. He looked down and spotted his rifle laying on the ground, the strap torn from its stock. He fetched it, for all the good it would do. He could at least get to a safe spot before the Lev's bomb wiped out the city. Someone had to report what had happened here.

When he turned to hobble back the way he came, he spied a green streak flitting around in the distance. It grew brighter and larger, until it was a roaring ball of light headed straight for him. Another Lev weapon? No, something more familiar.

Then he remembered the green fire of Baba Yaga.

In a flash, she was upon him, riding atop a glowing, chrome bowl like some sort of insane horseman. She brought her vehicle to a halt, and he got a better look at the thing, spying all manner of controls and gauges lining her chair.

"Taking a break, I see," she called down to him, extending a hand.

He took it without hesitation. Agony crackled over his ribs as he climbed aboard behind her. "You've got more tricks, then?"

She smirked. "Of course. This is the core of my house, the part that actually travels through time. You may have heard of Baba Yaga's Flying Mortar?"

"Where's the pestle?"

Zehnya gave him a mischievous wink. "That's a weapon best reserved for when I have something to grind."

She twisted the throttle and they shot into the night sky. Vasily would have appreciated it more had he not been the coldest he'd ever been in his life. The low, patchy snow-clouds unfolded before him like scenery on a stage to reveal a glimmering backdrop of stars clinging to the pearlescent moon. A bright patch under the distant clouds represented the sprawling imperial capitol, with all its history and beauty, its gas lamps alight for another peaceful evening.

"There it is!" said Zhenya, pointing to an orange streak on the horizon. The Duck shot across the night like a comet, no doubt considered an ill portent by the peasant farmers below.

"Get us closer," said Vasily. He checked his rifle. Two rounds left. He stowed it neatly beside him.

"I'll swat that thing out of the sky." She closed her hand around another flight stick, this one containing a trigger.

"Stop! If you shoot it, it could detonate."

The craft made a whirring noise as she depressed the trigger halfway. "Better here than the capitol."

He reached around and stopped her. "There is always another way."

She looked back at him, fury in her eyes at his presumption to touch her craft. He let go of her hand, showing his palms. "Think of the innocents already below us," he said.

"You've got ten seconds to convince me, or I'm bringing down the Pestle."

There was an alternative, yes? Surely they could spare the countryside. But what could they do? If the bomb got into Peter, the whole Russian government would become unseated. The Tsars were not nice men, but an age of darkness could follow a power vacuum that great. They needed to move the Duck far from this place. Somewhere...

Remote.

"Two seconds, farmboy!"

"How do you travel through time?"

Her finger twitched, but she didn't fire. "What?"

He tried to hide the panic in his voice. "The next place you're going is Tunguska. How do you get there?"

"The Mortar is the engine that actually does the time traveling. If we can get it into contact with the Duck—"

Vasily nodded. "We can send their bomb into the middle of nowhere."

She considered his proposition. They could see the spider web of roads that formed the outskirts of Peter gathering below. Zehnya laid into the accelerator, and he clung tight to her to avoid being thrown from the craft. They streaked toward the Lev aircraft with a speed meant only for gods, and the Duck grew in their view from a tiny speck of light to a blazing rocket.

"He's not going to simply let us ram into him, Vasily."

"Leave that to me." He shouldered his rifle and took aim down the scope.

The nose section had the portholes from the Hare, and for that, Vasily felt thankful. He could put a bullet through those. Through the windows, lit by the dim glow of dials and indicators, the agent spied his Lev nemesis. The man leaned forward, oblivious to Vasily's presence, and flicked a switch on his console. Strains of Anton Arensky's *Elegea* from his first Piano Trio saturated the air through loudspeakers, so deafening as to be heard for miles around. The melancholic tune was almost like an apology to the innocent people of Peter for the fate about to befall them. The soldier-king relaxed and closed his eyes, letting the sounds of the music take him to his final destination.

Vasily always hated the melodramatic villains.

"Can you make this shot?" asked Zhenya.

"Of course, I can," he bit back, but once the anemometer on his scope popped up, his certainty melted away.

The scope's windage spun far too fast to get a measurement. If he fired, it would have to be on gut instinct. He tried to imagine the bullet's path, but he found himself aiming far in front of the Duck, hoping the arc would bring the shot back into its airframe. He threw back the cockbolt and took comfort in the feel of the round chambering. He sucked in a deep breath. With a moonlit cloud as his mark, he counted down, then fired.

They saw a tiny spark as the bullet clanged off the Duck's hull, but all its windows remained intact. Through his scope, Vasily saw the soldier-king startle upright and look in his direction.

The agent let out his breath as the Duck took evasive manoeuvres, diving straight at the city. "Oh, bollocks."

"Idiot!" hissed Zhenya, and Vasily's stomach flipped as she raced downward after the Lev craft.

His rifle lost its weight as gravity, his long-time friend, abandoned him. His hair floated, his pockets emptied, and he held tight to Zhenya, trying not to scream in her ear. They raced through the clouds toward the falling Duck, and sparkling Peter appeared in their view, majestic like a bed of gold coins. A million lamplights—each of them a house, or a person, or a family—spread below them. The Mortar had grown close to the Duck, and Vasily choked on the sulphur fumes of the Lev rocket engines.

One more round. Maybe, if he could hit the centre point of the nozzle, he could make it lose control. What good would that do? Would it blow up? Would that be better in the air than on the ground?

He levelled his rifle for his final shot.

"Not yet!" screamed Zhenya. "Wait for it!"

She cranked a lever all the way, and Vasily nearly fell out of the Mortar as it streaked downward, past the Duck, coming to hover directly in its path. Vasily had a straight shot up into the portholes, and he could see the surprised whites of the soldier-king's eyes.

"Now!" she cried.

With a pull of the trigger, the viewport glass spider webbed with crimson strands, and Vasily knew his bullet had found its mark. With its pilot dead, all that remained was the Duck and Koschei's wrath...

...crashing straight at them.

"What's the plan?" he shouted.

The Duck spun lazily, chasing them toward the city. The exterior of the Mortar began to sparkle with strange energies, and Vasily smelled ozone. Zhenya's hands deftly flickered over the controls as the diving crafts developed an incessant scream. The bomb was a mere ten feet away, and he could see the dead soldier-king's face through the cracked glass. He looked from Zhenya, to the Duck, back to her, back to the bomb, and he knew he was shouting something, but he couldn't tell what it was, because everything seemed to take a left turn all of a sudden. All sensations became only noise.

June 30, 1908
Podkamennaya Tunguska River Basin
14 Years Later

With a strange harshness, Vasily Zinchenko found that he could speak and move normally again. His disorientation caused him to drop his beloved rifle, which tumbled over the edge of their aircraft.

It became mild of temperature, shockingly hot to a man used to Russian winters. Weight finally returned to him as the Mortar levelled off and shot in the direction of the rising sun. The Duck fell behind him toward the black pines, which were a lot closer than he'd hoped. He didn't know how the detonation on the Lev bomb worked, but he knew it would blow when it hit the ground.

"We're too close!" he said.

"I don't know where the next time jump point is."

"It doesn't matter! Just go there."

She began to frantically work the controls again, and Vasily watched in horror as the Duck tumbled toward the forest. Energy once again shot through the ship. A flash blinded his eyes from where the Lev craft had fallen, and a sudden heat warmed his skin. Vasily could only hope it was the summer sun. He closed his eyes.

"Just jump!" he cried.

June 30, 1908
Podkamennaya Tunguska River Basin
26 Minutes Later

White. All was white.

The Ministry agent tested all his limbs for the second time in twenty-four hours, assuring himself of their presences. Hot wind tousled his hair, and he inhaled the sharp scent of smoke. He couldn't see anything through his blind eyes, and he rested his cheek against Zhenya's warm back.

"Miss Babikov?" he whispered.

"Yeah?"

"Are we alive?"

He felt her let out a long sigh through the fall of her shoulders. "Yeah, just a few minutes into the future," she said. "Damn crack shot, you are."

"And you're not bad at... What is it you do? Time travel, I suppose?"

"That, and prepare for the worst," she said, looking around their Mortar. "We have just enough shielding around us to keep the heat at bay."

The light gradually became shadow, and Vasily opened his ailing eyes upon Hell. Pine trees had been laid low like piles of corpses, and granite had been blasted into orange glass for miles around. A tremendous column of smoke reached toward them as they flew, surveying the damage. Hot winds whistled past them, carrying clouds of cloying dust and flaming debris.

He swallowed dryly, thinking of the million people back in the intended target. Fourteen years prior. "My God... That could have been Peter. All of that, just to kill a few politicians."

"But they failed, thanks to us."

For minutes, they flew around the countryside, surveying the damage. If the gods had been looking for a place to chain forsaken Prometheus, they would have found it in Tunguska. The thought of what the Lev had nearly done to the imperial capitol would haunt Vasily's dreams for years to come.

Zhenya eventually steered her mortar away from the devastation and out over Lake Baikal. The clear waters did much to calm Vasily's mind, and soon, the agent felt peace return to his bones.

"I imagine my superiors will be surprised to hear how this all played out," he finally said.

Zhenya gave a gruff laugh. "I hate to tell you this, farmboy, but they'll never hear the story."

He recoiled. "What?"

"No, I'm not going to kill you to preserve my secret," she chuckled. "I don't have to. Did you just forget what just happened? We time travelled. Into the future. By fourteen years." She glanced at one of her panels and added, "And thirty-one minutes."

"So the Ministry thinks—" Then Vasily nodded. "You can't take me back, can you?"

"I don't know how to say this, so I'm just going to say it. The next time jump will take us to New York City, for the 1964 World's Fair. I don't know what the old hag wanted us to do there." She bit her lip. "Or I could just let you out here. I'm sure you could find your way back to some sort of sanity."

Maybe it was because he couldn't be surprised anymore after his fight with the Lev, maybe it was because he didn't want to go home, anyway; somehow, though, he couldn't bring himself to be angry, disappointed, or even dismayed about the fact that he was fourteen years removed from everyone who knew him. *Well, almost everyone*, he thought, resting his cheek on her back.

For the second time in his life, he'd been abducted by Baba Yaga. This time, it suited him just fine.

"And you'd have me with you?"

She shrugged. "You're a decent enough shot, and the guns only get better in the future. Maybe you could be my bodyguard. You're certainly hideous enough."

He smiled and she grimaced. He remembered his missing front tooth, and closed his mouth. "Maybe the dentists are better in the future."

"Maybe so," she said. "Only one way to find out."

He nodded his head, and the Mortar disappeared into the blossoming sky, the sun stained orange with the smoke of the impact.

Our Lady of Monsters

Delilah S. Dawson

Paris, France
1889

When the shop girls screeched that a gorilla in a bowler hat was eating all the croissants, Anne-Marie fetched her gun…

As usual, she was disappointed by reality. He was just a man, albeit an enormous one, hunched over the *boulangerie's* single table beside the baguettes, slathering croissants with jam and butter and shoving them into his maw with fingers the size of sausages. The shop girls cowered behind the counter. But not Anne-Marie Bouvier, for she was more than the average baker. And she hadn't put away her pearl-handled revolver yet.

Anne-Marie pushed sweaty, blond curls out of her eyes, settled her spectacles firmly on her nose, and rounded the counter to face the brute. Her arms were crossed casually, the gun held firm in floury fingers. He simply had to leave; he clashed horribly with the lavender walls and Anne-Marie's matching lilac gown.

"Je suis a vous, monsieur."

The gorilla looked up and grinned, an unsettling streak of intelligence in his coffee-coloured eyes. Dabbing his lips with his cravat, he stood and loomed over her in his cheap, brown suit, ignoring the gun.

"If you're really at me, love, I'll take a pot of tea. These Frogs can't seem to pull it off. Dunno what's so hard about it. Water and leaves, roight?"

His accent was rough and lower class, utterly East End and a fair match for his scarred knuckles, grotesquely crooked nose, and dark-haired wrists. She'd known bruisers like him when she'd lived in London as a child. They'd tried to kiss her, and she'd run them all off. Crying.

"You're speaking to a *half*-Frog, *monsieur*. And this is not a restaurant. Time to settle up."

"Already paid. But maybe this'll even things out, love?"

He fished around in his pocket and pulled out a familiar-looking ring. Anne-Marie gasped, her heart clamouring against her corset. Was it finally time?

"Where did you get that?"

His grin widened. "From Doctor Sound of the Ministry of Peculiar Occurrences, of course. These are the latest model so you might want to replace that antique you're wearin' currently, love." When he held it out to her, she noticed a matching but much larger one digging into his own pinkie finger. He knotted his brow. "Well, supposed to be wearin' anyway."

"Dropped mine in the dough." Heat rose in her cheeks as she snatched the ring and shoved it onto her finger. "Is there something more? He could've sent it by pigeon."

"No need for *par avion* since I'm here, now is there?" He leaned in too close for comfort, and she caught the scent of cheap shaving lotion and Earl Grey lingering in his lapels, plus the smoke of a hypersteam train journey. "Time to wake up, Miss Bouvier. Ministry's finally changing your status to active. It's been twenty years since your agent training. Have you stayed sharp?"

Anne-Marie struggled not to shriek with joy. She'd been waiting for this moment, hoping for some message from whomever was in charge—Doctor Sound, he said the director's name was—that would justify half a life spent languishing beside a hot oven, eating too many éclairs and hoping to someday follow in her mother's footsteps as a field agent. Finally, she had her chance.

And this walking caveman wanted to know if she was still sharp?

Quick as a blink, her fist shot out and popped him in just the right place to knock the wind out of his gut. He doubled over, goggling like an eel.

"I've stayed sharp enough," she said, a smirk bending her mouth

He stood, rubbing his ribs. One arm shot out in a blur while the other whipped across her so fast, all she felt was a rush of air and a stinging sensation against her opposite arm. She blinked, and her gun was suddenly in his hand.

"Rule one: Hold on to your gun," he grunted. "Rule two: Don't punch your partner."

"Partner?"

He spun the tiny gun around a thick finger and held it out, butt-first. "The Ministry don't expect you to handle your first investigation alone. You got the lay of the land and the language; I've got the brawn, the experience, and the assignment." He stuck out his hand, and she reluctantly let his huge mitt envelope her smaller one. "Agent Joseph Tipping. Call me Joe."

"Anne-Marie Bouvier."

"I know."

She smiled so wide her cheeks hurt, giddy as a girl. "Just give me a moment to get ready." With a little skip, she turned to head for her upstairs apartment—and the rooftop hutch that held the passenger pigeons with which she conducted Ministry business.

He caught her wrist, but gently. "We don't have time. Got to hurry. It's about to rain, and all the blood will wash away."

"What blood? Wash away from where?"

"From the cobbles under Notre Dame. Turns out gentlemen have taken to leaping off the cathedral's roof to their deaths."

Joe held open the door to the bakery and waggled his eyebrows at her. Anxious to please, Anne-Marie tucked the gun away in her skirt pocket, untied her apron, rolled down her sleeves, grabbed her hat and lavender umbrella, and all but skipped outside. With those few quick changes, the jovial baker became a field agent, ready for action.

"Deaths at Notre Dame? I read the papers every day and haven't heard a thing to that effect."

He eyed the thunderheads and hailed a cab.

"That's because all three of the lads was British and the Frogs covered it up. Let's go."

The hansom was far too tiny for them both and offered no privacy, but it was better than an hour's walk under heavy clouds. Anne-Marie was bursting with questions by the time they'd alighted in the shadow of Notre Dame. Joe silenced her with a hand.

"Here's the scoop, love. We have three sons of Britain found dead on the cobbles, bones broken as if they'd jumped from the roof, not a mark on 'em otherwise. None of 'em were churchgoers, and the bodies were found along the North façade, meaning—"

She pointed to the rose window and tall wall. "They couldn't have jumped."

Joe nodded. "That's what's so very peculiar about it."

They walked along the cobbles until Joe spotted a patch of street where the stones were darker and glistening with soap. Rusty stains dotted the mortar between the bricks.

Anne-Marie looked up. "Dropped from ornithopters, perhaps?" Joe hunkered down beside her. It rattled her being so physically close to a strange man, especially one so menacing. The man wore barely suppressed violence like a tailcoat. She knew from her training that successful partners working for the Ministry often grew close, but Joe unsettled her. She'd waited forever to be needed, but this wasn't exactly what she'd had in mind.

"Not ornithopters," he said. "Someone would've noticed. The motors are loud enough to draw attention. This ain't London."

"There are gliders—"

"They can't carry two people."

"Perhaps they were thrown?"

He jerked his head to the high wall and sloping roof. No stairs, no ledge; only a gutter. "Where would a man stand to accomplish that, eh?"

"*Touché.* But it was clearly murder. Why are there no gendarmes here? Why wasn't it in the papers?"

He grunted in disgust. "Gendarmes dumped the body in the Seine, washed away the evidence. We wouldn't have known, but one of 'em snitched. The three lads in question were troublemakers, without powerful friends or ready money. Yesterday's victim was Ned Gilly. Before that, Badger Leeds, and Dickie Edgington. Easier to pretend it never happened than waste time and francs on an investigation for lads as wasn't welcome." He stood and spat on the cobbles. "Blasted Frogs."

She stood stiffly. "If you hate France so much, why are you here?"

His flat glare met hers, his lip still curled. "I'm on a mission, same as you. Don't mean I like it."

Anne-Marie gave him her iciest, most Parisian silence; and he fiddled with his hat and looked up at the grand masterpiece of architecture.

"Too bad them gargoyles can't talk," Joe murmured, wistful. "Tell us who did it."

She followed his gaze and adjusted her spectacles before saying, "Grotesques."

"What'd you call me?"

"Not you. Them. Gargoyles are what you call the ones that shunt water away from the roof; hence why 'gargoyle' sounds like 'gargle'. The grotesques are simply statues. For decoration."

He snorted. "You'd think they'd decorate wif something pretty. Or at least religious."

"Demons *are* religious. Notre Dame was meant to scare as much as inspire."

He grumbled, his expression of interest quickly displaced by one of annoyance. "I got a better bit of inspiration. Let's find out where Ned Gilly was last seen."

A few raindrops plunked on Anne-Marie's hat, and she opened her umbrella. "That name is familiar. Was he a poet?"

Joe blew a raspberry and adjusted his bowler. "A bad one."

She knotted her brow, whispering the victim's name until finally she had it. "Ah, yes, now I remember. Gilly wrote the script for a folly at the Folies Bergere. A total flop. Opened two nights ago...the night he was apparently murdered."

"Heard about that play. Involved an orgy onstage."

He waggled heavy eyebrows, and she rolled her eyes, flapping a dismissive hand.

"Oh la la," she groaned, "*Simulated* orgy. *C'est la France,* after all. *Allons-y!*"

"Allen who?" Anne-Marie sighed, pinched the bridge of her nose for patience. "It's French for *let's go*, you ignoramus. Honestly, did any of your cultural training pierce your gorilla skull? We're going back to the bakery, and then I'm going to Montmartre to ask after Ned Gilly."

He huffed like an angry bull, his huge fists twitching at his sides. Anne-Marie pointed out a closed, waiting carriage in which they could talk privately. Joe hailed it but didn't help her up. Once inside, he hunched in a corner, tense and red with rage, refusing to talk until the horses' hooves clopped on the cobbles.

"Look, love. You don't want to make me mad. Much as I appreciate your take-charge attitude and haughty Frog act, it's clear you ain't a professional. Next step's to talk to his friends, toss his flat. Not head right into a whorehouse and start jawin'. Not as I mind whores."

Anne-Marie shrugged, her indifference causing him to sit up a hint straighter. Exactly as she wanted.

"Agent Tipping, just because it took the Ministry twenty years to activate me doesn't mean I'm unprofessional. Considering the French government doesn't know I'm on her Majesty's bankroll and keep a cache of illegal weapons, 'jawin' with whores', as you say, is better than charging around like a bull in a China shop or stooping to burglary. The murders must've occurred before dawn. Do you think Ned Gilly was dragged from his bed, or do you think he was caught on his way home from the cabaret?"

Joe rubbed the stubble on his jaw and gave her a measuring sideways glance. "Possible." He paused, then added, "You're not what I expected. Pretty thing like a plump hen, all ruffled and lacy but sharp as a schoolmarm and walks like a..."

"I'm wearing four knives and still have my gun."

"Bloody good that'll do us if your aim hasn't improved. I read your evaluations." He shook his head and then looked her over from head to toe. "You just don't seem like a Ministry girl, is all."

She flicked her fingers at him. "That's the whole point of keeping me here on inactive duty; no one should suspect I'm anything but a middle-aged Parisian baker. My mother was a Ministry agent, and my father was a French spy. I'd have been in the field already, if not for being mostly blind and having a useful pair of ears. I know I appear out of shape, but I've kept busy with several important fact-gathering missions to earn my keep. It will take more than murder and courtesans to give me the vapours."

"You think they'll let us walk into the Folies Bergere at breakfast, just like that?"

"Not you. Just me. You may go rustle around flats, if you wish."

A single eyebrow arched. "And let you handle your first interrogation alone?"

She smirked and adjusted her glasses. "These ladies are my customers, *monsieur*. I know the way to their hearts."

Anne-Marie balanced a tower of lavender boxes in one hand, knocking on the unmarked door with the other. When it opened a crack, she bustled right in.

"Petit dejeuner." Anne-Marie opened the top box, continuing in her best street French, "Compliments of an anonymous gentleman."

A few sleepy-faced girls hunched over thin porridge at a long table, only to look up licking their lips as soon as the scent of hot bread and powdered sugar wafted from the open boxes.

"You bake these?" one of the girls asked, mouth already stuffed with *pain au chocolat.*

"*Bien sûr,*" another girl said. "Runs a *boulangerie* on Lepic, *oûi?* I saw her giving milk to a cat with kittens, once."

Anne-Marie smiled and urged them to eat, making polite conversation as more and more girls appeared and fell to the pastries. After her brief time with Joe, she was more than happy to slip back into French. She knew a few names, had been sure to bring their favourite treats. Finally, when they'd mostly forgotten she wasn't one of them, she settled down between two girls and nudged the redhead on her left.

"Did you hear about Ned Gilly?" she asked, pulling a box of éclairs closer.

The girl shrugged and helped herself to a sweet. "What about him?"

"He was found dead yesterday morning. At Notre Dame."

The girl crossed herself with bitten fingertips. "Good riddance to bad rubbish. Great, nasty brute. Gave me this last week." She pulled down the shoulder of her shift to show a yellowing bruise on her clavicle.

"Did you know Badger Leeds and Dickie Edgington, too?"

A younger girl nodded. "Dickie was my first. Didn't pay."

"He wasn't as bad as Badger was, with the cigar burns."

"Sound like a nasty bunch," Anne-Marie said. "And all Englishmen, too."

The girls nodded, their mouths full and their fingers sugar-rimed.

The youngest girl piped up with "Mistress hates the English. One of those three monsters killed her daughter, but we don't know which one. We're all glad they're gone."

One of the other girls hissed at her, and she clapped a hand over her mouth.

"Is your mistress here? I've been wanting to talk to her about some half-priced baked goods."

The girls stopped chewing and stared at Anne-Marie. The redhead beside her snorted and tossed her oozing éclair on the table. "Tastes funny." She glared daggers at Anne-Marie. "But thank the anonymous gentleman for his kindness, just the same."

Anne-Marie shrugged and rose, leaving the ravaged boxes behind. The redhead followed her to the door, slamming it on her lavender bustle. Unless Joe found something better, her money was on the Folies Bergere and the cabaret's mysterious mistress.

Anne-Marie did her best thinking while baking. By the time Joe squeezed through the front door, her face shone with sweat and her arms ached from furious kneading. She led him into the office where she did the bookkeeping.

"What'd you find?"

"Don't bark at me, *monsieur*. What did *you* find?"

He sighed and emptied his pockets onto her spotless desk. "Receipts, bills, bits of his bloody poetry. No reason for the poor lad to be murdered."

"The girls hadn't heard about Gilly's death. Described him as a nasty piece of work. They didn't care for Dickie or Badger, either. Said their mistress hates the English and one of the three dead was responsible for murdering her daughter." Joe grunted and pawed through the crumpled papers, holding up a wine-stained bill.

"He owed the Folies Bergere a decent sum. Payable to Madam Allemande last week. Guess it might be worth keeping the debt to get your revenge."

She tapped the piece of paper. "We know they were all customers. We know they were all suspects, according to Allemande. Should we visit Dickie and Badger's flats next?"

Joe removed his bowler to run a hand through wild brown hair. "Forget them. Worry about Gilly. We find how he was murdered, we know what happened to the others."

"Is that the usual Ministry procedure?"

He bristled. "You correcting me? On the job less than a day, and you're telling me what's what?"

She calmly raised an eyebrow.

"*Bien sûr*, I'm telling you. This is my city, my home. Until you're the head of the Ministry, I do not work *for* you. I work *with* you." They locked eyes, and she refused to look away. He blinked first. "But in this case, I think perhaps I do agree. Did you bring a dinner jacket?"

He grunted. "I can get one."

"*Bon.* Tonight, we're going to the Folies Bergere, and you're going to chat with the other Brits, see what they know."

"Let's say I agree to it, just out of curiosity. What are *you* going to do tonight?"

She grinned.

"I'm going to pick every lock in the cabaret until I find Madam Allemande."

He thought a moment and nodded. "Roight."

"You're giving in, just like that?"

"File says you're good with locks, love. Besides, what man wouldn't want to spend a night at the cabaret?"

Anne-Marie looked him up and down, contemplating how one found a behemoth-sized dinner jacket in just a few hours and whether it was possible anyone would believe him a gentleman. "Are you sure you can pull this off? You never told me of your past training or specialties."

His grin was as crooked as his nose. "Don't worry, pet. Undercover *is* my specialty."

That evening, as she went to turn the sign in the window from *Ouvert* to *Fermee*, Anne-Marie couldn't help noticing the figure posing across the street. The suit fit him perfectly, and with his hair slicked back under a gentleman's topper, he looked less like a bare-knuckles brawler and more like an aristocrat— or two aristocrats stuck together in a black sack. Seeing her gaping, he tipped his hat and grinned. She hurried upstairs to change into her own guise for the night.

He was sitting at the bakery table when she emerged, her cheeks hot with a blush.

"Don't laugh."

He looked up, face blank. "Why would I?"

She smoothed her hands down the black leather corset and over her fitted trousers. They were far too tight, blast it all. Thanks to the bakery's bounty, her stealth uniform barely fit. But she couldn't sneak undetected into the cabaret in her usual frilly dresses, so she would just have to hope her pants didn't split up the back. Still, it felt good to put on men's boots and pack her waist belt with gear she hadn't had call to use in years, guns and knives and poisons and gadgets. She was ready.

But was he?

"What's your play?" she asked, and he stood and bowed.

"Reginald Cumberbatch," he spoke in a manner that gave her a start. "A humble shopkeeper on holiday from London."

The stuffy accent was flawless.

"*Touché.* Undercover really is your specialty."

He grinned. "You underestimate me."

She tried to bow in mock apology, but the seams on her pants creaked dangerously.

"Of course I underestimate you, *monsieur*, that means you're a good agent. We'll meet back here at midnight. Agreed?"

"Agreed." Joe went to open the door, but she stopped him with a tentative hand on his jacket sleeve.

"Wait." Her fingers hovered over the Ministry-issued ring, a slightly different fashion than the one she had been assigned twenty years ago. "How do these new rings work? If I'm in trouble, will it alert you?"

He nodded. "If you push it, I'll know."

"But how will I know if *you're* in trouble?"

He pulled back his jacket to show a pair of derringers, their chased brass accented with wood so polished that they'd clearly seen their share of Ministry action.

"I never am," he said in his usual, gruff manner.

Anne-Marie slipped into the shadows like it was a warm bed on a cool night. She was out of shape but bristling with determination. The air was brisk against her cheeks, and the exhilaration of her mission kept her moving.

When she'd been at the Folies Bergere earlier, she'd noticed convenient climbing niches in the bricks outside. She skittered up with a prowler's grace, glad that she'd kept her hands from going soft. As part of her dedication to keeping Ministry training on her mind, she gave herself the same birthday gift every year: a midnight trip past the Louvre security to enjoy the works of art on her own. She used a different and more challenging entrance strategy every year, and she'd touched the Mona Lisa with bare hands more than anyone since Da Vinci himself.

At the top of the building, she pulled herself onto the roof of the Folies Bergere and skittered over to a cracked window. Wrenching it open, she squeezed through. It was an attic of the most depressing sort, with rows of small and dingy beds meant for servants.

Anne-Marie's soft-soled boots whispered across the boards and down the stairs to the next level. The long hallway housed themed rooms decorated in glitzy excess. Perfume hung heavy in the air, and Anne-Marie held a handkerchief over her sensitive nose.

As she crept down the next staircase, the air warmed, and the sound of voices and music thumped through the cracked walls. The song ended to thunderous applause, and a woman's voice boomed as if heard underwater. Anne-Marie stopped, one hand to the wall.

"*Mes amis,* are you ready to meet Madame Allemande's Jewels of Paris?"

Whistles, stomps, and applause answered her.

Anne-Marie looked up and found a copper tube bolted to the ceiling, pointing down the dark hallway.

"Oh, la la! These girls need more of a welcome that that!"

The voice had definitely come from the tube, and Anne-Marie followed it as it snaked past red velvet curtains and disappeared into another wall beside a narrow door. She had the lock picked in moments, opening it silently onto a hall lit by green lanterns.

"The Folies Bergere is proud to present... the can-can!"

Anne-Marie hurried faster when she realised she didn't just hear the echo of the pipes but the actual woman's voice. Just ahead, a door was cracked, showing a thin line of light. Gun in hand, she pushed it open just enough to see inside.

The room was large, lit with gas-lamps and filled with ornate parlour furniture, bizarre statuary, and a low, annoying ticking sound. A strange hodgepodge of scents made Anne-Marie's nose twitch: oil, metal, and expensive perfume. She slipped through the door and hid behind a sofa.

A thin woman in a taffeta gown of emerald green stood with her back to the room as she spoke into an amplifying box, the source of the copper pipe. She paused to peer through two holes at eye level in the wall, watching the cabaret on the other side. After another round of deafening applause, the woman turned and spoke to an empty corner.

"I see a new Englishman out there. Perhaps he'll be the one to finally admit to murdering my poor darling Lizette. We know just what to do with him, don't we? Come, Maurice. Come, Fabrice. Murderers must be punished, *n'est-ce pas?*" Her accent and the way she spat *"Anglais"* marked her as a native Parisian. Anne-Marie felt panic rise behind her corset as she thought about Joe in the crowd, unsuspecting.

Something large moved, some metal contraption that squealed and clanked and then... purred? Anne-Marie ducked around the sofa to see what sort of clockwork padded to the woman's side, but a heavy weight landed on her back, shoving her flat. Her gun clattered to the ground, and she felt the bone-jarring weight of metal on her spine and arm as claws spread over her leather corset and wrapped around her shoulder. Pinned as she was, she couldn't reach any of her weapons. Struggling to turn her head, she saw a blinking yellow eye and a demonic, gibbering face.

Footsteps rounded the sofa. Anne-Marie could barely see the woman looming over her, a metal creature at her side.

"Ah, the curious baker. Inject her, please, Maurice."

Anne-Marie felt the cool pinch of a needle in her arm and struggled to turn over, to reach the knife in her corset, to do anything but lay there helpless like an idiot. She failed. Numbness spread quickly from her belly to her extremities as the injection took effect.

"You wish to know what happens to meddling Englishmen who enter my city unwanted? Who hurt my girls and refuse to pay my bills? Do you know which of those monsters murdered my poor daughter? If you are on the side of the English, you will meet their same fate." She leaned close, sniffed deeply, and sneered. "Half English, at least. You stink of tea and broken promises. Come. My pets will show you the most beautiful views in Paris." Her grin was skeletal, mad, her wrinkled lips painted red. "Starting with the tunnels in the catacombs."

Just before her eyes fluttered shut, Anne-Marie remembered her tracker ring and managed to push it with her clumsy thumb.

"If I'm in trouble, will it alert you?" she had asked Joe.

"If you push it, I'll know."

But how long would it take for Joe to receive the signal? How long?

It was the wind that roused Anne-Marie, tearing at her hair; that, and the odd, mechanical movement of whatever carried her. Her body instantly recognised that she was very high up, that she was uncomfortably dangling from rigid arms. Although her instinct was to go stiff and fight, she recalled Madam Allemande's words and the rusty stains dappling the cobbles in front of Notre Dame just that morning. She opened her eyes on a moonlit night, the stars impossibly close.

She thumbed the switch on her tracker ring again and again. Why had Joe not come when he'd promised her he would? Was her partner cozied up to some cabaret girl in the Folies Bergère, unable to hear or see the tracker's alarm amid the dizzying crowd?

But no. A soft beeping told her exactly why she had not been rescued. She let her head loll sideways, and her vision filled with the tails of a dinner jacket. Joe jounced ahead of her, tossed over the back of a clockwork beast like a sack of cake flour. The creature was like nothing she'd ever seen, with a twisted, nightmare body like a monster out of a painting by Hieronymous Bosch. Two horns sprouted from its head, while great silver wings sprung from its back with razor-sharp feathers; Joe flopped between them, unconscious. Taloned feet squelched through the cathedral's gutter, marching toward the grand spire.

Anne-Marie let her head fall the other way, her eyes following the riveted seams upward to the same hideous goblin face and gold-glowing goat eye she remembered from Madam Allemande's quarters at the Folies Bergere. It was so very familiar, and yet so very wrong. Glancing down to judge the distance to the cobbles, she solved the mystery behind the Englishmen's deaths.

Plated in grey metal that matched the original stone, the demonic automatons were nearly identical to the famous monsters that guarded the cathedral. No wonder no one had noticed them, then—they were part and parcel of Paris, of Notre Dame. Anyone spotting animated grotesques on the roof would assume they'd had too much to drink and go home to sleep it off.

Anne-Marie knew she had maybe a collection of seconds before her new partner was just an extra-large splatter on the streets of Paris. Regardless of her time away from Old Blighty, she was a Ministry agent with a cool head, and she had no plans of dying on her first mission. She would find a way out of this mess.

At least the grotesques were lurching along the lower gutter instead of the slippery iron plates of the peaked roof. With a deep breath, she turned as a restless sleeper might and allowed her body to partially fall from the creature's arms, steeling herself to grab for random bits of architecture should it drop her completely.

The grotesque froze and scrabbled to catch her with steel talons. She let her body weight slump into the cold slurry of the gutter. As the clockwork beast reached for her, Anne-Marie slipped a tin from her belt, flicked it open, and removed a glass ampule. Her gloves wouldn't be enough to protect her, but desperate times called for desperate measures. Turning her face away, she smashed the glass pill against the gargoyle's chest and whipped her hand away.

For a moment, the creature stubbornly persisted in trying to hoist her over one shoulder, but then the deadly mixture of corrosive acids bloomed with a rusty red that resembled an arrow to the monster's heart. Anne-Marie didn't dare look at her own hand, knowing full well that the acid had eaten into her glove and would soon sink into her numb skin, hunting for bone. A hand was a small price to pay against two agents' lives.

When the grotesque shuddered and dropped her completely, she had only one good arm with which to catch herself as she rolled perilously close to the gutter's edge. The creature was more rust than metal now as the acid spread. Its arms fell off, shedding bolts like fleas. The golden light in its eyes went out, and it toppled slowly over the edge of the cathedral. Anne-Marie didn't bother to lurch up and watch it crash against the cobbles. She barely had time to mutter a prayer before the other grotesque latched on to the spire, hell-bent on climbing to the top and tossing Joe to his death with a machine's heartless accuracy.

Much as she hated to admit that the English brute was right—Anne-Marie had always been a bad shot, and her spectacles were of little help. She had one more ampule of acid, and she didn't have a chance in heaven of hitting the bugger—she might even hit her partner—but watching the clockwork creature inch up the spire with Joe flopping over its wing, there were no other options.

She lobbed the little glass pill.

"Joe!" she managed. "Wake up, Joe! Wake up and hold on!"

A tiny clink let her know the ampule had hit something; but even squinting, she couldn't quite see if it had found its mark. She struggled up to her elbows and pulled herself closer toward the corner where Joe would fall, if he did fall, half-glad and half-furious that her extremities were still numb from the injection. It's not like she could catch him, even with two good hands. The grotesque carrying Joe paused and shook its foot, and she finally saw the growing flower of rust spreading along the creature's metal talon. Unfortunately, part of the insidious acid had also found home in the iron plating of the roof, and if she didn't get Joe away quickly, both he and the dying grotesque would fall through the collapsing ceiling and splatter inside the church instead of outside on the street.

The clockwork demon lurched sideways, dropping her mammoth partner, who slid down the roof with frightening speed. Anne-Marie balled her numb hands into fists and crawled through the gutter until she was directly below his sliding bulk. She braced herself for the impact, and the gutter shuddered beneath them. Metal shrieked on metal as the second monster slid down the slope, talons raising sparks. It landed on top of Joe with a heavy thump that drove the air from her lungs. Joe grunted and flexed as she struggled.

"Feeling bitey? Such a naughty girl," he said in the cultured British accent he'd used before departing for the cabaret.

She gasped and swallowed. "That's not me. There's a dying clockwork gargoyle trying to eat through your jacket. Shove him off so we can go home." Joe went completely still and pressed her more firmly into the gutter as he reached back to pry the monster off his back and toss it over the edge.

"It's not a gargoyle, it's a grotesque," he murmured sleepily. "Why am I numb?"

"It'll wear off shortly. I can already feel my hand burning. I need to get away from this water, and fast."

She tried to hide the fact that she was panting and whimpering as the pain spread to her palm, but he was too close to ignore it. With care she hadn't seen of him, he edged off her body and into the gutter, wiggling backward toward the corner where the handholds began.

With her arms finally free, she rolled onto her back and pulled a different tin from a different pocket. She would only have one chance to stop the acid from spreading before she lost her hand entirely and could look forward to a mechanical one from the Ministry engineers. In a flash, she'd opened the tin and shoved it right up against her palm, hissing as the powder instantly neutralised the acid and halted the burning. The pain didn't abate, but the worry did.

"Better?"

Anne-Marie spoke through gritted teeth. "A little, thanks to Our Lady of Chemistry. Now all that's left is to climb down sixty-nine meters of rain-soaked stone at midnight half numb and wounded without dying."

Joe chuckled darkly, his voice back to Cockney.

"Wrong. We still have to put an end to the murderer. Allemande."

"You mean capture her and deliver her to the Ministry."

He paused before answering. "Roight. Of course that's what I meant."

The climb down had been a nightmare, but Joe's urging kept her moving. The sun was just turning the sky a cheerful pink as they hobbled into the bakery. Her shop girls stared, their mouths in perfect Os, but Anne-Marie merely flapped her good hand and demanded a box of éclairs, which she gave to Joe before pointing upstairs. He took it in ruined but expensive gloves, and only as he preceded her up to her apartment did she notice the bloody rips in the back of his jacket where the grotesque's talons had torn into muscle.

They spoke little as they tended to each other's wounds with the dusty medical kit she had never opened before. Her hand would always bear a shiny pink scar across the palm, but it would still function. His back required a few stitches, which she was able to manage. He grilled her on Madam Allemande: how to find her room, how many statues were there and whether they were all clockworks; and what she had said about tunnels, and catacombs, and Englishmen.

"Are you sure?" Joe asked for the tenth time.

Anne-Marie pulled the suture too tightly and snapped, "Of course I'm not sure, you oaf! I was drugged and nearly thrown from Notre Dame by a clockwork grotesque. We'll go after her first thing tomorrow."

"Tomorrow's too late."

She snipped the thread and held up her raw, scarred hand, and he fumed silently but didn't press the matter. Still, something about the way he kept staring at the clock and her door didn't sit right. Just in case he had ideas about apprehending Allemande without her, Anne-Marie waited until his back was turned to twist open a sleeping pill and pour its contents into one of the éclairs. Within moments of devouring the pastry she presented on a doily, the giant oaf was snoring on her floor.

Ever since being assigned to Paris twenty years ago, Anne-Marie had dutifully written up her report every month and sent it on to the Ministry office in London. And every month, the same pigeon had arrived with her cheque, thanking her for her service to the Queen.

It took her some time to compose the report for her first real assignment, and she drank cup after cup of black coffee to the tune of Joe's snores while she attempted to record every victory and flaw of their escapade. Finally satisfied that she'd provided the most accurate and honest account possible, she limped to the roof. Slipping her missive into a metal tube, she released the pigeon and watched it soar into the clouds toward London. Her heart was a scramble of feelings: had she done well, or had she very nearly failed? Would she remain active and work as Joe's partner, or would she go back to being a boring baker, forever waiting for excitement to walk through her front door? Would they wait for word from this Doctor Sound or move on Allemande tomorrow? If Joe truly wanted to take down the mad cabaret owner, would Anne-Marie be strong enough to stop him and ensure that he followed protocol?

As she closed the wire door, she noticed an unfamiliar squab pecking at crumbs among her brood; one of the shop girls must've found it and forgotten to tell her. She pulled it out and unrolled the message.

Dear Miss Bouvier,

Status: Activated

Your mission: Theodore Gilly, a member of the House of Usher and an enemy of the Ministry, is en route to Notre Dame de Paris to investigate and revenge the death of his brother, Ned Gilly. He will be traveling under an alias, but his size and gorilla-like visage are difficult to hide; an image is included. Gilly is adept at accents, disguises, interpersonal manipulation, hand-to-hand combat, and weaponry. Intercept him at the Gare du Nord; full bodily harm is allowable. In this case, always shoot first; he'll kill you if he thinks you're a threat. As we are unable to get a second agent into Paris in time, we are promoting you to an active status, and sending in our closest agent, currently stationed in Callais. Agent Joseph Tipping is half a day behind Gilly and will assist your investigation upon arrival. Agent Tipping is also delivering a replacement tracking ring. Please send this bird back with a message to confirm status and compliance.

Welcome to active duty! Your mother would be proud. Be careful.

Doctor Sound

The Mystery
of the Thrice Dead Man

In Which Agent Books Takes a Paid Holiday

J.R. Blackwell

One Thousand Twelve Feet above the Atlantic Ocean
September 8, 1894

Wellington clung by his fingertips to a freezing metal pipe on the outside of the giant airship *Hammarström* as it zipped through the sky. He chanced a look down, to see the clouds floating below him, and below that, the wide expanse of the rolling ocean. From the balcony above him, where he had been so unceremoniously tossed, beyond the rush of air outside the ship, he heard the crackle of electricity and a loud shriek.

"Not a real mission," he muttered, clinging to the cold pipe. "Practically a paid holiday," he growled, and looked up towards the ship full of pirates that waited for him if he could find his way inside.

The Ministry Archives
London, England
September 3, 1894

Agent Wellington Books, Archivist to the Ministry of Peculiar Occurrences and the greatest solider that no one had ever heard of, wound the knob on his pocket watch, smoothed his lapel, dusted a speck off his shoulder and opened the first of the three folders in front of him.

Wellington was adding an extra layer of depth to the archives, noting files not simply by agent and region, but also by city, and notable individuals who had been involved in the various missions.

This new practice could allow for greater ease of research in existing cases. His detailed data extraction had led him to three cases that each bore similar names. It was when he was entering the name into his analytical engine that he realised that there were multiple entries, the only problem being that each noted the name as "deceased." This morning he pulled the three files to review them for the circumstances of these deaths. It could be coincidence. Or it could be an indication of sinister deeds.

In the folder was a field report from an agent active in the West Indies, where a wizard had been reported to be holding captives and making them work in the mines. As Wellington read, he could see the scene play out before him. Though case files were dry reading to some, for the Archivist, they were little operas, and they breathed their stories into his brain as he read.

September 5, 1891
The Great Mines, Matabeleland

I am Agent Mary Land, and I do not believe in magic. I believe in justice. It was justice that brought me to the remote Matabeleland mines, justice that lead me to uncover Dragomir Negrubine's slave trade, and justice that lead me to the entrance of the open mine during the deluge.

Negrubine, the wizard of the great mines, had already kidnapped many sons and daughters in the small village when I arrived. They said that Dragomir Negrubine used the young men and women as slaves for the mines, keeping them captive with terrible magic, the manipulation of lighting and fire.

I might not have made it to the mines if the albino giant hadn't been my guide. He instructed me to call him by his Christian name, Joseph. He told a story of a lost sister who had been kidnapped, and later, found dead, grit and blood under her nails. He had sworn vengeance against the wizard, and it was only he, among all the villagers, who dared to go with me to oppose him.

The rains were coming down in dreadful floods, an inch of water at our feet, pushing us back, our feet sticking in deep mud as they trudged onward. My weapon was useless in this flood, but there were slaves at the mines, locked by Negrubine's strange weaponry and the fear of his magic. The women of the village had presented me with a sword before I left and told me to avenge their stolen daughters. I had no intention to kill the wizard. I believed in justice and would see him delivered to the law.

Dragomir Negrubine was waiting for us by the open maw of the mine, his face lit from below by the fire at his feet that burned a blue flame despite the downpour. He had long black hair that was tied back from his face, and he wore a long, purple robe. His blue eyes had dark circles under them, as if he had been robbed of sleep by his evil deeds. He sneered at me as I unsheathed the sword.

"Dragomir Negrubine!" I cried. "You are under arrest for trade in slaves, theft, and illegal occupation." I could feel the water matting hair to my face.

He laughed, his head tilting backwards, manic with joy. "Oh, and you think that you'll take me in, little Mary, quite contrary?"

How did he know my name? I pointed the sword at his chest. "You don't call me by that name," I proclaimed. "I am an Agent of the Empire, and you are to face justice."

The wizard opened his arms. "Then run me though, and we'll see this drama ended. Because you'll never take me alive!"

I shook my head "There's been enough death, I am taking you to the law where you will answer for your crimes."

Joseph held up a jagged knife. "No, he dies today!" he cried. I ran to stop him but the giant was too fast, and he ran the wizard through, the blood spurting from the wizard's chest and on to their hands, washing away in the rains of the monsoon.

"I'm sorry," the giant said, "But I couldn't allow—not after what he did..."

I looked back towards the village, where tiny lights flickered in the darkness.

Wellington closed the file. Joseph had escaped justice, fleeing into the night. Agent Land, alone in unknown territory with a group of slaves to free from dangerous conditions had to choose between going after him, and freeing captives. She, rightly, chose to free the victims, but when she resumed her search, Dragomir Negrubine was gone. His body was never recovered. Since the "wizard" engaged in the terrible slave trade was dead, the case had been closed and the file rightly put in the archives.

But then, there was another case file, one year later, from Agent Gerrold Collins of Scotland.

September 10, 1892: Scotland: On the moor of Obin

The children of the town of Obin had disappeared in the night, their bodies found, mangled on the moor. Some said an animal dragged them out of their beds. Others said that it was a cursed creature, half animal, half man, possessed of a demon.

I am a man of reason, of logic, and I was sure the face of such a horror could only be that of a man. "I will prove you this," I had said as the men of the town and I trudged across the moor, "that despite what you think you've seen, there are no such creatures as werewolves."

A terrible howl rose from the mist and the five men who accompanied me trembled. "Dragomir is real," said the old man who had guided me to the moor. "Believe or not, he runs with a pack of wolves, and they devour those unwise enough to meddle with him."

"He may be a killer," I said, turning towards the echoing howl, "but he is only a man."

Then there was a flash of lighting, and outlined against the hill was a shape, a hideous shape whose top half was wolf, and bottom like a man. He was running in a strange loping gait. In front of him a child ran, screaming a high-pitched wail. Someone pressed a rifle into my hand. "Silver bullets," were the words whispered, but all I knew in that moment was that a murderer was after a child, and I raised the rifle and took the shot.

The bang echoed in the moor, and the creature fell. The young doctor, who was with me, a fresh-faced blond young man who was as mild as he was tall, ran towards the fallen creature. I arrived at the scene as the doctor was opening his bag, bringing out bandaging. Laying before us was a half-naked man, a blood-filled hole in his chest. Blood pooled under his tall, lean, body. His long dark hair spread around his head.

The man looked up, his ice-blue eyes focusing on me. "You. . .freed me," he croaked, and then exhaled. The doctor leaned over, and pressed fingers to his neck "Dragomir is dead," he declared.

Wellington looked up from the file. "Dragomir," he said, tasting the name. That the name had appeared twice could be coincidence, but it was this third file that tied events together. Perhaps this was all too invigorating. It was time for mid-morning tea.

He had programmed the Analytical Machine precisely to make him the perfect cup for each time of day. For morning, a fine English breakfast, brewed loose-leaf in a special ceramic teapot that was exclusively for black teas. This would not be dulled with milk or sugar, but experienced head-on, the faint scents of honey, clove and lemon, to awake the senses for the day ahead. His tea would be brewed to specifications, to exactly the temperature of one hundred degrees centigrade, and only too steep for exactly four minutes. Later, there would be be an Earl Grey in the afternoon, a definitive mix of his own devising, or, should he be feeling particularly adventurous, a darjeeling, the astringency of which left a calm awareness over the soul. The Analytical Machine, a steady sweet hum in the background of the archives, sung a little melody, and the tea was ready.

Wellington regarded his domain, the archives as they lay before him, silent and organised, all things just-as they should be. Except, of course, for the three files on his desk. The last file of the three, only a year old, stared at him. He needed to review it before he brought it to the attention of Doctor Sound, to be sure that what he had to share was relevant. He took a sip from his cup and opened the last folder from Agent Sylvia Rodgers.

```
September 7, 1893: The Carpathian Mountains,
Romania

     I faced Baron Negrubine at the edge of the
cliff. The Priest stood behind me, holding up
```

his cross like a shield. I had tried to dissuade the Priest from following me, but he insisted it would be folly to face the "monster" alone.

The wind whipped the Baron's long dark hair and his red cloak billowed around him like an angry cloud. "You are too late," he said, his fingers curling under the chin of the beautiful young woman in front of him, "It's already been done. She has married me, and her lands are mine!"

I pulled my Remington-Elliot Derringer and declared, "No marriage entered under duress is lawful." I hope he heard me over these damnable winds. Strands of red hair were tickling my cheeks as they flew around my face.

The Baron's blood red tongue slid over his teeth. "I am not of law," he said, his voice strong despite the powerful wind. "I am of Hell itself!" He thrust the girl in front of him, his gloved hands tight on her small shoulders. "Would you take the shot, Agent Rodgers, and risk killing my beautiful wife?"

The Priest stepped in front of me and raised a crucifix. "God will judge you!" he cried.

The Baron shoved the young woman to the side and backed away, hissing. I tried to aim my Derringer, but the tall, broad-shouldered Priest stood in my way on the narrow precipice. I dared not try to move him, for fear of shoving him off.

"Out of the way!" I ordered.

"God," cried the Priest, "and the sun!" In the distance, over the eastern mountains, the sun peaked on the horizon, a sliver of gold in the blanket of the velvety purple sky. Smoke curled from under the cloak of the Baron, and he screamed, his voice high, like an evil bird.

I couldn't see clearly as the smoke reached me, stinging my eyes, making them water. The blond Priest approached the Baron, holding his crucifix high, and the Baron toppled backwards off the great mountain cliff.

I coughed, blinking away the stinging tears and crawled to the edge of the cliff to peer over the edge. Below, in the shadows, I saw nothing but smoke and mist.

```
    "The demon is dead," said the Priest, putting
his hands around my shoulders, pulling me away
from the edge. "Now, let us tend to the living."
    "He wasn't a demon," said the girl, looking
up at us as if noticing us for the first time.
"He was a man. And his name was Dragomir."
```

Wellington stood up. Two was a coincidence, three was a connection. These cases needed to be reopened, which could only be done by the highest authority. It was time to go see Doctor Sound. He took the elevator to the administrative offices, folders in hand.

Books arrived just in time to see Agent Campbell, his face a deep scowl, emerge from the Director's office.

"Ah!" said Wellington, "Agent Campbell, Good afternoon—"

Campbell grunted and brushed past him. "There's no sense in that man," he growled.

Miss Shillingworth held open the door for the archivist and motioned him to enter. Doctor Sound stood, pushing his portly frame from his seat when Wellington entered, and they shook hands. "Agent Books, please have a seat." His tweed suit was well-fitted to his frame. Wellington always admired good fit on a well-made suit.

On the desk facing Wellington, there was a jumbled place setting, as if a mad waiter was preparing for service. The napkin was messily folded on the wrong side, and the soupspoon was placed on the inside of the other settings, nearly under the plate. He sat in front of the place setting, eyeing it curiously. "Agent Campbell appeared quite upset," he remarked as he moved the soupspoon into the correct location and adjusted the water glass to the correct side of the wine goblet.

Doctor Sound, nodded, learning forward. "Unfortunately, I had to pass on his involvement with a mission. He simply wasn't qualified."

Wellington folded the napkin and laid it, carefully, next to the plate. "Interesting. I always thought him a most capable field agent, although his field reports could do with more..." He paused, cleared his throat. In for a penny... "...relevant details."

Doctor Sound folded his hands together on his desk. "No doubt of that whatsoever. I have utter faith in his abilities. It's just that he lacks a very specific skill for a very particular mission."

Books pushed the end of the salad fork with his finger so that it was perfectly in-line with all the other utensils on the table. "It must be a very specific mission then," he said.

Doctor Sound stood. "Agent Books, why did you ask for this meeting today? Is this about the new data filing system?"

"No. Actually, it's about these case files." He placed the three files on the desk. "We've been killing one man for three years." Doctor Sound paged through the files as Wellington continued. "Similar names but the same description."

Doctor Sound looked at Wellington, startled. Then his face quickly changed into a grin. "Interesting," he returned, "but hardly a pressing matter. Likely just a common false name used in the underground."

"Respectfully, sir," started Wellington, "I don't think so. The descriptions are the same. It cannot be a coincidence. If my calculations are correct, he attempts some nefarious scheme every year at about this time, and even now he may be preparing—"

Doctor Sound waved his hand, cutting him off. "Let it go, Books. We have something else to discuss." He waved his hand over the now, perfectly arrayed, place setting. "You've always been very reliable," he said. "Which is why I think we aught to send you on a little trip. After all, you did pass the test."

Wellington raised an eyebrow. What test would require proper setting of the table? "What will be required?"

"You will go on a trip where you will be required to travel with another agent, by airship, review a certain situation, and report back to me."

A chill swept through him. "With all due respect, sir, I'm not a field agent."

"Correct," said Doctor Sound, "you are not a field agent, and you are not going out in the field."

"Just to clarify," said Wellington, hoping Doctor Sound could not hear his heart pounding against his rib cage, "I am simply going out on an airship, to carry out specific duties and reporting back. Which is, somehow, not field work."

"Exactly. If you were a field agent, we'd have to pay you more."

"Sir—"

But his words failed him as the building shook and a rumble wormed its way through the floor. "Ah!" said Doctor Sound. "That must be Agent Blackwell, perfecting her new device for this trip."

Wellington leapt from his chair. "Doctor Blackwell! Sir, you can't be serious."

"Of course! She will need a valet on the airship."

"I—" This was most certainly not why he had left the Archives. "—beg your pardon."

"A giant airship christened the *Hammarström*, one of the biggest of its kind, is currently a hundred miles from Britannia's shores. Destination: The Americas. It stopped in Southampton to receive a group of upper class ladies who are gathering there to discuss the suffragette movement. Agent Blackwell will go to mingle with them and check the delicate instruments of the engine to make sure it is properly functioning. If the engine were to break and the airship fail, it would be the ruin of the upper class. These ladies are from the richest and most respected families of London. This is a mission that is just to double check that everything is working as it should, without alarming the ladies."

"Then why do you need me?"

"I need someone respectable, someone who can uphold decorum, someone unlikely to cause any explosions." Doctor Sound motioned to the perfectly arrayed place-setting. "And you, Agent Books, meet all the qualifications to be Doctor Blackwell's butler." Doctor Sound walked around his desk and put a hand on Wellington's shoulder. "Don't panic about this, my good man. This is a trip to a fancy airship filled with harmless, upper class ladies who are far more likely to hurt themselves than anyone else. It's basically a holiday. Now get down to R&D, find Agent Blackwell and be on your way."

R&D, or Research and Design, or, as Wellington sometimes liked to think, the Madhouse filled with Exploding Bats, had black smoke pouring out of it. Researchers were scuttling out the door into the hallway, coughing.

"It's all right!" came a muffled voice from inside the smoke-filled room. "It was just a little explosion."

Wellington steeled himself before turning the corner into the room, covering his mouth with his handkerchief. Inside he saw the familiar figure of fellow Ministry agent and scientist, Doctor Josepha Raven Blackwell. She was holding a small silver raygun with a shattered chamber. She was also wearing a mask over her mouth with a giant black tube, and blue goggles that were lit from the inside. Emerging from the acrid plume of destruction, with her dark brown hair, pale skin, and a curvature she covered like an old matron, she appeared as one of Death's own harbinger. With the bird skull entwined in her hair as part of an elaborate decoration, her apocalyptic demeanour was only reinforced.

"What happened here?" he asked, pulling a lever on the wall that activated the internal fans.

Agent Blackwell darted towards him, and pulled off her goggles. A ring of soot marked her face, highlighting her pale skin and ice-blue eyes. "Oh, Agent Books! This is most exciting. I've made a new weapon for our trip." She held out a silver gun. It was a small thing, a barrel like a pen attached to a tiny, blue snowglobe and a silver handle. "I call it The Nipper!"

"Does all this smoke have something to do with the new weapon?" Wellington asked. The fans whirred, and the smoke began to clear from the room.

Josepha pulled off her mask, revealing her wide, smiling face. "Yes!" she said, delighted. "I was testing a bit of material to see what happened when I over-heated the light cache coils, and it turns out that they will explode."

"Clearly," he replied.

"Oh, not like this," said Agent Blackwell. "This was just a small sample, the actual explosion would be much larger."

Wellington rubbed his forehead. "Why would you *want* a gun to explode?" he asked. "Isn't that the opposite of what you'd want in the field?"

The scientist tilted her head. "I don't understand the question."

Wellington sighed, feeling the gentle foreshadowing of a splitting headache. This was going to be a long trip.

He adjusted his tie in his mirror so that it was perfectly centred. He checked his coat for any stray lint. Once more, he passed the comb through his hair. While his father would be in a right panic seeing him in such a position, Wellington found the work of a butler to be most satisfying. It was all so precise. It also helped that Agent Blackwell required very little of him. So far, he had carried a few bags, set the table, and ironed some things just to keep up appearances; but mostly, Wellington was able to catch up on his reading, even sketch out an idea for an ambitious automotive creation.

Agent Blackwell even refrained from impinging on his person during the trip, which was a delightful change of pace.

The small airship he was on with Agent Blackwell was about to reach the *Hammarström*, which was so large that this smaller airship could actually dock there to drop them off. Looking from the docking port, the ship was like an estate in the sky, brandishing grand balconies, great windows and gilding, as if it was a palace set among the clouds.

Wellington held the bags as they docked. The formal attire of the butler reminded him of his infantry uniform, everything just so and in its place. The circular door opened between the two ships, and Wellington followed Agent Blackwell onto the large docking bay of the *Hammarström*. They were to be greeted by the organiser of the conference, Lady White of the Taylor-Whites.

A tall, severe woman was waiting for them, her arms crossed in front of her. She was a giant of a woman, her weathered face hardly softened by her long, stringy hair wrapped in a tight bun. She wore a high-necked walking dress, gripping a large book in one massive arm.

"Baroness," she said, her face a tight frown.

Wellington felt a stone in his throat. Why did she have to choose such a high rank? It would clearly cause suspicion. Why not a simpler, lower rank, or just claim wealth? That was easy enough to fake.

"I am pleased to be here," Agent Blackwell replied coolly, holding out her hand in greeting. "I presume you are Lady White?"

The woman did not extend her hand. "You presume wrong," she said. "I am Ms Crux. I am here to make sure that everything operates as it should. You say you are Baroness Blackwell. A high claim."

Wellington slowly took in a breath, his face struggling to betray no emotion. It might be that their mission ended here, before it truly began.

"I am Baroness Josepha Raven Blackwell," she stated, her back straightening.

He cursed to himself. She wasn't even impersonating an actual Baroness. She was using her *real* name?

Ms Crux opened the book in her hand. "If you truly are who you say you are, then I don't suppose you will mind us looking you up."

Wellington caught the name on the cover: *Burkes Peerage*. His eyes examined the room for any exits.

She flipped open the pages. "Blackwell, Blackwell," she mused to herself. Then her eyes widened. "Daughter of?"

"Raven Katherine and Christoff Corax Emilian Blackwell."

"Town of birth?"

"Zakopane," Josepha replied.

Ms Crux's eyes widened, "Then you are she," she said, and curtsied deeply. "My apologies, Baroness."

Doctor Blackwell smiled magnanimously. "I understand having security," she said. "I commend you on doing your job." She looked back to Wellington. "Come along," she said.

Arriving in their suite, his curiosity overtook him. "How did you manage to exchange the *Burke's Peerage* books? Did you do it before the journey or did you somehow—"

"I didn't switch them, Books."

He gasped. That Doctor Sound would tamper with a book as important as *Burke's* just to add in a few agents was beyond the pale. Tampering with some records, yes, but with *Peerage*? "That is beyond—" Wellington stammered. "That Doctor Sound thinks he has the right to tamper with *Burke's Peerage*. Ministry or not that is just—"

"He didn't tamper with anything," she said, her cheeks blushing just a hint. "I'm in it." Josepha smiled sweetly. "But please don't spread it around the office. Being around a Baroness does seem to make people uncomfortable."

Wellington swallowed. "You? A Baroness?"

"Why yes," she said.

"And you work at the Ministry?"

"The Empire needs me," she stated quite matter-of-factually, "and I am very patriotic."

This was all too much. Wellington had to go sit down. And have a brandy. Or three.

Serving as a silent valet, Wellington accompanied Doctor Blackwell to her meeting with the charming Lady White of the Taylor-Whites, a tall, woman who greeted Doctor Blackwell like an old friend. Lady White, in turn, escorted her to a series of talks, including a tea-service, panel discussion and group meetings where ladies discussed the current state of women in the Empire, the world, and current politics.

Doctor Blackwell gave a rather graphic presentation on "Independence though Self Maintenance." Wellington had to excuse himself from the room in order to maintain his dignity. He was well aware Josepha made devices for the relief of hysteria in women. He knew all too well as during one rather upsetting night, she had made a mould of his forearm for one of her devices, a fact that he tried, repeatedly, to forget. The very idea that women all over the Empire were doing, God knows what, with his *arm*, was a horrifying thought.

Well, most of the time.

Still, on this grand airship, the sea beneath them, the sky around them, it was invigorating. The women bustled and talked, the smell of excellent tea around all of them. Wellington adored the archives, but this wasn't nearly as bad as he thought it would be. Sometimes, he forgot how the world of the living could be so stimulating.

At exactly five o'clock, Doctor Blackwell retired to her rooms to dress for dinner. This was the time that they would set their mission to action. They decided that she would arrive fashionably late, after checking the engines to make sure they were clear of fault. Many of the servants would be busy with dinner preparations, so it would be an excellent time to sneak into the engine area, check for faults, and then return to dinner.

After that, it would be only two more days of panel discussions and dissertations. Fortunately, Wellington had brought reading, and with any luck, Doctor Blackwell wouldn't set off any explosions.

Doctor Blackwell flung open the door to his rooms and caught him with his tie undone.

"Agen—" but then he caught himself. "Baroness, while I am but a humble butler, please do knock!"

"It's an emergency," she said. Josepha was wearing a deep, crimson dress with a plunging neckline, her hair piled on her head. "I simply cannot get myself into this dress, and we only have a short window that the engine room will be unguarded." She turned around to reveal that the back of her dress was open, a jet-black brocade corset under the dress.

"Baroness!" hissed Wellington. "This is most inappropriate. To see another Agent in their undergarments, let alone a—"

"Surely you know how to use buttons," said Doctor Blackwell, looking over her shoulder.

"Of course I know how to use buttons!" he replied. "That is hardly the point!"

"Time is running out."

Wellington sighed. "This is most inappropriate," he muttered as he slid each little silk covered button into its fabric hole. The dress closed around Doctor Blackwell, hugging her curves.

"Done," he declared, with a sigh. She turned to face him and he saw, at her throat, a small cameo. It was not the sweet coral that most women wore, but black and opalescent, bearing the face of a dragon.

"You are going to have to carry a Nipper," she said, thrusting the weapon towards him. "I've made two for the trip, but mine isn't easily accessible in this dress."

"Where is it?" asked Books, then stopped himself. "No, wait. I do not want to know."

"Excellent," she said, taking his hand boldly. "Let's go!"

"Decorum," he reminded her, extricating himself from her grasp, and they exited the suite.

Agent Blackwell smiled warmly (as best she could, most of her smiles were laced with a sort of wild madness) as they walked through the ships corridors before slipping unseen into a service corridor to the Engine room.

"Someone checks in the Engine room every half hour," whispered Doctor Blackwell, "more than enough time for me to check on the mechanics, repair anything that needs assistance, and be back well in time for appetisers."

Wellington shifted on his feet, watching though the porthole from the Engine room to the corridor. "Do be quick," he said.

"Agent Books, I am always efficient," she said, and opened a panel, examining the innards of the engine. Wellington glanced over. He had to admit, the technology was fascinating. An engineer himself, he was delighted by the inner workings of such great machines. Agent Blackwell danced around the engine room, opening a panel here, touching a piece of machinery there. She picked up an oil can and squirted it into a funnel, but a splotch of oil fell from the lip of the can to her dress, right on the front.

"Doctor Blackwell," scolded Wellington, shaking his head, "Do be careful." He took out his handkerchief and carefully dotted the drop away. Unfortunately, oil is oil, and a handkerchief, no matter how good, can only do so much. "Ugh," he groaned, "bit of a mark there. You'll have to change again before dinner."

"This is why I usually wear black, you know," sighed Josepha. "Far easier to hide the stains."

"Certainly oil stains," he agreed.

"And blood," she added, turning back to the engine. "We are done, Agent Books. Everything is in excellent shape and the ladies of the Empire are safe. We have plenty of time to—"

There was a huge bang, a rumble from above the decks and the engine room rocked, throwing Josepha to the grate on the floor, and knocking Wellington's head against the doorway. His world blurred for a moment, but he could just make out Josepha pushing herself up on her hands. Both of them smelled smoke.

"The engine!" cried Books, and both of them dived towards the controls, quickly checking the integrity of the machine. Fortunately, the engine was functioning perfectly. They looked at each other.

"It wasn't the engine," Agent Blackwell said in amazement.

There were hard footsteps outside, clapping against the metal floors. Books reached into his pocket for the Nipper. Doctor Blackwell put a hand on his arm. "No, none of that. We'll just tell the crew that I got lost. We can talk our way out of this."

But it wasn't the crew that opened the door, it was a group of pirates.

Wellington hated to stereotype. Being an agent of the Ministry meant being exposed to different cultures and viewpoints, and certainly, agents were an unusual group of individuals in and of themselves. It wasn't in his nature to draw quick conclusions about entire groups of people.

But these people were most certainly pirates. With their motley collection of weaponry, from curved sword to rapier, raygun to a clearly repaired brass-gear fist-knife. The three men and one woman who took them captive wore an assortment of clothing, from workmen's boots to fine (obviously stolen, and ill-fitting) overcoats. The pirates were a patchwork, but a *well-armed* collection of patchwork.

Wellington and Josepha were lead away from Engineering to the ballroom. The ladies were huddled together on one side of the room, where the pirates snatched the jewels from their throats, wrists and fingers. Lady White was nowhere to be seen, and Wellington shuddered to think of her fate. As they were pushed towards the crowd by their captors, he surmised the difficulty within this crowd of ladies for them to slip away, or perhaps plan an appropriate counter-attack. It was unlikely, out of the hundred women on the ship, that they would be noticed as missing.

Then a heavy hand fell on Josepha's shoulder. Turning, they both looked into the stern face of Ms Crux. Except this time, she had shed her stern bun, and replaced her corsets and skirts for pants and a shirt that was well-open to the navel, revealing the broad and sculpted chest of a man.

"Baroness Blackwell," he said. "We were wondering where you slipped off to."

She frowned, her skin blushing. "For my jewels? Don't bother, I don't have any of worth."

"Oh, Baroness Blackwell. Did you think our aim was to steal the jewels from a bunch of aristocrats? We came here for you!"

"What do you want with the Baroness?" Wellington said, stepping in front of her.

The former Ms Crux sized him up. From his military days, Wellington recognised this as a precursor to fist-a-cuffs. As this was a pirate, Queensbury Rules probably wouldn't be the fighting style of choice.

From over his shoulder came Josepha's voice. She must have been standing on her toes as Crux's steely gaze disappeared on hearing her say, "If your Captain thinks that my family has any wealth left for a ransom, you might as well kill me now. There isn't a penny left in the treasury, and the rest of my family is dead."

Wellington turned to her. "Josepha," he whispered. "I had...no idea."

She looked down. "A terrible accident..."

Crux snapped. "You are both coming with us!" he declared.

The pirates grabbed Wellington and shoved him—and Josepha from the sounds of the scuffling and commotion behind them—along the corridor toward the grand balcony of the ship. The French doors to the grand marble balcony swung open to reveal a breath-taking panoramic view of stars interrupted only by mountains of clouds illuminated by moonlight. A figure stood at the railing, and as he was clothed in black he appeared as a cut-out. This cut-out turned and stepped into the light, revealing a man wearing a military suit with a high neck and silver buttons, and a long, crimson cape that flapped in the wind.

Wellington heard Josepha gasp. He was surprised he himself did not gasp as well on recognising him from the tinotypes in the Archives.

"Baron Dragomir Negrubine," he said.

The man bowed slightly, strands of his long, black hair slipping over his face. He smiled and held out his hand to Doctor Blackwell. "Sister," he said, with a smirk.

Now it was time for Agent Books to gasp.

Baron Negrubine looked up at Books. "My full name," he began, "Is Baron Dragomir Corb Corax Emilian Negrubine. You must be lax on your Eastern European languages, because otherwise, dear sir, you would not be so surprised. My last name, roughly translated is—"

"Blackwell," he whispered, cursing silently to himself.

Dragomir laughed. "Very good," he said, "if a little slow."

"You're supposed to be dead," Wellington insisted. "The Ministry killed you. Three times."

"Oh, he's very good at dying." Josepha narrowed her eyes on her brother. "He pretends to be a vampire or a wizard and then tricks people into thinking he's dead with smoke and mirrors."

"A bit more than that," said the Baron. "Also, my faithful companion does help me to fool your stupid agents." Crux bowed and the Baron continued, pacing the balcony. "Your agents watch as I am stabbed, shot, or fall from a cliff. Your operatives close their little cases and I go about my business."

Wellington nodded. "Clever."

The Baron turned to Josepha. "Dear sister…" he started.

She folded her hands over her chest and turned away from him. "You don't get to call me that, not anymore, not after what you did."

"I am insulted." Dragomir place a hand on his chest, his tone of shock far from convincing. "Really, have I truly done worse than blowing up a boarding school?"

"Yes!" she bit back. "Most assuredly, yes! You used our countrymen, you enslaved citizens and you burned our family name."

"Wait," Wellington interrupted. "Come again? *Blowing up* a boarding school?"

They ignored him.

"Dear sister, I know that you've been trying to use your powers for the public good," Dragomir said, "but it never does quite come together, does it?"

"That's not true," Josepha returned. "I've done much good since—"

"But you could do so much more if you weren't subjected to silly rules. Join me, sister, and we will take to the skies. Between my abilities to manipulate and your technical knowledge, there is no limit to what we could accomplish."

"I have committed myself to unselfish goals. You would never understand."

"This seems private," Wellington offered, turning to the door. "I'll just leave you two to talk it out."

Dragomir motioned to the door and three pirates stepped in front of it, blocking his way.

"This one," and Dragomir took in Wellington as if just noticing him. He leaned in, his smile wide. "I am quite gifted at reading people, but you..." He walked around him, and Wellington suddenly felt as if he were a butterfly pinned against a board. "I see through this scrawny, intellectual façade a super-soldier, here to protect you from harm. Inside this man is one that will give me quite an entertaining fight, now won't he?"

"Agent Books?!" Josepha burst out into laughter, making everyone's head snap to her direction. "No, Dragomir. No. He's just an archivist."

A wash of relief swept through Wellington.

Then Dragomir spoke, and Wellington's anxiety returned. "That is sad, sister. I had hoped for a good fight out of him." He shrugged and unsheathed his sword, "But I'm sure even a bad fight is better than no fight at all."

Wellington opened and closed his fists. The shadows could prove useful, but unarmed was not the best way to start a fight, especially against an opponent who was skilled at dying.

Josepha suddenly threw herself between them, her arms outstretched. "No, Dragomir, no." She hid her face in her gloved hands. "Alright," she said. "You win. I'll come with you. I promise. Just don't hurt him."

"Now was that so hard?" asked Dragomir, taking her hands away from her face. He motioned to the pirates who opened the French doors back into the airship. "Dearest sister," he cooed, "we will conquer land and sea together, and hold the mighty in our grasp!" He waved his hand, motioning to Wellington. "Of course, with so much to do, we simply cannot have excess baggage." Dragomir nodded to Crux.

The man was on Wellington in a moment, grabbing him by his arms. Another pirate grabbed his feet and Wellington sailed over the balcony and into the night.

The last thing the archivist saw was Josepha's horrified face, her hand outstretched, reaching towards him, enough air between them to be an eternity.

Defenestration, thought Wellington, was a ridiculous word. As much as he liked having words for very specific things, who could possibly have occasion to use a word for being thrown out a window? But here he was, tumbling backward through open sky, defenestrated out of an airship by pirates, betrayed by a fellow agent, and tumbling towards the certain doom of the icy water that would break his body and swallow him whole.

Time slowed, and as it did so he saw, coming towards him, a metal pipe outstretched from the ship. He reached for it with both hands. One hand slipped immediately off, but he caught the pipe in the crook of his right arm. His body yanked violently against the metal, banging against the side of the ship, so that he slipped to his fingertips. Looking below, dark clouds floated serenely underneath him. He looked upward, the air of the ship rushing past him, and heard the crackle of electricity and a loud shriek.

"Not a real mission," he growled, clinging to the cold pipe. "Practically a paid holiday." He shifted his grip and kicked upward, wrapping his legs around the support. From above, smoke, fire, and pirates waited for him, if he could actually find a way back inside. He inched up along the pipe, his eyes looking around for entrance back into the ship. A handhold away was a window. But where did the window lead? An empty bedchamber? More pirates?

The window opened, and Lady Kristiana White, of the Taylor-Whites, stuck her head out the window. "Oi!" she cried. "What are you doing out there?"

Wellington looked around him, then back at her. Did he really *need* to give an explanation? "Pirates?!" he yelled, his voice straining against the wind.

"Thought as much!" said Lady White, holding out her hand. "Give it here, chap! Let's get you inside."

Their fingertips barely touched as Wellington reached towards her. "Give a little push!" she assured him. "I've got you."

While it was hardly wise to trust the aristocrat considering Crux's deception, the cold truth was he couldn't remain out here forever. He pushed off, and felt a strong hand catch his. Lady White hauled him up into the window with an immense strength, and dumped him, unceremoniously, onto the floor of the ship's kitchen.

Around him several women gathered, helping him to his feet. "You are—" *Tact*, Wellington thought. "—stronger than you look." His heart was beating hard in his chest.

Lady White flexed her considerable muscles. "I used to be a strong woman!" she said, "In the Traveling Circus of the Oswalts."

He coloured. "You! A Lady?"

"Oh tosh," said Lady White. "We all have pasts."

Wellington nodded. "Yes," he agreed, "that we do."

He withdrew the Nipper from his pocket, thankful that it had remained there this entire ordeal. "Lady White, do you know how to use one of these?"

She chuckled. "I can use any gun. I'm a hunting champion."

"Excellent," and he gingerly passed the weapon to her. "There are only a few pirates, and many of you. If you gang up against them, using this, you should be able to overwhelm them."

"Where did you get this?" she asked.

This "paid holiday" was resembling more and more like a mission with each passing second. "What if I said I took it off a pirate?"

"I wouldn't ask any more questions," said Lady White with a wink. Then she took his arm. "And what will you be doing, while we overtake the pirates?"

"They took Baroness Blackwell," he said. "I intend to get her back."

"Well, you should run off and get her," Lady White returned, patting him on the shoulder. "We all know what trouble she would be, if she fell into the wrong hands."

Wellington's brow knotted. "You do?"

"Blew up her boarding school," said Lady White, nodding along with the collected ladies. "Well known. In the right circles, of course." She turned to the group of ladies around her. "Now then, Women of the Empire, let's go show these pirates what we're made of!"

And, much to Wellington's horror, she hiked her skirt up, revealing bright, blue stockings, kicked open the door, and charged into the Ballroom. The pirates were quickly overwhelmed by the angry aristocrats, thanks in no small part to the Nipper, and the Lady with an amazingly accurate shot.

Wellington remained close to the shadows, working his way out of the Ballroom towards the Bridge. Through one of the *Hammarström's* observation windows, he saw the pirate's vessel, stuck to the edge of the grand airship like a black tumour. He rushed up the stairs, watching the retreating pirates as they crossed a wooden plank connecting the two ships. From the scant light coming from the *Hammarström*, Wellington could just make out Josepha Blackwell, in her stained red dress, pushed ahead of Baron Dragomir.

"Josepha!" he called out to her. "Don't go with him!"

Baron Dragomir pushed Josepha behind him. "You are too late," he bellowed. "She knows who she is. She's my sister, and my family—well, we create our own rules."

Wellington was about to run for him when he saw Doctor Blackwell behind her brother, reaching up her own dress. He had to delay him. Just for a moment. "Baron, the people we work for have a lot of money. We would be able to pay you for her."

The Baron laughed, shaking his head. "You cannot pay for blood," he said, and motioned to his crew. The connecting plank attaching their two ships began to retract.

The Nipper discharged from behind Baron Dragomir. Her shot went wild, out into the sky. They grappled for the gun, but Dragomir overpowered her in moments, wrenching the gun from her grasp. Wellington's hand gripped a distress chute on seeing Josepha leaping out over the open sky, her skirts flying, like she was made of electricity and light.

Then she rolled into Wellington, and it was very clear that she was made of flesh, bone, and squishy stuff. Particularly when they landed hard against the *Hammarström's* deck.

"Your loss!" cried Dragomir, as his ship floated into the sky. He gave a little bow, holding the Nipper in his hands. It was glowing brightly.

"You might want to shield your eyes," Josepha warned just before the darkness disappeared in the wake of a terrible explosion, light and heat washing over them as their own airship listed dangerously.

It was several minutes before they could see or hear again, and by that time, Dragomir's pirate ship was just so much ash in the air.

Despite the pirate attack, Lady White had insisted that the conference continue. The ladies were energised from driving off the attack. Doctor Blackwell, however, had remained silent for the remainder of the voyage. A trait Wellington knew was not normal.

In their final day, Wellington served Josepha tea, poured another setting, took a seat opposite of her, and made his confession. "I'm going to have to include this in my report to Doctor Sound. It not like we can keep an attack by pirates a secret. Especially since so many others serve as witnesses."

"But Agent Books! If it's known that my brother—"

"Now then," Wellington interrupted, enjoying his tea, something he desperately needed after this experience. "I don't think it necessary that your relationship with the Baron be mentioned."

Josepha's pallid complexion appeared to regain colour. "Truly, Agent Books?"

"Indeed. And this time, we saw him die."

"But Agent Books, that is hardly an assurance, he has faked his death many times and—"

Wellington knew taking her hands in his was not only most forward but hazardous in the case of Josepha. He did so anyway, assuring her softly, "Agent Blackwell, someday, you may have to face him. But that is not something the Ministry can make you do. It is something you must seek out on your own."

She looked out the window "You're right, of course."

"Yes, well, of course I am," he said with a shrug. "It's only proper."

"We wouldn't want to be improper, would we?" she quipped.

"Indeed," he stated, finishing his cup, dabbing his mouth with his napkin, then straightening his cuff. "Now, Baroness, you are due for a seminar. Ready?"

With a nod from her, they walked together to the dining room as the airship glided above the deep waters of the Atlantic.

The Clockwork Samurai

Jack Mangan

Otisburgh, Vancouver
British Columbia, Canada
1891

The Samurai knelt on the Canadian hilltop, blade pressed against his stomach. His breathing was relaxed and measured, even as the nearby ironwood tree shuddered in the pre-dawn breeze. Kuro stood over him, ready to fulfil his duties as second, fitting his katana into the grip of his brass right hand. The Pacific spoke softly in the distance.

"Lead with your left," the kneeling man said, the cold vapour of his breath billowing with each word. "I want you to feel this as much as possible."

"Hideo—"

"I am enamoured of the beauty of the stars, filling the sky like grains of sand on a black beach. Yet even now, the tide of dawn washes them away into the coming light. I shall step into those waves and allow the sea to carry me with honour into eternity." Hideo's voice was calm and resolute. "Were you not so enamoured of that light-haired American woman, you would sit beside me, Kuro, to perform the last noble act of your life." He inclined his head toward the scaffold tower of their keep, visible over the ridge to the south.

"Miss Beverly is a fine swordsman. Swords*woman*. Nothing more to me." Kuro felt his face redden. He tried to match Hideo's stillness, but his voice wavered in the cold breeze. "We obeyed Master Ueda's final order, before he committed *seppuku*. We have remained Samurai in this foreign land, continuing our ancient ways without persecution, serving under Master Toranaga for the noble House of Usher. There is no dishonour in the paths we have chosen, Hideo-san. Would you have preferred to become one of Emperor Meiji's bureaucrats?"

"Toranaga was a good man," Hideo agreed. "Since his death, we have taken orders from the barbarian, Scharnusser. There is no honour in kidnapping children."

Kuro made no reply, only recalled the fear in the seven-year-old boy's face as the Usher Samurai had stolen upon him on his father's island beach. Kuro still saw the terrified question in his eyes as he'd been bound and boarded into the shadow zeppelin.

Hideo sucked his breath in sharply, dimpling his exposed belly with his blade. The first golden crest of light appeared above the eastern hills. Far from his home, Hideo gazed a final time upon the rising sun.

Kuro raised his brass right forearm, adjusted the sword hilt in his left hand.

Twenty-four hours later

Her cooled steamsword clattered against his wooden katana, glimmering in the courtyard gaslight. Sweat ran freely from his hair in spite of the cold. She chewed her lower lip, as was her custom when concentrating. Tufts of long blonde hair stuck out at random points from beneath the rim of her knit cap. The duellists were both alive with purpose and determination, continuing to trade hits and parries, even as the steam whistle summoned the morning shift to their posts. Sunrise had only just begun to peek over the half-completed stone wall.

The work of converting the old Monastery to moated, modern fortress had fallen behind schedule, and a week earlier, Roderick Scharnusser had made grisly examples of three stonemasons to show his displeasure. Eight men in parkas went now to the exo-goliaths parked in the wall's uneven shadow. They watched the swordplay, laughing and talking softly amongst themselves. One by one, the men dispersed to climb into their giant cockpits, and began the tasks of firing the boilers.

Wood struck steel, their weapons locking near their hilts, drawing the combatants in tight. He felt the softness of her hair whip across his chin. The gears in his forearm chattered busily as he tightened his grip on the wooden pommel.

"This won't bring him back, you know," she said, her breaths coming hard.

"I pray nothing does," Kuro replied. "Hideo died a warrior's death. It was my honour to act as his second." With a light shove, the two separated. The wooden practice sword felt almost the same weight as his steel blade in his clockwork hand. He'd kept that katana sheathed, since cleaning it yesterday of Hideo's blood. Around them, the 10-foot-tall biped machines lurched into motion, the night's accumulations of dewy ice sliding from their frames. They walked awkwardly, deliberately across the yard to their tasks. With a drawn-out whine of pistons, the machine closest to them bent down to lift a heavy stone.

Its worker leered at them through his cockpit scaffolds, emboldened by his mechanical height and strength. "Hey, I thought there were no Chinamen left?" he shouted.

The goliath-driver nearest him responded with a laugh.

Beverly dropped her fighting stance to stand upright, visibly overcome with rage. "How dare you? A thousand of you in your machines are not worth one of these Samurai!" Her fury was as frightful and sudden as a thunderbolt. Kuro counted himself lucky that he'd never been the target of her anger. She turned away from him to focus on the labourer. "Attend to your duties, grunts. Speak again and you'll answer to my cousin."

The workers blanched. The nearest one said, "I'm sorry, Miss—"

She pointed her sword and he silenced, pulling his exo-goliath's levers to stand upright with the stone.

Kuro sighed. "He'd have died for such disrespect in my homeland. I am destined for a common death here in shame, many years down the road as an old man, surrounded by these savages." he said, then saw her dark expression turn to amusement. He bowed his head. "Pardon me, Miss Beverly. Present company excepted, of course."

"You can always go seek your noble death back in Japan," she said.

He shook his head. "I was barely a man the last time I saw her shores, and there are grays in my top-knot now. When Hideo and the rest of us left, the Emperor had turned the Samurai into *Shizoku*, bureaucrats wielding quills while the ink rusted their swords. I am the last now of the Samurai in America, maybe the last of my kind in the world."

"Well, my cousin's move with little Percy Amboy is bound to tick off his father. You may see some glorious battle soon," she said, lunging suddenly with her steamsword. His parry was more reflex than conscious action. The sword kiss brought her mischievous grin in close again to his startled face. "If you can survive practices with me." Their blades drew a circle in mid-air, danced for another five steps, until his smile matched hers.

Kuro had watched the late afternoon commotion from a frosted second story window, had seen the Ministry agent stride through the gates under the eyes of the Usher guardsmen's rifles. The tall man was a figure of masculine bravado in dust, goggles hung loosely about his neck, smirking at the confused henchmen as he surrendered to them. His appearance at the compound had apparently been a surprise to everyone.

Kuro blinked with surprise when the porter arrived and summoned him to stand watch for the prisoner interrogation.

Roderick Scharnusser was a strikingly large man. He'd parked his bulk outside his study doors, flanked by nervous lackeys. He said nothing as the Samurai approached, but frowned and gestured to the door handle. Kuro led Scharnusser in, who nodded to his men inside to exit, leaving them alone with the Ministry agent.

"You still haven't shaved off that neckbeard, Rod? I hope it keeps you warm up here in the snow." The man remained seated, staring Scharnusser down, his hands bound before him. His own facial hair looked more sculpted than neglected; and even with his wrists bound, he adjusted his cuffs, showing off a pair of elegant gold cufflinks. "This meeting is supposed to be just you and me, mate, one on one. Lose the Chinaman."

"Mr Campbell, I can hardly be alone with a man as dangerous as yourself, can I? My guardian here is a relic, freshly imported from Japan. He doesn't understand American English, and could never decipher your walkabout dialect." Kuro blinked at the lie. "You can speak freely."

"Call me Bruce. I'm pretty unhappy to have been airshipped across the Pacific, mate, just because you've gone and stolen O.S.M. Amboy's son. My superiors believe you're settling old scores, so I'm here instead of our North American field agent. Let's have it out, so you can return Percy to his father and I can go home."

Scharnusser's smile was thin. "A few clarifications, Bruce. Zachary Amboy is no longer with the Office of Supernatural and Metaphysical. He now runs a small colony with his wives, a few miles offshore from here."

"Yes, I stopped there on my way to your place. Half-finished inventions everywhere you look, people of all sizes and colours tinkering with his crazy machines." Campbell reached inside his jacket. Kuro stepped forward, and the man froze. In this opponent's eyes smouldered courage, bravery, duty. For a moment, he saw the spirit of Hideo. With a quick arch of a single eyebrow, he pulled out a crumpled fold of paper. "Got a note from him right here, in fact. It's long, but I'll read some of the highlights." Campbell pulled the goggles up from beneath his chin, framing and magnifying his eyes dramatically. "Cor, these things are blurry. The vision's the first thing to go, you know. Let's see… it says:

Return my son unharmed immediately… face my wrath… This is your only warning… I'm a bloody lunatic.

"OK, I added that last bit meself, but you get the point. I think you'd prefer to deal with me than him, sensible and level-headed man of action that I am. Here are your choices: accept a trade of the boy for me, or refuse, and be shocked and angry when I leave with Amboy's junior, and you have nothing."

Scharnusser frowned, paced slowly along a wall of books, bringing his bulky frame to rest at an unfamiliar marble bust mounted on a pillar. Bruce Campbell looked around blindly for a few seconds, then pulled the goggles back to hang at his neck.

"Mr Campbell, while you did play a role in the events of my father's murder, I recognise that you were blameless in the act. There's nothing to settle between us. I likewise don't hold your Ministry of Peculiar Occurrences responsible for my twin brothers' deaths. The guilt lies solely with Zachary Amboy. Each night, a raven flies in here and lands upon this bust, speaking my father's name, taunting me with his death. Amboy will answer for it. His son will not be released; he will die before his own father's eyes, when Amboy shows that he's man enough to come here himself."

Campbell looked directly at Kuro. "Seriously, mate. Everyone in the Americas is buggering mad, aren't they?" The Samurai made no reply. "So Roddy, this kidnapping isn't actually Usher business, is it? You've gone rogue with some personal revenge scheme? How are your superiors going to like that?"

Roderick struck the marble bust with his fist. "Enough! You have wasted my time, Mr Campbell. I shall send a courier to your ex-O.S.M. friend informing him that his son will be executed at twilight tomorrow. He can come and watch with you if he likes. In the meantime, you can rot in a cell. Samurai," and with a wave of his hand, motioned for Kuro to take Campbell away.

Kuro bowed. The Australian locked eyes with him, but stood and allowed himself to be escorted.

Beverly was waiting outside, tendrils of blonde hair escaping from tight braids to cascade along the pale white of her neck. Campbell's height and muscular girth loomed large over them both. His eyes immediately fell to the expanse of flesh from her collarbone to her corset. "Well, hell—"

"Can it, Agent Outback," she said, her voice taut.

Puzzlement mingled with his charm. "Have we met?"

"Yes, two years ago in Arizona, on my uncle's train. The day he was killed. Walk." The three of them began down the staircase nearest the study.

"No, miss, begging your pardon, I'd have noticed you."

"You did. You shook my hand."

Campbell's mouth hung agape now. "Cor, I do recall now. Blimey! From gentlewoman to hired muscle, how did that happen?" He looked at them both a moment, and his mouth dropped again. "And wait, you're with the little guy here? My lord, really?"

Kuro blushed, but otherwise betrayed no reaction.

"Keep walking, Outback," Beverly said. To his surprise, she looked equally flustered. "If you give us information on Amboy, you might just survive this."

"What's to tell that you don't know? Retired from service a few years ago for unknown reasons, left Arizona for a little island off of Vancouver. He's madder than a croc dentist. The O.S.M. must miss his inventions, though; I'll give him that. As clever a clankerton as the Ministry's wanker of an archivist. Zachary's wagon ornithopter was a pretty amazing piece of work, before your ninja boy here and his mate blew it up on their kidnapping mission. But you should see what he's done to his little gunboat. Hell of a ship."

"Which would be a problem if we fought him at sea, or on his island," Beverly said. "You'll notice that our fortress here is five miles inland."

"Be that as it may, you're fools to provoke that lunatic. Especially with no government agency to leash him."

Bruce then looked around. "Speaking of your rice-powered help here, where's the other one?"

Kuro glanced at Beverly. After holding her gaze for a moment, he looked forward. "Enough chatter, Outback," she said. He raised his hands in mock surrender.

They continued in silence across the compound, into a gas lit hallway lined with closed doors beneath another monastery building. The samurai's thoughts went to Hideo's burial mound, on the nearby hilltop where he'd taken his own life.

"All right, I can't hold it back any longer," Campbell said, staring at Kuro's brass right forearm. "What happened here? Did your hand go bad?"

Kuro replied in English, without hesitation, "There was an incident in my homeland. Your Ministry colleague, Kitty O'Toole, was there when it happened. You should ask her about it."

Bruce moved quickly, grabbed the metal hand, held it up to his face. Kuro's left hand went to his sword grip, Beverly drew her pistol; but Campbell only gave the glove an inquisitive look.

"I will, mate," Bruce replied. "I'll also ask her about the English teachers in the Land of the Rising Sun. You got a real command of the language there."

Now it was Kuro's turn to arch a brow. This one was far more clever than he led others to believe.

"The rubber grooves on the fingers give me a secure grip," Kuro said, snatching his hand back from Campbell. He unlocked the third cell door and held it for him, thankful that Amboy's son in the next room made no noise.

"That arm chugs louder than a locomotive, mate." Bruce snorted as he stepped into his cell. "I guess you Japanese will never be known for your technological devices."

"Our koala guest is quite impressed with himself," Beverly said. "Is he a worthy opponent?"

Kuro looked Campbell from head to toe. "Agent Campbell carries himself like a true warrior. But I don't think there'd be any honour in dying by his hand. He's too—"

"Foul? Uncouth?" she suggested.

"Crude."

"I'll take that as a compliment," Bruce said, beaming.

Miss Beverly's smile was colder. "We'll meet again, Mr Campbell."

The agent stepped into the cell. "Planning to keep me company tonight?" He winked at Beverly as the door shut in his face.

They nodded to the guard on watch and ascended the basement steps. Kuro walked in silence, his thoughts returning to the bombastic adventurer locked away in the depths of the Fortress. The man cast a shadow across his duty that unsettled him.

"What do you think about his warning?" she asked, snapping him out of his reflection.

Kuro paused, squinted in the grey twilight. "I fear that we have woken a sleeping giant."

Kuro felt no surprise to be woken at three o'clock in the morning to the clamour of alarms and whistles.

He dressed quickly, wound the gears in his arm, and bound his long black hair with a rawhide cord, recalling the days in Japan when he'd shaved the top of his head, in the chonmage style befitting a Samurai. Beverly met him in the hallway. She somehow looked even lovelier to him in her half-awake state, bedecked in long cotton nightclothes, tousled hair clinging to her scalp. He was tired enough to consider telling her, but neither said a word.

They instead went silently to the basement cellblock, where Roderick Scharnusser stood listening to a visibly quaking guard's report. The doors all appeared intact and locked, save for two. These both hung ajar on their hinges, severe scorch marks around where the bolts had been. Two other guards lay inert on the floor near each of these.

The lone conscious guard held up a pair of goggles with shattered lenses for his employer to see, his hands trembling. Kuro recognised them as Campbell's. "We did search him, but the goggles—there were two lenses in each frame. The cufflinks were keys, and they unlocked the frames." Kuro's eyes darted to the goggles, and protruding from the curve of each frame were Campbell's fine gold cufflinks. "Hidden inside each of the compartments must have been some explosive compound."

Absent his usual air of menace, Roderick smiled gently through the entire report, nodding encouragement to the young soldier. He said, "I understand that our two prisoners have escaped through a gap in the incomplete wall?"

"I think s-so, sir."

At the word, "think", Roderick Scharnusser's face switched from kindness to fury. He grabbed the guard by the throat. The young man's eyes rolled, a sickening sound in his throat as his body shook with convulsions, and that was when Kuro caught a glimpse of the Tesla-gloves under Scharnusser's coat sleeves.

The guard fell from his grip, slumped to the floor, the only sound in the hallway was the crackle of the deadly gauntlets. His face still twisted in a rictus of anger, Scharnusser looked up and pointed directly at Kuro. Sparks of blue leapt from his insulated finger. *"You,"* he snapped. "You were with me when he put those blasted goggles on in my study. You should have seen the threat. So now you will lead a team to fetch me Campbell and the Amboy child. Dead, alive, slightly unwell—it don't matter. You make this right." His hand lowered, but his cold gaze never left Kuro. "This is family business, so take my cousin with you. And you better make sure you don't kill the boy unless Zachary Amboy is there to see it. You all hear me?"

No one spoke. No one moved.

"Get to your goddamn shadow zeppelins," he barked. *"NOW!"*

Their small airships were prepping for flight at the compound's modest landing field when they arrived. A light snow-drizzle deepened the November morning chill. The other henchmen went straight to the two-seater cockpits of their craft. Kuro spotted Beverly by the airfield's hydrogen pump, watching his approach across the gravel. He'd taken the time to return to his room and put on his Samurai armour before meeting her. The weight of its metal plates felt right, along with the leather scent of its bonds and padding. She smiled appreciatively, looking him up and down, and whacked him across the arm with her cold steamsword; steel ringing off of brass.

"You'd better ignite your weapon," he said.

"Not near the hydrogen-filled balloon, thanks," she said. Her smile was radiant in the gaslight glow.

"Do we have a plan?"

"Not exactly. How about—" Her eyes suddenly grew wide, and she flung herself upon him, burying her face against his breastplate, speaking with exaggerated, breathless desperation. "Oh, Mista Campbell, sir. My cousin and that awful Chinaman are keeping me prisoner back there. Please take me with you, oh please!"

Her hair smelled of lavender. He could feel his face growing hot. "Do you think he's that much a fool?"

"All men are. Present company excepted, of course." She smiled, pulled her knit cap onto her head. "Now let's go out there and find us our worthy opponent."

A signal flare ascended into the early morning sky, and the dozen mini-zeppelins created a chorus of turbines and propellers, rising into the black-purple pre-dawn sky.

The rapturous scent of lavender lingered in Kuro's memory. They flew west in a loose formation, watching the terrain below for movement. The silence inside their own craft was deepened by the winds and light snowfall.

"There. There's a boat crossing English Bay." He saw the lights of the vessel when she pointed. A flag of dense white smoke flew from above its sole smokestack. His brow knotted. "What are those things sticking out of its sides?"

There were four large protrusions on its port and starboard gunwales, two astern and two near the prow. They looked almost like squat barrels, striped with bolted-on iron bands and cables.

"Could that be the gunboat that Campbell warned us about?" Kuro asked. "If we fly too low, they'll just shoot our zeppelins out of the sky."

"I love the way you say 'zeppelin,'" she said. "They're still close enough to shore. We'll get the other blimps to land with us at the water's edge. That lake's half-frozen already; with this cold, we can show Amboy that he's not the only one with mechanical tricks." She motioned for Kuro to take the stick for a moment as she sent out on her heliograph landing orders. The snowy eastern lakeshore didn't offer much room, but the mini-zeppelins all managed to stake down without trouble.

"Get the hoses into the water! Work those pumps!" she shouted from the cockpit, their henchmen scrambling to obey. With the autumn dawn sleeping in late, they were forced to plan their assault by lantern-light. Stepping out of the zeppelin, the narrow belt of shoreline sand was packed and hard beneath his boots.

Hoses plugged into ports on the mini-zeppelin balloons, leading to waist-high brass and iron welded boxes, which fed cannon-sized tubes that the men were dipping into the water. The lackeys toiled in pairs at the see-saw pumps protruding from the boxes sides, causing embedded needles and gauges to flutter wildly. "The hydrogen converters are experimental Usher technology, a pet project of my uncle's that Roderick carried on after he died. Half-science, half-sorcery. A chemical reaction inside those cauldrons converts the hydrogen to a hyper-freezing agent, which gets pumped out of those hoses there," she explained to Kuro. "It was intended for the moat we dug around the monastery, but it should cover this small lake too. At least long enough for our purposes."

Sure enough, even as she spoke, the calm lake surface began to crystallise. Kuro watched with amazement as a sheen of ice began to freeze around the submerged tubes along the shore. The henchmen looked up at her excitedly from their contraptions. "Not yet!" she shouted back. "Keep pumping! Get the ice firm enough to support your fat arses!" The taut zeppelin chambers began to deflate as the hydrogen drained into the converter boxes, into the solidifying lake.

Beverly picked up a few stones of varying weight, threw them and watched them skid across the ice surface. None broke through.

"The boat has stopped moving!" shouted a henchman. "It's stuck in the ice!"

Her smile was triumphant, vapour escaped her lips with a relieved exhale. "The low air temperature should help keep the ice in place, yes?" she said, raising her eyebrows to add the question mark. Kuro shrugged. She and he both looked over his heavy suit of armour. "Well, for most of us, at least." Beverly shouted back to her crew, "OK, that's enough, lay off the pumps! Charge the gunboat before they get free! Recapture that boy!"

Scharnusser's henchmen powered up what Kuro recognised as Edison-Wesson rifles, rapidly spinning the cranks bored into their stocks. Three dozen men stormed from the beach onto the lake surface, yet most of them skid, slid, and fell on their arses as soon as their boots hit the ice.

"And this is what happens," Beverly sighed again, "when you don't prepare properly." She turned to Kuro. "The Gatling is in our cargo hold. I'll aim, you feed the bullets."

"With deepest respect and apologies, I cannot help you with this weapon."

Beverly straightened as if she were just slapped in the face. Kuro did not care for her posture or expression. "What?"

"A true Samurai does not use guns, in any form. It would be a dishonour I could not bear."

He'd seen fury before in her face, but had never seen it directed at him; it was unsettling. She stepped up to him, her nose nearly touching his. "Damn your honour, we have a duty to our boss, to *my* murdered uncle."

He felt the heat of her rage, felt Hideo's disappointment in contrast. "I apologise, Miss Beverly. Perhaps one of the men can—"

"Let's get something straight, Chinaman—" and coming from Beverly, the insult cut him to the quick. "—you *serve* me, and I don't take kindly to problems with my tools in the field. Are you a problem, or a solution?"

Kuro forced back the bitter bile building in his throat. "I thought you understood my way, Bev—"

"Just go get onto Zachary Amboy's boat," she snapped. "If the father is on-board, then your duty is to kill the son before his eyes."

Kuro felt his own jaw set now with anger, the give of Hideo's neck beneath his blade tingling in his brass hand. "I will find the Amboy child and deliver the Australian back to Master Roderick, as ordered."

I will harm no child, Kuro pledged silently.

Neither moved for a long moment further, each sculpting the cold frustration between them. Beverly finally broke eye contact and singled out the nearest of Scharnusser's henchmen. "You two! Come help me with the Gatling gun."

The treacherous ice surface threatened to upturn him countless times, but Kuro managed to hold his balance and cover a sizable distance across the lake. The morning sun had finally begun to stir, adding grey and hue to the shadows, but still withholding its warmth. Soon, the boat was close enough for him to read the name, *Sheila*, stencilled across the rear hull, just above where the icy crust had frozen to its iron and timber.

A half-hearted volley traded between the Usher lackeys on the ice and a trio of shipboard riflemen at the stern railing. Two henchmen lay prone, bleeding on the ice, but the exchange was otherwise mostly ineffectual.

Fortunately for Kuro and the Usher men, the boat's bow and its large primary cannon were safely frozen forward, away from the advance on foot across the water. Kuro could see a flurry of activity on-board, with clusters of men working near the four round barrel-like protuberances spaced around the hull. A thick flag of white smoke billowed skyward from the lone stack. A shot caromed off of his brass forearm, sparking away to chew a hole in the ice at his feet. He felt nothing from the hit, but still startled and fell, sliding forward. He heard Beverly shout his name from the beach. Once he'd slid to a halt, he looked back to see her running across the icy lake top for him, leaving the two henchmen behind to finish assembling the Gatling on its stand. He waved to show he was unhurt, but still she pressed forward.

Kuro was momentarily overcome with humility, watching her display of selfless concern. "No, Beverly," he murmured, far too softly for her to hear.

A great staccato of machinery came to life from the *Sheila*. Kuro looked back to see compartments unlocking and sliding open in the four round barrels on the gunwales. Long, jointed limbs of wood and iron unfolded from within, touched down roughly on the ice coat that had ensnared the craft. Kuro then realised what the protruding barrels truly were: shoulders for legs that Amboy had appended onto his gunboat. The crew could be seen working intently; the boat's four limbs began to stamp with alarming strength upon the frozen lake. He spotted young Percy Amboy, their former captive, among the three crewmen working the rear portside leg from the safety of the deck.

First one, then another, then another of the *Sheila's* legs broke through, scattering massive, misshapen plates of ice across the black water around it.

"Shit." He'd heard the word countless times from the labourers at the Scharnusser camp. Common as the word was, it seemed appropriate here. In less than a minute, the gunship had sprouted four limbs, transforming to a great, walking beast. Its squat stance reminded him slightly of the komodo dragons his former lord had kept as pets in his homeland. The Japanese man watched wide-eyed as the massive, mecha-creature struggled to rise out of the water.

The Gatling gun awoke from the shore, its circle of barrels spinning, adding its red-hot fire to the discourse. The intensity of its attack was a stark contrast to the riflemen's scattered exchange. *Sheila's* crew hunched low to avoid the lead storm. Kuro watched a heavyset man move faster than his girth should have allowed to shield Amboy's junior, watched him cut down in front of the child.

More Ushers fell from return fire, even as a few managed to scramble from the ice up onto the deck. Kuro pressed on, drawing nearer to the boat, watching now as the integrity of the ground at his feet began to compromise and crack. He was aware of Beverly rushing behind him, catching up. Young Amboy pried his horrified stare from the bloodstained corpse of his saviour, locked eyes momentarily with Kuro.

The boat was using its limbs and internal steering to affect a slow revolution, turning around, cracking the ice that had held it. The ice squeaked and fell apart beneath his feet; jagged fissures spread outward from the *Sheila's* heavy footfalls on and through the surface. Five feet of water rippled now between the nearest rim of ice and the corner of hull behind the rear port leg. Kuro drew his *wakazashi* short sword in his left hand, hit the last piece of solid footing, and leapt from the edge of the world, hitting the gunship's hull, landing in the numbing embrace of the cold water. His short sword blade stuck and held true in the wood between the slats of the ship's iron plating. Two short meters up, a rifleman stuck his head out over the rail, grinned down at the Samurai. That common word came again to Kuro's lips.

The Gatling's deadly scrawl travelled the gunwale with a thunder of sparks and noise; its trajectory passing just over Kuro's head, sending the rifleman back to the deck. Using the wakazashi and the grip of his brass hand, Kuro began to ascend the outer hull the short distance to its deck railing. He chanced a look back, spotted Beverly on a small island of broken-away ice just behind him, her dozener pistol firing up into the *Sheila*.

"Go, Samurai! I'm right behind you!" she shouted. One of the embattled Ushers already on-board tossed a rope over the low sides for them, then turned and locked arms with one of the Amboy crew. Beverly leapt from her frozen plate just as it split and sank, catching the dangling rope. "Go!" she shouted, and the two of them climbed up to scale the railing at the same time.

Once on deck, chaos embraced them.

Beverly pointed to a man mostly obscured by his trenchcoat, goggles, and hat, holding the wheel steadily, positioned just behind the bulky cannon platform. Crewmen swirled around him, either fighting invaders or working to keep the ship moving. The boy they'd come for cowered wide-eyed around the man's feet, watching the carnage on the level below.

"Amboy," Kuro said.

"Father and son," she replied.

The *Sheila's* legs pulled the massive body upright, back out of the water, taking steps on top of the sturdy ice shelf, edging its nose toward the shore. The deck lurched with each stride, as if they were daring the frigid bay underneath to take them to its murky depths. Kuro could hear the Gatling still rattle its deadly report, but now Amboy had rotated his vessel nearly enough that his gunners were excitedly prepping their own weapons.

A number of Ushers had gained access to the deck by now, evening up the numbers against Amboy's Spartan crew. Not far from where Kuro and Beverly had boarded, Bruce Campbell was squared off against three henchmen, clearly enjoying the crackle of Tesla knuckles on his hand. A similarly-dressed man stood next to him, not quite as tall, twirling knives dexterously in both of his hands. He kicked his nearest foe overboard and looked up to see them.

"Bruce?" the bladed warrior said, his mouth a deep frown.

"What is it?" Campbell growled. "I've got three tasks to—hold on—*Yah!*—two tasks to dispatch here, mate. Is it urgent?"

"Possibly."

"A pleasure to see you again, Agent Hill," Beverly said.

The man answering to "Hill" cocked his head to one side, his eyes blank. "Have we met?"

"Oh, her. You've met her before, Brandon. I said the same thing. I'll explain later. Watch out for the Chinaman."

"Samurai are Japanese, Bruce," Hill quipped.

Kuro liked Hill already.

The two Ministry Agents charged them. A flurry of steel and sparks ensued. One of Agent Hill's knives glanced off of the Samurai shoulder plate; Campbell grabbed Kuro's right forearm with the Tesla knuckles, coursing painful voltage through his body. "I know you feel that!" the big Australian shouted, before he had to duck Beverly's steamsword.

Kuro was vaguely aware of Captain Amboy shouting from the bow, his voice cracking as he hollered at the shore, "You want to play with cycle guns? Try a Gatling cannon!" Two of his men, with Amboy stooping to lend his own strength to theirs, worked a massive crank on the cannon apparatus.

The ensuing booms were unsettling, each cannon blast coming less than a second apart. The deck shuddered with each shot. Kuro's attention was focused on the Tesla knuckles and spinning knives before him. It was difficult not to marvel at the gunship's main cannon retrofitted with a cycle of barrels, which spun and fired with precise, high-speed timing. Amidst the fray and the lingering burn of the Tesla jolt, he revelled of the battle thrill in his chest.

Meanwhile, the ship continued its odd, four-legged crawl across the lake ice, getting closer to the lakeshore, while continuing to discharge eight-pounder shots. Dawn's clouds glowed enough now to light the whole scene clearly. The Usher Gatling men fled their post, just seconds before their weapon was blown to fragments. The *Sheila* cannonmen then rotated the gun platform just slightly to focus their destructive fire on the staked zeppelins. Cannonballs spit from the barrels at high velocity, pelting the narrow beach. Amboy's son jumped up and down with each hydrogen explosion, cheering as each blimp collapsed in a heap of smouldering aluminium, hemp, and wood. Violent eruptions of sand and splintered wood burst all across the shoreline. He and his father seemed oblivious to the battle raging on the deck. Usher henchmen versus Amboy crewmen, Ministry Agents versus Samurai and Scharnusser.

"Bloody crazy Yanks," Campbell muttered through gritted teeth, his electric fists clamped around Kuro's blade. "Hey Zack, you want to—" But his shouted request would never finish. The ship's rear leg suddenly stumbled and broke through a weakness in the ice; the craft tipped abruptly backward, turning the deck into a slide. The combatants staggered, fell, and slid into each other, changing the game like the tipping of a chessboard. Kuro caught Brandon Hill in an awkward embrace. Campbell fell into a risqué position on top of Beverly, but she flung him away.

"Cease fire! Cease fire!" Amboy's voice could be heard over the commotion. Battle roars turned to shouts of alarm. The boy's high voice rang out clearly over the rest. Ice around the boat shattered and flaked. *Sheila's* other three legs continued to pump, but only squeaked and slid, alternately finding thin ice and water, their multiple joints struggling to adjust to the slippery, unsure surface.

Kuro momentarily lost his opponents, his balance, and his focus, sliding and slamming hard into the stern railing, only vaguely aware of Brandon Hill climbing free. He shook his head, trying to clear the daze, struggling to track the Ministry agents, distantly expecting to feel the burning dig of a bullet or blade into his flesh at any moment. The ticking of his arm sounded thunderous in his head. There was a new timbre to the shouts that cut through his haze, the foreign words making sense again as clarity returned.

"Don't hurt him!" Was that Hill's voice?

"Hold on, hold on!" Campbell's voice. No doubt.

Kuro looked up to his left. Beverly held Amboy's son in her arms, her pistol against the boy's temple as her steamsword lay hissing with heat next to her leg. The boy's face looked just as frightened as on the evening when Kuro and Hideo had stolen him from his father's island.

"Beverly," Kuro said softly.

The Ministry agents stood silently nearby, holding their empty hands out to plead calm. The Ushers and Amboy crew around the deck were stock still in place, not daring to move. Ice sculptures for this moment in time.

It was the laughter—the wild cackle of a madman—that grabbed Kuro's attention away from the tableau.

Zachary Amboy, holding tight to the wheel during the slide, chortled and guffawed at the grey sky above him, then retrained his gaze upon Beverly holding his son. The vacant anger in his grin set a profound disquiet upon Kuro's soul.

"You will let him go, you know," Amboy said, laughing.

"Does he deserve more mercy than my uncle?" Beverly shouted, pulling back the hammer on her dozener pistol. "Mikael Scharnusser sends his regards from hell!"

Percy—held tightly against her—sobbed, calling out for his father.

"He's only seven," Kuro pleaded.

"Quiet, Samurai," she hissed, her anger feral.

He swore silently in Japanese, his affections for her reeling amidst the peril and horror of her threat to the child. Campbell and Hill had both inched almost imperceptibly closer. Zachary Amboy was still chuckling quietly, madly, coming down the slight companionway from the bow.

"Beverly, we'll die here if you do this," Kuro said. "There will be no honour in these deaths."

"We have as many men as they do. Don't be a coward. My family will be avenged…" and Beverly said more, but he'd stopped listening. He allowed a momentary sigh, squeezing his eyes together wearily, then reopening them.

It was a precision strike that he'd have performed in younger days with unthinking, easy confidence, when his sword hand was still flesh and bone. Yet, even with the clockwork uncertainty of his artificial forearm, Kuro moved quickly, flicking his katana tip in close, inches from the boy's face, nicking Beverly's fingers and knocking the pistol from her grasp. It fired once over Percy's head, eliciting a scream from the boy. Shouts sounded out from all around the deck. Beverly clutched her bloody fingers, her expression plummeting from surprise to pain to anger.

Percy wriggled free, sprang toward the security of Bruce Campbell's knee. Beverly scooped up the steamsword and lunged, but Kuro stepped in the way, easily parrying her strike with his katana. She roared frustration and rounded on him.

The swords locked in an aggressive kiss, her strength and push driving him back; he locked in a stance, rounded his blade free, stepped back toward her. The two exchanged heated blows, sparks and heat flying from each parry. Each knew the other's moves intimately from their monastery courtyard practices, although neither had ever seen such ferocity and strength from the other. Beverly's sword had always been cool; Kuro's had always been made of wood.

The boat lurched as it found its footing and clambered up to walk the ice again, its systems running automatically, a crewman on the wheel deck now, driving them toward the shore. The Ushers and Amboy crew had not returned to their own skirmish, still entranced by the duel, but had backed away to give the swordfighters berth. The boat's rocking was gentler this time; everyone managed to remain upright.

"Anyone else feel like we're eavesdropping on a lovers' spat?" Campbell asked no one in particular. One of Amboy's crewmen tried to push past Campbell, who shoved him roughly back into the crowd. Someone responded with a punch, and the temporary calm was utterly shattered. Shouts of surprise and alarm swelled around the decks like turbulent waters preluding a storm.

Kuro and Beverly continued to circle, strike, and counter, unheeding of their surroundings. Their swords drew them in close again, their faces close, their eyes locked, their feet fixed firmly near the railing, neither saying a word. Beverly's hair whipped forward, brushing the Samurai's face through his helmet.

Kuro felt a warrior's instinct to turn around and face a new danger, but dared not take his focus from Beverly's smouldering blade. "Here goes nothing," he heard from behind, the Australian drawl unmistakable.

Something large, hard and muscular slammed into him, thrusting him up against Beverly, taking them hard into the railing, momentum spinning them up and overboard. All three of them—as Kuro realised Campbell was with them—hit the ice hard. Beverly skidded a few meters away. Kuro's heavy armour shattered the ice, plunging him into the frigid waters below. He did not have long to react to the needles of pain surrounding him as a large hand grabbed the Samurai by his arm, and pulled him up to the surface. He lay on his back next to Campbell for two quick breaths, knowing that anything longer would be fatal.

Beverly's steamsword arced down from above, missing by less than a second as the men rolled apart, carving a channel into the ice where they'd just been. Kuro was soon on his feet, sliding, leaping at her with an off-balance katana counterattack. Bruce scrambled on all fours until he was a safe distance from the combatants, the treacherous surface refusing the purchase of his numb fingers. The *Sheila* continued its fast-paced tread across the thawing ice surface, moving away from them where they'd fallen, bearing quickly down on the shore. More and more Usher henchmen were pitched over the rails as it stepped onto the narrow beachhead, reflecting the turn of the deck battle in Amboy's favour.

Kuro breathed heavily, watching Beverly for some sign of emotion, but her face was void of all but anger. Her eyes saw him, but were as lifeless and mechanical as his ticking arm, as if she'd retreated somewhere deep inside, leaving her body to function as a remorseless war automaton. Her breathing was coming as heavy as his, the vapour mingling with the rising mist from her steamsword. Hideo had been right. He knew the path they had chosen led to dishonour and darkness. Kuro understood now, but refused to die by his own hand. He would die for what was right.

End of pause. They fought across the lake's slippery surfaces, leaping from broken ice plates to sturdy shelves to half-submerged sheets, each as watchful of the treacherous, brittle footing as they were of their opponent. The sulphuric scent of her sword pommel's boiler was strong in the air; it hissed with each steel touch of blades. Three grunts of effort from Beverly, three strikes, eliciting three parries and three steps back from Kuro. She chewed her lower lip, immersed in focus, again reminding him of their morning practices.

It was a crack in the ice that finally betrayed him.

She grunted with three forceful high strikes, driving Kuro back. His foot broke through a weak patch in the ice, plunging his backward step into the frozen watery void. He flung his arms up, off-balance, his left boot submerged. His brass arm flung in front his chest, just in time to shield the piercing thrust of her steamsword. The blade tip drove easily through, skewering gears and cords, protruding far out through the other side of his forearm. Kuro pulled his right foot free, adjusted his footing, and fell forward into his arm with a deep-throated cry, the super-heated swordpoint driving unchallenged through his armoured breastplate. Steel dug through cold steel and leather, then flesh and bone beneath.

Beverly gasped, her cold resolve dropping away to panic, awareness dawning of what had just happened.

Kuro had taken numerous glancing sword blows and cuts in battle before, had even lost his arm and endured the surgical attachment of a brass prosthetic; but nothing had been like this. The scalding pain was unlike anything he'd ever experienced, radiating from a core deep inside his breast. Smoke rising, the pungent scent of scorched flesh assailed his nostrils. His right arm remained stuck before him, unable to move, unable to pry the smouldering steamsword from its lodging inside his ribcage. Beverly's hands let go of the pommel, went to her face in horror, her mouth open in a silent scream, tears falling freely to the surface of the ice. Before her, the Samurai fell to his knees, the sword still lodged in his arm and his torso. Blood flowed freely beneath the cloth and steel of his armour, running crimson rivulets into the ice.

"What have I done, Kuro?"

She fell to her knees to meet him, touched his skewered brass forearm, gently pulling to unsheathe the hot blade from his chest. The katana remained fixed in his grip, but both swords fell uselessly away as the dead arm slumped to his side. She pulled the helmet from his head and touched his face, already gone as pale as the frozen surface below. She leaned her forehead into his.

"What have I done?"

He dropped the gauntlet from his left hand, weakly touched her hand on his cheek. "I have been felled by the most worthy of opponents," he wheezed, pulling his head back to look at her, to truly see her one final time, her face haloed against the rising sun. "This…is…an honourable death. *Arigato,* Miss Beverly."

He struggled to forge a bloody smile, grateful for the compassion returned to her eyes.

A good memory to take with him to the other side.

Bruce Campbell sat a distance from her weeping embrace, not counting the time. The *Sheila* was gone from the lake now, although the trail it had trampled through the woodland beyond the shore was clearly visible. When the lady turned to him, he knew she was ready. Bruce gently extracted the Samurai's body from her arms, hoisting the armour-clad man across his shoulders to carry him to the shore. Beverly followed silently after him, weeping abated, her face now a tear-streaked mask of regret.

He laid Kuro inside one of the few mini-zeppelins still able to fly. Bruce drove Beverly's steamsword into the ground before offering her the passenger's seat.

"We're not leavin' him out here," Bruce assured her. "We do need to reach my mate on board *Sheila*. Are we clear?"

"Crystal," Beverly muttered.

The mini-zeppelin's engine's spun up, and the three of them were airborne, following the trail left by the walking boat.

His fingers splayed around the pilot's stick as ahead of them, clouds of dark some mushroomed in the distance. Bruce glanced over at Beverly who was staring out of her own window, her eyes empty, aloof. He saw in the armrest between them a small wireless and connected its leads, bringing a current to the small device. He tapped in the first word of his recognition code, tapped in the second...

"*Klaatu...Barada...*bugger me," Bruce grumbled. "What is that last bloody word?"

Again, he tapped in the first word of his recognition code, tapped in the second...

...and he took his best guess at the final word in the sequence.

Their mini-zeppelin glided over where the Scharnusser Fortress had once been. In its place now was a smouldering ruin of bricks, timber, and ash. *Sheila* stood triumphantly nearby, as a predator stands over its prey. Even after they landed without incident, Beverly barely seemed moved by the destruction of her home. Early evening chill had settled in, dragging the temperature down to below freezing; but she remained standing vigil outside the mini-zeppelin, staring at the Samurai through the window.

Bruce spotted Brandon Hill in the cockpit of an exo-goliath, in spite of the cold, piloting it through slow, awkward dance steps to the delight of some ship's crewmen on the ground.

"Good Lord, Campbell," Brandon scolded, climbing out of the machine, "when will you learn that bloody recognition code properly? *Nicto!* The last word in the sequence is *Nicto!*"

216

"The important thing, Hill, is that you recognised enough of it not to shoot me out of the sky." He motioned at the destruction around him. "So this is how you keep an eye on barking mad Zachary? Where is the yank, anyway?"

"Captain Amboy and his son are safely aboard *Sheila*, inside the main cabin. I wouldn't go in there at the moment, though. He's in a bit of a state. All of this demolition was seemingly for naught, other than the fall of an Usher house," Brandon said, producing his favourite smoking pipe. "Roderick Scharnusser managed to escape. Probably a private shadow zeppelin. You think Amboy was a madman before? You should have seen him when he found Roddy's taunting escape note. But my word, Bruce. You should have seen that Gatling cannon take down the fortress walls. It was incredible."

Hill stuck his pipe into his mouth, looked over Beverly, then shot Bruce a non-verbal question. Her eyes remained downcast, unseeing. Campbell only shook his head in response.

"We'll bring Scharnusser to justice, mate, of that I'm sure. But it's probably best that he escaped Zachary Amboy's clutches here." Campbell noted the snow starting to fall. Beverly still remained stock still outside their mini-zeppelin. He walked over to her, removed his overcoat, and laid it across Beverly's shoulders. She looked up at them both, noticing them as if for the first time, and nodded slowly, her eyes glassed with fresh tears. "There's been enough death today."

Hill lit his own pipe, tingeing the air around them with the sweet scent of his tobacco. "So," he said, giving his posh Gourd Calabash a few puffs, "we settle things here, then back to London?"

"Not yet. We got to get the boilers topped off on this bird here."

"Wait just a—" Brandon spluttered, motioning to the remnants of the monastery around them. "You're going to make me deal with all this alone?"

"You'll be fine, mate," Bruce said, slapping Brandon's chest with the back of his hand. "Go on—would I ever put a fellow Ministry Agent in danger?"

Brandon huffed, placed his pipe back in his mouth, and after a few agitated puffs, disappeared into the settling mayhem, calling out directions, attempting to direct Amboy's crew to some semblance of order.

Bruce watched the airship crews tending to his mini-zeppelin before returning to Beverly. "Got an errand to run, don't we?" he asked.

She nodded, her reply tight and strained. "Satsuma."

A Nocturne for Alexandrina

Tee Morris

London, England
Buckingham Palace
1839

For the first time since becoming queen, Victoria—unequivocally—was not amused.

Today was just one of those days where being queen really was more trouble than the title warranted, and certainly there was a lot of trouble to being queen of the British Empire. First, you needed to look like a queen. That went without saying. Getting up early enough to dress the part. Then there was the pomp and circumstance on the tiniest of life's most mundane details. Just making it to the table to enjoy a hearty breakfast with her beloved betrothed, Albert, practically demanded an act from Parliament. Then came the maintenance of the Empire itself. Petition upon petition from her overseas representatives, all imploring the crown for more money. Many of these "imperative missives" from ambassadors were about as dodgy and as superfluous as a man trying to sell high quality sand to a Persian desert gypsy. This, however, did not try her patience so much when compared to the explorers wanting to "expand the Empire" with her financial help.

Antarctica? Really? Why in the name of God would anyone wish to claim any part of that frozen wasteland?

She then felt a light trickle against the back of her neck. *I'm the Queen of the British Empire,* she seethed, *and with all this technology in my realm they can't keep this palace cool in the summer? It's not even two years old! Bloody hell.*

Suddenly conquering Antarctica struck her as a good idea. A summer retreat there sounded quite nice. Perhaps this was the price of being "the first" of anything—a sacrifice of creature comforts.

What gave Victoria a real chill of dismay was that she had only been queen for just over two years. And this miserable, droll routine would be her life for the next few decades. No, becoming queen had not come as a *complete* shock to her. Victoria's entire life and training had been leading to this, but certainly this predestination did not make the transition any easier. Good Lord, just the news reaching her had hardly been an easy process. She could still remember that night involving a rather delightful dream of a Scotsman from good breeding, fine manners, and the kind of calf muscles, just visible from his kilt, that promised thighs and accompanying backsides a woman would take great delight in having within reach. She was enjoying a day's riding and then a lovely tea—and that was when she knew it was a dream, of course, as a Scotsman, no matter how fine the breeding, would not enjoy a tea, nor describe an Assam as delightful. He was about to become quite forward when she was awakened at the break of dawn by Mamma, informing her that the Archbishop of Canterbury and Lord Conyngham were in her sitting room, awaiting an audience.

How disappointing. She would have preferred to return to her rather saucy dream, but instead she was to accept the charge of Queen of the British Empire.

Now, Alexandrina Victoria, crowned Queen Victoria, merely tightened her smile and gave the most imperceptible of sighs through her nose. Yes, even queens woke up on the wrong side of beds, even ones as plush and as comfortable as the ones in Buckingham Palace. She had to find a silver lining to this day, or remain trapped in this rut. For the rest of her life. She was queen; but she was human, too. Currently, she was bored and frustrated to the point of tears.

"Finally," spoke her Lord Chamberlain, "we have a request for an audience."

Then he paused. Queen Victoria crooked an eyebrow, inclining her head to the Lord Chamberlain. *Yes. Yes. Out with it.*

"This request is — well…" He went to speak again, but his words appeared replaced by a clumsy silence. "He wants permission to establish a new branch of Her Majesty's government."

"I see," Victoria acknowledged with a nod. *Let's see,* she thought, suppressing a wry grin as she dreamt up new ministries. *We are in need of a*

Ministry of Truly Appalling Pub Songs. We have no Ministry of Tweed. I think there are some patterns that are in desperate need of regulation. And then of course there is the priority to establish a Ministry of Silly Wal—

"Your Majesty," the Lord Chamberlain spoke, his voice shattering her witticism. "This branch he proposes would cover the entire Empire. It would be a global entity."

That caught her full attention.

"Does this petitioner have a name?"

"Professor Culpepper Source." The Lord Chamberlain paused to look over the papers in his hands, and then added, "He's a scientist."

"Is his name registered or recognised in any of our Royal Societies?"

"No, Your Majesty."

She turned to look at him. "And the reasons behind how he made it this far in the petition process and why I am seeing him this afternoon?"

"It is the evidence he has presented to his patrons and, in particular, to me personally."

"Are you saying you yourself have entertained this Professor Source?"

The man's complexion blanched as he spoke. He looked so pale in that moment that Victoria believed he would succumb to the vapours. "I cannot impress upon you the importance of seeing this man."

Perhaps Victoria's silver lining was at hand. "We shall see this man straight away then."

She was a tad disappointed at catching a glimpse of the petitioner when he came around the corner. The closer he drew, the fatter he became. He was a portly gentleman, with a rather bushy moustache that in some odd manner flattered him. The receding hairline, however, she found slightly irritating. Perhaps with a full head of hair, she would have found him quite dashing. In a rather plump sort of way. The suit seemed common enough. Not of any fashion she recognised, but of a tweed that did not speak of any fortune or elevated station.

A scientist. That is exactly what he looked like. A kindly scientist.

On this deduction, she gave a long, low sigh. *This day, I fear,* she grumbled inwardly, *is not going to get any better.*

"Your Majesty," he announced, giving a deep bow. When he came up, he paused, taking in a deep breath.

"Something amiss, Professor Source?"

He blinked. "Beg your pardon, mum?"

Mum?! Victoria asked, her back straightening slightly. *Did he just call me 'Mum'?!*

She began to worry about her appearance; she was only twenty, after all!

The man then released a little cough as he began what appeared to be a case of some sort. "Do forgive my impertinence, Your Majesty. I'm just a bit nervous, is all. I did not expect to see you upon such short notice."

On that, Victoria softened. An honest man. What a refreshing change. "Well, professor, it would seem that Fortune favours you as we are having a rather slow day here at the palace. Still, our time for an audience with you is fleeting."

"That it is, Your Majesty, so let us not bandy about." He clapped his hands together and then motioned to her. "I desire your company tonight, and yours alone."

That gave the collected court quite a shock. Victoria, on the other hand, raised an eyebrow. A bit bumbling. Sincere. Mindful of manners. And now, forward. With her.

This ought to be fun.

"This is a bold request you make of your Queen."

"Yes. So bold that you may wish to have me thrown in irons, but what I wish to bring to your attention—more importantly, what I have to show you—are matters pertaining to you and only you."

"Are these matters pertaining to the preservation of the Empire?"

The odd man nodded, his two chins jiggling as he did. "Of course."

"Then why not share these matters with my Privy Council, with those whom I trust with my life and with the direction of the Empire?"

"With all due respect and honours, Your Majesty," Source began, "you may trust them. I, however, do not."

Her Lord Chancellor stepped forward, and Victoria started at the deep hue of red his face had turned. "How dare you, sir! You did not tell me of this outlandish—"

Professor Source spoke over his tirade. "Sir, may I remind you of our previous luncheon, or should I reveal those daguerreotypes shared in confidence?"

That stopped the Lord Chancellor. Quickly. His red blush receded to a ghostly pale wash. He swallowed, glanced towards Victoria, and then took a few steps back.

"Is this true?" Victoria asked the scientist.

"Did I lie to your Lord Chancellor, Your Majesty? No. I am no cad. Did I withhold a few details in my petition?" His eyes twinkled. "Yes. I am a bit of a rogue, on occasion I am afraid."

She had worn a smile often in court, but this one was the first in a long time that was truly sincere.

"And why should we trust you?"

"Because I am the only one you can trust concerning the darkness that threatens your empire." He gave his odd cravat a slight adjustment and then tipped his head back proudly. "I have been witness to things unparalleled and unexplainable, and while some of these revelations are fantastic and inspiring, there are phantasms and evil forces beyond our collected comprehensions that counter their purity and benevolence."

Victoria felt herself shift from intrigued to positively enthralled.

"You are a most peculiar man." She rose from her throne, and gestured him closer to her, though her guards flanked them as they walked. "You also have conviction."

"Shall I expect for your company then upon the hour of nine?" He reached into his pocket and checked the time. "That should give you ample time to dress in something appropriate. Something that would allow for movement and—considering who you are—anonymity." He then paused, as if a thought suddenly came to him. "Dress warm."

She crooked an eyebrow at that. "Warm? But it's summer."

"I know," he said with a nod. "Trust me. Dress warm."

Victoria pursed her lips, looked to either of her guards, then leaned in and whispered, "Outdoors, are we?"

"Avebury Circle."

"At night?" She glanced over to one of her guards. He looked poised and ready for an order. She leaned forward to make certain her guard couldn't hear her reply to the odd man with "Sounds like a lovely evening."

The professor reached into his coat, and produced a small folded parchment held between two fingers. "I will be by the fire, waiting for your arrival, Your Majesty." His eyes darted to the present gentry, and then he whispered, "Alone."

"We can make no promises."

"Nor do I expect you to." He gave a wink, extending the parchment to her. "I could be mad. Or an anarchist. Or both."

"Doubtful," she retorted, taking the paper from between his fingers. "You are far too clever."

He beamed in reply, stepped back from the Queen, and spoke to her again in a full, proper voice. "Your Majesty, my gratitude to you and your devoted court for your time." He took up the small case by his feet, and then with a few more steps back, his body remaining in a slight bow, the man turned on his heels and walked out.

"Your Majesty?" the Lord Chancellor spoke finally, causing her to start. "Your Majesty, I am sorry, I had no idea—"

"He shared something with you?" Victoria asked. "Exactly what, may I ask?"

His complexion paled even further. "Documents."

"Really?" She felt her twin shadows follow her up to the man. He flinched as she leaned into him, his eyes seeming to bore into the floor underfoot. "These documents must have some hold upon you."

"Your Majesty," he spoke, his voice hard and brittle. "What I saw…"

Tears welled in the man's eyes, and Victoria stepped back. Now she was to be the one stunned to silence. She was queen of the most powerful nation in the world; yet an odd man armed only with a suitcase, it would seem, could win himself a private audience.

She read the time and place on the parchment, and then folded it back up neatly.

Yes, a bit of intrigue was in order. Things were getting unbearably dull in court. Now free of Mamma's influence and ruler of the British Empire, it was high time for her to stretch her legs and have a bit of fun.

No one paid her a second glance once she walked into the humble tavern just outside the stones of Avebury Circle. The hearth was modest but managed to give a hint of warmth in this quiet corner of her empire. Just as promised, Culpepper Source sat in a lovely, high-backed chair, and he stoked coals in the fireplace. Victoria tugged the lapels of her black coat tighter and walked across smooth, worn planks that groaned lightly as she closed on him. She did not concern herself with stealth or with grace. Her attendants were all enjoying a lovely deep sleep thanks to a delightful laudanum concoction that her Mamma used on Victoria when she was younger. She was as he wished her to be—alone, which could have been an invitation for the downfall of the crown. Only two years into her reign as queen and to be kidnapped or worse, assassinated, and the British Empire would be thrown into chaos. And yet, here she was, the Queen of the Empire, in The Red Lion, unattended, meeting what her attendants in court—all save for her Lord Chancellor—believed was a madman.

How thrilling, she thought with a delightful rush.

He placed the poker back into its holder and then sat back into a reclining position. "I would stand upon ceremony," he spoke over his shoulder softly, "but even with the collected subjects here, few as they are, that is attention neither of us desire, now is it?"

She gave a giggle and took the seat opposite of him. Victoria crossed her legs, taking a moment to enjoy the outrageous outfit she currently wore. The thigh-high boots, even with their dull finish, caught the light of the tiny fire as did the leather trousers she wore. The clothes would have appeared more appropriate for riding, had she decided that black suddenly suited her as a colour. He looked at her and smiled approvingly. No doubt, he found the cleavage she was sporting with her cinched corset and waistcoat most unexpected as well as most appreciated.

"I took you on your word," Victoria purred, her breath appearing for just a moment before disappearing as wisps of æther, "and dressed appropriately."

"Indeed. You look hardly ladylike or appropriate." His eyes sparkled in the firelight. "I approve."

Victoria gave her lapels another tug and looked around her. "And thank you for advising me on dressing warmly. I had no idea—"

"The chill you are feeling has nothing to do with the weather or even an odd day of the season." He looked over his shoulder, fixing his eyes on the publican for a moment, and then glanced around at those sitting at tables, many of them enjoying a soup or a pint. When Source spoke to her, his voice had dropped to nearly a whisper. "Your Majesty, what I have to show you tonight are those responsible for the anomaly."

"Those responsible?" Victoria considered that turn of phrase, and then asked, "You're saying this cold is the work of man, not God?"

Source went to answer but paused as if remembering something important. He pulled out his pocket watch and clicked his tongue lightly. "Actually, Your Majesty, it would be easier if I got on with it and showed you." He stood, and then slipped a large haversack across his shoulder. He patted it for good measure, and motioned for the door. "Shall we?"

Victoria looked at the door of the Red Lion and felt something in her slowly recoil, much like a cat feeling growing danger and slinking back into a corner. Stepping through that door carried a cost, something akin to that fateful night when she was first addressed as Queen of England. She knew following Professor Culpepper Source would completely change everything.

Source was standing there at the door. He was far from the hearth, but his eyes still twinkled.

Victoria placed her palms gently on her hips, feeling the two concealed Derringers that the Lord Chancellor insisted she have upon her person. Instinct told her she would be using them tonight, but that same instinct told her she would not need them against the professor.

When she reached the door, he handed her a pair of Starlight goggles, leaned in, and stated quite plainly, "Do not leave my side, no matter what this evening offers. I wish to return you to the throne in one piece, and cannot guarantee as much if you gallivant off without me."

What cheek! Whatever made Source think he could address her in such a fashion?

She would have voiced her outrage, had it not been for the look in his eyes.

Victoria nodded, slipping the goggles around her neck and giving him a reassuring "Very well."

The affirmation, however, did not sound all too convincing to her.

At first, there seemed to be no need for the Starlight goggles. They kept to the path defined by the outer circle's larger stones. While still visible under the light of the full moon, the Red Lion was growing farther and farther off. As clouds began to block out the moonlight, however, the quaint pub seemed to wink out of existence.

When her Starlights revealed the thick darkness, it dawned on her that it had been a crystal clear night moments before. A full moon. No sign of any cloud in the sky. Now, they were both plunged into a thick darkness where even the goggles were struggling to grant her vision. She looked up to see a rippled, tumultuous cover suspended above her. Not a single ray from the pale goddess of night pierced the heavy sky now over them.

"Victoria," came a whisper.

Hearing such presumption ripped her gaze from the obscured heavens back to a pair of Starlights looking at her.

"All will be made clear to you," he whispered. "Just stay close and not a word until we are well-hidden."

Well-hidden? Calling the queen of the empire by her Christian name? And a cloud cover that appeared from nowhere?

This intrigue was more and more exciting with each passing moment.

Taking her gingerly by the wrist, he guided her to a tree growing just at the top of a deep ditch. He checked his watch, and then adjusted the goggles as he studied the clearing before them. He freed from his pocket a small flask and took a quick sip.

"Care for a nip?" he asked Victoria pleasantly.

When in Rome. *"C'est bon,"* and she took a swig.

Whatever was in the flask tasted of nuts, and gave her body a delightful warmth a few moments later.

"Direct your eyes to this open field before us," he whispered, slipping the flask back into his coat pocket. "The party I wish for you to see should be appearing momentarily."

A deep rumble sounded in her ears, but instead of casting a glance to the far-off thunder, she concentrated on where Source assured her "all will be revealed."

Wind rustled through the nearby grove. Again came a threatening rumble of rain. Why was it so bloody cold? She dared to look back up for that full moon she remembered shining over the Red Lion when something caught her attention. Something in the forest. Running. Drawing closer, fast.

Whatever they were, the beasts were about to emerge from the wood just off to their right.

The shadows leapt across the ditch to land softly in the clearing, but the creatures stepping into her enhanced sight were not what she expected. They were human. Women, it seemed, by their gait. Three of them.

She could hear another pattering of feet and then the noise ceased. Coming to meet them from the opposite direction, also dressed in some odd cloak, was a man.

"Professor, they seem to be talking to one another."

"Yes, yes," he muttered, and then offered her what appeared to be a palm-sized suction cup. "Place that on your ear, if you please."

When she did as told, a woman's voice could be heard as if Victoria stood next to her. She followed the cable connected to the earcup, and it ended at what appeared to be a small wax cylinder with a strange bell device running from it that pointed in the direction of the gathered in the clearing.

"What is that?" she asked.

"What I sincerely hope will become a tool of the trade," he whispered, placing a similar cup to his own ear. "But please, Your Majesty, we must be quiet."

She turned her Starlights back to the clearing, and now saw a woman closing on the man. "Are you certain it is to be this way, Matthew?"

"It must be," he told her in reply. "The only alternative we have is to live in hiding, and I have grown tired of it. We strike, and we strike now. The patronage of the House of Usher will give us everything we need."

"We have never needed the help of those outside our coven," the woman in the middle protested.

"It is a new world, Evanna," Matthew conceded. "The Industrial Age is bringing upon us changes that we must understand, that we must exploit, before society does so. Then can we return to the true power we once held in this land."

Victoria felt herself bristle at that. "Not very pleasant people, are they, Professor?"

"Your Majesty, please," he whispered before placing a pudgy finger to his lips.

Her mouth opened with a reminder to whom he addressed, but the words caught in her throat on hearing the third woman in the clearing ask, "Did you hear that?"

The four faces turned in their direction, motionless save for the wind that tousled their cloaks. Victoria felt something in her stomach roil. Outlandish as it was, some instinct whispered to her that these four could hear her heartbeat.

It was Matthew that finally broke the silence, turning to the elder woman and assuring her, "Merely the Goddess, Miriam, whispering her approval through the trees. Nothing more."

Victoria finally released the breath trapped inside and her muscles relaxed.

The chill suddenly kissed the back of her neck, raising goose flesh on the nape of it and down along her arms. The professor's hand gently touched hers, and she saw him staring at her through his own goggles.

"The wind," he whispered.

In her Starlights, the one called Miriam snapped her head back in their direction. She was sniffing the air.

"A man. And a woman. Over there. And…" Her voice trailed off. "Something metallic. I smell grease."

"Right then," Source muttered. "Time to leave."

"Not just yet," Victoria whispered. "You should give my guard a moment to intervene."

"Your what?" And both the Professor and she returned their gaze to the four treasonous strangers.

Behind them, the shadows were taking forms of featureless grey men. The closer they drew, the more details appeared in their Starlights.

"You really didn't think the Queen of England would go unattended to Avebury Circle in the middle of the night?" Victoria said with a toss of her head. "If you did, you really are mad."

The four traitors turned to the advancing soldiers. They had only taken three steps when the Queen's guard stopped, shouldering their rifles, calling out, "Halt in the name of Queen Victoria!"

They kept walking. In the Starlights, Victoria watched them slip free of their robes, their pale skin giving them semblances of phantoms closing in on her loyal subjects.

"I command you to ha—"

That was the last utterance from the soldier as the man named Matthew disappeared, his form moulting, pieces of flesh peeling away from him as he walked, revealing something like a dog, or something that could have passed for a dog had it not sprouted bat-like wings and borne the posture of a small bear. The enormous size of the beast did not hinder its movement as it was on the soldier a moment later. There was no shot in defence, nor was there a scream.

It was all over in seconds.

"Your Majesty," the professor said, tightening the strap of his Starlights, "whatever I tell you to do, do not question it. You must trust me. Secure your goggles. You will need them."

Victoria gave her own straps a few sharp tugs, feeling the goggles press deeper into her face. They were going to make a run for it, a tactic she would be hard pressed to hold in question as she watched the three women shimmer in the same grotesque manner Matthew had. With their massive wings cutting through the air, the four creatures made quick work of Victoria's elite, then looked back where they hid. Through her goggles she could see small voids, where, no doubt, amber eyes would have stared back at her, narrow on her. Around their monstrous snouts were dark patches of what Victoria deduced was fresh blood and gore, now smeared into their own sheer pelts. Their heads jerk upward ever so slightly, nostrils flaring as the wind carried her fear to them.

"Follow me. Stay close."

Professor Source leapt free of their hiding place, running *towards* the beasts, setting quite the pace for such a rotund gentleman.

"Bloody hell," Victoria hissed as she bounded into the night on the Professor's heels.

The queen could hear their footsteps pounding against the grass, but her eyes were focused in front of them on the four beasts, muscles underneath their smooth, shiny pelts bending and rippling underneath folded wings as they closed the distance. In her Starlights, she watched details emerge with each step. The beasts' breath appearing for only a moment before the night's chill claimed its warmth. Long, thin mouths that could not completely conceal such protruding curved teeth.

Closer.

Closer.

The alpha male, Matthew, leapt upward, his wingspan extending fully to catch an invisible wind, causing his fantastic form to reach vertically into the night.

Victoria felt Source take her by the arm. He called out, "Slide."

On feeling him tug, she followed his lead, repeating his command to herself as she tucked one leg underneath her and reached forward with the other. Their momentum and the evening's moisture underfoot carried them onward, sending them underneath the flying monster and between those flanking him. Over the shrill, squeaking sounds of their bodies sliding on the wet grass, Victoria could also hear the dark beasts slipping and stumbling over themselves. Whatever precious seconds they had would be enough to stay ahead of them.

His grip tightened on her arm as they stood.

"Professor?" No need to whisper now. They were completely in sight.

"Your Majesty, you must trust me," he said, pulling a small rod from his coat pocket. His other hand snaked inside his coat's outer pocket, but his eyes never left the pack of four creatures regrouping before them. "Look above us—are the clouds parting?"

She looked behind them, and up. Much like a curtain rising to reveal Macready's boy-king overlooking the field of Agincourt, the blanket of clouds were thinning, and suddenly they were awash in moonlight. She squinted from behind the Starlights, and then removed them all together. Victoria could now see the four beasts pacing slowly, sizing up their prey for a final attack, only a pale illumination cutting them free of the night's canvas. She swallowed, and flinched at how dry and grating her throat felt.

"Yes," she whispered.

"Hold your ground with me," Professor Source spoke over the packs' low, undulating growl. He still kept his eyes on them, even as he affixed a perfectly clear crystal onto the end of what now Victoria could make out in his hand to be something like a brass spike.

The pack leader—Matthew, Victoria had no doubt—did not look to either of the three she-beasts. He did not bark a command, or even paw at the ground. He gave a snort, conjuring a veil of breath that concealed his head for a heartbeat. When the warm mist dissipated, Matthew leapt forward, his only sound being his panting. Even. Rhythmic. Controlled.

With a tiny *click*, the crystal locked into place.

Victoria could hear a quick, soft snarl accompanying each breath now. The creature's eyes flared crimson in the full moonlight.

Then came the small explosion of steam from Professor Source. His hand was pressing a small button in the brass rod, and now the rod extended to the length of a quarterstaff. Source reared back, and drove the metal staff into the ground.

On entering the grass and earth underfoot, Victoria watched the other three beasts flinch and melt quickly back to their human forms, their naked bodies pale and ghostly under the moonlight. They were now on their knees, grabbing at their stomachs and chests, wailing in pain.

Matthew appeared far too determined to slow down, even though his growl told Victoria he had been struck hard by something. It pushed on through whatever pain had stricken his followers, threatening to overtake them in a moment.

Victoria started back when the beam appeared. It was as brilliant as a noonday sun, only pure white in its colour. The blast lifted Matthew off the grass and held him in the air, suspending him in time and space. She was not certain how long the winged creature remained frozen above the ground; and in this grandeur, Victoria became aware of Matthew's nightmarish form. He had still not reverted to a human shape like his companions. She watched him fall, but his body never hit the ground. The beam exploded out from its back, splitting in three to strike each of the wailing women. As it had been with Matthew, the women swayed back in a slow, languid manner, defying the natural way of things before winking out of existence with a sudden crack of thunder.

From above Victoria's head, something popped and sizzled. She looked up to see the quartz obelisk at the tip of the staff emitting light wisps of smoke. It seemed to be glowing faintly, its colour reflecting the moon high above it.

His eyes betrayed nothing. The skin around them tightened for a moment, the only indication that he himself had not been frozen by whatever force he had conjured mere moments ago. A mist appeared under his flaring nostrils, and his grip on the brass staff in his hand tightened.

Victoria looked around her. Only mist and moonlight touched the grass of Avebury Circle. The stones remained standing as silent sentinel in the night.

"Your Majesty," Professor Source spoke gently, "I believe we should return to the pub. Warm ourselves by the fire. And," he chortled, managing a friendly grin, "perhaps indulge with a wee drop of sherry."

Flames danced merrily in the hearth. Pint glasses of stout, ale, and bitter mimicked the overflowing conversation, a delightful mingling of mirth and laughter. From the kitchen came sweet, succulent smells of dishes far heartier than anything found in her royal kitchens. Victoria thought absently that perhaps, on nights when she craved something simpler, she should request from her cook a Shepard's Pie. Any chef worth their salt would have a good recipe for Shepard's Pie.

The diminutive glass of sherry was placed ever so gently before her. Two fingers then slid it closer to her hand. She picked it up, and that was when she noticed the tremble. She was no longer cold, but still shaking.

Victoria downed the sherry in one gulp, and groaned as the liquid burned its way down her throat. She much preferred her sherry sweet. She kept staring into the fire. She would not cry. She would not scream. She was Queen of the Empire, and would not falter.

The second sherry was placed next to her empty glass. "Do have a care, Victoria, and make this one last. I would loathe to have someone of your station in a state when I escort you home."

"You are far too familiar, Professor," Victoria seethed.

"Due to the rather crowded nature of the pub, I'm afraid necessity will out." The professor settled back into the high back chair in front of her, interlacing his pudgy fingers across his rotund belly. His once hard, cold eyes now seemed to glow with warmth. "So, your questions?"

"Who were those—" She meant to say "people" but that was not quite right, was it? They were completely and utterly horrific. "—things?"

"Hellhounds," he said quite factually. "Or I should say, a small coven of necromancers that, through some dark sorcery, possessed the ability to change themselves into hellhounds. I have been tracking them since stumbling on one of their ceremonies in West Yorkshire where I was on the trail of a cursed talisman, completely unrelated to them, I should add."

"West Yorkshire? A far cry from Avebury Circle," she chortled.

"I am tenacious in some things," Source quipped. "Matters such as this, I hold as high priorities."

"Matters?" Victoria asked. "You mean, there are more of those abominations out there?"

The professor smiled, the corners of his eyes crinkling as the firelight softened his plump features. "Have another sip of sherry." She did so, but her eyes never left him as he spoke. "This coven was, perhaps, one of a more darker nature. Wiccans prefer a more peaceful life, as would a Christian, a Hindu, or any other follower of a faith." Source gave a slight sigh as he glanced out of the window, as if he were returning to the circle of stones just outside. "As it is in any faith, there are some that are *forward thinking* in their manifestos. They wish to enact peace by their religion through violence. A Holy War, as contradictory as the term Civil War." He produced the quartz that had come to their aid, and placed it before her. "Another coven offered me this as a weapon against Matthew's black magic. They call this Luna's Prism. They entrusted me with it much in the same way you will, following this evening, entrust me with the means and resources to preserve the empire."

Victoria knotted her brow at that bold conclusion. His smile never faltered.

"The coven who held on to Luna's Prism, were in need of a special branch of Her Majesty's Empire. They trusted me as I assured them such matters would no longer be dismissed by either Palace or Parliament after tonight."

"And how were you so sure?"

Professor Source took a sip of his own sherry before motioning to the barkeep. The man gave a nod and produced from around his neck, a key. He disappeared for a moment in what could have been a corridor to the kitchens, or perhaps storage, Victoria could not be certain; but she concluded it was a private room of some sort when the publican emerged from the back of the pub again, the key was no longer in sight and the small case that the professor had upon his person at their palace appointment was now in the publican's hands. Placing it at Source's feet, he gave them both a tip of the hat and then returned to the bar.

There was still a good amount of conversation and din around them, but she started at the sound of the clasps flipping open. The professor slid the box closer to her and motioned to it. "If you would indulge me, Alexandrina."

Feeling that it would be needed, Victoria took a long sip of her sherry, savouring it before she bent down and opened the box in front of her. Her eyes went wide for a moment, and then jumped back to the mysterious man opposite her. "Is this—?"

"If you have to ask me, then you already know the answer, don't you?"

She shook her head, but it was no illusion. No mirage. It was real, and her fingertips resting gently on it, only confirmed as much. "How is this possible?"

"There are more things in heaven and earth than are dreamt of in your philosophies," he quoted. "When these things call for the attention of the Crown or threaten the preservation of the Empire, this is where and when your new ministry will step in and intervene." From his coat's inside pocket, he produced what appeared to be a modest proposal, perhaps five pages or so, folded neatly and held together by a deep blue ribbon. "A clandestine organisation specialising in that which defies explanation. We will employ the brightest and most resourceful men and women representing every corner of the realm, dedicated to the preservation of the Queen, Her country, and the Empire."

The queen looked up from the bound decree, whatever shock, fear, or confusion she felt festering within her now gone. "Just like that?"

Source cast his eyes to the open case, then back to the queen. "Do you need more proof?"

She hooked her foot under one of the case's open lids and flipped it up. Both lids closed like a small creature clamping its leather-encased mouth around a snack. She gave the case a slight push and slid the box back over to Source.

"Yes, I could have simply presented this evidence to you in court, but I needed to know if you were the monarch that would undertake such a venture; and you did." His eyes narrowed as he continued, "There are dark forces at play, and I will not rest until I return these villains to the shadows from where they were spawned."

Victoria looked down to the proposal still unopened in her hand, then back to the professor. "I barely know you, sir, but I believe you will." She raised her sherry glass. "As decreed by Her Majesty, Queen Victoria of England and the British Empire, I raise a glass to your new charge…"

And then she paused. Her silence became a small chuckle of delight, and she raised her glass a fraction higher.

"A toast, to the Ministry of Peculiar Occurrences."

On their glasses touching, just over the chatter and jocularity of their pub, a lone dog cried out in the night.

UMBRIS OCCULTATI, CONTRA FUROREM

Our Agents

Jared Axelrod is an author, an illustrator, a puppeteer, a graphic designer, a sculptor, a costume designer, a podcaster and quite a few other things that he's lost track of but will no doubt remember when the situation calls for it. He is the author of *The Battle of Blood & Ink*, a steampunk graphic novel published by Tor, as well as the writer, producer and main voice talent of the companion podcast *Fables of the Flying City*. Both of these works led to Jared's nomination for the 2013 Philly Geek Awards for Comic Creator of the Year. He is writer and producer of the science-fiction podcasts *The Voice Of Free Planet X* and *Aliens You Will Meet*, a founding member of the groundbreaking daily flash-fiction website *365 Tomorrows*, and his works has been published on the website *I Should Be Writing*, as well as the anthologies *Have Blaster Will Travel, Gimmie Shelter, Podthology: The Pod Complex,* and *The Sovereign Era: Year One*. He currently resides in Philadelphia with his immensely talented wife. He is not domestic, he is a luxury, and in that sense, necessary.

J.R. Blackwell is a writer of short fiction, appearing in the anthologies *We Are Dust* and *By No Means Vulgar;* and an ENnie award-winning game designer for her live-action zombie role-playing game, *Shelter in Place*. J.R. is also an accomplished editor, her skills bringing together authors for highly-acclaimed collections such as *Gimmie Shelter* and *The Lost*. She is also a celebrated photographer, her works featured in the dark narrative *Her Side* by

Mur Lafferty, and magazines, newspapers, journals, blogs, book covers and book-jackets across the country and around the world. You can find out more about her work at jrblackwell.com.

Karina Cooper, after writing happily ever afters for all of her friends in school, eventually grew up *(sort of)*, went to work in the real world *(kind of)*, where she decided that making stuff up was way more fun *(true!)*. She is the author of dark and sexy paranormal romances, steampunk adventures, crossover urban fantasy, and continues to write across multiple genres with mad glee. Her award winning steampunk series, *The St. Croix Chronicles*, is the RT Reviewers Choice Awards recipient for Best Steampunk Novel 2012.

One part glamour, one part dork and all imagination, Karina is also a gamer, an avid reader, a borderline hermit and an activist. She co-exists with a husband, a menagerie and a severe coffee habit. Visit her at karinacooper. com, because she says so.

Delilah S. Dawson is a native of Roswell, GA and author of the Blud series for Pocket, including *Wicked as They Come* and *Wicked as She Wants*, as well as two e-novellas, *The Mysterious Madam Morpho* and *The Peculiar Pets of Miss Pleasance*. She has a short story in the *Carniepunk* anthology and an e-novella called *Follow Me Boy,* set in the Shadowman universe for Amazon's Kindle Worlds. Her first YA, *Servants of the Storm,* is a creepy paranormal set in Savannah, GA and will hit bookshelves in summer 2014. *Wicked as She Wants* was recently awarded the May Seal of Excellence from RT Book Reviews, who called her "a wonderfully fresh new voice!" and "on the fast track to the top of the genre!" Delilah enjoys horseback riding, cupcakes, and geekery and lives with her family in Atlanta. Visit her at delilahpaints.blogspot.com.

Glenn Freund is a biologist and artist who graduated from the University of California, Berkeley and is part of LoS Productions LLC a southern California based Production Company. While at Berkeley he studied Neuroscience, Animal Behavior, and Endocrinology, later applying those skills at Pomona college in immortality research. While in Southern California he became one of the founding members of the Jr. League W.A.T.C.H. a community building organization which is a spoof of the Jr. Park Rangers and the Neighborhood Watch, bringing in the tongue and cheek nature of The League of S.T.E.A.M. He is also the producer and engineer for the *S.T.E.A.M. Geeks* podcast, a bi-weekly podcast, which discusses a variety of topics in and around steampunk. The podcast can be found on Twitter at @steamgeeks while Glenn can be found at both @DrGlennClock and @jrleaguewatch.

Lauren Harris is a fantasy writer, voice actress, and the co-creator of 2012 Parsec Finalist, *Pendragon Variety Podcast* for aspiring writers of genre fiction, where she is known as "Scribe." Her voice acting can be heard on Audible.com as well as fiction podcasts such as *EscapePod*, *The Dunesteef Audio Fiction Magazine*, and *The Drabblecast B-Sides*. On occasion, she can also be seen cosplaying in a variety of steampunk fashions. Though she spent three years living in Tokyo, Lauren currently resides in a renovated tobacco shed in rural North Carolina, where she is pleased to have running water, wifi, and all her teeth. Find out more about her voice, costume, and editorial works at lscribeharris.blogspot.com.

Leanna Renee Hieber is an award winning, bestselling author, an actress, and playwright who graduated with a Theatre degree and a focus in the Victorian Era. Her debut novel, *The Strangely Beautiful Tale of Miss Percy Parker* won two 2010 Prism Awards, and is currently in development as a musical theatre production. *Darker Still: A Novel of Magic Most Foul*, was named an

American Booksellers Association "Indie Next List" title and selected for a Scholastic edition as a highly recommended title. Leanna's short fiction has been featured in *Wilful Impropriety*, on Tor.com, and in *Queen Victoria's Book of Spells: Tales of Gaslight Fantasy*. Her new series *The Eterna Files*, launches in 2014. A member of Actors Equity Association and SAG-AFTRA, Leanna works often in film and television on shows like *Boardwalk Empire*. When not writing or on set, she's telling ghost stories, cavorting at Goth clubs, corset shopping, channelling Narcissa Malfoy, wandering graveyards and adventuring about New York City, where she resides with a wonderful gent and their beloved rescued lab rabbit. Take a look at all she is up to at leannareneehieber.com.

Jack Mangan is an author, podcaster, musician, smitten father, and considered by the editors as "The Iron Man of Podcasting," born in New Jersey, but now residing in Arizona. "The Clockwork Samurai," featured in *Ministry Protocol*, is actually a sequel to his first Ministry story, the 2012 Parsec-nominated "Night's Plutonian Shore." Aside from the Ministry writings, Jack's fiction and non-fiction works have appeared in numerous online, print, and podcast venues, including such prestigious outlets as *Interzone Magazine, Podthology: The Pod Complex,* Michael A. Stackpole's *Chain Story, Theme and Variations, 2020 Visions, Variant Frequencies*, and *Tales of the Talisman*. His words and worlds have also appeared on independently-produced audio productions at *Wander Radio, Variant Frequencies,* and *Beam Me Up Radio*. His novel, *Spherical Tomi*, was among the first wave of podcast fiction releases, and was the first number one title at Podiobooks.com. His Deadpan Podcast has enjoyed a diverse, fun, weird history and a dedicated following since 2006. More info about Jack Mangan and his work at: jackmangan.com.

Dan Rabarts lives in New Zealand and has been writing since he was big enough to hide a torch under the blankets at night and scribble stories in the back of his Maths homework book. Because who needs Maths, right? His fiction can be found in *Beneath Ceaseless Skies, Andromeda Spaceways Inflight Magazine, Aurealis,* and in the anthologies *Dreaming of Djinn, Bloodstones, When the Hero Comes Home: Volume 2,* and *Regeneration.* His stories have been podcast on the *StarShipSofa, Tales to Terrify, Tales from the Archives* and *Wily Writers'* podcasts. Most recently, he has put on an editor's hat to compile a chilling, thrilling collection of flash-length horror tales called *Baby Teeth: Bite-sized Tales of Terror.* He has been a finalist for New Zealand's Sir Julius Vogel Awards multiple times, both for fiction and non-fiction. Find him lurking on the web at dan.rabarts.com, or in the dusty corners of the house, bleeding words across a page.

Tiffany Trent is the author of the young adult steampunk novels *The Unnaturalists* and *The Tinker King,* as well as the Hallowmere series. She has been published in numerous other venues, including the anthologies *Corsets & Clockwork, Magic in the Mirrorstone,* and *Willful Impropriety.* When not writing, she is usually out playing with 60,000 bees. Visit her at tiffanytrent.com.

Alex White grew up in the Deep South, where he still resides. He writes and produces his podcast, *The Gearheart,* which is a three-time Parsec Finalist. He also holds the distinction as to being the biggest contributor to the Ministry of Peculiar Occurrences, having designed the Ministry coat-of-arms, composed and performed the theme to the Parsec-wining *Tales from the Archives* podcast, created the covers for this anthology and *The Ministry Initiative* roleplaying game, and written "The Boy, the Bomb, and the Witch Who Returned." An artist and composer during the day, Alex has plied his trade for a US President, many major corporations, and most importantly, other authors. He asks too many questions of strangers and may be terminally curious. Alex can be found at thegearheart.com.

Peter Woodworth is a New Jersey native and resides there still, happily teaching English at a small local college. The first two books in his post-zombie-apocalypse *Dead Heroes* trilogy, *Runner* and *Domino*, are currently available on Amazon, and the final volume *Knockout* is scheduled for release in late 2013. His short fiction has appeared on websites such as *Terrible Minds* and *365 Tomorrows*, as well as in several anthologies: *Gimme Shelter; We Are Dust; Have Blaster, Will Travel; The Lost* and more. A longtime game designer, he has written a stack of role-playing books for both tabletop and live-action play for the likes of White Wolf, Evil Hat, West End Games and Eschaton Media. Peter's next project will be writing the supplement *Rogues Gallery: The Ministry's Most Wanted* for *The Ministry Initiative* from Galileo Games. When he isn't grading papers or writing novels, he reads a lot, runs too many RPGs, is seriously addicted to Fantasy Flight board games, and LARPs whenever he can swing it. You can find him online at peterwoodworth.com.

Our Field Directors

Pip Ballantine, New Zealand native, Fantasy writer and voice talent, is the author of Ace Books' *Books of the Order* and Pyr Books' *Shifted World* series. She has also contibuted to both fiction and non-fiction collections such as *Clockwork Fairy Tales* and *A Taste of True Blood*. She is also the co-creator with her husband Tee Morris of *The Ministry of Peculiar Occurrences* novels. Her awards include the 2011 Airship Award for Best Steampunk Literature, a 2012 Parsec Award for Best Short Story, the 2013 Steampunk Chronicle Reader's Choice for Best Novel, and a 2009 Sir Julius Vogel Award for her podcast of *Chasing the Bard*. Today she continues to podcast alongside Tee with both *The Shared Desk* and *Tales from the Archives*. She currently resides in Manassas, Virginia with husband, daughter, and a furry clowder of cats. You can keep up on what is currently occupying Pip's writing desk at pjballantine.com.

Tee Morris has been writing for over a decade, his first novel, *MOREVI: The Chronicles of Rafe & Askana*, a nominee for the 2003 EPPIE for Best Fantasy and the first novel to be podcast in its entirety in 2005. In 2008, Tee won the Parsec Award for Best Audio Drama for *The Case of the Singing Sword: A Billibub Baddings Mystery*, and wrote and edited for several short story and essay collections like *Farscape Forever: Sex, Drugs, and Killer Muppets*, *So Say We All: Collected Thoughts and Opinions on Battlestar Galactica*, and Dragon Moon Press' *Complete Guide to Writing Fantasy* series.

In 2011, Tee penned *Phoenix Rising: A Ministry of Peculiar Occurrences Novel*, written with his wife, Pip Ballantine. The title went on to win the 2011 Airship Award for Best Steampunk Literature and become a finalist for Goodreads Choice Awards for Best Science Fiction of 2011. Tee and Pip returned to the Goodreads Choice Awards in 2012 with *The Janus Affair: A Ministry of Peculiar Occurrences Novel*, and received Steampunk Chronicle's Readers Choice for Best Novel. While working on the third installment, *Dawn's Early Light*, Tee and Pip continue to produce podcasts with their Parsec-winning *Tales from the Archives*, a podcast anthology featuring short stories set in their steampunk universe; and *The Shared Desk*, a light-hearted look at the life of a writer. You can find more about Tee's upcoming releases and works in progress at TeeMorris.com.

TS (Tee) Tate received a Master of Arts in English in 2008 from Southeastern Louisiana University. She has studied under Edgar nominee Tim Gautreaux, Booksense Pick novelist Bev Marshall, and Clarion West graduate and World Fantasy nominee Cat Rambo. She has more than ten years of editing experience and is currently the Editor-in-Chief of LitStack.com. She has spent the past nine years in the corporate environment as a Technical Editor and has previously edited for Christine Rose, Phoebe North, Heather McCorkle, Laura Pauling, Anne Riley, Christine Fonseca and UF writer Carolyn Crane. With Heather McCorkle, Tee co-founded the #WritersRoad chat on Twitter.

A SFWA member, Tee is currently working on several creative projects, including her second novel and various short stories. Her flash fiction, "Street Noises," was included in the Pill Hill Press anthology *Daily Frights 2012: 366 Days of Dark Flash Fiction (Leap Year Edition)* and her short "Til Hunt Be Done," was included in the *Winter Wonders* anthology from Compass Press. A diehard New Orleans Saints fan and no stranger to the Humpty Dance, Tee lives with her family in Southeast Louisiana.

16253517R00142

Printed in Great Britain
by Amazon